The Party

The Party
Elizabeth Day

4th ESTATE • London

4th Estate
An imprint of HarperCollins*Publishers*
1 London Bridge Street
London SE1 9GF

www.4thEstate.co.uk

First published in Great Britain in 2017 by 4th Estate

1

A catalogue record for this book is
available from the British Library

ISBN 978-0-00-819426-0 (hardback)
ISBN 978-0-00-819427-7 (trade paperback)

Printed and bound in the United States of America by LSC Communications

Find out more about HarperCollins and the environment at
www.harpercollins.co.uk/green

For Jasper

party

noun

1. a social gathering of invited guests, typically involving eating, drinking and entertainment.
2. a formally constituted political group that contests elections and attempts to form or take part in a government, e.g. 'faction', e.g. 'the party's election manifesto'.
3. a person or people forming one side in an agreement or dispute, e.g. 'the guilty party'.

I.

THE INTERVIEW ROOM IS SMALL AND SQUARE. A table, three plastic chairs, a high frosted window, the glass grimy with dust, strip lighting; our faces cast in dingy yellow shadow.

Two cups of tea: one for the female police officer, one for me. White with two sugars. Too much milk, but I'm not in a position to complain. The rim of my cup is patterned with indentations where, a few minutes previously, I bit into the polystyrene.

The walls are off-white. They remind me of the squash courts at the RAC on Pall Mall where, just a few days ago, I demolished an opponent who was several positions ahead of me in the club rankings. He was a banker. Florid face. Baggy shorts. Surprisingly lean thigh muscles. I dispatched him fairly swiftly: serve, slice, smash. The rubber thwack of the ball as it pinged into concrete, a dark green full stop at the end of each rally. Grunting. Swearing. Eventual defeat. Aggression contained within four walls.

The police station has a similar feel: a sort of bristling masculinity even though only one of the two officers interviewing me is male. The woman has clearly been designated 'good cop'. It was she who offered me the tea, said it would be beneficial. She also suggested two sugars.

'You know,' she added, meeting my gaze, 'after the shock.'

It's true, I hadn't expected the police to turn up on my doorstep this morning. It's only the second time in my thirty-nine years that I have found myself interviewed by the authorities. On both occasions, it has been because of Ben. Which is odd, really, given that he's my best friend. You'd expect best friends to take better care of each other.

The female police officer is short with rounded shoulders and a pleasant, freckled face. Her hair has been dyed that indeterminate colour inexplicably beloved of middle-aged women, which is neither brown nor blonde but somewhere in between. A kind of beige. Brittle at the ends.

Her colleague is tall. One of those men whose height is his defining feature. He stooped when he walked through the door, holding a sheaf of papers in hands the colour of supermarket ham. Grey suit with a white mark on the lapel. Toothpaste, perhaps. Or the left-behind smear of a baby's breakfast. He is, I'd guess, in his early thirties.

The two of them sit across the table from me, backs to the door. The chairs have moulded seats with letterbox apertures in the back. We used to stack these chairs for school assemblies and end-of-term concerts at Burtonbury. A lifetime ago, and yet no time at all. Sometimes it seems as close as the next minute. Pencil shavings and plimsoll rubber, the scuffed mark of a trainer against the classroom skirting board. Dormitories with sagging beds. The creak of a spring as a boy shifted in his sleep. That constant feeling of unease. That was before I met Ben, of course. Before he saved me from myself. We've been saving each other ever since.

On the table, to one side, is a large tape-recording machine. Too big, really. I find myself wondering why it has to be so big. Or why, indeed, the police still insist on using cassette tapes in this digitised era of sound-clouds and podcasts and iTunes.

I've declined a lawyer. Partly because I don't want to fork out the necessary funds for a good one and I know, given the circumstances, Ben won't pay and I refuse to get stuck with some snivel-nosed legal aid type who can't distinguish his arse from his elbow. I don't think Lucy's parents will stump up either. After everything that's happened, I suspect my in-laws might also be disinclined to help.

'Right then,' says the woman, hands clasped in front of her. Short nails, varnished with clear polish. A tiny ink stain on the fleshy part between thumb and index finger. 'Shall we get started?'

'By all means.'

Beige Hair presses a button on the giant recording machine. There is a long, loud bleep.

'This interview is being tape-recorded at Tipworth Police Station, Eden Street, Tipworth. The date is 26 May 2015. The time is 2.20 p.m. I am Detective Constable Nicky Bridge.'

She glances at her colleague, who then identifies himself for the tape.

'I am Detective Constable Kevin McPherson.'

'Mr Gilmour,' she says, looking at me, 'would you introduce yourself with your full name and date of birth please?'

'Martin Gilmour, 3 June 1975.'

'Is it OK to call you Martin?'

'Yes.'

She clears her throat. 'You've been offered the services of a duty lawyer and declined – is that right, Martin?'

I nod.

'For the tape, please.'

'Yes.'

There is a pause. Grey Suit shuffles his papers. His head is lowered. He does not look at me. I find this curiously disconcerting, the notion of not being worth his attention.

'So, Martin,' Beige Hair says. 'Let's begin at the beginning. Talk us through the events of the evening of 2 May. The party. You arrived before the other guests, is that right?'

'Yes,' I say. 'Yes, we did.'

And then I start to tell them.

It begins with a door that wouldn't open at the Tipworth Premier Inn.

2 May

'I DON'T KNOW WHY they couldn't have put us up in the house,' Lucy said, slipping the plastic card key into place. 'Not like they don't have enough rooms.'

The light beneath the door handle flashed obstinately red. Lucy tried again, impatiently shoving the key into the slot and taking it out too quickly. I could see her getting annoyed but trying not to show it – that tell-tale flush across the back of her neck; the square set of her shoulders; a triangle of concentrated tongue just visible between her lips. I watched as she made several more clumsy attempts, my irritation rising. Who was it who said the definition of madness was doing the same thing over and over again, but expecting different results? Aristotle? Rousseau?

'Here,' I said, finally able to bear it no longer. 'Let me.'

I took the plastic card, still sweaty from her fingers, and slid it into place, leaving it for a few seconds before smoothly removing it. The light went green. The door clicked open.

'That's exactly what I was doing,' Lucy protested.

I smiled, patting her on the arm. There was a minute retraction in her pupils. Almost imperceptible.

'Here we are, then,' she said, too brightly.

We rolled our suitcases into the standard suite. Calling it a suite was optimistic. The floor space was almost entirely swallowed by twin beds. A reproduction of a bad watercolour depicting ladies on a beach hung skewed above the headboards. By the television, there was an electric kettle and a jam jar filled with teabags. Plastic packets of UHT creamer lay scattered around its base, as though some invisible milky tide had swept up and left them there like pebbles on a seashore.

Lucy immediately unwound the cable and took the kettle to the bathroom to fill it from the basin tap. It is the first thing she does on arriving anywhere. When we travel abroad, she will take a foil packet of English teabags with her.

I sat on the edge of the bed, feeling the friction of man-made fibres against my chinos, and slipped off my loafers. I checked my watch: 5.37 p.m. Ben wanted us at the house by 7 p.m. for pre-party drinks, so we had a little over an hour. I eased myself back onto the pillows and closed my eyes, hearing Lucy bustling around as she put on the kettle and unzipped her case, unfolding the swishy evening dress she had brought to wear and hanging it in the bathroom where, soon, I knew she would draw a hot bath in the hope that the creasing would magically erase itself in the steam.

These are the things you learn over the course of a marriage: other people's habits. Those incrementally acquired ways of being: a gradual evolution from attractive quirk to something pointless, stupid, illogical, obsessive and finally maddening. It takes someone else to pick up on them, to be driven to the edge of sanity by their repeated appearance.

'I mean, how many rooms do you think they have in their new mansion exactly?'

I ignored the question for a few seconds, hoping to fool her into thinking I was asleep.

'I know you're awake, Martin. I can tell. Your eyelids are flickering.'

For fuck's sake.

'Sorry,' I said, and sat up. 'I don't know.'

'Well I bet it's plenty. And you're his oldest friend, after all.'

'Mmm.'

The kettle boiled, sending a bloom of condensation halfway up the mirror.

'Has something happened between you two?'

'God no.'

This was not strictly true but, at that stage, I didn't feel she needed to know the particulars. It would have involved too much explanation and, to be honest, I didn't have the energy. There were things my wife – my pliant, adoring little wife – would never understand about the bond between two men.

'They've got loads of family staying,' I said, unbuckling my trousers in preparation for getting changed. 'Not just Ben's but Serena's lot too. I don't think Ben wanted to inflict that on us.'

Lucy, a mug of tea in one hand, came over to me. She tilted her head. Moist brown eyes looked at me expectantly. A pulse beat in the purplish semi-circle beneath her left socket, as it always did when she was nervous. She placed her free hand tentatively on the small of my back. I could smell her tea-rose perfume. I used to find that fragrance deeply charming. It was, like Lucy, modest and unshowy. That night, it caught in my throat. Too sweet. Too soapy.

'I'm sorry, I'm—'

Lucy dropped her head and withdrew her hand.

'Of course,' she said. She turned away. 'Only ...' I could see her weighing up whether to say what was on her mind. 'It's been months.'

Not this again.

'Has it?'

She nodded.

'I've had a lot on my mind. The new book.'

I had just delivered a lengthy manuscript on post-Impressionism to my publishers. They hadn't been especially enthused by the idea but my agent had talked them round. Pointed out that there was a major Manet retrospective coming up at the Tate and who better to write the definitive work on it than esteemed newspaper art critic Martin Gilmour? I had something of a reputation. My first book, *Art: Who Gives a F**k?*, published five years previously, had established me as an enfant terrible of the art world, the critic who dared to call out bullshit and say things as he truly saw them.

In truth, the contents were not particularly explosive. The title had been my agent's idea. Credit where it's due: it sold by the truckload. It became the kind of book people give their trendy friends at Christmas. I've seen it in the downstairs loo of some fantastically fashionable, architect-designed house (curtain walls and basement studies). I'm pretty sure no one actually read it from cover to cover. Apart from Lucy, that is. Lucy is loyal to a fault. Always has been.

We met thirteen years ago when I was working on the *Bugle*, London's pre-eminent evening newspaper (although, admittedly, there was no competition at that stage. The free-sheets and the morning *Metro* only came along later). I had wangled myself a position as maternity leave cover for the deputy arts editor and Lucy was the desk secretary. In those days, you could still smoke in the office, something I did regularly and self-consciously, only too aware that when I took a drag on a cigarette my twenty-something cheekbones were highlighted becomingly to anyone who might be looking.

I didn't notice Lucy for several weeks. She existed as a pleasant blur on the periphery of my vision. She was a plump, prettyish girl with owlish spectacles and shoulder-length brown hair that was neither straight nor curly but instead manifested itself unsatisfactorily in the liminal space between. Her hair, I would subsequently find out, was a source of constant frustration. The rain had only to glower threateningly from an unbroken grey cloud for it to start frizzing at the ends. On wet days, Lucy wore her hair up in a velvet scrunchie as the Duchess of York used to do. There always was something delightfully out of step about Lucy. She was in floaty florals when everyone else was in figure-hugging pencil skirts. She wore men's brogues and had thick, sluggish eyebrows. She was of a different time. Part of her still is. I have never worked out which time, exactly. It could be that the one she belongs to hasn't been invented yet.

Anyway, back then, Lucy hadn't made much of an impression other than of being someone who answered the phone and said 'hello' when one walked into the office. Did the odd tea round. Once, I saw her return from her lunch break with her fingernails painted a glossy black and this had momentarily sparked my interest. More going on there than meets the eye, I thought. But then I forgot about it, turning back to my keyboard to bash out five hundred words of guff on the latest insufferably pretentious graduate show from Central Saint Martins or a Hollywood actress of negligible talent who had some hold over the newspaper's proprietor.

It wasn't until my second, or even third, month there that Lucy made any sort of lasting impact.

I had been asked by Ian, the section editor, to knock up a piece on the return of the 'Great American Novelist'. There was some tenuous peg, I seem to recall – a debut by a muscular young author who had been hailed as the new Tom Wolfe. I had tried to farm out the writing of the piece to a willing freelancer, but it was just before Christmas and none of my regulars had been available so I'd decided to have a go myself.

I was sitting at my desk, discussing who should be included with Ian.

'There's an argument to be made for Jay McInerney,' he said.

I nodded, as if I were already across that. 'And DeLillo, of course,' I added. 'Wolfe. Can we get away with Franzen?'

'Definitely.' Ian leaned back in his chair, folding his arms across his rumpled shirt. 'You've got Philip Roth, I'm guessing?'

'Sure, sure,' I said, even though I hadn't thought of Philip Roth and hadn't, at that point in my life, read a single one of his books.

There was an audible tsk-ing sound from the other side of the desk.

'I mean, if we're going back a bit further, we could look at Salinger …' I continued.

The tsk-ing turned into a loud, impatient grunt. Ian's lips twitched at the corners.

'Do you have something to say, Lucy?' he asked, amused.

'No,' she said, face flushed. 'Actually, I mean, sorry, yes, yes I do.' She coughed and a pink dot appeared in the centre of each cheek.

'Please …' Ian said, motioning with one hand that the floor was hers.

'Well, have you thought of, you know, including any women in your list?' she asked, her voice gathering momentum and volume as she spoke. 'It's just always the same boring, old, white, men. I mean, soon you'll be citing John bloody Updike.'

I scoffed, while mentally reminding myself to include John Updike. How could I have overlooked John Updike? It was those kind of mistakes that made me stand out. That made me look like a boy who didn't have a home full of packed bookshelves but who instead relied on his mother's *Reader's Digest* for reading material.

'… who basically write everything with their dicks out and who all congratulate each other on being so fantastic,' Lucy was saying, 'when really their "state of the nation" novels are just family dramas repackaged with extra testosterone. You know, there are incredible female authors in America who, just because they write about families and have these … f-f … awful covers with close-up photographs of children and sandcastles, they just get ignored all the damn time.'

She dropped her head. Hair fell loose across her pale forehead.

'Sorry,' she said. 'I just …'

I smiled at her. How sweet it was, I thought, to feel so impassioned about something. She caught my eye and smiled back, lips parting just enough for me to see her precise, straight and entirely sensible teeth.

'Blimey,' Ian said. 'Didn't realise we had Emmeline sodding Pankhurst sitting here. So who would you suggest, then?'

'Anne Tyler, Joan Didion, Donna Tartt,' Lucy said without looking up. 'And that's just for starters. That's if you even agree with the fundamental premise of there being something that is "The Great American Novel". Which I don't, by the way.'

Ian chortled. 'Thanks, Luce. Remind me, what did you study at Bristol again?'

'English,' she mumbled. 'And it was Durham.'

'Thought so.'

'I actually think it's a good idea,' I said, surprising myself at the sound of my own voice. 'We should include some women.'

Lucy grinned. Her glasses had slid down her nose and she pushed them back up with a single nail-chewed forefinger and I noticed, as she did so, that her hand was shaking.

'Thanks, Martin,' she said and she looked at me with shining eyes.

The more I got to know her after that, the more I was charmed in spite of myself. She was so respectful, so admiring of me, so fundamentally grateful that I would pay her any attention. And I, in turn, found her intelligent and interesting company. She knew a lot.

We started taking lunch together. At first, it was just a hurried sandwich in the staff canteen but soon we graduated to the restaurant across the road from the office where we sat in wooden booths and drank wine from a magnum that the waiter would mark off at the end of the meal, charging us according to how many inches we had drunk. It was only a matter of time before lunch turned into an after-work drink in the pub – me: a pint of Guinness; Lucy: a gin and tonic. (I never liked Guinness. I only drank it when I was trying to give the impression of blokeishness.) After six months, we were having dinner. We both had a penchant for Persian food and would seek out the best places for a night-time meal of aubergine stew and lamb with barberries at the wrong end of Kensington.

And then she kissed me and I didn't know how to say no. It was on the pavement outside a brightly painted eatery called Tas or Yaz or Fez or something similar. We were standing under a streetlamp, dank drizzle coating our faces like wet muslin and I found myself looking at her face, at the speckles of moisture on her unfashionably large glasses, at the discreet jiggle of extra flesh just underneath her chin, at the double freckle on the lobe of one ear so that it looked as if she had got them pierced even though she was one of the few women of my acquaintance who hadn't.

'Too scared of infection,' she had said, explaining it to me once. 'Too scared of everything.'

She isn't stupid, Lucy.

It was as I was looking at her that Lucy's expression changed. Her eyes – brown, lively – acquired a liquid quality, as though their brownness could seep out if left unguarded. I realised, too late, that what I was seeing in those darkened pupils, was lust. She leaned in, clasping her hands behind my neck and I succumbed because it was easier than anything else. And would it do so very much harm?

Her lips were soft and doughy. The kiss became moister and more enthused. I could hear a faint moaning sound coming from Lucy's throat and then I pulled away, hands on her shoulders, a firm, paternal, 'We shouldn't be doing this.'

She looked at me sadly.

'Why not?'

'I … well, look …'

'We get on well, don't we? I mean, I like you.' A meaningful little lacuna. 'I *really* like you. Can't we just … see where it goes? I'm lonely. I know you're lonely …' This came as news to me. The truth was, I did feel alone but I thought I had masked it sufficiently well from prying eyes in the office. At that stage, Ben was getting more serious with Serena and I was increasingly at a loose end in the evenings. Whereas, previously, the two of us had frequently gone drinking in Soho, starting off in a private members' club before graduating to dinner at Quo Vadis and a nightcap at the Atlantic, these days Ben was more likely to stay in cooking pasta and watching films with Serena. He had asked me to find my own place so that she could move into the mews house I had shared with him since we graduated.

'Time to grow up, mate,' he had said, slapping me on the back. Touch came so easily to Ben. It was something I both hated and loved about him.

So perhaps I was particularly vulnerable to attention when Lucy came along. I realise now that is not an excuse.

I walked her home that evening. She lived in a surprisingly nice flat off the North End Road. I say surprisingly because I had assumed, from the dowdiness of her clothing and her penchant for buying men's jackets from charity shops, that money was tight. It turned out I was wrong about that. Lucy's parents were quite well off, in a hearty, middle-class kind of way. They had sent their three daughters to private school and lived in a red-brick farmhouse in Gloucestershire. At Christmas-time, they attended the carol concert at Tewkesbury Cathedral.

I deposited her at the door.

'Come up,' Lucy said, tugging at the sleeve of my coat.

I shook my head, feigning regret.

'No,' I said, trailing my fingers down her cheek. 'That wouldn't be right. Next time.'

I kissed the top of her head, inhaling Timotei and light sweat, and walked away, raising one arm aloft as I went.

'See you tomorrow,' she called out to my retreating form.

For whatever reason, the evening with Lucy had left me experiencing an uncomfortable surge of different emotions. I thought of my mother, of the way she looked at me when I told her, when I was back from school one Easter holiday, that she shouldn't say 'settee' but 'sofa' and that the way she pronounced 'cinema' without elongating the final 'a' was embarrassing.

I found myself walking towards Brompton Cemetery and although it was late and I knew the main gates would be closed, I also knew from previous visits that there was a point in the wall on the Lillie Road where the stones had come loose and you could crawl through quite easily on your hands and knees.

This I did, the palms of my hands gathering up bits of twig and pine cone and leaving a latticed indentation of dirt across my skin. I stood, brushing myself clean. A piece of lichen had lodged itself in my hair. I shook it out.

The cemetery stood in the gloom of night, half lit here and there by a weak streetlamp. Gravestones and silhouetted stone angels loomed out of the shadows. Some notable historical figures were buried nearby although I'd never tried to seek out their graves. My favourite gravestone (if one can have such a thing) was to mark the passing of a young man called Horace Brass who died at the age of sixteen in 1910. His name was carved in looped art nouveau cursive.

I started walking towards it, hands in my pockets. A man fell into step beside me. I glanced to one side and saw that, no, this was not a man but a boy. A teenage boy, like Horace Brass, pale and thin as a silver birch. He had greasy hair and spots around his mouth.

'Looking for company?' he said.

'No,' I said too loudly. 'No I don't … I mean, I'm not.'

A fizz of anger in my solar plexus. I doubled up my pace and walked swiftly back the way I had come.

The next day, I was late into the office. I had a migraine, I recall, and with every step I took, the ground felt too far away for my feet to make contact with it. I sat at my desk, shading my eyes from the sunlight spooling through the windows, and flicked through the latest issue of the *Art Newspaper*, pretending to concentrate on the words. When Lucy came in, she smiled at me and I remember this internal surge of relief that she still liked me. In Lucy's mind, I was still the man she had kissed outside her front door, the man she had wanted to come upstairs, the man she respected and liked and enjoyed spending time with. In her mind, I was the nice Martin Gilmour. I was the Martin Gilmour I wanted to be.

I smiled back at her. That day, we went again for lunch together, taking our supermarket sandwiches to sit on our coats in Kensington Gardens. I kissed her, taking her face in both my hands, conveying a tenderness I almost felt. She tasted of prawns and mayonnaise. I felt no stirring, no passion, no love. But there was affection there, and fondness too. And there was an understanding of sorts. I am sure of that. I did not pull the wool over her eyes, as my mother might have said. Lucy knew what I was. Really, she can't complain.

Of course, nothing is as easy as it first appears. I used to like Lucy so much, truly I did. Over the years, that like has been dulled: brass left unpolished. The same qualities that drew me to her: an uncomplicated view of the world, her mild eccentricity, her un-groomed refusal to make the best of herself and above all, her adoration of me, now set me on edge. And then there's the children thing, naturally. I'd always told her I didn't want any of my own and she accepted it in the beginning. But that was before her friends started popping them out with alacrity, posting twelve-week scans and pictures of bleary-eyed newborns on Facebook with humdrum frequency. Our socialising changed – it was no longer nights in the pub but picnics in the park surrounded by screaming toddlers, or early-evening barbecues, the timing of everything defined by when babysitters could be relied upon to arrive and leave or when Isadora or Humphrey or Matilda could be put down for their naps.

Oh, and isn't Lucy wonderful with kids? Look at how she plays with them! Forever kneeling down to meet their eyes; taking them by the hand; running after them in a game of tag, her floral dress breezing round her knees. She had six godchildren. But every time she went to Tiffany to buy a silver charm bracelet or engraved tankard for yet another christening, something within her hardened. She lost that yielding softness she once had.

I suppose it didn't help that Ben and I were so close. Difficult for any woman to come into that situation and hope to get my undivided attention. But, as I often told her, that's the way it had always been. Ben and I went way back. Best friends from school. So close we had, at one stage, been informally christened by his mother as 'Starsky and Hutch'. Later, Ben's wife Serena had coined a different phrase.

'You're always there, aren't you, Martin?' she had said. 'Ben's little shadow.'

For whatever reason, the moniker had stuck. Little shadow. Even Ben calls me it now. I'm in his phone under 'LS'.

The real reason we weren't staying at the house on the night of the party was that Ben hadn't asked. Lucy was right: there were more than enough rooms to accommodate a small army of guests even on the night of his fortieth birthday. And, yes, I had been offended by this omission. I'd left it too late to book anywhere decent. Their new house was in Tipworth, a bucolic Cotswold village overburdened with twee shops selling novelty oven gloves and packets of fudge, but severely under-served by decent hotels. All the nice boutique places were fully booked when I tried, by other guests, most of whom, presumably, would have got their PAs to do it for them. Ben's fortieth was going to be a grand affair. Le tout WII in attendance.

In the end, the only place available was a Premier Inn just off the motorway roundabout. The room cost £59.99, which seemed absurd.

'Are you sure?' I had asked on the phone when the receptionist recited the price list.

'Yeah. Breakfast not included. But there's a Little Chef across the road.'

The glamour!

And now, here we were. Lucy upset in the bathroom. Kettle boiled. Me standing trouserless on scratchy carpet. As I unpacked my dress shirt and bow-tie, I didn't explain why Ben hadn't asked us to stay. It unsettled me to have to stare it in the face.

Although it would have taken us less than ten minutes to walk to the party, Lucy insisted on a taxi.

'Shoes!' she said, pointing down to a pair of bright red, spar-kling, strappy heels.

'Very nice,' I lied. 'Are they new?'

She flushed with pleasure.

'Yes. I got them off eBay.' She twirled her right ankle, the better to show off how truly garish they were. Like every conventional woman, Lucy likes to pretend she is unconventional by buying attention-seeking shoes. In all other respects, she was playing according to type: a long A-line dress in a stiff, dark green material with two thin straps, her shoulders covered by a pale red pash-mina. She held a tiny evening bag in one hand. I knew, without it being opened, that it would contain a folded tissue, a lipstick worn down to the nub, a pen, a compact mirror and our hotel room key. She would always insist on carrying a hotel room key.

'Have you left the key at reception?' I asked, by way of a test.

She shook her head. 'You know I never like to do that. What if they go in and steal something?'

'You do realise they have a master key?'

'Well,' she said, climbing indecorously into the taxi. 'Still.'

The cab driver turned back to look at us.

'Tipworth Priory?'

'Yes,' I replied. 'How did you know?'

He chuckled. 'The way you're dressed sort of gives it away, mate. Not normally that much call for black tie around these parts.'

Ben and Serena Fitzmaurice were famous for their parties. It was a point of pride for them. This one was ostensibly Ben's fortieth but was doubling up as a housewarming. They had bought the seventeenth-century Tipworth Priory a few months previously. It was their second home.

During the week, they lived in a white, stucco-fronted house in the expensive part of Notting Hill. At the weekends, or so they had told me, they needed 'more space' for the children.

'We just want to get away,' they had said, as they pored over glossy brochures from estate agents with three names and no ampersand. It baffled me as to quite what they were getting away from. Still, it wasn't for me to try and fathom the desires of the super-rich. I had nodded and murmured sympathetically when they talked in this way and soon enough they'd stumbled across Tipworth Priory in a picturesque part of Oxfordshire that had fields and sheep and all the requisite trappings of the countryside, while also comprising cafes that served soya lattes and organic mackerel salads in light-filled converted chapels. An outpost of a Soho private members' club had just opened up nearby, doing wonders for the local economy, if not the local inhabitants, who promptly complained to the reporters at the *Tipworth Echo* that they were being priced out of their own villages.

In fact, Ben and Serena had had their own run-in with the local press at the time contracts were exchanged, involving a kerfuffle over the eviction of a handful of elderly monks who still lived in the Priory. The Fitzmaurices confided that they felt it had all been terribly overblown and the monks became, in their retelling, a light-hearted dinner-party anecdote designed to highlight the amusing narrow-mindedness of benighted country folk.

(I read subsequently in the *Echo* that a new location was found for the monks in a nondescript Oxford suburb. They are now housed in a purpose-built block sandwiched between a multi-storey car park and one of those discount stores that sells value packs of pickled onion crisps and more plastic clothes pegs than anyone could reasonably need over the course of an average lifetime.)

With the monks out of the way, Serena and Ben were able to set to work on the interior. They did a lot of things involving faux-rococo marble fireplaces, built from monumental stone veined with grey like the bloodshot white of a wide-open eye. The chandelier in the main drawing room was imported from Italy – a splintering waterfall of glassy splendour, which, on closer inspection, revealed itself to be constructed entirely from upended wine glasses. It was, Serena and Ben thought, a humorous accent; a sign that although they recognised beautiful design, they were not ones to take themselves too seriously. But I knew that the chandelier had cost £250,000. More, if you count the packaging and transport costs. I couldn't help but admire the grandiosity of it. The sheer, unthinking excess.

I hadn't seen it since the renovations had been completed, over three weeks ago. In spite of myself, I was intrigued to look at what they'd done to the place. I wondered whether Serena's somewhat déclassé penchant for white lilies and plush carpets and luxury hotel fixtures and fittings would have denuded the building of all its character.

As we approached Tipworth Priory that evening, the taxi indicating into the long sweep of driveway, the overall effect was impressive. Our route was lined with spherically trimmed box hedges, each one encircled by a purple halo of light. The Priory exterior was Grade-I listed so, much to my relief, Serena hadn't been able to get her paws on it. The resplendent Cotswold stone was intact, emitting a warm buttery glow in the dusky sunshine. There was still stained glass in the windows. On the front lawn was a large marquee, bedecked with flowers in purple and white. A fountain featuring a stone boy with an urn tilted forwards on his shoulder had purple and white petals floating in the water. As the taxi came to a halt, we heard the electric whir of a generator and the facade of the house became sharply illuminated. I got out of the car and noticed that a giant 'B' and 'S' in the same shade of virulent purple were now being projected from some unseen source of light onto the wall. Typical Serena.

'Yes,' said Lucy. 'They don't like to do things by halves, do they?'

The taxi driver snorted.

'You can say that again, love.'

I shot her a look. She started to pick at the tender flakes of skin edging her thumbnail. The fare was £6.60. I handed over a ten-pound note and waited for the precise change.

'You should have given him a tip,' Lucy said, as we walked up the steps and tugged on an ornate pulley system to ring the ancient bell.

'At that price? Not likely.'

I could hear footsteps echoing on flagstones and then the door opened and Ben was there, arms flung wide, shirt untucked, bow-tie undone round his neck, hair a wild mess of curls, broad smile on his face.

'Hello, my dears!'

He ushered us in, embracing Lucy and giving her a kiss on each cheek, then crushing me into a bear hug and slapping me on the back. 'So pleased you could come early,' he continued, leading us through a hallway strewn with Moroccan rugs which occasionally parted to reveal a series of gravestones. Lucy's heels click-clacked against a 'Dearly Departed' and when I looked down, I realised I was standing on 'Emily, beloved wife of ...' How strange, I thought, to end your life like this. Buried in a priory graveyard and now merely flooring for a rich man's party.

'Forgive the chaos,' Ben said. 'Pre-party madness, you know how it is.'

We passed a group of girls in black skirts and white shirts with their hair pulled back in ponytails of varying degrees of severity. One of them smiled as we went. Another one bobbed, almost a curtsey.

'I'm just so glad I get to see you guys before it all kicks off,' he was saying. 'We both are. There's never enough of a chance to chat at these things, is there? Not to the people you really want to talk to, anyway.'

He was breathless in his chatter. Charming, as ever, but underneath there was an accent of nervousness. It was unlike Ben to be nervous. Probably anxious about the guests arriving, I thought.

'This place is spectacular, Ben,' I said.

'Yes,' Lucy added. 'Really ...'

Ben paused for a second and raised his head, as though sniffing the air.

'It is, isn't it? We got super lucky. It's going to take months to do up properly though. Months. We haven't even started on the chapel. I'll show it to you, LS. I know you love your architectural history.' He clutched Lucy's arm conspiratorially. 'Such an old fuddy-duddy, isn't he, Luce? That's why we love him.'

It was a source of amusement to Ben that whenever the two of us went anywhere together, I would seek out the local church and find a point of interest: an unexpected fresco of St Peter holding the keys to heaven; a war memorial erected to an only son called Arthur; and once a pew cushion embroidered with 'This Too Shall Pass'.

We followed Ben to the end of a wide corridor, the walls adorned with black and white family photographs in uniform clear perspex frames. This led into the kitchen, where Serena stood, surrounded by half-unwrapped bouquets of flowers, the stems a tangle of bloom and pollen. Around her stood a group of waiters and one man wearing a floppy khaki hat and a safari jacket with countless pockets.

'Serena,' Ben purred. 'LS and Lucy have arrived.'

She looked up, her face vague. It took a moment for her gaze to click into place.

'Of course! Of course! Sorry, sweeties, totally slipped my mind. Hang on a sec.'

She turned to the man in the jacket. 'Tom, these are great, thanks. Much better than the other flowers.'

'We'll have to re-plant,' he said gruffly.

'Mm-mm. I know, darling. We will.'

Tom exited the kitchen, his boots leaving a speckled trail of mud as he went.

All at once, Serena was a flurry of insincere compliments.

'So gorgeous to see you! Martin' – she had a way of saying my name which stretched all the vowels to the point of snapping – 'you look very smart. Oh, and Lucy, what a … what a …' She gave a tiny pause. '*Pretty* dress. Where's it from? Is it Donna Karan?'

'No,' Lucy said. 'Monsoon.'

'So sorry we couldn't have you to stay. Just. You know how it is. Family. Extended family. Friends flying in from abroad.'

'Of course we do,' I said. 'It's no problem. We're just delighted to be here. And to see this, this …' I made a great show of looking around in an awestruck manner, 'palace. Truly, Serena, you do have the most impeccable taste.'

She didn't reply but gave another dazzling smile. Serena hadn't yet dressed for the party and still managed to look more glamorous than any of us. She was wearing cut-off jeans and a loose white blouse that somehow managed to be both shapeless and sexy. Around her neck, a silver chain, the heart pendant fitting snugly in the gap between her clavicles. Her hair was in rollers and her eye make-up heavily done – black-brown smudges the colour of a bruised nail – but she wore no lipstick and, as a result, her face had an untethered quality, like one of those children's picture books with different panels to flick through for amusing variations on face, torso and legs.

'I said I'd show LS the chapel,' Ben said. 'You girls will be able to make your own fun for a bit, won't you?'

I glanced at Lucy, who was standing in the corner next to an enormous Smeg fridge, holding her pashmina tightly, her mouth set in a mutinous line.

'Of course, sweetie,' Serena said. 'But at least get them a drink first!' She laughed – a tinkling sound like teaspoon against saucer – and poured us all a glass of Veuve Clicquot that was already chilling in an ice bucket by the industrial-sized sink.

Ben took our glasses and led me back the way we'd come.

'We're still waiting for some of the furniture,' he said as we came to a halt in front of a stone fireplace. The mantelpiece was the same height as our heads. The central recess had been filled by dozens of altar candles, waxen wicks pulled straight and ready to be lit. 'Stuff Serena picked up in France. Some bigger pieces from a friend she has in Bali.'

'Not tempted to light a real fire?' I asked.

'Ha! No. Serena wanted it all to be candlelit tonight. Adds to the—' He broke off, lowered his voice and assumed a cod French accent, '*ambience.* So I'm told.'

He put his arm round my shoulders and drew me to him. He was still grinning. Still determined to show what a jolly time he was having and how relaxed this all was and wasn't it all just good clean fun between friends. Perhaps he forgot how well I knew him. I had, after all, made a lifetime's study of the planes of his face. Tonight, there was a twitching light to his eyes, a kind of fevered alacrity that meant his gaze kept shifting over surfaces and people, never once steadying to meet my own.

He dropped his arm, took a gulp of his champagne and waved me into a narrow corridor, darker than the others, which led off from the main aspect of the house.

'I think you'll like this,' Ben said. He pushed open a door, the hinges blackened and creaking. There was a lingering smell of incense. In the half-gloom, I could make out the hulking form of an altar and a font.

'Sorry guys, don't mind us,' Ben said, stepping across a cable. Two men in black T-shirts bearing the words 'Sono-Vision Inc.' above a logo of three interlinked circles were applying miniature screwdrivers to a series of speakers.

'Quite a production,' I said.

'Ha!'

The chapel looked almost entirely as it must have been when the monks had left. There were open hymn books on the shelves, the pages fluttering in the draught of a closing door. It was as if the former residents had been forced to leave halfway through a service, abandoning all their possessions in their rush to escape.

It reminded me of Victor Hugo's house in the Place des Vosges in Paris: untouched since his death, everything still in its rightful place. But then you saw Hugo's death-mask, placed casually in a box on top of the desk, and you realised how macabre it all was, how strange the human impulse to keep everything stagnant, frozen in aspic. When my mother died, I couldn't wait to be rid of her. I arranged for a swift cremation and when the notice came from the funeral directors that her ashes were ready for collection, I ignored it. What do they do with uncollected ashes? I never found out.

'Spooky,' I said.

'You have no idea, LS. No idea. There's a ghost, you know.'

He went on to say that the ghost was said to hang about the medieval graveyard, just by the ornamental maze they had planted to entertain their four children – Cosima, Cressida, Hector and Wilf (known to the family as Bear). The ghost was referred to locally as 'The Brown Monk'. He was believed to walk through the walls of the house making a soft, low, moaning sound.

'You don't believe in all that though, do you?' I asked.

Ben shook his head. 'No, but … Serena. You know how she is …'

Yes. Yes, I did.

The first time I met her, at a restaurant situated at the top of one of London's newest skyscrapers, Serena had leaned across the table and clasped my forearm. She did it so quickly, I had no chance to remove my cuff from her grasp and so we sat there, uncomfortably, while she looked at me earnestly with those chlorine-blue eyes and said 'Ben's told me so much about you. I already know we're going to be kindred spirits.'

I gave a non-committal smile. The non-committal smile is one of my specialities.

'I can see the child in you,' she said and as she spoke, a strand of blonde hair stuck to her lip gloss and stayed there, bisecting the lower half of her distant, beautiful face. Behind her, I could see the dark sweep of the city: the carcass of recently erected scaffolding illuminated by a foggy moon and the red twinkling lights of Canary Wharf, sequenced like the LED display of an unreadable digital watch.

'It's so important, isn't it?' she said as the first course arrived. 'To keep that childlike wonder about the world.'

She removed her hand, pleased with herself. There was a single wrinkle on her smooth forehead and it seemed to have been placed there expressly to denote concern and empathy.

Serena was the latest in a long line of girlfriends. But even I had to acknowledge she was different. Prior to this, Ben had had a type. He was handsome and came from money. His life had been almost too easy – public school, Cambridge, hedge fund manager – and as a consequence, he sought out difficulty in his personal attachments. He liked neurotic girls with ripped jeans who smoked too much and cut their own hair. They never lasted for more than a few months and Ben had always been the one to end the liaison.

Often, I would have to mop them up afterwards. They would come to me, these girls, a muddied mess of tears and eyeliner, and I would always tell them the same thing: that Ben just wasn't ready to settle down and who knew if he ever would be and it wasn't them, it was him, and he adored them in his own way but he couldn't help it, he just wasn't ready. And they would nod and bite their lips and then, after a cup of sugary tea and a few crumbs of cake (they would never eat the whole slice), they left my flat, never to be seen again.

I liked these girls, probably because I never felt threatened by them. They had no designs on my friendship with Ben. They respected our unbreakable bond. We knew each other better than anyone else in the world, you see. No woman could compete with that. Like I told them: not their fault.

Until Serena.

Serena, with her casual confidence, bowled him over. They met on a skiing holiday. Of course they did. That's where people like that meet. It's either Verbier or St Tropez.

She was blonde and tall and striking. Lean muscles. A sugary scent. Hair that swung from side to side as if advertising itself. She worked in an art gallery, although as soon as they got engaged, she gave up the job. She was the kind of person I had always assumed Ben would find boring. We used to laugh about the dull Sloanes with their made-up careers and their reliance on Daddy's trust fund and their weekends in the country in Hunter wellingtons and padded body-warmers.

But I underestimated Serena. Because although she looked boring (beautiful, yes, but undeniably boring) she possessed this unspoilt quality. She was deeply naive. It wasn't stupidity, not exactly, but rather a sense of other-worldliness, as if she had never quite found her place on the planet. A more unkind word might be 'ditzy'.

For whatever reason, Ben was smitten. I realised, that night, when I looked across the table at him, desperately wanting him to look back, that Serena was there to stay. Ben turned to her and, with the pad of his thumb, stroked the stray strand of hair away from her mouth, then kissed her with excruciating tenderness. And I knew things were going to change.

It wasn't a perfect marriage. They had the requisite children, each one precocious and adorable in a slightly different way from the one that had come before, and as Ben broke away from the company he had worked for since graduation to build up his own business, they spent more and more time apart. Serena, ever vague, never understood the pressures of his work. Ben, increasingly preoccupied, had no time left over to devote to the emotional maintenance of his wife. She grew harder. The naivety I had once noticed became polluted by a certain world-weary assessment of things and people – of their value; their cost. Ben loved her still, of that I was sure. He just wasn't in love with her.

I don't think either of them really cared. They put on a good show. Serena had aged well, thanks to the judicious use of fillers administered by a discreet plastic surgeon and the unparalleled youth-preserving tactic of having very little to do. She became one of those glamorous, wealthy women who don't have enough to occupy their time and who attempt to fill it with charity lunch-eons and a nebulous search for meaning. She went on Ayurvedic retreats and meditation weekends, leaving the children in the care of two full-time nannies and a dedicated housekeeper who wore a dark uniform designed to look not too like a uniform. She spoke a lot about 'connections' and 'auras'. Ben was kind to her. In public, they made a good pair.

But she still had her 'ideas'. And one of these, Ben told me as we stood in the chapel, was to do with the ghost at Tipworth. He said she had arranged for a local exorcist to come and perform some charade that would 'release the negative energy'.

'How does one find a local exorcist?' I asked. 'Do they advertise in the *Yellow Pages*?'

Ben laughed. 'Fuck knows. I mean, does the *Yellow Pages* even still exist?'

'Trust Serena ...' I let the thought dwindle, unanswered.

We stood side by side for a few seconds, as the light outside slid into paleness. The coloured panels in the windows sent rhombuses of pink, green and blue across the worn stone floor.

'You're not drinking,' Ben said, accusingly.

I looked at my champagne flute. It was true. I hadn't taken a single sip. My fingertips were clammy from the accumulated moisture on the side of the glass.

'Sorry.' I smiled, then raised the glass. 'Here's to you, Ben. Your new home. And, happy birthday.'

'Thanks LS.'

We clinked. But I felt again, looking at the studied vacancy of his face, that something was amiss.

'My oldest friend,' I said, trying once more to elicit some sort of spark of recognition. But he shuffled uncomfortably and still couldn't look at me.

'Listen, LS. We need to talk.' His voice was dry and reedy. 'About …' He gesticulated broadly with his free hand, as if painting treble clefs in imaginary sand.

I waited. One beat. Two. Blood pumping. Muscles clenched.

'I've got a business opportunity I want to discuss with you.'

Relief. The flush of it almost physical.

'Oh,' I said, trying not to think of all the things he might have said. 'Interesting. Tell me more.'

I made an effort to keep the pleasure out of my voice. Ben had never asked me to join him in any kind of business venture before. I'd always been a little offended at his failure to do so. Of course, in the early days, I didn't have the necessary funds. But since the publication of *Art: Who Gives a F**k?*, my bank balance had been conspicuously healthier. Published in twenty-one languages. In the *Sunday Times* bestseller list for twelve solid weeks. The royalties kept rolling in.

Now that he was offering me an in, I was delighted. It meant he trusted me. It meant I was just as good as any of his trustafarian friends.

'It's a little investment idea I have. A new casino-style resort in Montenegro.'

'Ah. Montenegro: the new Monte Carlo.'

'Ha!' he said again. 'Very good, LS. Yes. Should use that as a slogan, really.'

I took a sip of champagne. The bubbles pricked my tongue.

'Of course. When do you want to have this chat? Not now, surely?'

He shook his head, the curls in spasm.

'No, mate, no. We'll find a quiet time after the party. With the wives.'

I raised my eyebrows.

'I mean … it will involve them too.'

'How intriguing.'

'We can do it once the guests have gone.'

'I suppose it would have made even more sense for us to stay the night then. I mean, the Premier Inn has its charms, but …' As soon as I spoke, I realised I sounded defensive.

Ben groaned. 'I knew you'd be pissed off. I said as much to Serena.'

'I'm not pissed off.'

'You are, LS. I can tell. Listen, it's a family thing. We've got all these aunts and uncles and in-laws. You know what it's like.'

I walked up the aisle of the chapel, trailing my hand along the edge of the hymn-book rails. When I got to the altar, I noticed dust on one fingernail. *You know what it's like.* One of his phrases.

'No, Ben,' I said, turning back to him, my voice reverberating off the vaulted ceiling. 'No, I don't. You seem to forget I have no family.'

In the failing light, I could no longer see his expression. His glass, empty now, hung lazily from his hand.

'You're it,' I said, but too quietly for him to hear.

Notebook of Lucy Gilmour

WHAT WAS IT ABOUT HIM I LIKED?

When I first saw him he just stood apart. It was the way he was dressed. Martin always wore impeccable clothes. He was in well-tailored suits when everyone else at the newspaper was in jeans and loafers. Even when he tried to be casual, he couldn't quite manage it. Corduroy and cashmere was about as relaxed as he got.

I remember seeing him in the staff canteen, sitting by himself, a copy of the *Financial Times* folded with precision into a rectangle, comfortably sized so that it could be held easily in one hand. I noticed his fingers: elegant, long, the nails freshly cut and clean. He was eating a salad from one of those clear plastic containers. I watched as he forked limp rocket leaves to his mouth and ate them in small, delicate bites.

He looked up occasionally, as if he wanted to be noticed and, at the same time, his demeanour suggested he didn't care what anyone else thought. I admired this. I was twenty-two, just out of university, and I questioned everything about myself. I had no faith in my instincts. I needed constant affirmation just to prove I existed. I liked to lose myself in the company of others, hoping that if I found safety in a big enough group, no one would expect me to talk. The idea of sitting on my own in the middle of the canteen and not minding who saw me was completely alien. I would rather have walked naked down Kensington High Street.

Later, when I got to know him a bit, I realised Martin was the most original person I'd ever met. I asked him so much and yet, by the end of each conversation, I would have learned nothing new about him. He had no back-story. He didn't talk about his family. Unlike most men, he didn't particularly seem to want to talk about himself. The only person he mentioned with any regularity was his best friend, Ben, and he would refer to him in just that way: 'my best friend Ben', as if the label were part of his official title.

I found the mystery interesting. I had just come out of a two-year relationship with a boy I'd known from university and the whole thing had been suffocatingly intense. My ex wanted to share everything. He wanted to hold hands in the street. He wanted to kiss me in public. He wanted to tell me how he imagined us growing old together. Once, he had cried in the cinema at a film about an elderly woman with dementia whose husband struggles to care for her. I was embarrassed for him.

'It's just,' he said afterwards, handkerchief moist, 'it made me think of us and what would happen if …'

He never finished his sentence but I knew what he meant and although I took his hand, although I told myself how lovely this was and how lucky I was to be loved this way, part of me felt uneasy. An internal voice that said: what a fool he is to feel so deeply for you. You're not worth it and soon he'll find out and then where will you be?

Martin never sought to know me, not really. He was interested in my opinions and I think he enjoyed talking to me on an intellectual level, unwrapping the layers of my brain like a Christmas present. But otherwise, it was all surface – at least, to begin with. And this appealed to me. I liked being made to feel smart without having to commit to anything else. Martin took pleasure in the present tense of my company, without needing it to have a future or a past conjugation.

Do you know how rare that is? Very. I've never met anyone else with that capacity.

He wasn't my type, physically. I'd always gone for stockier men with strong arms and big hands and shoulders that looked as if they could lift a car but then, look at where that had got me. I told myself it was time to try something different. Martin was slender, his chest almost concave. He was tall, with fine brown hair parted to one side in an old-fashioned way. He wore glasses and his face was long, the planes of it delicate and handsome. When he smiled, it managed to be both impish and vague. He had narrow hips and the cheekbones of a teenage model.

Later, I would discover Martin had an ability to change his appearance to fit whatever social setting he found himself in. It was never anything I could put my finger on. It was simply as if his surface changed colour to melt into the environment. A chameleon.

At the start, it was a friendship between work colleagues. We went for lunch together. Once, at Maggie Jones, we ordered two globe artichokes and the house white, which came in a huge bottle. The waitress marked it off with a pen to show how much we'd drunk. Martin kept filling my glass slightly more than he filled his.

'You should do something different with your hair,' he said, tearing off a crust of bread and popping it in his mouth.

It was the first time he had ever mentioned my physical appearance. I reddened under the scrutiny, immediately self-conscious.

'Well!' I tried to make light of it. 'That's very forward.'

'Those velvet scrunchie things …' Martin waved his hand as if ridding the room of a smell. 'Why do you put it up all the time? Let it fall to your shoulders and frame your face.'

I was flattered that he had put such thought into it. That, by extension, it meant he had been studying my face. It was Martin's form of a compliment, I realised, and I seized on it gratefully, immediately sliding the scrunchie from my ponytail and shaking my hair out, tucking it behind my ears.

He reached across the table, untucking it. A breadcrumb from his finger stuck to my cheek.

'There,' he said. 'Much better.'

I didn't like my hair down because it was neither straight nor curly. It was frizzy and never looked intentional. But under the warm glow of Martin's approbation, I started seeing myself differently. At his desk, he had a postcard of a Lord Leighton painting propped up against a pile of books. Perhaps, I thought, he saw me as one of those pre-Raphaelite heroines whose hair (now that I brought it to mind) was wavy too.

'Thank you,' I said.

'Pleasure.'

When I got home that evening, I studied myself in the mirror. My eyebrows were too thick. My cheeks too full. I tried sucking them in and squinted, attempting to make myself look thinner. I played with my hair. It fell on my shoulders and I wished it were longer and glossier and easier to manage. I had a small scar on the side of my nose from a bicycle accident when I was a child and I worried that it looked like a spot. I sighed. I put my hair back up in a scrunchie and, even though I wasn't seeing anyone but was just going to spend the evening watching television, I dabbed some concealer on my scar. It made me feel better not to see it.

The next day, I put concealer on in exactly the same place. I left my hair down. I passed the mascara wand over my lashes. I never normally wore make-up in the office.

When Martin came in, he had headphones on. Not the in-ear ones that most people wore, but the old-fashioned kind that used to come with Walkmans. I tried to catch his eye but he didn't notice me. At lunch, he left without asking me along. It was only in the afternoon, when I handed him a page proof of an interview he'd done with a young actress, that we spoke.

'You look nice,' he said.

I flushed.

'Hair,' I replied, stupidly.

He smiled. 'A marked improvement.'

That day, we went for a drink after work. He ordered Guinness, I remember, which sat oddly with his slightly fey aestheticism. I thought of him like a languorous cat: elegant but distant. He had these tortoiseshell glasses with round rims that reminded me of a writer from a different era. He took them off and rubbed the bridge of his nose, leaving them folded by a soggy beer mat on the table between us.

When he got up to go to the loo, I picked up the glasses. I don't know why but I tried them on. They sat tightly around my skull and I was surprised to notice they weren't prescription lenses, just plain perspex.

Before Martin, my own personal appearance wasn't something that ever bothered me, partly because my parents never cared that much. They were lovely people and I had a lovely upbringing. Lovely. I remember an American friend of mine once saying 'lovely' was such an English word – 'Like you're describing a picnic,' she said.

But it *was* lovely. My older brother took up most of my parents' time and pride. He was the brainy one, the sporty one, the popular one. I was happy to sit on the sidelines of his success. I'd always been the not-quite child. I got Bs in exams, not quite As. I didn't quite get into Oxford so went to Durham instead. I wasn't quite pretty, but I was pleasant-looking and I was taught that those kinds of things didn't much matter. It was what was inside that counted. I made myself pliable and easy and nice to be around. I was helpful.

'You see what needs doing before it has to be pointed out to you,' my mother once told me as she heaved a roast chicken out of the oven. 'You anticipate.'

That was my thing. *Lucy: she looks after people.* And it was true. All through my teens, I anticipated what others wanted from me and then I shaped myself accordingly. I was shy and quiet and never a threat. They liked me for it.

Except for Martin. Martin was a tougher nut to crack.

I used to do the tea round for my desk at the *Bugle*. I knew everyone's orders: milk and two sugars, no milk but a slice of lemon, Earl Grey not English Breakfast. Martin never wanted one, no matter how many times I offered. Eventually, I plucked up the courage to ask why.

He pursed his lips. He had pale lips that always made his face look cold.

'That stuff they serve in the canteen?' He rolled his eyes. 'Please. It's hardly worthy of the name.'

'I can get coffee if you'd rather.'

'Even worse,' he said, returning to his computer screen.

It wasn't rude, the way he did it. He delivered his opinions as statements of fact: not aggressively, just as if they were indisputable.

Every time he dismissed me, I simply wanted him to notice me more. That evening, after work, I got the bus to Knightsbridge. I went to Harvey Nichols and I bought a specially packaged box of expensive teas. I left them on Martin's desk the next morning. He never mentioned it in person. Instead, he sent an email. It read simply: 'Thank you for the tea.' And then the box disappeared and he returned to refusing all hot drinks.

How intriguing, I thought. How different.

My friend Neesha at work couldn't understand it.

'What do you see in him?' she asked.

We were standing outside the building, shivering in the wind as we took a fag break. They had just declared we were no longer allowed to smoke inside the office. Neesha smoked more than I did. She was secretary to the editor and had the most stressful job in the building. Mostly, I came outside just to keep her company.

'Who?'

'Martin, dummy.'

Neesha passed me her cigarette. Her red lipstick circled the butt. I took a drag.

'He's interesting.'

'You can say that again.' Neesha chuckled. 'There's something not right with him, Luce.'

'Don't be mean.'

'I'm not. You must have noticed, love. The other day Ian had to say his name eight times before he showed any signs of life.'

'He's just in his own world,' I said, surprised at how defensive I felt.

Neesha sniffed. 'Thinks he's better than us, more like.'

'It's not that.'

'Oh please, Luce. I know his type. Public school, Oxbridge, acts like his shit doesn't stink. Cares more about … I don't know … his fucking gold cufflinks than about actual people.'

I laughed.

'You're too nice, Luce. You always think the best.'

This wasn't strictly true. I was good at appearing nice on the surface but my special skill was getting people to like me whether I liked them or not. With Martin, it was different. Because I wasn't sure where I stood with him. It was the unavailability that lured me in. I flattered myself that it was simply a disguise worn by a scared little boy who needed looking after and I was the one he would let in.

Neesha finished her cigarette and ground the butt into the pavement with the edge of her spiky high heel. 'Just be careful, that's all I'm saying. He doesn't care about you the way you care about him.'

'I think—'

'He's never said a word to me, you know. Even though he's in and out of the editor's office every week, he's never once said hello.' Neesha loosened her coat. 'You can tell a lot about someone by looking at how they treat secretaries.'

I didn't listen. I kept seeing Martin. Our lunch appointments turned into dinner dates. The tea run became after-work drinks. The days turned into weeks which turned into months and soon I found I looked forward to each day more if I knew I was going to see him. The weekends dragged because they were devoid of his company.

I concede, looking back, that I was the one who made most of the running. Martin seemed either too polite or too shy to initiate a kiss, so I was the one who lunged one night after we'd been out for dinner at a Persian restaurant in Kensington. I didn't much care for Persian food – too many fragrances and the crispy rice stuck in my teeth – but Martin loved it, so I went for him.

The kiss was dry and chaste. I tried to wriggle the tip of my tongue into his mouth but he resisted. I drew back and looked at him.

'What's wrong?' I asked. 'Don't you like me?'

He held his head back.

'Of course I like you, Lucy.'

'Well then.'

I kissed him again and this time he responded, but cautiously, as though evaluating each reflex and twist. I clasped the back of his head, running my hands through his hair, and gradually he relaxed. I was moved by his nervousness. Martin, who was so particular in every other respect, so certain of the right way to wear a tie, so unquestioningly sure of what constituted good taste, seemed to have no parameters for this. I wondered how many times he had been kissed before me. It crossed my mind that he might be a virgin.

And instead of repelling me, his unworldliness was appealing. In this one area, I thought, I was superior. He could teach me about art and beauty and the best way to do my hair, but I was the one who would take the lead physically, who would show him how it was done.

Under the light of the streetlamp, I reached down and slid my hand under the waistband of his trousers. He was limp. I brushed against it gently with my fingers and then, rhythmically slid my palm up and down until I could feel him stirring.

'No,' he said. I ignored him. 'No, Lucy, don't.'

He stepped away from me, removing my hand.

'Sorry,' I said.

Martin held his breath for a moment. I wondered what he was thinking. He seemed to be wrestling with some inexpressible thought and then I saw his face relax and he smiled.

'It's just …' He bent forward and kissed the top of my head. 'Too fast.'

I nodded, relieved.

'Yes, yes, of course.'

I drew back. He went home and I returned to my flat. Over the next few weeks, I was careful not to crowd him. We continued going for dinner but I didn't try to kiss him again. We held hands, his palm cool and smooth. Once, he came back to my flat and we slept next to each other without touching.

I told myself it was an old-fashioned courtship and when, at the end of six months of this, we did finally have sex, it required some subtle manoeuvring. It took a while for Martin to get hard. He needed me to be in a certain position. Again, I told myself it was sweet to be with someone so inexperienced, so needful of my help.

I'd had enough of men who took me as if I were their due, who woke me up with an erection and grunted their way to a satisfactory orgasm. I found Martin's tentativeness delicate and respectful. He treated me like a piece of fragile china. I was sure, once he got used to me – to us – the sex would become more relaxed, less mechanical. I was beginning to love him, not for his physical prowess but for his mind. I wanted to hear what he thought about everything.

By the end of the year, we were engaged. I felt proud. I had won him over. Me. Lucy. The not-quite. And I was happy, too. Very happy. He saw something in me I failed to see in myself. How lucky that was. How I loved him for it. And how I loved thinking I could be the one to protect him.

Neesha stopped asking me to go outside for fags. We still said hello and goodbye and smiled at each other warmly but I knew it wasn't the same. It didn't matter to me as much as I thought it would. I told myself: she doesn't see the Martin I see. She can't understand what he's like away from the office, in those quiet moments where I catch him on the sofa looking sad and lonely and I wonder what's going on in his head and I reach out and stroke the soft hair at the back of his neck and slowly, he comes back to me, and we kiss and I know there is no one else who can do this for him. Only me.

Martin

Epsom, 1985

MY MOTHER'S NAME WAS SYLVIA. You don't get many Sylvias nowadays, do you? A shimmery, slippery name for such a big-boned woman. Recently, one of Ben's children introduced me to a fuzzy-faced toy and told me with pride that it was part of his collection of 'Sylvanian Families'. I'm not sure whether the animal in my hand was meant to be a rabbit or a mouse or a non-specific mutation of both and although it looked soft to the touch, when I pressed it between my fingers I realised that underneath the thin coating of fur, it was hard plastic. That tallied more with my notion of my mother.

My mother was a perpetually disappointed woman. Her husband – my father – proved the ultimate in unreliability by having the temerity to die before I was born. The worst of it was that his death was entirely unexceptional, thereby denying my mother the one pleasurable thing she might have got out of it – namely, a good story.

It was December and my father had been dispatched to post a clutch of Christmas cards in the letterbox at the end of the road. The weather in Epsom had been bitterly cold, falling below zero the night before, and as he turned left out of the house, my father's foot made contact with a patch of ice and he slipped, falling over onto his back and hitting his head against the kerb, triggering a cerebral haemorrhage.

A neighbour found him, dead in a spreading pool of his own blood, and alerted my mother who was eight months pregnant and in the process of making a fish pie for supper. I don't know what my mother's reaction would have been and, not having been a witness to my parents' marriage, I have no idea as to the extent of her affection or otherwise for her husband. From what I know of her now, I can't imagine her being in love, but perhaps she was and perhaps it was my father's death that made her into the bitter woman she became. Allow me to give her the benefit of the doubt on that.

She never spoke to me of my father, of the kind of man he was. There were no pictures of him around the house. He existed in my head as a gap: a burnt hole in a non-existent family photograph which I could not fill with any kind of recognisable physical detail, no matter how hard I tried.

My mother told me the story of my father's death only once, when I was old enough to have found the words to ask her. I must have been eight or nine. For all of my childhood up to that point, my father's absence had been explained away by two simple syllables: 'He died'. This would usually be followed by a sigh and a sense that this had made things very difficult for her and that was all I needed to be aware of.

It had taken me a while to pluck up the courage to ask for further elaboration. I remember I chose my occasion carefully. It was at the end of the day, when my mother had come back from her much-despised job at the local cafeteria and she was sitting by the gas fire, sipping from a mug of Horlicks that I had warmed for her in the microwave. 'How did my dad die?' I asked.

She wrinkled her nose.

'I was wondering what took you so long,' she said. And then she relayed the whole episode with a sturdy matter-of-factness. I remember not looking at her as she was talking, but instead focusing on the fire's fake flames sending leaping shadows up the flock wallpaper and the overripe-pear smell of gas as it seeped into the room.

One detail of Sylvia's story stuck in my mind (she was always Sylvia to me, never 'mother'). I still think of it now, some thirty years later. My mother told me that after she had called the ambulance, she had gone outside, wrapped up in her outdoors coat, and she had bent down by my father's lifeless form and she had gathered up the scattered Christmas cards from the pavement and put them in her pocket to send the next day.

'But …' I said. 'Did they have blood on them?'

'What kind of a question is that?' She took a slurp of Horlicks and looked away. 'I wasn't going to waste my time writing a whole new set, was I now?'

I wonder what they thought, those people who received those blood-spattered cards.

My father's death meant that it was just the two of us from the start. There is a peculiar kind of claustrophobia that comes from being the only child of a single mother. You learn, quite quickly, that nothing you do will ever be enough to fill your parent's yawning need for filial devotion. What starts off as love rapidly turns into a sort of inescapable hatred and the hatred is even more needy, even more trapping than the love was. It sucks you dry from the inside.

I think my mother's obsessive love for me co-existed with contempt for her own vulnerability. She was dependent on me for affection and yet she denied that she needed it. I never met her standards because I never knew what they were. They seemed to shift and change on a whim. All I knew was that I was a source of near-constant disappointment.

I could read this disappointment in the wrinkles at the corner of her mouth, bracketing her lips downward. I could sense it in the way she looked at me sometimes, sideways on as I was doing the washing-up or watching *The Generation Game* on the television or sitting naked in the bath, a trail of goosebumps down my spine because the water was never hot enough. When she looked at me in this way, she seemed to be analysing me, trying to work me out, like a sceptic attempting to understand another person's faith.

There was some oddness. There always is in that kind of relationship. For instance, she insisted on dressing me each morning, long after I was old enough to do it myself. She would hold open my underpants so that I could clamber into them, kneeling on my bedroom carpet so that I was uncomfortably aware that my penis was at her eye level. She would brush my hair brusquely and tie my shoelaces and prepare my packed lunch: Mother's Pride triangles with Marmite and cucumber (which I disliked but never told her I disliked) and then she would walk me to the bus stop on her way to work, waving me off as I took my regular window seat and made the short journey to the local primary school.

I returned from school earlier than she got off work, so I would let myself in. She expected me to make my own supper and then to prepare something simple for her, a chicken kiev or a can of baked beans on toast. When she came back through the front door, I could evaluate her mood from the tread of her feet on the kitchen lino. If it had been a bad day at the cafe, she would find fault with everything.

'Why are you wearing that stupid old jumper? Why have you made me green beans when you know I hate them? What are you, a bloody retard? I haven't raised you to be a simpleton, have I?'

She would never hit me, but she would nitpick and carp until I felt physically assaulted. Only once did she pinch the tender flesh on my forearm, twisting it anti-clockwise between her fingers until I yelped with the burning pain of it. There was a mark there for days.

You might have thought school was my refuge. My mother, the beneficiary of a generous life insurance policy after my father's death, had decided to send me to a fee-paying preparatory and it was true that, for a time, I enjoyed the rough and tumble of playtime, the rambunctious whoops of the other children as they scampered around the sandpit. But, fairly quickly, I began to stand out. I was never sure why. Perhaps it was something to do with my face. I have been told I have a tendency to look disapproving or unhappy when I think my features are simply expressionless and relaxed.

Perhaps it was that I ran out of patience fairly quickly with the other children. I began to feel detached from them, older somehow. I've always felt older. After a few weeks of watching them sift sand through a red plastic square with holes in the bottom and shriek with displeasure when said red plastic square was removed so that someone else could play with it, I found that I couldn't understand what it was about the red plastic square that was so appealing.

I tried to evaluate it logically. Was it the physical sensation of the sand siphoned through the small apertures? Was it the idea of having achieved something, of having transmuted a seemingly solid substance into a liquid river of grains? And, even assuming it was either of these fundamentally trivial motivations, why was that so completely absorbing? Why did the red plastic square assume such proportions in these children's heads, the idea of it expanding to fill all available space, all their angsty desire, their desperate need to play and experiment ... how could all of it be subsumed into a single unexceptional item with 'Made in Taiwan' stamped on its underside?

The red plastic square tormented me for weeks. I felt there must be a piece of me lacking, a talent for childishness that I didn't possess. I just didn't get it. It annoyed me that I didn't. Believe me, I wanted more than anything to be an unthinking, easy child. I wanted to belong. And at the same time, I knew that I didn't.

So maybe that goes some way towards explaining what happened next. It was the incident that was to change the course of my life although, naturally, I didn't realise it at the time. It was to do with the bird.

A sparrow. A defenceless sparrow who had fallen from the sky onto the bricked surface of the playground. Wing broken. Mewling from its beak. Flapping senselessly. Heart pitter-pattering frantically inside its feathered chest.

A girl called Jennifer was the first to find it. Jennifer was blonde and tall, with ungainly limbs and a clumsy way of running which, she confessed to me once in an unguarded moment, was modelled on the way Bobbie ran in the film of *The Railway Children*. She was one of those children forever destined to be mildly despised

41

for her inelegance and, indeed, when I looked her up on Facebook a few years ago, she still had those unfortunate broad shoulders and a pitifully small number of online friends despite her emoticon-strewn status updates.

Jennifer found the bird as she was playing tag. She stopped, almost tripping over her own shoes, and tears sprung to her eyes. It just so happened that I was sitting on a nearby bench with a book in my hand, and when I saw her standing there, whimpering, I got up to see what was going on.

'What is it?' I asked.

Jennifer was breathing heavily, a half-asthmatic wheeze in the back of her throat.

'It's ... it's ...' She pointed at the bird's prone form. 'I think it's dying.'

I knelt down and peered closer at the sparrow. It looked at me, moist eye swivelling in its socket. I extended one finger and prodded it, feeling the silky feathers part with the pressure.

'Don't touch it, Martin!' Jennifer was saying. 'We need to tell the teacher.'

The teacher was duly told and the bird was scooped up by adult hands and placed in a makeshift nest of cotton-wool and pipe-cleaners. This was then put on a high ledge in the hallway, just above a radiator and next to a window overlooking the street outside. The ledge ran parallel to a flight of stairs which led up to our classroom.

For the next few days, when the bell went for morning lessons, an excitable gaggle of schoolchildren would file up the staircase and peer into the cotton-wool nest to see how the sparrow was faring. The teachers seized upon this set of circumstances as a way of educating us about 'nature'. (They were a bovine lot, those primary school teachers, with barely an original thought between them.)

So it was that some time after that, there was a competition to come up with a name for the 'school sparrow'. I forget who won it now or what the eventual name was – let's say it was 'Sammy'

– but by christening the bird, I noticed everyone felt closer to it, as though it were a form of mascot. Then, we were encouraged to draw pictures of the blessed thing – coloured pencil doodles which were Blu Tacked on the walls like sacrificial offerings. More than once, our homework consisted of finding out 'facts' about Sammy. This being the pre-internet era, I had to waste more time than I would have liked poring over *The Observer Book of Birds* in the local library.

We had been told not to touch the sparrow and not to disturb it with our gawping. But each time I passed Sammy while walking up the stairs, I wanted to reach out and squeeze him in my cupped hands. He was such a small, insignificant thing – barely bigger than a tennis ball. The more the other children stared and whispered, the more they monitored every tiny movement of Sammy's body for signs of recovery, the more angry I became. It was so stupid to attach such importance to a brainless creature.

But what really made me snap was overhearing Jennifer one morning. Ever since the discovery of the sparrow, she had assumed a possessiveness over it. She appeared to think that her self-appointed guardianship gave her an insight into what the bird was feeling and how long its recovery might be expected to take and she would treat us all to smug reports on its progress. Her father was a vet, as I recall – a fact she took every opportunity to mention.

On this particular morning, she had been invited to the front of the class by the teacher to tell us how the sparrow was faring.

'I think Sammy might be flying again soon. His wing is almost healed.'

Jennifer looked pleased with herself. The teacher, a woman appropriately called Mrs Love, was smiling benignly, nodding her head in agreement. I think it was this that finally sent me over the edge. Because it was all so bogus. The sparrow hadn't shown any signs of recovery. Its wing was still as uselessly snapped as ever. Its eyes had acquired a dull patina. The kindest thing would have been to break its neck in the playground.

'It's probably going to die,' I said. I spoke without putting my hand up first and when the words tripped out of my mouth they were louder than I had anticipated. Jennifer took a surprised step backwards. Her lower lip wobbled. The teacher glared at me.

'Martin. What a terrible thing to say.'

'It's not,' I protested. 'It's true.'

'That's enough, Martin.'

I felt a hot bullet of anger lodge itself in my throat. I think it might have been the first time I'd ever been told off by a teacher and I felt it keenly. I vowed to myself I would never, ever forget this moment, the indignity of it, the unfairness and the dumb, unquestioning way in which the teacher sided with ignorance over truth simply because it was easier. Who cared about imparting actual knowledge when you could keep everyone quiet by making them draw pictures of a bloody bird?

(I've never liked animals. I find it sickening how we fetishise them with tartan dog coats and velvet cat collars and special tins of food with jellied rabbit chunks and how we invite them into our homes, these wild, unthinking things, and expect them to reflect all the human characteristics we most wish to see in ourselves.)

The morning after the teacher had publicly slapped me down, I told my mother I needed to go in to school early to help with the completion of a class project. She dropped me off at the bus stop an hour before my usual time. The school was dark, apart from one light coming from the headmistress's office. The front door was on the latch. I walked in, taking care to tread lightly so that my plimsolls did not squeak against the floor.

To one side of the hallway were the cloakroom stalls, their pegs empty apart from a single, discarded art-class overall. Beyond, I could make out the receding outline of Doris, the cleaner, who was pushing an industrial hoover along the corridor, swinging the flex from side to side as she went. She was listening to her Walkman, as I had known she would be, humming along to the indistinct tune piping through her headphones and swaying her arthritic hips as best she could in time with the silent beat.

I left my coat and my bag in the cloakroom, not by my normal peg but in a corner, stuffed behind one of the benches, where I could retrieve it later. I slid off my shoes, nudging them into the same cubby-hole. Then I tiptoed back into the corridor and up the stairs, carrying under my arm two volumes of the *Encyclopaedia Britannica* borrowed from the local library for just this purpose (you couldn't check out reference books, I seem to recall, so I must have temporarily stolen them). I took the steps slowly, one by one, clutching the weight of the encyclopaedias to my waist, feeling reassurance in their solid bulk.

I gazed up at the ledge, allowing my eyes to acclimatise to the early-morning gloom and then to focus on the blurry outline of the bird's man-made nest. Pipe-cleaners and twigs and strands of mismatched wool and cotton-wool. When I got to the top step, I placed the two encyclopaedias on the floor and climbed on top. I wasn't a very tall boy and I had known I wouldn't be able to reach the ledge without some help. Looking back, I can't help but feel a bit proud of my foresight. I think it shows a degree of maturity to be able to make such a plan and enact it under my own steam.

I stood on sock-covered tiptoe, leaning forwards with one hand placed flat against the wall to keep my balance but I still couldn't quite reach the nest. It was agonisingly close. I could brush the tips of my fingers against a protruding bit of twig, but I couldn't get the purchase I needed to remove it. I didn't dare use two hands in case I lost my balance and fell with a clatter down the stairs.

I stretched, pushing at the single millimetre of twig I could reach until I could feel a trickle of sweat running down my back, the moisture attaching itself to my school shirt so that the material stuck to my skin and made me even hotter. A bead of sweat fell from my forehead onto the grey stone floor and left a dark circle there. I began to get frustrated and then panicked and then angry and I knew I was running out of time and that the other children would soon start arriving in dribs and drabs and then in a stream of maroon and blue before the first bell sounded at 8.50 a.m. I tried one final lunge, jumping as high as I could, both feet spring-ing off the encyclopaedias, and as I leaped, I took my balancing arm away from the wall and grabbed at the nest with both hands.

I crumpled back to the ground, the books skittering to one side, my leg twisting under my weight. There was a thudding pain in my left ankle. But when I looked at the bounty in my hands, all this was forgotten. There it was: the nest and, inside, a startled, twitching Sammy.

The rest of it happened quickly. I put the encyclopaedias back under my arm, balanced the nest in my free hand, and crept back downstairs. I knew Sammy couldn't fly because of his broken wing. No escape. The bird's eye pulsated blackly: a squelching dot of terror. I stared at it, cupped in the nest in my hands, and although I had a vague instinct to talk to it in order to make it feel better, although I knew that's what other, more normal chil-dren would do, I remained silent. And I remember thinking: let it suffer. Let it learn what life is like. And that in thinking this, I felt less alone. Because there was something else, some other living thing, that was enduring an experience worse than my own.

I went back to the cloakroom, put the nest on the bench, deposited the books on the floor by my peg, slipped on my shoes and, picking up Sammy again ('Sammy' in my mind now: a thing worthy of a name), walked swiftly outside. I made my way towards the playground, but instead of going through the gates as usual, I tacked to the right and followed the fence around the perimeter. I could see the swings. The looming, inverted 'v' of the slide. In the distance, a lone car, its engine puttering as the passenger door opened and disgorged a child.

The school had been built in the middle of what must once have been rather a nice patch of greenery. Behind the playground was a copse of trees. We weren't allowed to wander here, but the naughtier children always did in order to experiment with ciga-rettes and kissing, so I knew it existed. By the time I reached the field in question, I was panting. I walked towards the central grouping of trees. The grass was wet from overnight rainfall and my plimsolls became stained with claggy brown mud. I would have to clean them later, I thought, before my mother got home.

At the centre of the trees was a small clearing, lined with discarded fag butts and empty crisp packets. At one edge were the ashy remnants of a fire, scraps of newsprint stuck to the underside of stones. I put Sammy in his nest on the ground. The bird was shivering now, straining to move its useless wing to no avail. Stupid thing, I thought.

I picked up a medium-sized rock from the undergrowth. I played with it in my hand, feeling the heft of it. And then, I slammed the sharp end of the rock down into the nest. The bird made no sound but when I withdrew my hand, I saw that its eye was still flickering, still sentient. Again, I punched it with the rock, throwing all my might into that single action. Again. Again. And again, this time emitting a scream for what I knew would be the final blow. I felt the crack of slender bones beneath my fist. A noise like the slow release of air from a flattening tyre. When I removed my hand, one knuckle was bleeding. The bird lay there, cracked and lifeless, the tremble of its eye finally stilled.

I told myself it had been a mercy, that only I, out of my cohort of classmates, could see the bird was suffering and needed to be put out of its misery as swiftly as possible. How frustrating it must have been for that creature, sitting on a ledge in a concrete building, gazing out of a window at the sky it could no longer fly through, beholden to these lumpen schoolchildren for scraps of birdseed. How undignified, I thought. How unfair.

As a child, I remember so very fiercely wanting to be grown up: to earn the privilege of being in control of my own existence, not by doing anything, but simply by existing for longer. I chafed against the arbitrary restrictions placed on my life. Lights out. Homework hour. Tidy your bedroom. Finish your vegetables. Stop reading. Stop fidgeting. Stop staring. Is that why I felt such a thrill when I killed the bird? We're not meant to admit to this kind of feeling, but let me tell you honestly: I felt its death with a visceral intent – the violent pleasure of having finally *done* something. It was the ultimate satisfaction.

There is no need to dwell too much on what happened next. You can guess most of it. There was a predictable flurry of activity when the bird was discovered to be missing. It was Doris who raised the alarm; Doris, the cleaner, to whom I had never paid much notice, who had always seemed a bit of a dullard with her vacant expression, her yellow dusting cloths tucked into the elasticated waistband of her jeans. Well, Doris told a teacher, who then told the headmistress, who then informed the entire school at assembly that the bird had disappeared to a general commotion of disbelief. Jennifer, sitting cross-legged on the floor in the row in front of me, started crying. Alan Munro patted her arm with his podgy fingers, fat knuckles blotted with dirt. Next to me, Susan Rankin gasped and pulled the cuff of her school jumper over her hand. I was still, head lowered, eyes fixed at a point just to the right of one of my maroon socks. There was, I reasoned, no point feigning emotion. I was not known for being an expressive child. Besides, I don't think I really cared about being found out. I think I already knew the game was up. I think I wanted it to be. I was so sick of them all, you see.

As the assembly continued, and we shuffled to our feet to sing 'Morning Has Broken', I could feel someone looking at me. When I glanced round, my eyes met the heated gaze of Mrs Love, her small features contracting.

She waited until the end of assembly to take me aside, grabbing hold of my arm with surprising force, her thin fingers pressing through my jumper.

'So, Martin,' she said in a low voice. 'Do you want to tell me what you did with Sammy?'

'All right,' I said. She looked surprised, then led me off to the staffroom which smelled of instant coffee and fig rolls and had old copies of the *Guardian* and a single dog-eared issue of *Horse and Hound* stacked up on one of the bookshelves. I confessed without much trouble. I glossed over the finer details of how I'd dispatched

48

the creature, saying simply that I felt it should be put out of its misery. Mrs Love's face turned from red to white to shiny as a sweat broke out across her upper lip. I could see that she didn't know what to make of me. She actually tried, at one point, to reach out and take my hand.

The headmistress summoned my mother and said that I was suspended with immediate effect.

My mother was not as furious as I had expected her to be. She refused to talk to me for the rest of the day and sent me to bed without any food, but that was pretty much par for the course. The next day, she didn't go to work but sat waiting for me in glacial silence at the breakfast table. I came down in my pyjamas and dressing gown, having not known what clothes to get dressed in. My school jumper lay wrinkled and empty: a shed skin over the back of my desk chair. I wondered if I would ever wear it again. I was intrigued, more than anything, to know what would happen next.

'Well, Martin,' my mother said as I took a seat and poured milk over a bowl of cereal I did not want to eat. 'I can't say I'm surprised.'

She looked at me over the rim of her coffee mug. There was a chip on the upper edge of the handle: a white arrowhead against the red.

'You've always been a wrong 'un.'

Her lips pressed together in a tight, crooked line.

'I've tried my best for you, I have, and it hasn't been easy, all on my own, but I've tried to raise you like a normal boy. I've given you a roof over your head and everything you could ever want. But you're not, are you? Normal, I mean.' She broke off and then added, more to herself than to me: 'There's something missing.'

I willed myself not to cry. Until this point, I'd felt powerfully immune from any kind of emotion. But my mother had always possessed the ability to wound me at the most tender point.

I nodded.

'Yes.'

She drained the last of her coffee.

49

'Yes,' she repeated. 'There we are.'

We lapsed into silence. My cereal became lumpy. I sipped at my orange juice. Outside, it started to rain, droplets of it trailing down the window in a race of their own making. After a while, my mother pushed back her chair and came round to my side of the table and then she did something I could not remember her ever having done before: she reached out and squeezed my shoulder.

They let me back into their drab little school. My mother spoke to the headmistress and, I suppose, gave her some guff about my dead father and how hard it had been for me. I returned after a fortnight's purdah. Jennifer never spoke to me again and the others kept their distance. But, I confess, I found relief in my exile rather than torment. The time passed peaceably enough. Events merged into each other; a soupy fog. Nothing interesting happened.

And then, one springtime morning, I found myself sitting the entrance exam for Burtonbury School. I think, from what I can recall, that my mother had been speaking to someone in the cafe about my predicament and they had told her I should try for Burtonbury. The customer in question had a troubled relative who had gone there and prospered. It seemed as good an idea as any. In any case, I liked exams and was good at them, and I knew about boarding school from Enid Blyton books so I was in favour of the idea. I wanted so very much to get out of Epsom. The only exciting memory I have of that place is of once having seen Lester Piggott fall off his horse while competing in the Epsom Derby.

I passed the Burtonbury exam, as we had both known I would, and was offered a full scholarship. My mother sewed name tapes into socks for what seemed like weeks. In the welcome pack sent to me before the start of the autumn term, there was a shopping list of necessary items for boarders. I was required to come with one full-size umbrella, one complete rugby kit in the school colours of brown and green (with three changes of Aertex shirts), a shoe-polishing set, a supply of stamps and – most bizarrely – a stiff straw boater with a ribbon which I would be expected to wear for formal occasions.

My mother ignored the approved outfitters and uniform suppliers, seeking out instead the cheaper bargains in charity shops. As a result, my school jumpers were always faded and my P.E. shorts were never white enough and the Aertex shirts had immoveable off-yellow stains under each armpit. The smell of other people's sadness lingered in the threads.

To this day, I have a profound aversion to second-hand clothes. I can't abide the new trend for 'vintage' outfits, the nipped-in 50s dresses sported by overweight ladies who live in east London running Scandinavian coffee shops and the rolled-up chinos favoured by bearded hipsters who work in digital marketing. I have a minimal wardrobe but I invest in key, tailored pieces that last. Although I can't really afford it, I have my suits made to measure by Ben's tailor, purely for the pleasure of knowing no one else has ever shrugged their shoulders into my jacket.

Despite my mother's obsession with cutting costs, the requisite Burtonbury boater defeated her. There simply wasn't an available supply of them in Oxfam, which must have been terribly frustrating. In the end, she was forced to go to Ede & Ravenscroft and spend an inordinate sum on a hat I would only wear three times a term, before consigning it forever to a cardboard box shoved in the back of my wardrobe.

The evening before the first day of my new school, my mother and I took the bus and then the tube to Paddington, armed with my boater and a suitcase full of clothes. My luggage was so heavy that the only way I could board the train was by mounting the stairs, grabbing hold of the suitcase handle and leaning back as far as I could without falling over. In this way, I managed to leverage my body-weight against its bulk before sliding it up into the carriage.

My mother did not wait to see me off. She stood on the platform and watched me take my seat. I glanced at her through the window: a broad woman in a shapeless beige coat buttoned all the way up to her neck. Her face was set. I raised a hand halfway to the window. I was going to wave but then didn't. I thought it might, for some reason, make her cross. She gave a little nod of acknowledgement, then turned and walked away, the low heel of her shoes sounding dully against the concrete.

As she left, I felt a wave of relief, as if a curtain had been lifted from my field of vision. The light flooded in. I blinked and allowed this new sensation to settle. I was on my own, for the first time in my thirteen years on this planet. Entirely, blissfully, permissibly alone.

The train pulled out of the station. The carriage filled with the sound of schoolboy voices and the pop of fizzy-drink cans and crisp packets being opened. I kept staring out of the window, unwilling to speak to anyone. The graffiti and bricks and metal of London slid past and gave way to suburban hedges and children's swings and washing lines which in turn transformed into an unspooling ticker tape of green fields and church spires.

As the train pressed on, I was aware of the importance of the moment. I watched myself, squashed in that train seat, with my untouched sandwiches still wrapped in tinfoil on the table in front of me, and I realised that my life was in the process of taking a different direction, plotted according to a new constellation. At the age of thirteen, my boat was setting sail across the beating tides of a different ocean. I would be starting a new school, one more befitting my character. But perhaps I also had some intimation that a more profound shift of fate awaited me.

Because, although I didn't know it yet, I was about to meet Ben and nothing would ever be the same again.

II.

I REACH ACROSS THE TABLE FOR MY COOLING TEA. My throat is dry from all the talking. My eyes, too, feel scratchy. I wonder if I could ask for some Optrex drops but one look at Grey Suit's downturned mouth suggests the request wouldn't be met in a generous spirit.

He still hasn't spoken. While Beige Hair has been looking at me in a frank, friendly fashion and interjecting with the odd murmur as I recount the evening's events, Grey Suit has been sitting impassively in his chair, arms folded across his stomach. No paunch. A hint of hard muscle beneath the gentle stretching of the shirt buttons.

I'm guessing you have to keep fit if you're in the police. There are probably regular tests where they have to run measured distances as a beeper goes off at shorter and shorter intervals. I can imagine Grey Suit in shorts and a loose T-shirt, perhaps bearing the faded crest of an American university he never attended, sprinting with all his might, his face as void of thought as it is now.

I knew people like him at school: boys who excelled at physicality and who never needed to try with anything else. Big, slab-faced boys with no personalities and an understanding of the world wholly predicated on who would win in any given contest. The kind of boy who would always initiate an arm wrestle in a pub. They were popular, these boys. I wonder if it's because we all have an innate need to be protected. So we seek out the bigger, brawnier specimens and we want to be around them because they will shield us one day when we most need shielding. They will man the lifeboats when we hit the iceberg. And for this, we are willing to overlook their complete lack of conversational guile or intellect.

'So,' Beige Hair is saying, 'you weren't staying at the big house. At Tipworth Priory, I mean?'

I can't work out whether this is a tactic or whether she really hasn't been paying attention.

'No. As I think I already said.'

Beige Hair nods. 'Of course you did, Martin. Of course you did.'

Grey Suit shifts in his chair.

'That didn't bother you, then?' he asks.

'What?'

'Not staying at the Priory? With Ben and Serena?'

'Not at all.'

In my account of the build-up to the party, I omitted a few of the more trivial details. There was simply no need for the police to know Lucy had been offended. Beige Hair keeps looking at me.

'They had lots of family members staying,' I say to fill the silence. 'It was just a logistics thing.'

'Right.'

I exhale more loudly than I intended, not realising I've been holding my breath. It's ridiculous, really, how nervous they make you feel. Even when you haven't done anything wrong. It's like those customs officials at American airports, scowling and rude and suspicious of anything you say.

Beige Hair is looking at me expectantly.

'I'm sorry,' I say. 'I didn't quite catch that?'

'Well, Martin, I was only saying that they seem to have a lot of bedrooms at the Priory. It wouldn't have been too hard for them to find space, would it? And you're such close friends, it just seems odd ...'

'I don't know. You'd have to ask Ben and Serena. Besides, there were security issues.'

'Of course. The VIP.'

'Exactly.'

I glance upwards to the ceiling, hoping to find something of interest there. In one corner, there is a hairline crack. A childhood memory comes to me unbidden: my mother washing my hair in the bath as I, hating every second, fixed my gaze on a crack in the yellowing ceiling, willing it to be over.

'Are you all right?' asks Beige Hair.

'Perfectly.'

'You look a bit upset.'

'Not at all,' I repeat. 'Just wondering how much longer this will take.'

She turns one sheet of paper over, shifting it to the other side of her folder and revealing another page of foolscap beneath, covered with scrawled black handwriting.

'So you and your wife arrived at the party before the other guests to have a drink with Ben and Serena,' she recaps. 'Did you think Mr Fitzmaurice was acting normally?'

'What do you mean?'

'Well, did anything strike you as out of character?'

I shrug.

'Anything on his mind, perhaps?'

'It was three weeks ago. I don't understand why you're raking it all up now …'

'You must know it takes time to gather together the relevant facts,' she says. 'As a journalist, I mean.'

I don't say anything.

She tries a different tack.

'How did Lucy think Mr Fitzmaurice seemed?'

'You'd have to ask her.'

'Oh, she's been very helpful with our enquiries,' Beige Hair says. 'But I wondered what *you* thought, Martin.'

She waits.

'Tell you what,' I say. 'Why don't you tell me what you'd like me to think was on his mind and I'll tell you whether you're right or not?'

For the first time, her expression hardens.

'We don't have time for guessing games, Mr Gilmour. In case it had escaped your notice, we've got a person lying in a critical condition in hospital.'

Mr Gilmour, now. No longer Martin. She stops. A note of irascibility is creeping into her tone and I can see her struggle internally to keep it in check.

'We just want to establish the facts,' she says, more gently. 'So that we can work out exactly what happened and then we can all go home.' She smiles. 'Wouldn't that be nice?'

Grey Suit sniffs his assent, but otherwise stays immobile.

I place the tea back on the table. They have given it to me without a spoon or a stirrer and the sugar has sunk to the bottom like sediment.

'I thought he seemed entirely himself,' I say.

Obviously, I am lying.

2 May

WE DIDN'T SAY ANYTHING as we walked back through to the kitchen. Our champagne flutes were empty. There was a distance between us, solid as concrete. I regretted my comment about not staying over. Stupid of me to say it. Stupid, stupid, stupid.

'So here, LS, we need your advice,' Ben said, pointing towards a blank wall at the bottom of a narrow staircase in the back of the house. It must have once been used by servants, I thought, staring at the stripped wooden steps. Although did monks have servants? I wasn't sure. It didn't seem a particularly monkish thing to have.

'Oh. How so?'

'We want a big piece of art. To lift it a bit, y'know.'

A few years ago, Ben started saying y'know, eliding the two words to form a seamless whole. It was around the time certain politicians started eschewing the glottal stop in order to demonstrate their man-of-the-people credentials. I suppose it was intended to denote a certain informality, a lightness of touch, a sense that, in spite of Ben's enormous pile of inherited wealth and his aggressively successful hedge fund, he was in truth just an easy-going guy. Someone you could talk to. Someone you could kick a ball around with. Someone of whom one could say, 'Oh Ben, he's great. One of us. No airs and graces.'

This reputation was important to Ben. At school, it came to him naturally. Later in life, it was one he cultivated, and I found it less convincing. As a teenager, he had been touchingly sincere. These days, he saw sincerity as a valuable asset and it wasn't quite the same thing. Admittedly, people who didn't know him as well as I did gobbled it up. Ben acquired friends with ease. He had never liked being alone. And now, in this vast house, surrounded by sound engineers and gardeners and waiting staff, anticipating the arrival of some three hundred and fifty guests to celebrate his fortieth birthday, he should have been in his element.

'What kind of thing were you thinking?' I asked, knowing Ben wouldn't have a clue.

'Oh, fuck knows. Something ... modern. And big.' He laughed, rubbing his nose. 'What's the name of that guy Serena likes so much? The guy who does the graffiti?'

So fucking predictable.

'Banksy.'

'Yeah. Him.'

'Mmm. Possibly a bit passé now.'

'Ha! I knew you'd know.'

'I'll have a think,' I said, knowing that I would do no such thing. It was clear no one would ever see this part of the house. Serena wouldn't dream of asking for my advice anywhere that actually counted.

'Thanks, mate.' He squeezed my arm. 'Let's get back to the girls.'

Always 'girls', never 'women'. It drove Lucy mad.

In the kitchen, Serena and my wife were perched awkwardly on high stools on opposite sides of a free-standing unit. The unit's surface appeared to be constructed out of four-inch-thick white marble but as I approached, I realised it was a sort of galvanised rubber. When I touched it, it had a texture like a fireman's hose. A lemon squeezer constructed out of chrome and resembling a rocket launcher stood ostentatiously in the centre.

'... nightmare, you can't imagine,' Serena was saying. She raised her head at the sound of our footsteps, giving a short smile that quickly dissolved.

'What are you two gossiping about?' Ben bent and started rubbing Serena's shoulders. She made a show of stretching her neck, moving her head from side to side.

'I'm soooo knotted up,' she said.

'I know, sweetie. You've been working too hard.'

'Has there been a lot to do?' Lucy asked. I caught her eye. We shared a flash of amusement. Neither of us can take Serena seriously when she talks about being busy.

'Don't get me started,' she replied. 'You just cannot rely on people doing what they're meant to do. And then there's all the added security we've had to—' She broke off. A warning look from Ben.

'What's that?' I asked.

'Oh, it's only … well, we weren't really meant to say anything …'

'No, darling. We were sworn to secrecy.'

'Oh come on, babe, it's only Martin and Lucy.'

I noted the 'only'.

'What security?' Lucy asked.

'There's a notion,' Ben started, 'but I can't stress enough, it really is only a notion, that we might be expecting a very important guest.'

He paused, full of self-importance. I refused to encourage him and turned to look out of the window at the kitchen garden, filled with terracotta pots of herbs and flowering jasmine.

'The Prime Minister,' Serena squealed, unable to contain herself.

'Darling.' His hand came to a stop on her shoulder, the fingers pressing down next to her collarbone so that the crescent moons of his nails turned white. 'We don't know whether—'

'No, no, I know. But he said he'd make every effort.'

'Wow,' Lucy said, with no enthusiasm.

'She didn't vote for him,' I explained.

'Did you?' Ben asked me. 'Or are you still pretending to be left-wing?'

'I'd say that was none of your business, Ben,' Lucy said, sharply.

He laughed.

'Sorry, Luce, sorry. You're right. No more political talk.'

The Prime Minister was an old family friend of Ben's. His name was Edward but as soon as he'd been elected leader, he had started asking everyone to call him Ed in the vain hope that everyone would forget about his Etonian background. His and Ben's mothers had known each other way back when. I had met him twice at Ben's dinner parties, long before he became smooth and polished and airbrushed, one of those public men incapable of shaking a hand without clasping it. I didn't have much time for him, truth be told. But Serena had always been pathetically impressed. She enjoyed proximity to power. I sipped my champagne. 'It'll be nice to see Ed again.'

'Oh, have you met him?'

'Yes, several times. At yours. For dinner.'

He nodded vaguely.

'Of course, of course. I'd forgotten.' Ben poured us all another glass of Veuve. 'A lot's changed since then.'

There seemed to be nothing to say in response. I took the stool next to Lucy, resting the soles of my shoes on a ledge that was too close to the seat to be comfortable. Ben stayed standing.

'Yes, there'll be plenty of people you know. Mark, Bufty, Fliss, obviously; Arpad and Seb. Oh, and you remember Andrew Jarvis, don't you, LS?'

I stiffen.

'From school. And Cambridge.'

'Oh,' I said, feigning nonchalance. 'Jarvis.' His name redolent of a smirk of thick muscle beneath a tightly buttoned school shirt. 'Yes, of course.'

'He's an MP now. One of Ed's lot. Junior energy minister. He and his wife have just bought a place down the road.'

'He found someone willing to marry him, did he? Wonders will never cease.'

'Oh come on, he wasn't that bad.'

'His wife's a sweetie,' Serena added.

'She is,' Ben agreed. 'She really is.'

I let it go. Ben has a bottomless capacity to reinvent the past. I think it's a calculated tactic. He rewrites a narrative to suit his needs at any given time and he's so casual about it, no one seems to care. It's an admirable skill, really, when one thinks about it.

Ben raised his glass.

'To us,' he said, one hand still resting on his wife's neck.

'To our dear friends,' I added. 'Ben and Serena.'

Ben, more at ease now in a familiar pose of bonhomie, gave an expansive grin. His top three shirt buttons were undone, revealing a sprouting of dark hairs. He was tanned. He was always tanned from a recent holiday or golf game or simple genetic good fortune. He smelled of oak and leather – the same aftershave he'd been wearing for years, ever since his father gave him a bottle when he turned sixteen. He was handsome in an unexpected way. His mouth was perhaps too large, a little loose around the lips. His nose was arguably a bit flat. There were wrinkles across his brow. But when you put it all together, it worked. There was a rugged-ness to his looks, a worn-in quality that suited the encroaching years. I had to admit: I'd never seen him look so good.

'Yes,' Serena said. 'Friends.'

Lucy tipped the glass back to a forty-five-degree angle and sank most of the champagne in one gulp. I laid my hand on hers. Her skin felt hot. She placed the flute back on the counter, fingers shaking.

There was a noisy clatter from the far end of the room and then the sound of childish squawking.

'Mama!'

A small, rotund shape bowled across the floor and launched himself at Serena's legs. This was Hector who, at three years old, was the most obstreperous of the Fitzmaurice children.

'My love,' Serena cooed. She bent to pick him up, straining the sinews of her yoga-toned arms as she did so. Hector was a barrel-shaped child with square head and un-charming features. His brow loomed over the sockets of his eyes, giving him the appear-ance of an elderly ape.

'Hello, Hector,' I said.

This unprepossessing lump was, I'm sad to say, my godson. To be frank, I was offended they had waited till their third progeny to ask and I've never wholly got over the slight. I am, however, punctilious in the observation of all my duties. He got an engraved silver tankard for his christening and has had a bottle of fine wine put aside for him every year since then at Berry Bros. Heaven knows what he will ever do to deserve it. He has none of Cosima's grace or Cressida's impishness. (The youngest, Bear, is still at the baby stage, so it's hard to tell how he'll turn out.)

'Gah,' the child responded.

Tucked cosily on his mother's lap, he looked glumly out at the rest of us, clearly wishing us all to be gone. He started pawing at Serena's blouse.

'Mee-ma,' he said. 'Mee-ma, mee-ma.' His voice rose to an un-ignorable pitch.

'No, darling, not now. Mee-ma for later.'

She removed his chunky, dimpled hand from her breasts. Serena believes in attachment parenting. She breastfed Cosima until she was four and had a full set of teeth.

'Could I have a top-up, Ben?' Lucy was reaching out with her empty glass.

'Sorry, darling. Should have noticed.'

He poured the champagne too quickly so that it bubbled up, almost to the rim, and he had to wait for the foam to slide back down. When her glass was full, Lucy took it and swallowed almost half of it in one go. I had noticed her drinking more over preceding months and I didn't want her to be drunk tonight. It would be embarrassing and, apart from anything else, I needed an ally.

I cocked my head towards hers.

'Don't you think—'

'No, Martin. No I don't,' she said, too loudly. Hector, startled by the sound of her voice, started crying.

'Oh baby, oh no, oh baby, don't cry,' Serena cooed. She stroked his hair with her hand. 'They didn't mean to shout, did they? No they didn't.'

Lucy glared at me. Then she leaned over and tapped the child's podgy leg with one hand.

'Hey, Hector.' Tap tap tap. 'Hey, hey. I'm sorry. Don't be a baby.' Tap tap tap. 'You're a big boy now, aren't you? No need to cry.' Tap tap tap.

When Lucy removed her hand, I could see a red mark on his thigh.

Serena turned her back to us, shielding Hector from our sight.

'Shall I take him?' Ben offered.

Serena stood without answering and walked out of the room with the screaming Hector. The sound of her rubber-soled espadrilles on the tiled floor as she left seemed designed to express her unvoiced fury.

Ben exhaled. He shrugged apologetically.

'Don't worry about it, Luce.'

'I wasn't,' she said.

Ben laughed. 'Good. That's OK then.'

He walked to the fridge, which loomed in one corner of the kitchen, emitting a low-frequency hum.

'Snacks,' he announced to no one in particular, sliding out a platter covered in cling film and bringing it over to the table. He took the film off with a flourish. There was a selection of soggy-looking salmon blinis, a few slices of hard cheese that looked like Manchego and some mini-sandwiches cut into triangles. A smear of brown in the centre suggested leftover chutney that someone else had already eaten. Leftovers, I thought. So that's all we're worth.

'You guys want some water?'

I reached for a blini. 'Yes, please.'

He came back with a bottle in a familiar shade of light blue. I immediately recognised the label: the cursive green writing, the line drawing of those hills I used to see every day when I walked to lessons. It was Burtonbury mineral water, said to be the finest in Britain and drunk by no lesser person than the Queen.

Ben twisted the cap, releasing a fizzing jet of air. As he poured, the splash of liquid against glass cracked the ice cubes.

Martin

Burtonbury, 1989

BURTONBURY WAS SITUATED ON THE OUTSKIRTS of a picturesque Midlands town which had flourished in the late Victorian
era thanks to an abundance of natural spring water. The school
building had once been a hotel for gentlemen afflicted with
rattling coughs or dyspeptic stomachs, and pale-faced women in
black lace suffering from attacks of the vapours who travelled up
from London with their valises and their maids in order to 'take
the cure'. It was the most fashionable place to be seen: the rehab
centre of its day, where faded personalities would disappear for
weeks on end in order to drink from the wells and soak in tepid
baths with hot flannel compresses strapped to their fevered brows.

For a time, a handsome young doctor from Adelboden in
Switzerland – called, rather wonderfully, Dr Schnitzel – took up
residence as the medical director. When I arrived, there was a sepia
photograph of him still hanging in the school's entrance hall: a
bearded man with curlicues of hair framing each ear, his eyes
hooded, like a lugubrious Russian novelist.

But the water cure, just like the cabbage soup diet, was a tran-
sient fad and, after a while, Dr Schnitzel returned to Adelboden,
the custom dried up and the red-brick, high Gothic Empire Hotel
fell into a state of disrepair. It was requisitioned during the two
world wars. In the 1950s, it was bought up by a couple from
Birmingham who made it into a care home for the elderly, ripping
out all the marble-floored bathrooms and hand-painted cornices
and replacing the luscious carpets with a thin, hard-wearing material in institutional green.

It became Burtonbury in 1960, a boys' boarding school designed initially to cater for the children of diplomats posted abroad. Through the years, it cultivated a reputation for middle-ranking academic rigour and some modest sporting success. It was a decent school, but it didn't belong to the higher echelons of private education. It tried very hard to be Eton or Harrow and yet, like a newly minted millionaire who buys a bright blue Rolls-Royce without realising it should have been a petrol-black Bentley, it never quite outgrew its arriviste status. Burtonbury always languished just outside the top twenty in the annual league tables. The *Tatler* Good Schools Guide was lukewarm about it on a perennial basis.

By the time I turned up – heaving my suitcase off the train, the cheese sandwiches swiftly disposed of in a platform wastebin – Burtonbury was undergoing something of a crisis of confidence. The paint was chipping off the skirting boards. The AstroTurf was peeling at the edges. The desks were still the old-fashioned kind, with swing tops and varnished ink splodges left over from an era when the Cuban Missile Crisis seemed as if it might genuinely explode the world. The teachers roamed the corridors with a look of resigned acceptance, like passengers on a ship they knew was about to hit an iceberg and sink, with agonising slowness, over the course of several years.

Into this, I arrived: a silent, sullen little boy relieved to be rid of the suffocating small-mindedness of his suburban upbringing; a boy who saw Burtonbury as an expansive academic canvas on which to make his mark. I was invigorated by the idea of reinventing myself. In my naivety, I imagined the school would be a modern-day version of the Platonic Academy, where like-minded young intellects could discuss profound philosophical ideas with each other. We would retire, at the end of each day, to pore over bookcases containing dusty, leather-bound tomes of Romantic poetry before gathering in the evenings for another energetic, yet respectful, discussion, perhaps in our pyjamas and flannel dressing gowns, eating hot buttered toast washed down with cups of cocoa and followed by a good night's sleep. That was my notion of boarding school.

Needless to say, I was wrong.

The first glimmer of realisation dawned as I was shown to my dormitory room by the matron, a sallow-faced little woman wearing spectacles sticky with dust. I remember being hypnotised by those glasses – by the notion that someone could either be so lazy or simply not care enough to wipe them. They depressed me. My mother failed in many respects, but she was an excellent housekeeper and the cupboard beneath the sink at home was always filled with plentiful stocks of Jif and Flash and J-cloths and those all-purpose surface sprays which had labels illustrated with gleaming tiles in blue and yellow. To this day, I have a horror of the taint of teacup rings on Formica.

The dormitory was a long, carpeted room lined on either side with two beds, four in total. The double window at one end was framed by curtains patterned with footballs and cricket bats. The walls were painted a mild, sunny colour. It was clear that an effort had been made to make it look homely and yet, paradoxically, this only served to emphasise its institutional strangeness.

When I was shown in, there were already three other boys in the room, unpacking their trunks. I mumbled a hello but no one acknowledged my presence. They were chatting loudly to each other about their holidays and I caught snatches of their conversation here and there as I shuffled to claim the bed in the corner closest to the window.

'Mate, she was gagging for it …'

'No she fucking wasn't.'

'I swear.'

'She told me—'

'Her sister was at the fucking Feathers. I'm telling you. She's a right slag.'

'Yeah, and there was that time at the Admiral Codrington and you were bladdered, geezer, bladdered …'

'*Such* a loser.'

They seemed to be talking in code, a conversational shorthand filled with names I could make no sense of. And although what they were saying was delivered in aggressive, foul-mouthed terms, they were laughing as they spoke, one of them occasionally breaking off to punch another one in the arm or slap him lightly on the back. The boys were taller than I expected and seemed older than me. They looked almost interchangeable: the same floppy-fringed hair, the same brown deck shoes, the same open-necked, deliberately un-ironed shirts and V-neck jumpers with threads coming loose at the cuffs.

My own clothes appeared outdated by comparison: neatly pressed suit trousers, polished school shoes and a plain white shirt buttoned all the way up to the neck. My assurance started to slip. My cheeks grew hot. The edges of my mind curled with uncertainty and I began to wonder whether my determination to get out of one life had led me to leap blindly into a worse situation. I knew, as I unzipped my suitcase (another thing I had got wrong – the other boys' trunks were brass-buckled affairs with stencilled initials underneath the handles), that I would have to learn a whole new set of rules if I were to survive.

I unpacked rapidly, largely ignored by my room-mates: jumpers and T-shirts in a chest of drawers, shirts and blazer in a rickety wardrobe with initials carved into the soft wood all the way down one side. I stuffed my boxer shorts into a canvas bag and bundled them under the bed. At the bottom of the suitcase I noticed, to my shame, that my mother had packed a small brown teddy bear without my knowledge. The bear was called Howard and had been given to me at birth by an elderly aunt I had never met. Howard had been my constant companion for many years, his checked waistcoat fraying slightly more at the seams each time my mother put him in the washing machine. He slept in my bed, propped up next to the pillow. I didn't pay him much attention and, indeed, had forgotten all about him in the exciting hubbub leading up to my departure for Burtonbury, but I suppose my mother, in a moment of uncharacteristic tenderness, had been concerned I might have noticed if he hadn't been there.

Seeing him squashed in the corner of my case, his arm out of kilter with the rest of him, elicited a series of complicated feelings. There was a surge of nausea, a clutching at my stomach which I think must have been homesickness, followed by a stab of embarrassment superseded by horror.

I wonder now, looking back, whether she did it on purpose. Whether she knew that putting it in there would make me squirm. Whether she wanted to remind me that however much I tried to escape her and the suburban house with the double-glazed windows and the stuffy sense of not belonging, I would never entirely manage it.

I tried to zip the case back up with Howard still in it, looking at me reproachfully, but one of the boys chose just that moment to come across.

'What's this then?' he said, leaning over and grabbing the bear roughly. 'Your ickle-wickle teddy bear?'

He lifted Howard up and moved the bear's arms with his fingers, in a parody of a puppet show. The other two boys snickered obligingly.

'Have you come to help your ickle-wickle master settle in to his big new school, hmmm?'

'Stop it,' I said, quietly. 'Please.'

The boy glared at me. His eyes were cold. He had a spot just below his left nostril which flared red from having recently been squeezed.

'Give him back,' I said.

'Him?' The boy sneered. 'Him?! Hear that, lads? The bear's a him. What? Does he get up in the middle of the fucking night and hang out with all the other toys for a fucking midnight feast?'

'A teddy bears' picnic,' one of the others suggested, guffawing.

'Yeah, exactly. A fucking picnic.'

The boy drew back his arm and, before I could stop him, lobbed Howard across the room. The bear hit the wall and slid to the ground, flopping face down onto the carpet. The other two boys picked him up, taking an arm each and subjecting Howard to a brief tug-of-war until one of them grabbed possession, ripping the bear's arm in the process. I glimpsed a plume of white stuffing unravelling from the loosened joint. Howard went sailing over my head again, pitched like a rugby ball from one end of the room to the other.

And although I should have just left them to it and walked out of the room and gone to find something better to do, my upset and humiliation rapidly calcified into something more stubborn. I began to feel enraged. Howard might be a stupid, childish teddy bear. But he was my stupid, childish teddy bear and I think, now, I must have objected to my possessions being treated with such arrogance. I was always so careful with my own things, you see. Never liked to share. I believe it's a trait of only children but, really, when you look at how callously people treat things, how they fail to discern their real value until it's far too late, how they knock over priceless Ming vases in museums with their oversized back-packs, it seems to me to be the only sensible way to behave. Protect your possessions. And, by extension, yourself.

I attempted to intervene, jumping up to try and intercept the looping arc of Howard's trajectory. The harder I tried, the faster the throws became. I was shorter than the other three and they knew they had the advantage. I could feel the pressing clamminess of tears. My vision blurred, then tightened, as if a sheet of cling film were being stretched across my brain, and I could feel the rage coagulating – a hard nugget of a thing, chipped and coal-black at the base of my spine, sprouting and twisting into fury which climbed up each vertebra, all the way to my heart and throat, sticking in my chest like a pool of warm tar. I could hear the snap and crack of the bird's bones underneath the crush of that rock and before I knew it, I was clenching my fist in readiness to smack their stupid faces and punch each one of those boys to the floor.

A draught. The dormitory door opening. Confident steps across the carpet. And then a voice: 'What the fuck are you doing, Dom?'

The boys stopped immediately. Howard the bear dangled from one of their hands. I raised my gaze from the floor and turned. There, standing in the square of the doorframe, was a curly-haired boy with a smattering of facial hair across his lower jaw. His voice had broken and when he spoke it was with absolute certainty that what he was saying was the most important thing anyone could be listening to at that given moment.

'Oh piss off, Ben,' said the boy with the spot by his nostril.

'Give it a rest, Dom. Leave him alone,' he said, talking as if I weren't there. 'Matron'll hear. I've got a bottle of vodka for later and I don't want her finding it, OK?'

The mention of vodka seemed to pacify Dom. He pushed a hand through his hair. The other two busied themselves with their unpacking. One of them started Blu Tacking a poster of a girl in a tennis skirt to the wall.

'Yeah, sure,' Dom said, the spot by his nose seeming to get redder with each word. 'Sorry.'

'Cool,' Ben said, turning to leave. Just before he did, he looked over his shoulder directly at me. His eyes, caught in the light, looked silver. 'You don't need a fucking teddy bear, OK?'

He walked out of the room. I snatched Howard back, wanting now to rip his stupid head off, and I stuffed him under the bed, behind the bag with my underpants. He would stay there, ignored, for the rest of term. I forgot about the bear until it came to packing up my possessions to go home for the Christmas holidays and then he emerged, cobwebbed in dust and flakes of dry skin, glass eyes hardened by resentment at his abandonment, and I threw him in the bin without a second thought.

Notebook of Lucy Gilmour

KEITH SAYS IT'S OK NOT TO DO THIS CHRONOLOGICALLY. He says the order in which things come back to me is 'in and of itself very interesting'.

It was Keith who suggested I jot things down as a way of processing what happened. To my surprise, I found it helped. My notebook has now become the outlet for all my most private thoughts. (To everyone else, of course, I offer up a more palatable version – and I include both the police and Keith in that.)

'The mind has a way of organising itself,' he said in our session earlier today. 'Sometimes the most important things will remain buried for a long time and we remember them only on a cellular level.'

'Muscle memory?' I said.

'If you like.' Keith was sitting as he always did on the leather armchair on the opposite side of the room. The bay window was behind him, the bottom half obscured by plantation shutters painted pigeon-feather grey. The sun had shifted during the course of our conversation and now his head was backlit so that I couldn't make out his features and I wondered, not for the first time, whether he sat this way deliberately, so that his responses remained forever unreadable.

'Muscle memory,' I repeated, the alliteration pleasing me as it tripped off the tongue. '*Muscle Memory: A Memoir*,' I said. 'By Lucy Gilmour.'

'Interesting,' said Keith. 'Why do you say that?'

I thought of the miscarriage, of the way it had come back to me a year later, almost to the day, and I had found myself crying at the steering wheel of the car wondering why and it was only later, when I worked out the dates, that I realised what it was.

Strange. When I was in hospital, the nurses were so sympathetic and I didn't think I deserved their attention. I didn't feel sad. I was shrouded by a kind of intellectual numbness. I processed what was happening to me on a logical level and this seemed to me to be very important: to remove the emotion from it. Of course your body isn't capable of holding on to a baby, the inner voice said; how self-indulgent of you to think it could.

I dealt with everything on a purely practical level. The cardboard tray they gave me for the discharge. The blood. The specks of something else, not yet formed, in the fluid. The sanitary pads, so thick they were comical. The pain, which came in waves that surged and then withdrew. Bent over double in the early hours of the morning, unwilling to press my buzzer because what I was going through wasn't real. It wasn't an illness. The pain wasn't unmanageable. You're making a fuss, the inner voice said; you're embarrassing yourself.

Martin wasn't there. I told myself it didn't matter, that there was no point in both of us having a sleepless night. And besides, wouldn't it be an extra thing to worry about? I'd have to handle him along with everything else. I'd have to worry about what his expression meant, about why he wasn't talking, about why he wouldn't hold my hand. I would have to explain his curtness to the nurses, to the doctors. I would have to neutralise his unintentional rudeness by over-friendly small talk.

The thing is – the thing to remember is – that he was capable of great charm. The first time I took him home to meet my parents, he was so brilliant at engaging them in conversation. He sat at the homely kitchen table, the wood of it knotted and stained over the years, and he asked solicitous questions of my mother, who was convinced no one ever wanted to talk to her and who blossomed under the attention. They were simple questions, obvious ones that normally no one bothered with – where did you grow up, what did your parents do, any siblings – and my mother, who too easily tended to think she wasn't clever enough, answered fluently because she could.

He was drinking tea, I remember, and I was worried it wouldn't pass muster, given his disdain for the builders' on offer at the office. I knew my mother made pots of tea with a combination of PG Tips and Twinings Earl Grey and I tensed myself for Martin's mouth to crumple with distaste when he sipped it. But when there was a lull in conversation he said with complete sincerity: 'Mrs Hillhurst, this tea is delicious.'

'Oh please,' said my mother, flapping. 'You must call me Pat.'

'Pat then.' He ran a hand through his hair, pushing back the front section that kept flopping forward. It was a gesture I had seen somewhere before and it took me a moment to realise what it reminded me of. Then it came to me: Ben had exactly the same habit. His best friend Ben.

My father was similarly taken. Martin, who never usually watched sport, sat through an entire rugby match on the sofa next to my dad and asked politely about what was happening and when and who the best players were and my father seemed pleased to be considered an authority. I watched them from the corner of the living room and felt content. Martin looked at me. I blew him a kiss. He smiled. I knew he was pleased.

'Thank you,' I said in the car on the way home.

'What for?'

'Making such an effort with my folks.'

He shrugged.

'They really liked you.' Martin didn't reply. He kept looking at the road, his eyes obscured by tinted Ray-Bans. And then, because secretly I wanted him to respond with some warm words of his own, I added, 'I mean, they liked you a lot.'

He flicked on the indicator. Tick tick tick.

'I'm good with parents who aren't my own.'

It didn't strike me until years afterwards that it was an unusual thing to say.

The miscarriage wasn't his fault. He had never wanted children. He had been open about this from the beginning, so I can't claim

I didn't know. This had been one of his non-negotiables and I had agreed, too readily, too keen as ever to fence off his love, to rope it down and keep it safe.

We had the conversation in the cafe at the Saatchi Gallery in Chelsea. An exchange over a bowl of sticky nuts and two Old Fashioneds (he liked to drink Old Fashioneds and complained if the ice cube was square rather than spherical). We congratulated ourselves on our rational ability to talk about difficult things without resorting to sentimentality.

'Why don't you want children?' I asked and then, worrying I hadn't struck the right tone, I added: 'Out of interest.'

Martin prised a shiny cashew nut out of the solidifying honeyed mass on the table between us.

'I'd be a disastrous father.'

'No you wouldn't.'

I reached across, tracing the shape of his knuckles with my fingers. He let his hand stay there, smooth and pink-brown as a bar of Imperial Leather soap. At that stage, I knew the barest outlines of his unhappy childhood. He had given the impression of neglect – a dead father, a distant mother, a boarding school adolescence cut off from parental affection – but without ever defining it beyond vague generalities. I read into the gaps, I interpreted the absence of detail as evidence of childhood trauma. It moved me. I could see why someone whose own childhood had been so tough wouldn't want to inflict that on their own flesh and blood.

'Besides, there are too many people on the planet,' he said, removing his hand to wipe it on a napkin. 'Not enough resources, and still we procreate. I rather like it just being us,' he said and I had that fluttery feeling in my stomach. Only Martin could make me feel like this. A compliment from him was like warm sunshine on my back. 'Don't you?'

'Yes.' I raised my tumbler and said 'Cheers' and waited for him to clink his against it, which he did, laughing in that way he had which always made it seem he was astonished to be laughing, as if

75

he was laughing in spite of himself and his facial muscles were temporarily beyond his control. I lived for that laughter.

Two years into our marriage, I got pregnant. By then, I knew I wanted a child and that I had been too hasty, too ignorant in accepting Martin's conditions. My friends had their babies and I was enamoured by their rosy dimpled knees and thin, soft tendrils of hair. I liked their smell of fresh laundry and buttercups. I liked holding them, my arms providing the necessary shell to their fragility. It was such a cliché. The biological clock. But it kicked in, despite my determination to avoid it. And soon I was looking wistfully at toddlers in the street, imagining how I would dress my own and wondering what it must feel like to be loved by a small person with unquestioning entirety, at least for a while. At least until they grew older and discovered you were a disappointment.

The pregnancy was an accident. Martin didn't like to wear condoms and I thought I'd taken the pill that morning, but I hadn't, not for a couple of days. I didn't think it mattered given how infrequently we had sex. It wasn't the first time we'd been careless. Each time, I subconsciously hoped it would end in pregnancy. Each time, I got my period and felt a pain I chose to ignore. This time, miraculously, my period was late. Martin didn't believe me when I told him.

'Are you sure?'

'Yes.'

He didn't raise his voice. He sat at the kitchen table, legs crossed. He unbuttoned his jacket and then said, calmly: 'Lucy. We agreed.'

'I know.'

'And – what? You just decided without consulting me you'd go ahead and do this massive fucking thing neither of us wanted.'

'*You* didn't want,' I muttered.

'Oh no. No. I'm not having that. I said before we got married. I *said* I—'

76

'I know what you said. But Martin, look, it was an accident. It's happened. And maybe … well …'

'Maybe what?'

'Maybe we should be happy about it?'

He got up, went to the fridge and poured himself a glass of water from the filter jug. Need to change the filter, I thought automatically. Must get one tomorrow.

I waited for Martin to come back to the table, but instead he walked out of the room. After a few seconds, I could hear the muffled headlines of the *News at Ten*.

Give him time, I told myself. It's a shock, of course it is. He'll come round.

I spent the rest of that night making excuses for him.

III.

'SO HOW DID YOU FEEL?'

Beige Hair cocks her head to one side. I wonder if she's been on some taxpayer-funded police training initiative for developing Core Empathy and Understanding Skills.

'Sorry, I don't quite follow.'

A thin smile. She waits.

Oh well done, I think. You've been told that leaving silences at key points often encourages the interviewee to talk. Slow hand-clap. Unleash the party poppers. If she thinks that's going to work with me, she's got another think coming. I'm a journalist. I know all about these tricks. The pause stretches until, finally, it breaks.

'Being asked in on one of Mr Fitzmaurice's deals,' Beige Hair says, relenting. 'Must have been exciting.'

'Not particularly.'

'Really?' She feigns surprise. 'I would have thought ... well, the chance to make some money, helping out your best friend at the same time. That's a pretty nice offer. Have I said something funny?'

'No, why?'

'You seem to be laughing.'

I rearrange my features. Increasingly, these days, I notice myself lapsing into a smirk without realising I'm doing it. I wonder how much of this is to do with the drugs, those few years after university when I did more coke than was strictly advisable. One of the salient things I remember about being high – along with the sense of enormous well-being; the giddy belief in one's own fascinating brilliance – was losing control of my facial muscles. I'd want to show concern and be grimacing. I'd try to smile and end up crying.

In the end, I went cold turkey in an expensive facility kindly paid for by Ben's parents (goose-down duvets; hand-roasted coffee; fig-scented candles). The tics stopped. One month of group meditation and therapeutic art classes did the job.

I haven't snorted a single speck of white powder since then. But other unfortunate aspects of my addiction have remained. I still have the occasional desire to rip things to shreds, to behave with abomination, to shock when I find myself in polite company. I still have a propensity for sudden squalls of anger, these days mostly contained – although poor old Lucy has borne the brunt of some of them. And now I've discovered I still have an inconvenient habit of showing inappropriate emotion on my face.

'No,' I say. 'It's simply that Ben wouldn't have asked me to invest in one of his schemes out of the goodness of his heart. It wasn't a selfless act of friendship, trust me.'

Beige Hair scribbles something on her piece of paper.

'How so?'

'Listen. Everything Ben does is guided by naked self-interest. He doesn't mean it maliciously. It's just this sense of entitlement you get when you're from a good family, when you have money, when you grow up in a stately home and go to public school and Oxbridge and you're good-looking and you've never had to fight for anything.'

It is the most I've said since walking into the interview and I realise too late my mistake. The trick is to talk as little as possible. Isn't that what every police procedural TV drama has ever taught us? Talk in monosyllables. Counter a question with another question. If all else fails, say 'No comment'. I see Grey Suit sit up straighter in his chair, his interest piqued. Beige Hair gazes at me neutrally.

I look into her plain, simple face. It is the kind of face that has grown used to not being noticed. It is a face with modest expectations, a face which says she'd be perfectly happy with a small house and two children and Ikea furniture and clothes ordered online from the Next sale and a DVD and a bottle of £4.99 rosé on a Friday night with the husband in front of a nice box-set, huddled up on a cosy sofa with a blanket knitted by her grandma when the youngest was born.

I see you, I think to myself. I see you for who you are. And I know that the thought of people like Ben and their unearned privilege sticks in your throat like a fishbone.

'You know what I mean,' I say, looking directly at her.

Beige Hair actually nods.

'Had he ever asked you to be involved in any of his business projects before?'

'No; I mean, the timing was never right. He knew I wouldn't be interested …'

'Did you think it was odd he chose the night of his birthday party to mention it?'

Yes, I say silently, yes I did think it strange. I knew that something was up, that he was using the Montenegro story as cover for another issue he wanted to raise. And it didn't take too much of a leap of imagination to work out what the real motive was likely to be. It was the great unsaid, the thing neither of us ever talked about, which lay between us like an expanse of uncrossable water. Lately, there had been a small but perceptible shift in Ben's attitude towards me. It started at around the time they bought Tipworth Priory. He was spending more days out of London, which meant I saw him less. His moods were trickier to monitor from afar. The whole situation became increasingly difficult to control.

The distance worried me. And whenever I get anxious, the memories start coming back, visions that press against my cerebral cortex like the slap of a wasp against a window. The sounds come first. Crunch of metal. Whirring of the car's wheels as they spin freely in the air. Then the smells: petrol, rainfall, smoke. Visuals are always the last thing to click into place. A girl, twisted and bloodied. Ben's face, white in the moonlight.

I always see the same two images, as if I have a spool of negatives with only a set number of pictures to be developed.

Taking drugs in my twenties helped push those things to an unexamined corner of my brain. Coke would speed up my thoughts; alcohol would slow them down; marijuana would give them a poetic lyricism. When I did all three together, in the right quantities, I became neutralised.

At first, I was scared about getting clean because I didn't want the recall. But, as it turned out, sobriety made me surprisingly calm – un-haunted, if there is such an expression. It's only relatively recently that the visions have started coming back. Unwanted ghostly fragments, rattling around like mismatched cutlery in a drawer.

'Martin? Did you hear me? Did you think it strange he mentioned this big investment opportunity on the night of his fortieth birthday party?'

'Not especially, no. I hadn't seen Ben for a while. The house move and all that – you know. It made sense he'd want to speak to me when he had the chance. To us, I mean.'

'Us?'

'He wanted Lucy to be involved too. Both the wives, actually.'

'Right.'

She notes something down. I am desperate to know what it is but I consciously look away. 'So, going back to the party,' Beige Hair says, 'after your drinks in the kitchen, what happened then?'

'That's when Fliss arrived.'

'Fliss?'

Grey Suit shifts, then – miraculously – opens his mouth.

'Felicity Fitzmaurice,' he says, in a Scottish accent.

'That's right.' I stare at him, challenging him to look away. He doesn't.

'Ben's sister.'

2 May

WE HEARD FLISS BEFORE WE SAW HER. Her voice, a mish-mash of throaty transatlantic vowels and upward swoops at the end of sentences, spiralled through the draughty corridors. It pinballed off the walls, bouncing through the house until it reached the kitchen where we sat, reverberating against the room's chrome and rubber surfaces until the final clattering syllables were swallowed by their own echo.

'Where the bloody hell's my little brother?'

'Oh my God!' Ben said, putting his glass down with a smash. 'Fliss!'

Soon the three of us were swept up in a flurry of Ben's enthusiasm and we started walking back the way we had come in, Lucy clinging on to her empty glass with such force I feared it might crack. Her clavicle looked more prominent than usual, her wrists snappably slight.

Fliss stood in the entrance hall wearing what can only be described as a patchwork cloak, constructed from sewn-together pieces of purple velvet and squares of lapis lazuli, dotted here and there with tiny circular mirrors that threw out spores of flickering light as she moved. She had a rucksack on her back, the kind favoured by teenagers on their gap years, with two thick canvas-weave shoulder straps and a thinner strap across the chest which she had buckled conscientiously into place. Her skin was leathery and sunned, with deep grooves at the side of her mouth and wrinkled hands which went baggy around the knuckles. Her hair was still long, but twisted at the ends, random strands of it plaited and punctuated with colourful wooden beads.

'Ahoy there,' she said, allowing herself to be hugged with crushing force by Ben.

'Sis, it's so great to see you. When did you get in?'

'Couple of hours ago,' she said, her voice muffled by his chest. 'Lemme out. I want to say hi to Mart and Luce.'

He chuckled, then released her.

Fliss turned towards us, green eyes alight.

'Guys, guys, guys.' She stretched out her arms. Both Lucy and I submitted to the inevitable show of Fitzmaurice tactility. 'How long's it been? Five years? Ten?'

'Eight and a half, I believe.'

She giggled. 'Oh, good old Mart, always the details person.' Fliss kept one hand on my wrist. 'What would we ever do without you, darling?'

Her voice was gravel and honey. She squeezed hard with her fingers, as if about to give me one of those expert Chinese burns she used to specialise in when we were teenagers.

'How are you, Luce?'

'Good,' Lucy said, shifting gently out of Fliss's reach.

'You look fantastic – really …' she searched for the right word. 'I dunno. Like, really, in tune with yourself, you know?'

Lucy shrugged. Neither of us knew how to react to Fliss. She was more grounded than Ben, partly because she had never done what was expected of her and, as a consequence, had more experience of real life. While Ben, the younger child, had been well behaved throughout his smooth academic career, apart from one notable blip at university, Fliss had got expelled from her boarding school for drugs and then astonished everyone by refusing to return to full-time education.

Instead, at the age of sixteen, she had gone to be a chalet girl in Switzerland and then a grape-picker in Provence and then, variously, an au pair in Australia, a waitress back in England (briefly; she hated it), a tour guide on an open-top bus in St Louis, a teacher of English as a foreign language in Italy, a barmaid in Sweden, a plucker of chickens in a factory in Croatia and, finally, a yoga instructor in Ibiza where she had spent most of her time, on and off, ever since. The last time I had seen her had been at a drunken dinner party at Ben and Serena's place in Notting Hill when the conversation had taken an aggressive turn over pudding. One half of the table was arguing with the other half about the rights and wrongs of the Iraq war, in that semi-detached, earnest way that moneyed people do, always safe in the knowledge no political outcome will really affect them.

In the middle of an increasingly antagonistic discussion, Fliss had slid her chair back, got up without a word and executed a graceful headstand on the tiled floor. The conversation had fallen silent. After a few seconds, she had unfurled herself and resumed her seat and everyone had burst into a spontaneous round of applause while she sat there, face flushed with the rush of blood to the head. That was Fliss.

'Where's Serena and the squidlets?' she was saying now.

Ben shrugged apologetically.

'Hector had a bit of a meltdown so she's taken him upstairs. They're all up there with the nannies.'

'The nannies! Fuck's sake, little brother! You're so fucking *money*.'

I laughed. Lucy's posture relaxed. Fliss had a way of making things better. I was never sure how much she knew about what had happened all those years ago. Despite her open manner, Fliss was pretty unreadable when it came to revealing anything intimate.

I had spent several exeat weekends with the Fitzmaurice family when I was at Burtonbury, never wanting to go back to the stifling bungalow in Epsom. My communications with my mother were stilted and increasingly infrequent – limited to letters detailing factual occurrences in toneless language and the odd uncomfortable call made from the communal pay-phone at school, consisting more of silence than speech. Besides, why would I choose suburban pebble-dash over the baronial majesty of the Fitzmaurice family pad?

They lived in a vast red-brick country house called Denby Hall, set in beautiful gardens with topiary and peacocks. The house had been built in the seventeenth century, shortly after the Restoration, by a minor aristocrat who had proven himself loyal to the throne during the civil war and was rewarded with an honorary title. The exterior was impressive: all white stone carvings and overblown fountains. Inside, however, the design was muddled. It was an edifice built by someone with a mania for corridors. I sometimes felt the rooms were added as an afterthought – squashed in proportion and huddled around a wide, central hallway that had no need to be as broad as it was. The walls were hung with ancestral portraits and still lifes of lobsters or decaying fruit. The grandeur co-existed with cheapness, in that way I have come to associate peculiarly with the English aristocracy. There were little bottles of shower gel and shampoo in each room bearing the logos of various hotels, and I had once discovered I was eating my dinner with a fork that had 'Cathay Pacific' engraved on the handle.

I was intimidated when I first visited Denby Hall. How could I not have been? By then, Ben and I were firm friends but his parents clearly thought me an odd little boy.

'I've heard so much about you,' his mother, Lady Katherine, had said when we were introduced. I shook her hand. Discreetly, she withdrew and wiped her palm on her calf-length skirt. 'You must make yourself at home here.'

'Thank you.'

She was a tall woman with a high forehead and light grey eyes. Her hair was so blonde it was almost white, cut into a neat bob which fell just below her ears. She stood with the poise of a ballerina and when she walked, she appeared to glide. My abiding recollection of her from those days was of distance, both physical and metaphorical.

She turned her gaze towards Ben. She had the strangest way of turning her head while her neck remained perfectly immobile. Like a snake, I thought.

'Perhaps you'd like to play some tennis before lunch, darling?'

'Yeah.'

'Yes,' she said, admonishingly.

'Yes, Mummy. Sorry.'

Lady Fitzmaurice looked at me.

'You've got your tennis gear, I assume?'

I had no tennis clothes. I felt a white-hot spasm of embarrassment.

'You can borrow some of mine,' Ben said, quickly. 'If you forgot, that is.'

'Thanks.'

'Lunch is at one, boys,' Ben's mother said. 'Your sister's home.'

Ben groaned.

'Heard that, little brother.'

And there was Fliss, suddenly in the room without announcement: a gangly teenage girl with braces on her teeth in a pair of cut-off denim shorts and a striped T-shirt which kept slipping from her shoulders.

'Who's this?' She assessed me, unsmiling.

'Martin.'

'Hello, *Martin*,' she said, over-enunciating my name as if it were a food she didn't like.

'This is Fliss,' Ben said. 'My sister.'

'Well I'm not your fucking girlfriend, am I?'

I laughed, in spite of myself. Fliss smiled, then realised she was smiling and stopped abruptly. I think, after that, she decided I was tolerable, more or less.

Fliss was just three years older than us but, at that age, it might as well have been a decade. By observing her, I learned a lot about girls, about their moods and intransigence, their curious mixture of defensiveness and vulnerability. In summer, the three of us used to walk to the lake in the grounds of Denby Hall, strip off to our underwear and launch ourselves into the water by swinging on a raggedy line of rope, slung round the branch of an overhanging tree.

When I think back to that time, I think of it with elemental fondness. Liquid coolness. Slivers of reflected sunlight smashed into pieces as we disturbed the surface with our impact. The brown water lapping and circling around the entry point and then coalescing, covering our tracks, making it all seem new for the next time we clambered up the bank and swung and jumped and dipped and screamed.

Once, when Ben and I were fourteen and Fliss was lounging around at home in between jobs, painting her nails black and listening to Bob Dylan albums, the three of us went to the lake and got caught in a thunderstorm. We sheltered beneath the trees until the sheeting rain had stopped. Despite our efforts, we were drenched through.

Fliss, leaning back against the trunk of an oak, slipped out a blue and silver tin from her back pocket.

'Something to warm us up,' she said, opening the lid to reveal five tightly rolled joints. She took one, lit it and inhaled, then passed it on to me. When I gave it to Ben, his fingers grazed mine. As he smoked, I saw his eyes become lazy. We started to laugh and then we couldn't stop and then it seemed obvious we should take our clothes off because they were wet, weren't they, and we were going to go swimming anyway, and what difference would it make?

Ben unbuttoned half of his shirt and then pulled it over his head. I took off my T-shirt, rolling it into a ball to play for time. I was stoned but I was still able to register my nervousness. Ben had never seen me naked and I felt, for reasons too difficult to explain, that the first time he did so should have some sense of occasion attached to it.

'Come on, slow-coach,' he said, pushing his boxer shorts down to his ankles. His buttocks were white, separated from his torso by a thin tan line. His penis rested against a thicket of dark, curly hair, the tip of it like a mushroom. As he dived into the water, I noticed a fish-like ripple of muscle from his shoulder blades down to the low cleft of his sacrum. He swam out of sight, round a bend in the water.

I turned to see Fliss standing before me, naked apart from her pants, her nipples tensed in the cold air. She walked towards me slowly and when she got close, she reached down and cupped my erection with her hand.

'That's nice,' she said, in that throaty voice. And then she leaned forward and placed her mouth on mine, parting my teeth expertly with her tongue. She tasted of weed and chewing gum. It was the first time I had kissed a girl and I tried my best to do what was expected of me, but the more she thrust her tongue against mine, the more she worked on me with her hand, the less turned on I felt. I lost my erection.

'I'm sorry,' I stammered. 'It's not …'

She drew back so I could see her face. A wrinkle of confusion appeared and then cleared. She laughed, the sound of it false.

'S'OK,' she said. 'Next time.'

She gathered up her clothes and her blue and silver tin and stalked off towards the house. There never was a next time and we never spoke of it again.

In the hallway at Tipworth, Fliss slid herself out of the rucksack, depositing it unceremoniously on the stone floor by the fireplace. Almost immediately, a silent girl came to remove it.

'Hey, where are you taking that?'

The girl froze.

'Chill, Fliss, they'll take it to the cloakroom. It'll be fine.' Ben grinned at the girl. 'You can go ahead and check it in, thank you.'

The smile stayed on his face a moment longer than it needed to. I watched him as he let his eyes follow the girl's receding figure. She lugged the rucksack out of the front door to one of the lawn marquees. At one point, the rucksack slipped from her grasp and she bent to retrieve it, her short skirt riding up her legs to reveal the tell-tale thickness of a stocking top. Ben took it all in greedily. Not for the first time, I wondered whether all was quite well between him and Serena. Ben's wife had never seemed a particularly sexual being. Beautiful, yes, but untouchable: a waxwork representation of what a stunning person should be.

Whereas Ben had always been intensely physical, as though his every movement were necessary, an act of explanation. The first time I saw Marlon Brando in the black and white film of *A Streetcar Named Desire* it reminded me of Ben. That same powerful agility, that same silent mastery, muscles coiled in readiness like a cat waiting to pounce. He still had that quality now. I looked at his broad shoulders, contained in his jacket, an implication of strength, and I thought back to his pale teenage skin, the slender width of his tapering waist as he launched himself naked into the lake.

I felt a jab in my side. Lucy was poking me with her finger. A black globule of mascara stuck stubbornly to the end of a single eyelash.

'What?'

Fliss, laughing, patted me on the back.

'Put your tongue back in, Mart. She's young enough to be your daughter.'

But … I wanted to protest … *but … I wasn't looking at her.*

We stood there for a moment, unsure of what to say to each other and then, as if on cue, there was an electronic screech, a fizzle of white noise and a distant thudding sound. The pounding got louder and then a singer's voice, high-pitched and frenzied, emanated from the marquee in the garden.

'Music,' said Ben, eyes fired up. 'What do you say we get this party started?'

Notebook of Lucy Gilmour

I'M NOT SURPRISED BY ANYTHING THAT'S HAPPENED. I feel bad for what I did, of course I do. But I wonder now if it wasn't inevitable. Something was awry as soon as I walked through the doors at Tipworth, into that ridiculously extravagant setting. The evening felt unbalanced from the start. That's not an excuse. But there were events leading up to what I did, events and slights and irritations going back years and years and years.

I knew Ben and Serena had a specific reason for wanting us there early. They had a game plan, it was obvious. It wasn't a friendly invitation. I'd never been close to Serena and relations between Ben and Martin had cooled in the preceding months. The regularity of those cosy foursome dinners in their well-appointed Notting Hill house had dwindled, much to my relief.

Those dinners.

Every time, Martin had been so keen to go but I could never understand it. It seemed clear to me that Ben got frustrated with my husband's puppyish devotion. At best, he found it amusing. At worst, it felt as though Martin was trying to ingratiate himself to the point of humiliation.

The last time we'd had dinner at their house had been almost a year before the party. Serena had sent me an email the night before, so it was obvious we were last-minute additions.

hi lucy, the email went (Serena didn't believe in capital letters, which always gave the impression she was simply too busy for them or that they were, in some sense, beneath her) *having a few people round tomorrow for a super-casual dinner. wondered if u guys wanted to come? be nice to see u xoxox S.*

It always annoyed me that just because I was the wife, I was automatically seen as the diary scheduler, the keeper of Martin's domestic flame, as if our incapable menfolk couldn't possibly do anything as onerous as making their own appointments.

The following night I had planned to go to the cinema to see a new film by a director I liked. I hadn't booked tickets, but when I told Martin I'd rather do that than schlep over to Notting Hill to make polite conversation with rich people, he looked gloomy.

'Why can't you see that it's *nice* of them to invite us?' he asked.

'I can't help it. I just think they take advantage of you. They think they can say jump and all you'll do is ask how high.'

'You can go to the cinema any time.'

'I know, but I wanted—'

'Life isn't only about what *you* want, Lucy.' His mouth was crooked. He seemed to be holding something in and I realised I'd upset him. I relented.

'No, you're right. We should go. It'll be nice.'

He relaxed. I reached out, brushed my hand against his arm. I reminded myself that Ben was the closest thing he had to family.

I didn't take my hand away and, because Martin allowed it to rest there, I slowly moved in to hug him, resting my cheek against his chest so that I could hear the quickening thump of his heart. After a few seconds, he put his arms around me.

When Serena said 'casual' she actually meant 'very smart pretending to be casual'. A beautifully cut jacket in the lightest suede. An oatmeal cashmere cardigan flung over the shoulders as an afterthought. Gold chain necklaces with hammered discs of jade and topaz. Jeans that cost hundreds of pounds because they were ripped and zipped in precisely the most flattering places.

There was no point in my trying to match up to Serena and her friends, so generally I removed myself from the competition by choosing the most plain, ordinary clothing I could find. I knew Serena thought I had no taste – so did Martin for that matter – but it was done on purpose. I didn't want my clothes to be the most remarkable thing about me.

For this dinner, I remember I wore a denim dress over black leggings. I had worn the same thing a few weeks ago and a woman in a shop had stopped and asked when my baby was due. The woman was mortified when I told her I wasn't expecting but I had found it amusing. And I liked the idea I could have been pregnant. I liked the idea that Serena might think I was.

'Don't you look sweet,' Serena said when she opened the door.

She kissed me on both cheeks, her skin silky against mine.

'LS,' she said. 'Glad you could come.'

'Oh no, listen, it's always a pleasure and, as always, you're a vision,' Martin said and he was already speaking too quickly and too much. 'We brought you this—' He handed over the bottle of wine we'd spent £25 on in Waitrose. 'And these—' A bunch of flowers in garish colours I knew Serena would hate.

Serena accepted them gracefully.

'You shouldn't have,' she said, turning and leading us along the hallway and downstairs into the basement kitchen. The room was filled with the smell of warm pastry. There were three people already seated at the table and one of them was Ben.

Serena put the flowers on the counter, dropping them with such carelessness they might as well have gone straight in the bin. A thin, young girl in a white shirt and black trousers handed me a glass of champagne. In the background, a man in an apron was sliding trays of salmon into Serena and Ben's top-of-the-range cooker. It was a monster of a thing in burnished steel with a baffling array of knobs and dials along the front. They had bought it a few years ago, insisting that they needed something this size to cater for their growing family. I'd seen one like it once in a food magazine which featured an 'at home' interview with a TV chef and I knew it had cost £75,000.

'It's super-relaxed,' Serena was saying now. 'Hope you don't mind, guys.'

'No, of course not, Serena. It's so much nicer that way. I always think, don't you, that—'

I silently willed Martin to be quiet.

'Darling, LS and Lucy are here.'

Ben turned. His face was blank. Then his expression shifted. He grinned broadly, threw his arms wide open.

'*Mes amis!*' he said, slipping into French for no discernible reason. It was a thing he did. I used to find it hilarious. Now it drove me mad. '*Vous êtes les bienvenus!* Come, come, take a seat.'

'*Un siège?*' I asked.

'Ha,' he said mirthlessly, hugging me close. 'Hi, Lucy.'

We sat down at the round table and were introduced to the other guests: Matt, a media lawyer, and Milly, who, like most of Serena's female friends, didn't do anything. The table was dotted here and there with small glass jars, each one containing a single white rose, cut down to length. The napkins were linen. The cutlery had faded yellow ivory handles.

I sat facing a wall dominated by a set of shelves, containing not books but scented candles and pieces of sculpture: a bronze dog in miniature; a tribal mask with cut-out eyes; a stunted tree whose branches were hung with tiny crystal spheres. On the central shelf was a silver-framed photograph of Serena and Ben's wedding. Serena was looking off-camera, smiling prettily, and Ben was grinning with his arms round her, his eyes crinkled at the corners. It was in black and white and I knew the photograph well because we had a copy at home. But our version was wider, expanding to show Martin standing at Ben's side. He wasn't in the photograph in the Fitzmaurice kitchen.

The evening was fairly unmemorable, except for one incident. We were talking about university, because there had been a news story that morning on the growing number of British teenagers applying to study abroad.

'That reminds me, Ben,' Martin said. 'Did you get the letter about the Queens' reunion?'

'Yeah. They're always badgering me for money.'

'It's a black-tie dinner. I thought it might be rather fun.'

Rather fun. He had this way of picking up Ben's turns of phrase and it never sounded right. I don't think Martin even realised he was doing it.

'God, really Martin? I can't imagine anything worse.'

Martin sipped his wine. He caught my eye. He seemed uncertain.

'It was only a suggestion,' Martin said. 'Thought it might be nice to go back, see some of our old haunts.'

'Why this obsession with the past, LS? I'm sick of nostalgia.'

Ben reached for the decanter of red. Serena lightly tapped his wrist. It was her signal that he'd had too much and Ben ignored it. He poured the wine high up the glass and then offered the wine to Milly, who shook her head and opened her mouth to say something.

'We've got to move forwards,' Ben said loudly, leaving Milly gawping like a fish. 'Move forwards. Think of the future. That's the problem with Britain,' he continued, making one of those wild cognitive leaps of which he was so fond. 'Backward-looking. Always wanting to remind everyone how much fucking history we have.'

'Ben,' Serena said.

'I happen to rather like history,' Martin continued, straining to keep his tone jolly. 'It was my degree after all.'

'Yes, yes, yes.' Ben leaned forwards, pushing his fork onto the floor with his elbow. 'We all know you did history and you got a double first and you're extremely bloody clever.'

Martin sat back as if slapped.

'Well, look—' he started.

'Are wives invited?' I asked. 'Or are the Cambridge colleges still as institutionally sexist as ever?'

Ben guffawed.

'Oh Lucy, what are we going to do with you?' He dabbed at his mouth with a napkin. 'You look so meek but you're so fucking feisty.'

'I went to Oxford myself,' Matt interjected pointlessly. Everyone ignored him.

'And I *love* it,' Ben was saying. 'I love that my best mate Martin ended up with you because, trust me, we really didn't think he—'

At this point, Serena stood and started collecting plates. There was a clattering sound as she stacked the china.

'Pudding,' she said brightly. 'Gooseberry fool. I hope that meets with everyone's approval.'

'Oh fab,' Milly trilled. 'I don't know how you do it, darling, and make it seem effortless!'

Staff, I wanted to say. That's how she does it.

Instead I said, 'You really didn't think he what, Ben?'

Ben looked at me, his face blank again.

'I'm sorry?'

'Just then, you said you were pleased Martin had ended up with me because you really didn't think he … something …?'

'Can't remember.' He gesticulated. 'I was talking nonsense. Sorry, LS.'

But there was something there, some unease or coolness neither of them wanted to tell me about.

'Fuck the reunion,' Martin said, desperate to be back in favour. 'It'll be full of wankers anyway.'

'Exactly,' Ben said, reaching across to replenish Martin's glass. 'No need to rake over old memories.'

Martin cocked his head. 'No.'

I noticed Martin's was the only portion of the table without a single crumb or stain around where his plate had been. He could have walked out of the room right then and there would have been no physical trace of his presence.

I remembered that dinner party this morning in my session but I didn't speak about it. That happens sometimes: I think I'm going to tell Keith about one thing and I end up talking about something else entirely. And often the something else seems trivial or superficial and it's only by talking it through that I realise it isn't and that each separate particle of my disastrous marriage is woven together by a complicated intermeshing of invisible thread.

'He bought the same shoes, you know,' I said. Keith, who specialises in never looking surprised by anything, ran the pad of his thumb across his top lip.

'Who?'

'Martin.'

I glanced at the mantelpiece to my left. Keith is careful not to let slip any personal details about his life so I have become obsessively observant about his surroundings, examining any clues with the forensic attention of an archaeologist. The mantelpiece was filled with small, irregularly shaped ceramic bowls.

'Lucy.'

My attention shifted away from the pots on the mantelpiece and back to Keith.

'Yes. Sorry.'

'You were saying about the shoes?'

'Martin. He bought the same shoes as Ben. A few months ago. I don't know why I'm thinking of it.'

Keith stayed quiet. As ever, I filled the silence.

'They were these awful, *awful* trainers …' I scratched at a hangnail. 'They had a fluorescent pink sole, designed by some hip-hop guy. So Ben bought a pair because apparently they were really hard to get hold of and cost hundreds of pounds or whatever. Limited edition, you know.'

Keith, impassive, didn't seem to know.

'And Ben wore them once to dinner at this Michelin-starred restaurant. To fucking dinner! He had on this suit, beautifully made, and then bright pink trainers on his feet.'

We had sat down to dinner and ordered a cocktail and the waiter came with an amuse-bouche that consisted of a tiny square of raw tuna coated in popcorn, and Ben started talking about the latest cabinet reshuffle and some review of a hotel he'd read in the *FT* and had we seen this play at the Royal Court yet because it was terrific, it really was.

'We'll have to get tickets,' Martin said, even though I knew he hated the theatre and thought the majority of modern plays were rubbish. The only thing I could ever remember him liking was a Terence Rattigan adaptation at the National. Something about the repressed emotion appealed to him and, to my surprise, he had cried at the end.

'But mate,' Martin continued, grinning. 'I have to ask. Those trainers ...'

Ben glanced up from the wine list.

'What about them?'

'Mate. The soles!'

Ben wasn't finding it funny. He could be like that sometimes: perfectly happy to take the piss out of himself and other people for months on end and then, without warning, the shutters would come down.

'Yeah? And your point is?'

Martin, wrong-footed, began to redden.

'I just ... I mean ... It's not your normal ... It's quite a vivid ...'

'They're limited edition,' Ben said. 'Had to get them imported from the States. Didn't you see Jay Z wearing them the other day? It was in all the newspapers.'

'Oh,' Martin said. 'I'm sorry, I didn't mean ...'

He was fiddling with the edge of his napkin, head bowed as if he'd been told off. I couldn't bear seeing him like this. How dare Ben make him feel so small?

'You had them imported from the States?' I asked. 'Are you actually kidding me?'

Ben smirked.

'Nope.'

'You should have told me,' I continued. 'I could have customised a pair of Reeboks with a pink highlighter pen for half the price.'

Ben shut the wine list. For a moment, it looked as if it could go either way.

'You're right, Luce, you're right,' he said, popping the tuna in his mouth and swallowing it in one go. 'At least I'll know for next time.'

Martin squeezed my knee gratefully.

Five days later, I came home to find a pair of pink-soled trainers on the shoe-stand in the hallway. I guess Martin had imported them from the States too.

'And what did you think?' Keith asked.

I laughed.

'That he didn't give a shit about my opinion.'

I looked at the pots again.

'It strikes me,' Keith started, 'that you saw yourself as Martin's protector.'

My eyes wandered from the pots to a jar of tulips, each petal obstinately purple.

'The illusion of power,' he said. 'But it was just that, wasn't it? An illusion, I mean?'

Silence.

'You were trying to please. But did you remember to ask yourself what *you* wanted in all of this?'

He let the question hang. For several minutes, neither of us talked. Then, Keith nodded and looked at the clock and said we'd have to bring things to a close.

'Remember to write,' he said. 'Anything that comes to mind.'

'I will.'

I walked out, leaving the door open behind me. There was an emptiness in my head. I suppose what I'd been trying to tell Keith in my roundabout way, is that over the course of those two dinners I finally saw what had been self-evident to everyone else for years. My husband wasn't in love with me. He was in love with his best friend and he always had been.

Martin

Burtonbury, 1990

HOW DID BEN AND I BECOME FRIENDS? I'd dearly love to tell you it was a natural meeting of kindred spirits, an organic flourishing of like-minded souls. But, in truth, I set out to win him over as if it were a military campaign. I was precise about my goals, viewing each small victory as a stepping-stone to a broader, eventual triumph.

A few months prior to my arrival at Burtonbury, I had chanced upon a copy of Sun Tzu's *The Art of War* in a second-hand bookshop. Its cover was bent back and faded and a corner of it was obscured by a scribble in ballpoint pen, the kind of thing a child would draw in a fit of pique to depict a thunderstorm at the upper edge of an angry picture. There was a short dedication: 'To Colin, Hoping you might find something of use in these pages. With much love, S.' and it was dated 'Xmas 1974'.

I still have that book now, the red spine squashed in between *Roget's Thesaurus* and Gombrich's *The Story of Art* in my study shelves. These days, when I thumb through *The Art of War*, I find it amusing that a man called Colin celebrating Christmas in 1974 might be needing advice on the pursuit of some vicious silent battle. What indignities had he suffered, I wonder? Who knows? One of those small mysteries lost to the vagaries of time. The evaporation of one man's personal history into thin air. Colin: now just a figment of other people's imagination.

Anyway, *The Art of War* was my guide when it came to inveigling my way into Ben's affections. It became obvious, after that first day, that he was one of the most popular and respected boys in the school, blessed with a quiet authority which most of us would spend the rest of our lives trying and failing to emulate. Teachers loved him. His fellow pupils seemed to respect his intelligence rather than despise him for it (that was a new thing for me: the idea that being clever was a badge of honour rather than something to be hurriedly disavowed). I realised, observing him that first week as he walked into morning assembly with his tie askew, his shirt just the right level of billowing looseness, that this would have to be a subtle subversion.

'Victorious warriors win first and then go to war,' wrote Sun Tzu, 'while defeated warriors go to war first and then seek to win.'

And so I planned it all to the very last detail.

The first thing to do was to find out what his interests were. This meant getting close enough to him to overhear his conversations, which was harder than it sounded. Although Ben was in the same house as I was (named Sullivan, after some long-forgotten benefactor, and abbreviated in the manner of all public school labels to 'Sullies'), he moved in a very different crowd. Well, to be more accurate, he moved in a crowd and I didn't. From that first day with Howard the bear, I had clearly been marked out as the wrong kind of person with the wrong kind of things.

Shoes, for instance. There was only one acceptable form of footwear and these were tan-brown Kickers with leather laces. You couldn't tie the laces in the conventional manner, you had to spiral them tightly around a pencil until they stuck firm in a tight coil like alien antennae.

And ties. You had to wear your school tie either far too long or far too short, gathered up in a thick tongue inches from the collar, with the excess material tucked through a gap in the buttons on your shirt so that it rubbed uncomfortably against your chest all day.

Then the language. Words were invented or mispronounced or simply meant different things according to who used them. 'Fit', for example, could be employed to denote a girl's general attractiveness but if it were said it with an ever so slightly altered inflection ('fut'), it meant the opposite.

Needless to say, during my first few weeks at Burtonbury, I was ill-equipped. My shoes were regulation brogues and I found the notion of wearing a tie like a child's bib faintly ludicrous. All of which marked me out. I didn't especially care. And, later in life, I have come to find there's a certain usefulness in observing from the outside. It allows you space to listen and examine and understand. And, once you understand a group dynamic, you can control it without anyone suspecting.

Ben was surrounded by friends wherever he went. He had an easy, placid manner. He wore his good looks lightly; there was no gel in his hair, none of those sideways glances at reflective surfaces so beloved of adolescent boys. When I saw him in a group of people, I noticed that he would initiate conversations and then withdraw, only interrupting when he had a point to make or an apposite joke to crack. In class debates, he would deploy the same tactic to great effect: positing an initial point of view with confidence and then keeping quiet while everyone else piled in with their half-baked opinions before coming in strongly at the end with an incisive summary of key points.

The first time I spoke to him directly was after an English class in which he had been asked to voice his thoughts on Shakespeare's portrayal of 'the other' in *The Tempest*.

'What do you think, Ben?' Mr Reynolds had asked, the tip of his nose perpetually shining with the onset or aftermath of a cold.

Ben stretched back, one sleeve riding up his arm to reveal a twist of thick blue vein. He tipped his chair, bit the end of his pen. 'I think Caliban is intended as a symbol of slavery.'

It was an obvious point, easily assimilated from the CliffsNotes study guide I'd seen him flick through in the corridor before the lesson started. But it wasn't unintelligent. In many respects, it was classic Ben: just enough to sate the request and yet never too revealing of anything truly important. I've got to know these Ben-isms well through the years.

'Yes,' said Mr Reynolds. 'Good. Anyone else?'

'He's kind of a retard,' said Conor Mayhew, who could always be relied upon to say the densest possible thing. 'He doesn't get what everyone else is on about.'

Ben raised his eyebrows. I watched him struggle between his desire not to say anything controversial in case it made him unlikeable and his disagreement with Conor's comment. And, after a few seconds, it was the latter impulse that won out.

'Sorry, sir, but I don't think that's true,' he said. 'Caliban isn't stupid. The other characters might think of him like that, but that says more about them than it does about him.' He paused, then added a plaintive: 'Doesn't it?'

A warmth spread across the base of my throat. Because looking at the nape of Ben's neck from my seat two rows behind him, at the gentle feathered 'V' of his gathering hair, I couldn't help but feel he was talking about me.

I put up my hand.

'Yes,' said Mr Reynolds, 'er ... er ...'

'Martin. Martin Gilmour.'

'Of course. Martin. Carry on.'

It was the first time I'd ever volunteered to speak in class at Burtonbury. My throat was cottony.

'Well ... Just ... I think that's right. I think Caliban probably is a bit like the fool in other Shakespeare plays. He sees the truth where no one else does.'

Mr Reynolds nodded pensively. 'Which other plays were you thinking of?'

Bastard, I thought.

'*King Lear*,' I replied, because what Mr Reynolds couldn't know was that my mother had once given me a set of Shakespeare cartoon books: each of his plays reduced to strip comics and graphic characters communicating in speech bubbles, and that these had provided me with a more comprehensive knowledge of the great playwright's canon than any number of stuffy English lessons ever would.

'Mmm, good,' said Mr Reynolds, turning to write something inconsequential on the blackboard which none of us would copy down.

After the bell, we all filed out to the canteen. It was break-time and a Thursday, which meant we got given packets of crisps and you had to be quick to nab the salt and vinegar, which always ran out first. I hurried along the corridor and then felt a tap on my shoulder. I turned and was surprised to see Ben standing there.

'Thanks for that,' he said. His face was open but unsmiling. There was a tiny blood-spot in his left eye, which served only to highlight the remaining perfection of his face.

I nodded, temporarily at a loss for words. 'That's OK,' I stammered. I couldn't think of anything else to add and after a few seconds, Ben gave a muted smile, shrugged and walked on by. But, I reflected as I ate my packet of cheese and onion (the exchange, although brief, had made me too late for my preferred flavour), at least the ice was broken. At least Ben no longer knew me solely as the boy with the teddy bear. He had noticed me. Better: he had noticed me backing him up.

The third time Ben and I exchanged words was on the rugby pitch.

I had never played rugby before, preferring the lack of bodily contact afforded by prep school football, but at Burtonbury, there was no choice about that kind of thing. I put on my games kit – green shirt, brown shorts – with the heaviness of a condemned man. I knew, without having to try, that I would be terrible at rugby. I disliked team sport for the reliance on other people and I abhorred physical contact. To be forced to do both things in the space of one hour was a particular torture.

We filed out onto the pitch, led by a games teacher called Mr Wilson who wore shiny tracksuits and had a flashy gold watch on his wrist. He was accompanied by Scott, an Australian student who was working as a teacher's assistant before starting university. Scott was an Adonis of absurd proportions: chiselled features; golden tan; calf muscles that protruded like rats from a python's stomach. Everyone had a crush on Scott without ever admitting that's what it was.

Several months later, Scott would be discovered *in flagrante* with Miss Edison, the slutty art teacher, and would be asked to leave the school. Miss Edison returned the following term but she was less friendly than before. The loose blouses she used to wear, with the sleeves that kept slipping off her shoulders, were replaced with plain cotton T-shirts. She seemed sadder. For weeks on end, we were forced to do still-life studies of four apples and a bowl. And then one day, she walked out of class and never came back.

There was a brief announcement about her departure in assembly the following week and rumours abounded that Miss Edison had flown to Australia to be with Scott and they were going to get married in spite of the age difference and have a brood of charming, dual-nationality babies. I think we took comfort in this story. We liked Miss Edison.

Years later, Ben and I ran into Scott in the bar of Duke's Hotel. We were drinking martinis (Ben liked his dirty, served with a jug of brine). We recognised Scott immediately. He must have been nearing thirty but he looked exactly the same as he had at eighteen.

'Scott,' Ben said. The Australian glanced up. 'You won't remember us, but ...'

Ben did the introductions. Scott's face broke from blankness into a grin. The two of them chatted.

'Whatever happened to Miss Edison?' I asked.

Scott stared at me.

'Who?' he said.

And that was that.

Anyway, on the day of my first rugby lesson, Scott remained on the edge of my consciousness. We were divided into teams by the teacher and then told to warm up, which consisted of aimless running around and the execution of twenty squats, followed by more running around and then some hamstring stretches.

No one asked if I had played before. I think it was simply assumed that I must have done. The prevailing Burtonbury belief that everyone was like them never ceased to amaze me. Although I suspect now that there are advantages to thinking like that. You don't need to ask as many questions. Assumption is the mother of all certainties.

But when I took to the pitch, I didn't know the rules. I thought the safest thing to do was to stay on the periphery of the action, making it clear I wasn't someone to be trusted with the ball. This worked for the first twenty minutes but then, without warning, there was a jostle of activity and a boy I'd never seen before came sprinting towards me, panting like a horse, chased by another boy who wore a mouthguard that was a slash of fluorescent yellow, and suddenly the ball was hurtling towards me. Instinctively I put out my hands and caught it.

Time seemed simultaneously to slow down and speed up. I was aware of the heft of the ball in my palms, the pleasingly solid sensation of having done something right but in the same moment, four boys were bearing down, running towards me with all their might. Self-preservation kicked in and I knew I needed to get rid of the ball immediately, so I threw indiscriminately without looking to see whether anyone was around to catch. As I lobbed the ball into the air, I felt a spasm of relief. There was an audible groan from my team-mates but I didn't care. Getting rid of the ball was the thing.

Just as it left my hands, I felt the full weight of a boy slam into my side. I tumbled to the ground. The boy had his forearm pressed against my neck and there was a pain in my ankle where it had been kicked. I felt the dampness of grass behind my head. Squinting, I could only make out the black shadow of my assailant against the sky.

I blinked. Sat up. The boy was smirking.

'Should be more careful, dickhead,' he said.

His face was densely freckled. The rim of one of his ears was folded over. His wide forehead glinted with sweat.

'Fucking hell, Jarvis, what the fuck?'

A familiar voice. Ben appeared from behind Jarvis's meaty head.

'What the fuck are you doing?'

Jarvis shrugged.

'Whatever,' he said, lumbering up to a standing position. He jogged back towards the action. His shirt was smeared with grass stains.

Ben glanced at me.

'You all right?'

I nodded.

'Come on, then.' He leaned forward and offered his hand. I took it, thumb criss-crossed with his, and he levered me up. I lost my footing, stumbled and fell into him. I felt heat rising from Ben's chest. He pushed me back.

'OK?' he asked.

'Yes. Thanks.'

He ran off. For days afterwards, I could recall the tender dip of skin between his thumb and forefinger, the touch of it as he lifted me up and helped me back on my feet. He must like me, I thought, to have done that.

It was time to capitalise on our three brief encounters, to forge a common connection.

The next obvious step was to work out what music he liked. Ben was often to be seen walking around with his Discman peeking out of his blazer pocket, the headphones either on his ears or slung casually around his neck, piping out a tinny bassline. I tried several times to sidle up and hear what it was, or to make out the spinning letters on the compact disc through the plastic aperture. Once, in the lunch queue, I nearly managed it. I stood behind him, only inches away, clutching my tray to my chest, and I could smell him: tang of soap and skin with an undertone of something oaky. Just as I leaned into his neck, craning each aural synapse to make out the lyrics, he turned and flinched and took a step back. He looked at me oddly. Then, releasing another one of his expressionless smiles, he resumed his place in the queue, readying his plate for rubbery slices of roast turkey and a paste of mashed potato.

When I realised that tactic wasn't going to work, I got smarter. Ben shared a dorm in Sullies down the corridor from mine, with two other boys called Mungo and Johnno. (Years later, when I mentioned this in passing to Lucy, she shrieked with laughter. 'You went to a school where people were called Mungo and Johnno? That's hilarious.' She caught sight of something in my expression. 'I mean,' she added hastily, 'I like Ben, but that is quite funny, you have to admit.')

Because they were just a few doors down from where I slept and because, essentially, I had no friends, I was able to devote a lot of time to tracking their movements. For a week after the lunch queue incident, I made sure that I woke earlier than my room-mates, slipping out of the dorm to the sound of their rattling snores, closing the door behind me on the musty fug of sweat and socks.

There was a shared bathroom in between my room and Ben's. I locked myself into a loo cubicle, propped myself up on the seat, and waited for the sound of Ben's voice. My plan was to come out at the appropriate moment, stand at the basin next to him while we brushed our teeth and somehow use the opportunity to engage him in conversation.

As it turned out, it didn't quite work like that. Ben came in, but he was trailed by his two room-mates and the three of them spread themselves across all the available basins so there was no space for anyone else. I came out of the loo rather sheepishly, wearing my blue-and-white-striped pyjamas. Ben, I noticed, wore boxers and a T-shirt with a Hard Rock Cafe logo on the front and a ripped neck. His friends were similarly attired. In place of slippers, one of them wore a pair of espadrilles, the fabric back worn down flat under his heel.

'D'you have any toothpaste?' Mungo was asking Ben. 'I've run out. Can I borrow some?'

Ben, eyes sleepy, hair pressed against his scalp where he must have laid it against the pillow, passed over a tube of Colgate.

'Don't borrow it. Have it. Don't want it back after it's been in your gob.'

Johnno snorted.

'Dick,' he muttered.

Mungo glanced at me as I walked past, barely registering my presence. I was irritated. There was no way I could get close to Ben now. Back in the corridor, I could hear a guffaw of shared laughter and could only think that I was the cause of it.

But then I had another idea. I crept down the corridor away from my own dorm and towards Ben's room. With all three of them in the bathroom, it seemed like too good an opportunity to lose.

I pushed the door and slipped inside. There were four beds, just like my dorm, but arranged differently – four of them against the same wall, so close to each other you could reach out your hand and touch the next boy's mattress. I could see that Ben's bed must be the one on the right, because there was a family photo on the chest of drawers depicting a girl who looked like him with her arm around a much younger Ben. The light in the photo was sunny and fuzzed. The girl had long brown hair and irregular front teeth.

I crossed the room, opened the top drawer. Boxer shorts. Vests. A packet of Marlboro hidden underneath a pair of socks. The next drawer contained random sheaves of paper; letters in opened envelopes with postmarked stamps; a postcard with 'Malibu' written across it in a yellow diagonal. I flipped it over briefly. Blue biro, girlish handwriting with circles above the 'i's, signed off with a single 'J' and a flurry of kisses. I stuffed the postcard into the drawer, feeling the corners buckle as I did so.

My heart was beating tightly. I was aware of the clicking of the clock, the hubbub from the bathroom dying down, footsteps on the carpet. I wrenched open the next drawer at speed. Four pairs of jeans (I had a moment to register the opulence of this: four pairs!), and there, at the back, was what I had been looking for: a few CDs in cracked plastic covers. I picked one out, the edges of it slipping against my sweating hand, and had time to register the band name: Run DMC. There was another one I glanced at just long enough to make out three initials: R.E.M. That would have to do. I shunted the drawer shut with my thigh. And then, without thinking, I opened the top drawer again and took out a letter at random. I slipped it down the waistband of my pyjama bottoms, pulled the drawstring tight and rushed out, leaving the door to bang behind me and hoping no one had heard.

I turned the corner just as one of Ben's room-mates was walking back down, his sponge bag swinging in his hand, his breath smelling of peppermint. The envelope crackled softly against my stomach. Its presence gave me a frisson of power.

Strange as it now seems to me, I didn't read that letter for several days. I was too caught up in the execution of my plan. And it wasn't even much of a plan. Still, it was all I had to keep me occupied. School was a doddle. In spite of my certainty that Burtonbury would be a place of intellectual stimulation and personal fulfilment, it turned out I was one of the brightest boys in my year without even trying. And because my schoolwork could be fairly swiftly dispatched, I had plenty of time to devote to the winning over of Ben. After my investigations in his dorm room, I put aside a precious portion of the extremely limited pocket money my mother deposited into a local bank at monthly intervals for the purchase of popular music CDs.

On Saturday mornings, we were allowed to walk into the nearby town of Burton in groups of four or more, as long as we signed in and out using the register on the table in the front hall of the boarding house. I remember that register so clearly: a green lever-arch file with loose-bound paper marked off by hand into rows and columns where spaces would be left for initials and times. A biro was attached by a blue piece of twine, the end of the pen secured by the over-zealous application of Sellotape by someone determined it shouldn't get stolen (matron, probably). And yet it always was stolen. Again and again and again.

For me, that single detail more or less summed up the sheer bloody-minded entitlement of those public schoolboys. There was no point to the theft. It's not as if there were a shortage of cheap writing implements at Burtonbury. It was more that the act of stealing something the authorities didn't want us to have and knowing the inconvenience it would cause made it worthwhile. And underlying it all was the fundamental belief – no, the inbuilt knowledge – that someone else would always be on hand to sort it out. Someone whose job it was to serve them.

I digress. Apologies.

In Woolworths, I went straight to the music racks. There were two Run DMC albums, each one stickered with a black and white label advising parental guidance. I picked them up and tried to think of myself as the kind of person who would choose albums like this, knowing my own taste without question, knowing with precision the sort of music I would like to listen to as I lit cigarettes and blew smoke rings, eyes half shut like Steve McQueen in *Bullitt*. I scanned the racks for R.E.M. There was only one of their albums. I grabbed it.

Back in my dorm, I had to beg my room-mate Dom to lend me his Discman in return for promising to polish his shoes every day for the rest of term.

I sat on the bed, placed Run DMC in the Discman, slipped the headphones over my ears and crossed my legs to get more comfortable. I envisaged myself spending a happy few hours taking in new aural sensations, a pleasing musical education of chords and melodies that would serve only to bring me closer to Ben, to understand the innermost workings of his mind. What I got, instead, was a clattering cacophony – thumping beats, and singing that wasn't singing at all, but more like rhythmic shouting. I took off the headphones in disgust and flung them across the bed. Was this really the sort of thing Ben liked to listen to?

I removed the CD and replaced it with R.E.M. I sighed, told myself not to pre-judge, and pressed 'play'. R.E.M. did, at least, seem to believe in a traditional approach to rhythm and the verse/chorus dynamic. Some of their songs were passable, if a bit self-consciously put together. At home, my mother was partial to Frank Sinatra and light opera. Say what you like about the Brat Pack, but they did at least know how to hold a tune.

I checked my watch: 4 p.m. Tea. I placed the CDs carefully back in their cases and left them, in plain sight, on the top of my bedside table. They were clearly the coolest things I owned.

In the dining hall downstairs, boys were huddled around the two giant silver toasters, each one capable of handling twelve slices of bread at a time. I took two slices of Mothers Pride and elbowed my way in gently.

'Oi, watch it fuckface.'

I turned and came face to face with the boy from the rugby field. Jarvis.

'Just trying to get to the toaster,' I said, as reasonably as I could.

'Just trying to get to the toaster,' Jarvis repeated in a feeble sing-song, his voice at a nasally high pitch, his fingers elegantly raised in mockery as if tinkling on some imaginary piano. 'We're all fucking waiting for the toaster, yeah?'

I don't know what it was about this particular interaction that affected me so. I had managed to keep my temper in check since arriving at Burtonbury because I was worried about cocking everything up again and, in truth, I was a little intimidated. But Jarvis was such a boorish, dense little prick that I simply couldn't let him get away with it for a second time.

'Fuck off,' I said, loud enough so that the group of a dozen boys around us could hear.

'What did you say, you fucking nonce?'

'I said: fuck off, Jarvis.'

I stared at him, drilling my gaze into his stupid face, and I could feel myself drawing up, shoulders pushing back like a bull readying itself for a charge. Heat pumped through me.

Jarvis started towards me, grabbing my neck with one hand and pulling back his other arm in one jerking motion. He sniffed, casually, as if he were already scenting victory.

I was not a fearsome opponent. I was of below average height and slim build and I was pale and effeminate and, until this point, no one had paid me much notice. But Jarvis, like everyone else, had underestimated me.

I ducked his first punch. The dining hall was filled with the sounds of boys jeering and cheering. Jarvis's face sweaty with effort. Doors slamming, chairs squeaking as more people joined the fray. A ring formed around us. Shouted encouragements. My back being slapped and pummelled. Jarvis, charging for me again. I stood my ground, feet wide apart, fists formed, and as he came for me, I punched him square in the jaw. The pain in my knuckles was pure electricity. Jarvis, stunned, reeled backwards. Ignoring the pain, I lunged forwards, punching his eye, the crack of bone against my knuckles.

'Fucking hell,' Jarvis said, dropping back, crouching, legs bent, head hanging forward as he put the palm of one meaty hand against his injured eye. 'What the fuck are you doing, you fucking lunatic?' But his voice was cracking, he was almost crying now and his words had lost their force. The onlookers were going wild at the underdog's unexpected triumph. My ears pounded with their roaring. The room came back into focus. I saw a mish-mash of smiling faces. Some of them were actually clapping. I caught snatches of speech here and there:

'Good one, mate.'

'Showed him.'

A slice of bread, thrown by an unknown hand, arced across the room and landed by Jarvis's left foot. Jarvis, seemingly undone by this final humiliation, limped out of the dining hall. And then, with an assurance I had never known I possessed, I walked towards the silver Dualit, picked out two slices of white bread, and pressed down calmly on the toaster lever.

'You've earned that.'

It was Ben. He was looking at me with amusement, a twitch of a smile playing over his top lip.

'Yeah,' I said. 'Guess I have.'

The toast popped up, sending a scattering of crumbs into the air. Ben stood there as I spread crunchy peanut butter across both slices and then dolloped on a spoonful of raspberry jam. We sat down. He had a cup of tea and a plate piled with two slices of ginger cake and a chunk of flapjack. I noticed that when he drank, he lifted the saucer in one hand. It was a gesture that seemed courtly and old-mannish.

He pointed at my hand, the back of it reddening.

'Should put ice on that, you know.'

'Yeah.'

'How're you settling in, then?' he asked.

I shrugged. 'Yeah, fine, thanks.' A pause. 'I mean, it's better than my old school.'

'Yeah?' Ben fiddled with his earlobe. 'Why's that?'

'Oh, you know. Just. My old school was full of wankers.'

Ben laughed. Encouraged, I continued.

'Not their fault. They were just really different from me, you know? No music taste or anything.'

'You into music then?'

'A bit.'

'What kind of stuff?'

'Um. The usual. Love the old classics. The Beatles. The Stones.'

Ben took a bite of his cake, uninterested.

'And R.E.M. ...' Was it too much to mention the other band as well? Would he be suspicious? I ploughed on. I might never get this opportunity again. 'Run DMC, that kind of thing.'

He looked at me with admiration.

'Really? Me too. I fucking love "Walk This Way".'

I hadn't got a clue what he was talking about.

'Yeah, totally.' I mentally scanned a remembered image of the R.E.M. CD cover to come up with a suitable track title. 'And ... "Begin the Begin". A classic.'

Ben leaned forwards. 'Shit, yes! Love that song.'

A silence fell, but it was companionable. Ben demolished the rest of the cake in two bites.

'Starving,' he said when he caught me looking at him. 'Rugby,' he added, his mouth still full. I watched the cake disappear down his gullet, the rise and fall of his Adam's apple, the faint line of gingery crumbs curved in a half-moon on the plate.

He wiped his hands on a paper napkin, then lifted it to his mouth. Every movement he made was done with total conviction of its rightness. Whereas I questioned everything: how I ate, how I spread my toast with peanut butter, how I spoke, and whether, at night, when I heard the shuffling underneath the other boys' duvets, followed by stifled half-sobs and groans, those boys were thinking of the same things I was. Curly hair. Muscular torso. The wispy spread of stubble along an adolescent jawline.

'You going tonight?'

It took me a moment to realise Ben was talking to me and that what he was saying required a direct answer.

'Um …'

'Tonight. You know. The bop with the BGC.'

BGC – not to be confused with BCG, which was an injection against tuberculosis I'd been subjected to in the sanatorium the previous week – was Burtonbury Girls College, the local girls' school. Every term, the two schools organised a joint disco known to all and sundry by the egregiously babyish monosyllable 'bop'. I had successfully avoided the whole thing by not buying a ticket and had planned to spend a quiet evening reading uninterrupted in my dorm room. I had a letter I needed to write to my mother, whose communications had become more querulous in response to my silence.

'Actually, I haven't got a ticket,' I said, immediately annoyed by my choice of the word 'actually', which I thought made me sound priggish.

'Oh no!' He looked genuinely disheartened on my behalf. 'Hey, listen, I know someone who's got a spare. And to be honest, mate, it's pretty easy to gatecrash.'

I opened my mouth, preparing an excuse for why I couldn't possibly attend.

'Come over to my dorm first, yeah? I've got this new album you'll lose your shit over. Honestly. It's fucking genius. And,' he dropped his voice, 'I've got a bottle of vodka. Just to, you know, get us in the mood.'

He pushed his chair back before I could say anything else. He lifted his plate, placed the balled-up napkin in the cup and stacked the saucer neatly on top.

'Cool,' he said, squeezing my shoulder as he passed. 'See you later. Around 7.'

Ben didn't tell me what dorm he was in. Of course, I was already familiar with its exact location. But, I thought to myself as I cleared my own plate, he didn't know that. It was that confidence again – the righteousness of the popular. Ben knew I'd know. He just did. And the thing was, he was absolutely right.

IV.

I HAVE FINISHED THE CUP OF TEA. Someone had left the bag in so that by the time I reached the final millimetres, it was stewed and tepid and bitter to the taste. I wonder if they will offer me another and decide that, if they do, I will request that they leave the bag out. Or at least that they give me a stirrer and then I can fish it out myself. But then, I think, where will I put the teabag? There is no saucer, obviously, and the polystyrene cup comes without a lid. It would have to be placed on the table, squashed and moist, leaving a patch of damp on the laminate, and I'm not sure that would be the done thing.

The idea of the second cup of tea begins to obsess me. I worry that if someone else takes out the bag, they won't leave it in for long enough so the tea will be watery and weak. Could I ask Beige Hair to ensure it was left in for a prescribed period of time? But how long would that be? I can only judge in terms of the look of it, not in seconds or minutes. When I make my own tea, I know when it reaches optimal strength from the colour of the darkening water. It is a colour that comes just after chestnut mushroom, just before polished teak. It needs to be conker-like, russet-tinged. When milk is added, it should be almost terracotta ...

'Mr Gilmour? Martin?'

'Yes. Sorry. Where were we?'

Beige Hair scratches her temple with the lidded tip of her ballpoint pen. She is disappointed in me, I can tell. She thought it would be easier than this. I wonder how much she knows about me, what the extent of her pre-interview research has been. I have a Wikipedia entry and I suppose she might have read it. I didn't write it myself and I'm not sure who did, but it has all the basics there, more or less accurately stated. For a while, it had me down as a year younger than I actually am and included some unfairly critical reviews of my book. I set up a fake profile to edit it, taking out the negative quotes but leaving in the incorrect year of birth. Then, when I checked it a few months ago, I saw someone had altered that as well.

It was simultaneously bizarre and flattering to read the biographical details about myself that a stranger (I assume it was a stranger, but who knows) had thought worth compiling. Astonishing to realise how much information about me existed online. And yet there was so much of merit that had been left out. My friendship with Ben, for instance, was not even mentioned. Neither was my mother, which was less surprising given that Sylvia Gilmour had never done anything of note in her unexceptional life, but it still gave me an oddly unbalanced feel to read this partial account of my existence.

'You were at school with Ben Fitzmaurice, is that right?'

Beige Hair's voice has acquired a bored edge.

'Yes, I believe I've already mentioned that. Several times.'

'We just want to be as thorough as we can.' She places her pen on the table, leans back in her chair, draws her lumpy grey jacket over her chest. 'And how would you describe Ben, the first time you met him?'

I am taken aback by the question.

'Really, I can't see why this is remotely relevant.'

Grey Suit pipes up again. Now that he's started talking, he can't stop.

'You can let us worry about what's relevant,' he says. 'Just answer the question.'

Beige Hair doesn't move. So that's how it is, I think. They're one and the same. The two of them, in league together, trying to trip me up. Bullies, just like Jarvis. The memory of my fist connecting with his jaw flashes in my mind. My knuckles begin to itch. I imagine what it would be like to lean against this table, draw my arm back, feel the muscles tense in readiness, and then slam my clenched hand into Beige Hair's face. Would I feel the crunch of her cheekbone? Would blood start to trickle from her nose? Would her head snap back on impact?

I smile at her, lazily.

'He was popular,' I say. 'Good-looking, clever, sporty.'

Beige Hair nods again. Grey suit stares at me coldly. There is a brief silence. And then Beige Hair asks me a question in such a soft tone of voice that it takes me a moment to register what has been said.

'Were you jealous of him?'

I break eye contact and stare down at the tea I have already drunk, thin rivulets of brown streaking the white disc at the bottom of the cup. I breathe in.

'I suppose I was.'

It is the first wholly real thing I have said since I came into this room.

2 May

THE RICH DO PARTIES BETTER THAN THE REST OF US. It's not just the money or the every catered-for whim or the superior quality of the alcohol and food. It's a certain unquantifiable atmosphere that comes from other people's excitement. We are turned on by wealth, us lesser mortals. We don't want to be and yet we are.

We are jealous, yes. Internally, we decry the excessive, absurd, narcissistic scale of a party like Ben Fitzmaurice's fortieth. But other people's money has a narcotic quality. It makes you high. It makes you forget your misgivings. You feel privileged, somehow exceptional to have been invited, as though the tiniest fleck of gold leaf from a giant glittering statue has smudged off on you and you can kid yourself you belong. That you are, for a single night, indubitably *One of Them*.

And it *was* quite a party. Important to remember that now, given all that has happened since. Important to recall how decadent the whole evening felt when we were in it, senses heightened, then dizzied by the free-flowing drink. The lychee martinis. The champagne cocktails. The Old Fashioneds made with aged tequila dating from the year of Ben's birth. And, in an ironic nod to his university days, trays of potent, sickly-sweet Bacardi Breezers and bottles of Hooch which prompted us all to laugh at this audacious joke of his which, in another context, would seem so common, so cheap, but because it was Ben, everyone agreed in a swooping hullabaloo of voices that it was 'classic', that he was 'a legend' and 'an absolute hoot' and 'jolly good fun'.

Drink. So much of it. A saturation of joy. The drink poured through the night, a liquid effervescence bubbling into the corners of the house, a rolling tide which swept over and dragged us under, heads thrown back, mouths gaping open with bright, luminous laughter, echoing into the promise of the night's stretching darkness.

The heady swirl of it: images snatched into focus then lost in an ever-spinning blur. Flash of sequins. Red-soled shoe. Shimmering diamonds. Lacquered nails. Hair shot through with shining dust. A backless dress, scooped low enough to see the tip of a private, fleshy crease. A bow-tie, uncoiled on a scatter cushion, edges curling.

After Fliss went upstairs to change and say hello to Serena and the children, the guests seemed to arrive all at once. Lucy and I, left on our own without explanation, stood in the shadows and watched as they traipsed through the door. Ben had disappeared to glad-hand the gathering crowds. Serena was nowhere to be seen.

'I mean, seriously,' Lucy said. 'What's taking her so long?'

I watched as a popular female television host whose face seemed to be ninety per cent teeth wobbled past in stiletto-heeled ankle boots, legs shaking like a newborn calf's. Much had been made of this particular woman's natural warmth and her easy, conversational manner when she first became famous as the presenter of a prime-time talent show. Her breakthrough moment had come when she interviewed a nine-year-old girl who had performed an operatic aria alongside a singing dog and who had been rejected by a panel of four judges. The girl had sobbed unhappily and the TV presenter had flung both arms around her and held her tightly in full camera beam, patting the back of the little girl's plaited princess hair. The next day, the presenter's picture had been on the front page of the *Daily Mail* and, underneath, the caption: 'Our Queen of Hearts'.

The whole episode had been nauseating. I had never been convinced by the television presenter's sincerity. We are so desperate to think ourselves empathetic these days, as if the exercise of tears is proof of our elevated humanity. In truth, our over-emoting is a selfish endeavour. We cry because we want to be seen to cry.

The television presenter had fallen out of favour in recent years, reduced to selling her own jewellery line on a cable channel and appearing as a guest panellist on discussion shows about other shows where the programme you had just watched was dissected in unnecessary detail and comedians you'd never heard of were allowed to make bad jokes you never wanted to hear repeated. You know the kind of thing.

'Excuse me,' the TV presenter said.

I realised I was standing in her way and she was trying to get past me into the next room.

'Terribly sorry,' I said, but I didn't immediately move to the side.

She smiled. It was a smile applied to her face like a sticking plaster. The longer I stood, the more the smile faded – incrementally at first and then slipping entirely.

Her voice turned hard. 'Could you please get out of my way?'

Without the smile, her face was haggard and old.

'Of course.'

I let her through.

Lucy looked at me wryly. She shook her head, suppressing a smile.

'Honestly,' she murmured. 'Can't take you anywhere.'

'Oh you know I can't stand her.'

'Mmm.'

I took a martini glass from a floating tray. Lucy followed suit.

A male model who had recently shot an aftershave campaign in his underpants strutted past. The billboards featuring his – for want of a better word – package had caused such a commotion when they were – for want of a better word – erected in various city centres that there had been several car crashes. Whiplash and minor injuries, I read on MailOnline (sadly, even I am not immune to the cheap allure of tabloid clickbait).

I could hear Lucy's deep inhalation as he walked past. The model was handsome – cheekbones, a well-trimmed beard, flinty eyes. But his face possessed a blankness that I found discomfiting, as if you could read anything you wanted on it; as if he would reflect whatever you most wanted to see.

On his feet, I spotted a pair of limited edition pink-soled trainers. I also had a pair, as it happened, bought several months previously. I'd seen Ben wearing them. They suited him, but not as much as I felt they'd suit me and I knew he'd be tickled if I got the same ones. Further proof of the closeness of our tastes, just like those CDs all those years ago.

They were tricky to get hold of, those trainers. I had to have them shipped from the States, at exorbitant expense, but it was worth it. When I put them on, they gave me a raffish air. I liked wearing them with suits. Style, I'd learned through the years, is all about the unexpected combinations.

Lucy seemed to take exception to the trainers. Said it was a waste of money. I didn't have the heart to tell her she wouldn't know style if it slapped her in the face. Besides, she couldn't understand the fraternal bond that meant men sometimes wanted to wear the same thing, almost as a tribal signifier. Poor Lucy. There were so many things that went over her head. She never needed to be as alert as me, who picked up clues like breadcrumbs.

'It's just rude,' Lucy said. It took me a second to realise she was still harping on about Serena's no-show. 'It's her party, after all.'

I sipped my drink. Ice-hot vodka thumped the back of my throat.

'Ben's, technically.'

'Oh come on. We both know Serena is treating this as a show-off-the-new-house-housewarming party. There'll be a double-page spread in *Elle Decoration* on Tipworth Priory before the month's out.'

I put my arm around her shoulders, squeezing her.

'Shush,' I said.

'Ow. You're hurting me.'

'Sorry.'

Another floating tray. Lucy took a tumbler of something orange with a glacé cherry, still on its stem, sitting at the bottom.

'Let's not get too drunk—' I started.

'Martin, I don't know about you, but I intend to get absolutely bloody hammered. It's the only way I can get through this.'

I let it go. Lucy has never especially liked parties and she has her particular reservations about the Fitzmaurice penchant for showy hospitality. In the early days of our courtship, she had been charmed by Ben, by his irrepressibility and his ease, by the way he made every occasion more fun simply by being part of it. Serena was different. She had always been more guarded and Lucy found her standoffish and cold.

But my wife had always been unfailingly, punctiliously polite. It was always Lucy who remembered to send cards at birthdays and Christmas, who bought the charmless Hector his presents, who knew the postcode off by heart to all their various properties.

It was only lately I had noticed this new, cutting tone and I wondered what had prompted it. Possibly it was Serena's greedy need to pop out children, one after the other like a trail of cut-out paper dolls. Her fertility seemed to stand aggressively in opposition to Lucy's childlessness.

'It's just so … so … unnecessary,' Lucy had said when I told her Ben and Serena were expecting their fourth. I knew what she meant. Everything about them had become unnecessary.

Waiters filed out from the corridor bearing platters filled with ironic canapés – miniature newspaper cones containing tiny portions of fish and chips; a satsuma-shaped fruit that revealed itself to contain chicken mousse when you bit into it; salted butter popcorn served in tiny boxes with 'For One Night Only: Ben at 40' printed across the front in red. The air was scented with sugared almonds and candyfloss. Could it be true, I wondered, that the rich have better smells than us too?

'Anyway, we've got our own reason to celebrate,' Lucy said.

I was mystified.

'Your book.'

She pressed her lips to mine. Dutifully, I brushed my mouth against hers.

'I'm so proud of you,' she continued. 'It's a work of genius. The definitive—'

'I don't think it is,' I cut in, more briskly than I'd intended.

'It is,' she said, hurt.

She deserved more, I knew. Lucy had always believed in me. I think, if I were to be honest with myself (always a dangerous idea) I would have to admit that she is the only person who ever truly has. From the first moment we spoke, she had complete faith in my ability. I had no idea where she got this from and yet, over the course of our marriage, I had come to rely on it. Lucy was the one thing in my life I never had to question. She was simply there, as solid as she always was.

I had taken her home once to meet my mother. Just the once. It was something I felt I had to do: some sense of filial responsibility lingered even then, even after I'd stopped going to Epsom for the school holidays. By the time I got to Cambridge, my reinvention as Ben Fitzmaurice's surrogate brother was so convincing to me, I'd almost forgotten I had a different past – one that involved gas fires and sausages in tins and bloodied Christmas cards dropped on an icy pavement.

We hadn't invited my mother to the wedding. Lucy and I had gone to the local register office and Ben had served as one witness and we'd asked Ian from the paper to act as the other and then the four of us had gone to the pub and had cheese and pickle sandwiches and ready salted crisps for lunch and got thoroughly, happily drunk. Neither of us had wanted a fuss. Or, to be more accurate: I had not wanted to invite anyone and Lucy had readily agreed. She wore a blue dress, fished out from the back of her wardrobe.

But, to my annoyance, a few months into our married life, I began to feel guilty about my mother not having been there. I tried to ignore the feeling but it kept catching up with me, like a

125

sprinting man trying to flag down a taxi, only just visible in the rear-view mirror. In the end, I gave in to it and Lucy and I packed an overnight case and drove our Ford Focus to the airless bungalow I recalled so vividly.

Nothing had changed, other than the size of my mother's television, which had grown bigger in my absence and which was now hung over the fireplace: a giant, leaking pool of black against the magnolia walls.

'Gosh,' Lucy had said brightly when she saw it. 'How impressive.'

My mother sniffed. Instead of responding to Lucy, she looked at me.

'What do you think of it, Martin?'

I thought it was an abomination. But I was nervous in her presence and found I couldn't speak normally.

'Very nice.'

'It's my eyes,' my mother said, glaring at us. Her skin was sallow, yellowing around the outer ridges of her nose and the tips of her earlobes. Her eyebrows were raggedy and overgrown, the hairs sprouting in competing directions. She had become old in my absence. But her age did not make her frail. Her frame was still broad, her arms hanging slightly in front of her chest like a gorilla or an athlete. When she walked, she used a single leg crutch, the name of the local hospital written in black block capitals down the central steel pole.

'Couldn't see the old screen. Couldn't make out the words on *Songs of Praise*.'

There was an uneasy silence. Lucy and I sat on the low grey sofa I remembered from my boyhood. My mother took the high-backed armchair opposite. She stared at us, unembarrassed by the lapse in conversation. Outside, the sound of traffic.

'Biscuit,' she said, pushing a plate of plain digestives sharply towards us.

I took one. It was mushy and stale. A granular paste stuck wetly to my teeth.

'So what are you doing here?'

Lucy pressed down her skirt with the palms of her hands and said: 'Well, Martin's told me ever such a lot about you and—'

'Has he really?'

'Yes, and I wanted to meet you for myself, Mrs Gilmour. Given that you are, after all, my mother-in-law.'

Lucy's voice had acquired a strangely precise quality: every 't' pronounced, every full stop adhered to as if she were a 1950s radio announcer. I realised it was a sign of her own anxiety and I reached out and patted her hand.

'Ahhh, that's sweet,' my mother said. 'Aren't you a *sweet boy*, Martin?'

She leaned back in her seat and even the set of her elbows against the chair arms seemed filled with ferocious intent.

'I don't know …' I started.

'You don't know what? You don't know what you're doing here? Well neither do I. Not so much as a word all these years and suddenly you turn up, all la-di-da and pleased with yourself, with your wet little wife who seems to think the sun shines out of your arse, and what am I meant to do? Give you a big hug and tell you everything's hunky-dory? Not bloody likely, son.'

I had never heard her speak like this before. The strange collo-quialisms she shot out like bullets. The aggression behind every word. The swearing. She had never sworn. And although she had been, for much of my childhood, unhappy or resentful or angry, she had always contained these emotions in my presence. She had been cold. But now the coldness had gone, replaced by wild anger.

The cup in my hand began to clatter against the saucer. I placed my biscuit, half eaten, back on the plate. I was struggling to get enough air into my lungs.

Then, Lucy stood. She reached out for me with her hand. I took it, gratefully, and levered myself weakly up from the sofa.

'Yes, Mrs Gilmour, yes, he *is* a sweet boy,' she said.

Lucy led me from the room. My mother followed us, her slippers shuffling across the carpet.

'You want to be careful with that one, dear,' she was saying. 'He's not right in the head. He's not like the rest of us.'

'Please be quiet. I'm really not interested in anything you have to say to me.'

'You should be, missy. He's not in love with you. He's not capable of it. There's something missing in there.' She rapped the side of her head with a knuckle.

We were at the front door. Lucy turned the lock with her free hand, still holding mine with the other. I gulped at the air from beyond the threshold, one foot on the step towards safety, the other still on the fitted carpet from which I had been trying, forever, to escape.

'He's pretending,' my mother was shouting now, waving the crutch in the air, the grey plastic stopper at its base swinging this way and that. 'He's pretending to be fucking human.'

We were outside. Lucy slammed the door behind us. We walked briskly to the car and I could still hear my mother's voice, even when Lucy turned the key and sparked the ignition, even as the engine kicked into action, even as we reversed into the road and shifted into gear and started driving, even when we were at home, miles away, unpacking groceries for a pasta supper, even as the water boiled in the pan, even as we clinked glasses of wine, even as we watched the *News at Ten* and even later, when the bath was running and the radio was on as we readied ourselves for bed, even then I could hear my mother's voice: a haranguing, insistent drumbeat of shame. I heard it even in my sleep.

Some time later, her neighbour called me up and told me my mother had been diagnosed with Alzheimer's and was being taken into care.

Within a month, my mother was dead from a stroke. I sold the house and paid for a junk removal company to take all her possessions so I didn't have to go back. I arranged the cremation and I never collected the ashes. And although I wanted to feel anger or sadness or anything, really, to prove her wrong, to prove that I did have natural instincts, that I wasn't simply pretending, what I felt instead was none of those things. It was relief.

I took another martini from a tray, downing it in two swift gulps. I looked sideways at Lucy, at her dress with its effortful, sensible attempt at glamour, at her chewed fingernails glinting modestly with pink varnish. Her pashmina was draped around her shoulders, the end of it trailing against the floor. The dress puckered around her stomach, which sagged and protruded and drew the material out of shape so that what line there might have been was ruined.

'Still no sign,' she said. 'Of Serena, I mean.'

'Probably wants to make an entrance,' I suggested. 'We should mingle.'

Lucy rolled her eyes. 'If we must.'

'We must.'

I gripped her firmly by the wrist and led her through to the next room. There was an internal balcony above our heads, lined with a carved wooden balustrade, and from this mezzanine level, a blur of semi-recognisable faces looked down on us, like Roman senators expressing their pleasure at the gladiatorial combat below. The light was sandy and we glowed with its beneficence. In one corner, a man in floral-patterned cowboy boots was chatting to a long-limbed supermodel who had been the first black woman to appear on the cover of Italian *Vogue*. She was wearing a strapless snakeskin dress, slashed to the thigh and revealing patent-leather shoes with platform soles and a spiked, dominatrix heel.

I noticed someone who from the back might or might not have been Andrew Jarvis, a hulking torso, the edges of it running to fat, a spray of ginger hair turning grey, but the man moved away before I could check. I had read about Jarvis in that morning's *Telegraph*. He had been appointed chair of some parliamentary select committee and was photographed with his wife, standing next to a gate at the end of what must have been a driveway into their picturesque constituency home. He had on a checked shirt, the sleeves rolled up to reveal elbows patched with psoriasis. No jacket of course. Like all politicians nowadays, he wanted to give the impression of a man at ease in his own skin who found the trappings of power unnecessary. The wife looked dull and as if she had once been pretty: the snub-nosed type who doesn't age well, whose freckles turn into liver spots and whose youthful, lithe flat-chestedness becomes bony and weathered as the years pass.

I hadn't read the interview – hadn't wanted to give him the satisfaction – but the headline was a quote from the piece: 'You shouldn't underestimate me.' Well, I thought, remembering his slow-moving lardiness, it would be pretty hard to overestimate him.

There were more drinks in the new room, long glasses set out in a looping semi-circle across the top of a sideboard, each one containing a white liquid topped with a slice of peach. I took two, passed one to Lucy.

'What is it?'

'No idea.' I sucked at it through a straw. 'Tastes good though. Strong.'

'Cheers,' she said.

We clinked glasses.

'It's so nice this, isn't it?' She gazed up at me. 'Spending time together, I mean.' She paused and I knew this was my cue to say something in response. When I didn't, she tapped me gingerly on the elbow, pinching the threads of my suit towards her: a child needing attention. 'You know,' she said playfully. 'Having some fun.'

'Yes,' I said, shifting away. 'It is.'

There was a rustling sound among the crowd, as if a pack of cards were being shuffled, and then Serena appeared at the top of the staircase. Silence.

'There she is,' I heard someone murmur.

She was a vision in silver. Her sequinned dress clung to her like a reptilian second skin. There were thin straps over each shoulder that one imagined could be snapped by the faintest pressure. The neckline poured downwards in a deep V, the edges of it sculpting

130

each breast and drawing just enough attention to her nakedness. The fabric gathered in a pool on the floor, as if she were emerging from a lake. Around her neck, a choker of diamonds. Her wrist was circled by another dazzling strap of jewels. Her hair was swept up at the back, tendrils of it falling softly to her neck.

'Bloody hell,' Lucy said. 'She looks amazing.'

Serena started to walk down the stairs, holding the banister with regal poise. Her nails were painted silver and, as she got closer, I noticed a tiny black dot in the centre of each nail, like an all-seeing eye.

'"A woman who was haughty and astonishingly proud in the matter of beauty",' I said.

'What's that from?'

'Plutarch,' I replied, pleased she'd asked. 'Talking about Cleopatra.'

Lucy shook her head.

'That brain. Too much knowledge for its own good.'

At the bottom of the stairs, a man wearing a kilt took Serena's hand and guided her to the centre of the room. I recognised him as a stand-up comedian. He had recently been touring the UK with a sell-out show. The posters were plastered all over the London Underground and featured the man in the kilt furrowing his brow and crossing his arms while inexplicably smoking a cigarette the wrong way round, with the filter pointing outwards. The tour was called 'Upside Frown'.

Serena floated past us without recognition.

'Martin!'

A booming voice sounded from behind my head. I turned and came face to face with Dennis Paulson, my former editor at the *Bugle*, a man I hadn't seen since he retired several years before. I had not felt the lack of his company in the intervening period.

'How the devil are you?' He pumped my hand with all the vigour of a dog wagging its tail. 'It's been fucking years. How many has it been? Didn't expect to see you here, old boy. What a fucking great surprise. How long's it been?'

'Eight years, I believe,' I said when Dennis had stopped talking. He was one of those men who made questions into monologues. He wasn't ever really interested in what anyone else was saying, but he enjoyed the pretence. During his editorship, he had been renowned for leaving every Friday afternoon for his house in the country and not returning until the following Tuesday lunchtime. Given that the *Bugle* was a daily London evening paper, this was somewhat inconvenient for all the staff. He always wanted the features desk to run pieces on country pursuits and they would have to remind him gently this wasn't what their metropolitan readership wanted. Undeterred, Dennis kept suggesting new angles on fox-hunting or salmon-fishing. He was famed for once having brought a brace of freshly shot pheasant into the afternoon leader conference. He had still been wearing his Hunter welling-tons at the time and dried mud had flaked off onto the carpet as he walked.

'Fucking eight years? Has it really? Fuck. Time flies, doesn't it? Must say I loved your book. The art one – what's it called? The one with all the pink on the front. Fucking great. So how do you know Ben and Serena? Never realised you guys were friends.'

A waiter came past with a platter of mini Yorkshire puddings. Dennis took a napkin and stacked up three in the palm of his hand. He ate them all in quick succession, each one in a single mouthful. As he spoke, we were lightly doused in a shower of spittle.

'I went to school—'

'So do you keep up with the old gang then? Toff. Buster. Binky. All that lot?'

I had no idea who he was referring to. Dennis had a tendency to give people nicknames they never wanted.

'I mean,' he continued, darting his black, amphibian eyes side-ways and back. 'Who do I have to fuck to get a drink in this place?'

I got him a glass from the sideboard. He clasped it to his chest. For a minute, I thought he was going to down it in one but he started taking surprisingly ladylike sips.

'And of course you remember my wife, Lucy,' I said, lightly pushing her forward.

'Course I do,' Dennis said, with a vague nod. 'Lovely to see you again. And looking so ...' He searched for the appropriate word. 'Lovely,' he said again, a hint of defeat in his features. 'Your book got quite a roasting though, didn't it?' he continued undeterred. 'Who's that chap who reviewed it, the one who said that you could learn more about art by watching paint dry than ...' He saw my face and then changed tack. 'Well, fuck 'em, eh? Easy to criticise. Difficult to do.'

'Actually,' Lucy said, 'Martin's book sold incredibly well.'

'Of course it did! No such thing as bad publicity! Bobsy!' he shouted, customary bombast resumed. Lucy jumped. 'Bobsy, darling, over here!'

A woman in a vivid yellow gown, slashed to her navel and stuck by some invisible force to her improbably pert breasts, started moving towards us.

'Listen, guys. Fucking lovely to see you both. I've just seen someone I know.' He slapped me on the back as he went. He'd probably have a heart attack before the year was out. Either that or gout would set in.

'I wish you wouldn't,' I said when he'd gone.

'Wouldn't what?' Lucy asked.

'Go on about the sales figures.'

I was embarrassed she had intervened with Dennis. I was not the kind of man who needed his wife to fight his battles for him.

'He was having a go at you ...'

'No he wasn't. That's just the way he is.'

'He didn't have a clue who I was,' Lucy muttered.

'Don't take it personally.'

'To think how hard I worked for that place ...'

'Not this again.'

'It just annoys me, that's all. No gratitude or sense of loyalty. Made redundant after five bloody years doing all the menial stuff no one else could be bothered with.'

'I'm going to find the loo,' I said.

'I was just saying …'

I walked away. The rest of her words were swallowed up by the crowd. Lucy has never got over what she perceives to be her mistreatment at the hands of her employers at the *Bugle*. She was let go at around the same time as I got a promotion to chief art critic. Surplus to requirements. They gave her a modest pay-off and, with my pay rise, it was enough to see us through. When I sold *Art: Who Gives a F**k?* a few months later, the advance gave us another cushion. Then it became a bestseller, which was even better for the bank balance. And, of course, there's always been the regular injections of cash from Ben and the Fitzmaurices. We're pretty well off, all things considered. Lucy doesn't have to work. You'd think she'd be grateful, but she still insists on doing meaningless bits of media consultancy for charities and non-profits. I don't know why she bothers. It strikes me as far too much effort to nurture a social conscience. Hearts were never intended to bleed.

I made my way upstairs, passing a huddle of three men in the corner, catching the phrase 'quantitative easing' as I went. When I turned back, I saw the former head of the Bank of England talking to the Chancellor of the Exchequer, who had recently plummeted in weight owing to something called the 5:2 diet, and a thin, bearded man in a velvet suit. The man saw me looking and raised an eyebrow. Our eyes locked. I nodded, put my lips to the glass, drank, moved on.

On the wall, there was a murky oil painting of an aged aristocrat in a frock-coat and a lace shirt, gathered with a pin at the neck. I wondered where Ben had got it from. The Fitzmaurice house in London was full of white sofas and chrome-legged chairs and contained not a single piece of art that dated from before 1950. It was a point of contention between us that each time I came round for dinner, I would bemoan their lack of appreciation for history.

'We can't all be as educated as you,' Serena said, the last time I brought it up.

There had been a sharpness to her voice, I recall, and I wondered if I had made the joke too many times. If her response to my affectionate reiteration had tipped over from intimacy to impatience. I wondered whether – dreadful thought – my repetition of it had actually become a private joke between Serena and Ben. Whether I, as an object of ridicule, provided a means of cementing their closeness. After all, joint opposition to something can be almost as unifying as mutual passion.

Serena had smiled. 'Don't look so serious, Martin. We weren't all lucky enough to go to Cambridge, were we?'

And then she had walked across the room and popped an olive in my mouth so that I could feel the dry softness of her fingers against my lips. Her face had been so close I could smell her face cream and the acrid undertone of a single smoked morning cigarette.

I reached the top of the staircase and went to the edge of the internal balcony to look down at the gathering swarm below. From up here, the guests looked smaller in scale, cartoon characters drawn into a complex computer game where the object was to collect drinks and friends and superficial gobbets of chit-chat.

I smoothed my hand down one sleeve of my suit to reassure myself that I looked smart and rich. That I gave the impression of belonging. That I had the right clothes. Because I knew, from past experience, it was important to look the part.

Notebook of Lucy Gilmour

I DON'T WANT TO GIVE THE IMPRESSION that it was all bad. It's hard now, viewed through the lens of everything that has happened, to remember that there were moments of happiness. It's hard not to feel resentful towards Ben and to blame Martin for allowing their friendship to assume such vital importance to his entire existence. It's hard not to think that I was competing in a battle I'd never signed up to, a battle everyone else knew I could never win but which I fought and fought and fought, attempting to persuade them they were all wrong.

But it's necessary for me to remember the good times. When it was just me and Martin: when he was removed from the pressure of being around other people, of having to perform for them and pretend he was somehow better than he was, we got on very well. There are many things I've questioned about my husband of late but when we were married and living together, I was supremely confident in the thought that he never once felt the need to pretend to me.

We went on holiday once, to the south of France, to a spot just up the coast from Cannes. I had booked a bed and breakfast in a small town overlooking a harbour and a pebbled beach. The B&B was simple but clean and our room had two large sea-facing windows which we opened every evening at dusk to hear the cawing of gulls and the murmuring pitter-patter of waiters in the cafe on the street below.

Our days fell into an easy routine. We would wake late, usually having missed the breakfast provided by the elderly *patronne*, and we would get straight into our swimming gear and take a bag with books and suntan lotion and towels to the beach. We hired two sunbeds. It was summer and the pricing was way beyond reasonable, but there was a tacit agreement between us that sometimes it was worth being ripped off.

We would lie there, side by side in companionable silence, reading our books and feeling the heat on our skin. Occasionally, Martin would get up and wander about and I would see him at the water's edge, bent over, examining shells and pebbles. When he returned, he would hand me one – a pearlescent scrap of a flattened oyster shell or a brown-grey stone worn feather smooth by the waves. He seemed less defensive there, less quick to take offence at imagined slights and, as a result, I was freer in my conversation. There were no topics to avoid.

In the afternoons, we would resume our position on the beach, angling our sun-loungers to track the movement of the sun across the sky. Sometimes, our talk would continue. And I remember it was on one of these afternoons, as I was immersed in a biography of Thomas Hardy I'd bought at the airport, that Martin said, out of the blue, 'I wonder if I'm like him.'

It took me a moment to engage, to realise he'd spoken. I set my book down and turned to look at him. He was staring out to sea, eyes masked by his Ray-Bans. His chest was still pale, pinker where his ribs dipped. Martin tanned in increments: the thin trail of hair from his belly button down to his waistband was bleached by the sun. On his face, the high part of his cheeks and the tip of his nose had gone red. He had lost some of his London greyness, but still looked very much the Englishman abroad.

'What was that, sweet?' I said. I always had endearments for him, I'm not sure why. It wasn't how I normally spoke.

'I was just thinking …' he trailed off. I waited. The pages of my book fluttered in the breeze. 'My father,' he said. 'I was thinking about my father.'

It was the first time Martin had ever raised the topic of his father. I had tried, in the early days of our being together, to get him to open up about it and he had always shut the discussion down, often in anger.

'But it must have affected you?' I'd say, ploughing on regardless. And he would shout and say I hadn't got a fucking clue what I was talking about and why did I have to make everything into a bad soap opera and why would a man he never knew, dying before he was even born, affect him?

In the end, I learned it was safer to drop it entirely. It was clearly too painful for him, I told myself. He should be left to deal with it or not deal with it however he wanted. I convinced myself it was really none of my business. What would I know, with my two living, breathing parents and my comfortable middle-class life?

Now here he was, on a sun-lounger on a beach in France, unexpectedly offering up this piece of information.

'What were you thinking, darling?'

I wanted to reach out and take his hand but I stopped myself. Martin sighed.

'I suppose ...' He started again on a different tack. 'It's odd when you've never known your father and never been told about him and then you grow up and one day, you're the age he was when he died and you think, "Am I like him at all? Is he the reason ...?"'

He broke off. Waves lapped against the sand. A child started crying in the distance, demanding ice cream. Its parent responded in hissed, rapid-fire French.

'The reason for ...?' I prompted.

'Oh I don't know, Luce.' He took off his shades and rooted about in the bag for his glasses case. When he found it, he took out the small square cleaning cloth and vigorously wiped each lens. The process took a few minutes. Then he snapped the case shut, slipped his glasses back on and said: 'The reason I've never felt I belonged.'

He looked at me then and I saw his naked vulnerability. The public Martin: the Martin who spoke too much at dinner parties, the Martin who was sometimes pretentious to mask his own insecurity, who clung to his friendship with Ben as if it were insurance against his own self-loathing, who wore sharply tailored suits and spent too much money on designer shoes as if to prove something to everyone else when the only person who needed to believe it was himself. That Martin was nowhere to be seen on that beach in France. Instead, I was left with the version I loved, the Martin who was honest about himself and who, instead of being angry, was actually just scared. Scared, as all of us are, of being found out.

I got up and went over to sit on his towel, my hot thigh pressed against his cooler one, and I leaned forward and kissed him lightly on the lips. He smelled of saltwater and coconuts.

'You belong with me,' I said.

He smiled and placed one hand on either side of my waist and he sat up and kissed me back, moving his hand up my back to my neck where he played with my hair, the ends of it damp with sweat.

'I do,' he said and he drew back; patted me on the thigh. He picked up his book and started leafing through the pages.

I sat there for a bit, telling myself there was no reason to feel sad that the kiss had ended sooner than I would have liked. He had confided in me, I thought; he had trusted me. He loved me. He needed me. He belonged with me because I gave him the space to be himself. There is no greater feeling, is there, than someone needing you that much? Than being the only person they can turn to?

I know now I was kidding myself. I look back and I'm astonished at how suppressed I was. How I was sacrificing all my needs and desires at the altar of this persuasive man. How I was losing myself without realising it.

I wanted so much to believe in my own importance, to believe I was enough, to believe I could make him better.

Stupid of me, I know.

Martin

Burtonbury, 1990

OF COURSE, I WAS WORRIED about what to wear. Ridiculously, the bop was considered one of the most crucial social events in the termly calendar and all I had were my jeans (deeply uncool because the waistband was slightly too high and the hems slightly too short) and a shirt with a light blue stripe. I did the best I could. Whereas, a few weeks previously, I would have tucked my shirt into my trousers, I now knew it was best to leave it casually half in, half out.

I tried repeatedly while standing in front of the full-length mirror on the wardrobe door to tuck it in and then pull it out precisely the right amount – enough but not too much. It was several minutes before I was satisfied. That's the thing about nonchalance. It takes an awful lot of bloody effort.

I couldn't do anything about my shoes. I was saving up for a pair of Kickers but was some distance from my eventual target, especially given the forty pounds I'd blown on CDs I didn't like. So I was stuck with the brogues again. I slid them out from under the bed with a sigh.

I was nervous, I realised, but not so much because of the bop. It was more the prospect of some uninterrupted time with Ben. The coaches weren't due to leave for BGC until 7.45. So that was at least forty-five minutes of one-on-one interaction with him in which to press home my advantage.

There were footsteps in the corridor and then the recognisable drone of Dom's voice. I slammed the wardrobe door shut, stuffed my wallet in my jeans pocket and made for the door, escaping before he had a chance to say anything.

'I thought you weren't going,' he shouted after my retreating form.

I checked my watch. It was 6.45. I knocked on Ben's door. No answer. I pressed my ear against the gloss-painted wood. Music snaked through the gap between the hinges. I pushed the door open.

'Mate!' Ben said, beckoning me in. He was standing against the window, arms propped against the sill, wearing an open-necked blue shirt, the buttons undone to reveal a strand of hair at the lowest point of the V. He grinned, the pink of his tongue just visible. On the little finger of his left hand was a signet ring, burnished gold and gleaming. Behind him, the sun was on the brink of setting, casting foreshortened charcoal shadows along the pale carpet of the dorm room. He made everything else seem dusty – in some sense not alive enough.

We were not alone. I was disappointed as I took in the other boys who were sitting on the edge of the beds, standing against the desk, lying on the floor so that a latticework of languid legs stretched out beneath me. The room smelled vaguely of smoke and when I tried to trace the source of it, I noticed Ben with a rollie pinched between his thumb and forefinger. He took a final drag as I watched, his lips pursed, eyes lazily closed, then he blew the smoke out of the window, wafting the final wisps of it with his cupped hand and stubbing the butt into a small fold of tinfoil before wrapping it up tightly and placing it in his jeans pocket.

'Come in,' Ben was saying. 'Make yourself at home. Olly, shift up a bit. Let Martin have some floor space.'

A boy on the floor with spots smattered across his forehead like raspberry seeds, moved to one side. If I couldn't sit next to Ben, I would much rather have stayed standing by the door. But with Ben looking at me expectantly, I was trapped. I shuffled into the room, slotting myself onto the available patch of carpet, my knees hoisted up underneath my chin. I tried to look as if this were the most comfortable position in the world, but after a while, my neck ached and sweat worked its way down my back and I was anxious there would be a damp patch on my shirt when I stood.

The room was ablaze with music and chatter but no one seemed to be speaking in full sentences.

'Fuck, yeah, and …'

'… fitter than you like.'

'Nah, mate, nah. Level three.'

'… football socks. Two pairs.'

'At least, you know, that's what Gadget said …'

'… such a dickhead.'

It was not what I had expected at all. This was not going to be an intimate tête-à-tête with Ben, swapping shared likes and dislikes and getting to know each other. In fact, he appeared to have forgotten I was there and was now arm in arm with James Lewis, a rugby player who was two years older than us and was renowned throughout the school for his sporting prowess. The two of them were snorting with laughter, whispering into each other's ears. The laughter subsided and Ben slapped James's back, whispering again, the sibilance cracking with semi-contained laughter.

What must it be like, I wondered, to have such an open soul?

'Here,' Acne Boy jabbed me in the ribs with his elbow. He held a hip flask in his right hand, monogrammed with the letters 'B.F.' I took it from him and placed it to my lips. Incredibly, this was the first time I had ever tasted anything stronger than undiluted lemon barley. My mother had been rigorous about never allowing wine at the dinner table, believing the mere presence of alcohol in the house to be a sign of moral slovenliness.

I tipped the hip flask back and felt the metallic force of the vodka hit the back of my throat like a left–right combination punch.

'Hey, hey hey,' Acne Boy was saying. 'Don't hog it, mate.'

But I hadn't finished yet. I gulped down my first swig and then tilted the hip flask again and let the liquid once more slip and weave its warm way down my gullet. There was the feeling, immediately, of something connecting: a clarity, an electric current of certitude. My synapses fizzed and hissed with the yes of it. Yes flooded my bloodstream. Yes, the platelets screamed, yes, yes, yes, more, more, more.

'Fuck's sake! This guy's a fucking nutter.'

I could hear Ben whooping as I drank.

'Down it, Martin. Down. It. Down. It. Down. It,' he chanted. I needed no encouragement. That first sweet-sour taste of vodka, the attention it brought me, had me hooked. It was as if I had spent all my life up to this point trying to fit the wrong key into a lock in the door and now, finally, I had stumbled across the right one and the metal teeth of it had slotted with beautiful smoothness into the precisely shaped cavity of my core.

This, I thought. This was the answer. Yes, yes, yes. More, more, more.

I handed back the hip flask. My cheeks felt numb and although my vision was blurring at the edges, it was also as if I were seeing everything with intense clarity, as though each movement in the room were being slowed down for my benefit.

The nerves dissipated. I was inhabiting my skin, aware of the physicality of each fleshy atom. I stretched my fingers, looking down to see the glorious efficiency of my hand: the economy of design, the beauty of it. And then I was interrupted again by another boy proffering a rolled-up cigarette and I took it and placed it between my lips and the paper of it was soggy from other people's saliva and the taste of it, when I inhaled, was brackish. I suppressed a cough.

'Keep it in, mate,' someone was saying. 'Don't fucking waste it.'

I took another drag, deeper this time, and then tried to hold the smoke in the pit of my stomach until I ran out of breath and as I exhaled I wondered if this was not, in fact, a cigarette, but something else. As soon as I'd had the thought, my eyes rolled back and the top half of my head seemed to crack like the shell of a boiled egg tapped with the back of a teaspoon. I ignored the swell of nausea in my chest. I took another drag.

The swirl of it: the sunlight, the raised voices, Ben's grin as he put my arm around his shoulder and walked me out of the room.

'Just breathe,' he was saying, 'just breathe.'

And then the slap of cold outside air as we boarded the coaches, the faint aroma of stale curry in the upholstery, jostling for space on the back seat, squashed in with people I barely knew, James Lewis on one side, punching my upper arm and laughing at something I hadn't said. More drink, this time decanted clear liquid in plastic water bottles, and my head was contracting and releasing and one moment I felt sheer panic at the loss of all familiarity and the next I found myself surrendering, relaxing into it as I would a wave in the sea, allowing the force of the water to carry me under.

At the girls' school, we stumbled out of the coaches in varying states of boisterous drunkenness. The teachers tried to shush us, threatening us with detentions if we misbehaved. They searched our pockets, looking for alcohol, but the water bottles escaped detection because, after all, we were allowed water and then we were inside the sports hall, bedecked for the occasion with streamers and sagging helium balloons.

Thump of music. Brash flashes of light. The noise of our chatter dropped without warning, a sail losing its wind. We stood along one wall in the darkest part of the hall, a homogenous puddle of male adolescence, slump-shouldered and staring at our feet and then there was a flurry of girls, appearing from everywhere and nowhere all at once in a blizzard of giggles and gloss and strawberry-scented perfume. They wore short skirts and tight trousers and tiny, strappy tops and T-shirts with provocative writing on the front and they entered the hall as if they possessed it, as if they already knew exactly what lay ahead, how the course of their evening would be charted.

They started dancing almost immediately, a swaying, sinuous forest of silver birch trees, and they pretended to ignore us even though I could see from the slant of their eyes that they were looking and looking and looking, the room filtered by the prism of their sideways glances.

Hours passed, or possibly minutes, and then two of the girls broke away – rebellious foals sauntering across to us, not making eye contact, shoulders bare, legs marked with small nicks and grazes.

One of them went up to James, the other to Ben and the girls were laughing because they knew they were being watched and their mouths were moving too quickly, too much, and I was hypnotised by the shape of those mouths, by the lips like elastic bands, stretched and loosened and stretched again to the point of snapping.

I had a bottle in my hand and as I saw Ben being led by the girls onto the dance floor, I called out to him, I said his name for the first time out loud, and I heard the single syllable of it drop like a marble onto the polished wooden floor and he turned and raised his eyebrows and I held out the bottle of vodka and wanted him to take it.

He shrugged and said, 'No thanks, mate,' and then he was on the dance floor and moving his hips closer to the girl's pelvis and she had her arms resting straight on his shoulders and her cheek nestled into the crook of his neck and I felt a drumbeat of anger at this sight, at my exclusion from it.

I squeezed the bottle tightly in my fist, feeling the plastic of it buckle and warp under the pressure, and I wished it was glass and that it would break and that shards of it would lodge in the palms of my hands and make me bleed.

I should have waited to read the letter. But when I got back to the dorm, I was still unsettled by the evening. And drunk. Yes, it should be noted I was very, very drunk. On the journey back, I concentrated on not vomiting and on not thinking of the image of Ben and that girl, coupled on the dance floor, the ridge of his cheekbones picked out by the green-white disco light, his hand in the small of her dipping back.

Back in Sullies, I traced my fingers across the paintwork to reassure myself that, despite appearances to the contrary, the building remained static. At one point, my chest heaved and I had to bend over, one hand cradling my stomach as I waited for the sickness to pass.

I got to the dorm. There my name was, a copperplate reminder of who I was: Gilmour. I read it to myself, mouth moving silently.

Dom and the others hadn't yet got back. I turned on the light, crashing into the wardrobe as I did so. There was a jangle of wire hangers. I hit the side of my head with the flat of my palm, thinking the noise was coming from some internal source. When I realised my mistake, I giggled stupidly.

I had an idea that it might be simpler to move if my centre of gravity were lower, so I got down on all fours and crawled towards the chest of drawers. I opened the bottom drawer, forgetting that my pyjamas were actually under my pillow, folded away carefully the way my mother had taught me. But once the drawer was open, the edge of paper caught my eye.

In my addled state, I didn't immediately remember where the letter had come from, that I had hurriedly stashed it in the waistband of my pyjamas during my reconnaissance mission to Ben's dorm. I levered open the flap, still gummy from where some unknown tongue had licked the back. The letter had been folded into three long rectangles.

I didn't recognise the handwriting. It was in blue fountain pen whereas my mother, on the infrequent occasions she did write, used a black ballpoint. These vivid blue lines were free-flowing and seemed to have been written in a rush, the ends of each sentence sliding down the side as if falling off a cliff, the dots over some of the 'i's forgotten in haste, the loop of the capital G becoming wayward and untidy. There was a smudge at the bottom left-hand margin.

I began to read.

The address was Denby Hall, Yorkshire. The date was 31 August 1989.

Dear Ben

From the floor, I levered myself up onto my elbows. It was difficult to keep my eyes focused. Unidentifiable spores floated across my vision. I blinked and continued.

I've been wondering whether to write this letter, my darling. I don't want to cause you any more upset especially now that you're probably all settled in at Burtonbury and having a whale of a time. I'm sure you've made lots of friends! I know you were a bit worried about leaving but home will always be here and we all love you very much.

It has been a terribly hard summer for all of us. I worry that you don't say much and I suppose I didn't want to keep asking – or nagging, as Fliss would say! – and sometimes a letter is an easier way of talking about things that are hard to do in person. I've definately always thought so.

I noticed the spelling mistake. My respect for the writer dropped several notches. With my attention diverted, the next sentence snuck up on me without warning.

You asked me a few weeks ago why I thought Magnus had to die. The answer, my darling, if there is one, is probably too difficult for us to understand. That's the kind of thing only God can know. But I've thought about it a lot myself and I wonder if there was something about Magnus that meant he was too good for us to keep. He was so sweet, such a happy boy and he made us all laugh so very much, didn't he? Do you remember he used to call you Bobo when he was very little and how much you hated it because you thought it sounded like Boobie? I'm laughing now thinking of that. Then Magnus saw you were upset and waddled over to you in his nappy and gave you the most enormous kiss on the cheek and after that, you couldn't be annoyed with him any more.

Perhaps, with little boys like that, who bring such joy and love to their families, there is only so long we get to hold on to them. So when he became very ill, it was almost more difficult for us and for you, darling, than it was for him. He was so brave. All the doctors said so, do you remember? There was a blotch on the page here, a dried-up splash of what must have been a wiped-away tear. The paper crinkled to the touch.

I suppose what I wanted to say is that we should try and focus on how happy Magnus was and how happy he made us, even if it was just for four short years. And he loved you and Fliss so much, Ben, and you were such a wonderful older brother to him. You were. I hope you know that.

I'm sorry your summer holiday turned out to be such a sad, sad time. If Daddy and I were preoccupied, it was never because we don't have time for you or because we don't love you very, very much. We do, my darling. We love you to the moon and back. Call us anytime – you have the number and the BT phone card. Lots of money on that so no excuse!

I will see you at exeat, sweetheart. Not long to go now. Please remember to brush your teeth properly and try to eat the odd piece of fruit, even if you hate it.

All best love, Mummy.

Mummy. I snorted. So childish. My mother never called herself by anything other than her proper name, as if she were nothing to do with me but merely existed as an individual who just so happened to be looking after me for a while. There were never any of those easy expressions of love in our tepid suburban bungalow. 'Love you to the moon and back.' I said the phrase out loud and then laughed, the sound of it hitting the walls like hail. What did that even mean? Sentimental nonsense, I thought, and at the same time, I felt sad that no one had ever said anything similar to me.

I did a quick calculation. August 1988. That would have been the month before Ben started his final term at Burtonbury House, the feeder school he and Jarvis had been to together. His younger brother had just died and his mother was sufficiently worried about him to send him this letter.

I folded the paper carefully back along its creases and replaced the envelope in my drawer. Tomorrow, I would have to work out a way to return it to Ben's possession. But before that, I would make a copy. Not now, not when I was incapable of holding a pen straight, but in the morning, before anyone was awake.

Why did I want a copy? I didn't understand my own motivation. But I think, looking back, it was insurance. Insurance against the future. I knew something about Ben he didn't know I knew. That none of the other boys at school seemed to know either. That was power. Sun Tzu: 'That general is skilful in attack whose opponent does not know what to defend; and he is skilful in defence whose opponent does not know what to attack.'

There was something else also. Some flickering spark of thought that was only just beginning to catch light. Because it would dawn on me, over the coming days and weeks, that there was an opportunity here too. Ben's much-loved younger brother had died. That meant there was a gap in his family. A gap I was only too willing to fill.

Notebook of Lucy Gilmour

KEITH ASKED ME THIS MORNING about the first time I'd ever met Ben. It was unusual for Keith to be so direct. Normally he gave me space to let my thoughts meander, interjecting here and there with a 'Yes?' or a 'Then what?' and sometimes, when he seemed impatient with my tendency to leave a sentence incomplete, a 'Finish that idea.'

But today he just asked me, flat out, and I was surprised because I didn't think we'd been talking about Ben that much. I thought we'd mostly been discussing my husband, which was the entire point of the exercise, wasn't it?

Keith's lips twitched.

'The point of the exercise?' he repeated. 'What do you think that is, exactly?'

I thought.

'To understand why I've become the way I have?'

I didn't want to say the word 'breakdown' although I know that's the official reason for my extended sojourn here. But it makes me sound like a rickety old machine, cogs jamming and turning to rust. Besides, I don't think it's true. Doesn't a breakdown imply you lose control and act irrationally? Whereas I have never felt so sane.

Keith nodded slowly, professorially.

'Good.' He sipped his coffee. Instant: I could smell it. 'And don't you think Ben might be a part of that?'

I sat there, tense, sitting straight so that my back didn't quite touch the chair. I waited. Keith waited.

'I don't want to talk about Ben.'

'Why not?'

'Because,' I said. 'I'm angry with him.'

There it was: unassailable, unarguable. After a lifetime of being reasonable, it seemed I was finally fucking furious.

I didn't want to talk about when I first met Ben because then I'd have to admit, out loud, that I had liked him. More than liked. He was so clever and funny and handsome and it was enough just to sit near him. He was the kind of man you couldn't help but want to impress.

And I was so determined not to be impressed when Martin took me to meet him. I'd been hearing about Ben Fitzmaurice for weeks and I was sick of him. Every conversation I had with Martin would somehow end up with his regaling me with a relevant anecdote or incident involving Ben or his sister Fliss or his parents or their beautiful family home in the countryside. He went on and on about him until finally I cracked.

'I feel like there are three of us in this relationship,' I said one night, after we'd been going out for a few months. I'd cooked a cod fillet with sauce from a jar and Martin had got this faraway look as he described a trip he'd taken in Italy and a dish he'd had with Ben in a tiny restaurant in the Cinque Terre.

'I mean, Ben speaks fluent Italian of course,' he had said.

'Of course,' I muttered.

'But even he couldn't make out any of what it said on the menu. So we ordered this pasta thing and when it came …' Martin clasped his forehead with one hand in a pose of would-you-be-lieve-it, 'it was fish fingers and peas.'

'Really?'

'Like you'd get in a Little Chef!'

'Hilarious.'

Martin cooled.

'You don't seem amused.'

And that's when I said the thing about there being three of us in the relationship. It was meant as a joke but Martin was offended and we had a long conversation about how Ben had been there for him and how he would never have got through school without him.

'When can I meet him, then?'

'Oh,' Martin said, a forkful of fish suspended midway between plate and mouth. 'Well. I suppose I could see if he's around this weekend.'

We went to a pub near Holland Park. Martin and I got there first and sat in a booth in the corner and, a few minutes later, the door swung open and Ben walked in, followed by a rush of cool autumn air.

'Maaaaate,' he said, drawing out the word until I thought it might break. 'So good to see you. And you—' he said, releasing Martin from a bear hug and turning to me, 'must be Lucy.'

I reached out my hand but he kissed me on the cheek. He was chewing mint gum.

'I've heard so much about you,' he continued, taking off his coat and moving his stool closer to where I was sitting in one fluid motion, 'but Martin forgot to tell me how fit you were.'

I blushed.

'Ben, mate,' Martin said. 'Hands off.'

This was the most un-Martin-like turn of phrase I'd ever heard him utter. I turned towards him, eyebrow raised and noticed my boyfriend's hand was shaking as he lifted his pint glass.

'I've heard lots about you too,' I said. 'Not how fit you are though. Sorry about that.'

Ben grinned, made eye contact, kept it.

'Well now you've seen for yourself.'

It was impossible not to be drawn to him. He had a handsome, mobile face. Quicksilver expressions. A mass of curly hair – longer then than it is now. He ran his hands through it frequently.

Martin seemed to relax in Ben's presence. When it was just the two of us, Martin did most of the talking, but with Ben, he hardly spoke at all. He was happy to laugh along at Ben's comic delivery of some long-winded story, interjecting here and there to remind him of a specific turn of events.

I didn't feel left out, not back then.

The way Ben spoke was both intense and light-hearted. He took other people more seriously than he took himself. His honesty struck me. He was unguarded in an unexpected way.

He's very different now. All those years in the City and being married to Serena have made him more wary of the world, more untrusting. The hint of mischief has gone, replaced by anxiety and pomposity. I suppose if you make millions and buy posh houses and start hanging out with the Prime Minister, that's the kind of thing that happens to you. Still, it's a shame.

That evening, though, Ben was kind and solicitous and paid for all the drinks. We stayed there for hours. The light dimmed outside. The barman lit an open fire. Tinny music filtered through from an unseen jukebox. When the opening chords of 'Eye of the Tiger' started up Martin groaned.

'I've got to change this.' He sidled out of the booth, swaying slightly as he made his way over to the other side of the bar.

Ben came to sit beside me, so close our legs were touching.

'You know you're the first girlfriend of Mart's I've met?'

'Well I hope it was worth the wait.'

He lifted his pint of Guinness and took a swig.

'Definitely,' he said. 'Martin's a very lucky man.'

I opened my mouth to say something. Ben stopped me.

'He can be a tricky bastard, but he's got a good heart, deep down, you know?'

His words seemed to float in front of me. I wasn't sure I'd heard him correctly and then I realised I was drunk and needed to eat something with sudden urgency.

'Peanuts,' I said. 'Need to get some.'

I wobbled over to the bar and by the time I got back to our table with a packet of dry roasted, Ben and Martin were deep in conversation again, side by side in the booth. I was about to make a joke about how they looked like the couple rather than Martin and me, but there was never a break in their chatter. I just sat on the stool and ate the peanuts and waited for them to finish talking.

*

Keith thinks I have a thing about men who withdraw their affection. He says the ready availability of love seems to unsettle me and he wonders if this might be because I have low self-esteem and therefore don't consider myself worthy of it. Keith has begun saying this, or versions of this, with more regularity in our sessions of late and I know he finds it odd that I don't respond. I realise that the sketchy outline I've given him of my upbringing – two loving parents, a secure and stable home – doesn't tally with his therapeutic take. I think he knows – because he's good at his job, Keith, he really is – that I'm not telling him the whole truth.

I'm not sure I want to. I've kept it a secret for so long that I've begun to think it's the source of some sort of unspoken power. That if I speak the words out loud, I'll lose a part of myself. So I thought I'd write it down here, sort of as an experiment. For my own eyes only. See if it helps.

It was at university. When I arrived at Durham to take up my English degree, in my floaty skirts and DM boots, I was unprepared for the sophistication of my fellow undergraduates. I had never realised, until freshers' week, what a sheltered life I'd lived. Up until that point it had been: nice family, local day school, stable friends, Sunday morning church and regular roast dinners.

But that first week at Durham was a whirl of vodka jelly shots and public snogging. Everyone seemed to be drunk, all the time. I was plied with pints of beer and double gin and tonics and alcoholic concoctions involving Red Bull and sambuca. At a social event to publicise a student drama society, I got so drunk I had to leave early and throw up in the loo.

It was in the midst of this spinning, semi-conscious state that I met David. He was stocky, muscular and short, coming up to my eye level if I wore flats, and had a cleft in his chin. He was from Lancashire and spoke with an unfamiliar flat northern burr. And he was confident, bordering on cocky, and inexplicably charismatic. Every time I walked into the pub, he was there, holding court on a battered leather sofa at the back by the dartboard.

He made the first move. I was in the pub one evening, waiting for a friend, sitting on a high stool at the bar reading a paperback copy of *Vanity Fair* as preparation for one of my essays. I felt his presence before I saw him, almost as if the air shifted to make room for his bulk.

'Hiya,' he said, taking the stool next to me and signalling the barman with a single extended finger. 'Pint of IPA.' Then turning towards me, 'I'm David.'

He put out his hand. I took it. His grip was strong and he held on to me for longer than he needed.

'Lucy,' I said. I was immediately nervous. I wondered if I should make a show of returning to my book, but I couldn't stop looking at his eyes, which were light green and flecked with grey and surprisingly delicate, I thought, for a man with such robust features.

'Lucy,' he said, as if playing with the sound. 'You should come and sit with me.'

He lifted my drink and his and, just like that, led me over to his group of friends and patted the space on the sofa next to him and I sat there, never once thinking to question it. He spoke with such authority that it seemed natural to do as he said. It wasn't charm, it was more straightforward than that: he knew what he wanted and he went and got it.

We got drunk. His friends kept buying rounds and I was drinking cider, for reasons I can't remember, but it went straight to my head and soon the room was swirling and the patterned carpet was wobbling underfoot. But it wasn't a worrying kind of inebriation where I felt out of control. Instead, because David was there, I felt sheltered and safe. I felt he would take care of things.

I followed him back to his room. It wasn't even discussed, it was simply assumed it would happen. And it did, that's the thing. I was a willing participant. I was collusive in it. I fancied him and I wanted to kiss him and I wanted to feel his strong arms around me and I had no sense of what was really happening at that stage.

He unlocked his door with a key he wore round his neck. I remember this so clearly because it was such an odd thing to do. He had rolled his shirtsleeves up beyond his elbow so that I could see the hairs on his arm, turned golden from the sun. From the back, I noticed the tight fit of his jeans over his buttocks. There wasn't a spare inch of flesh on him. Everything about him was muscled and hard.

Inside the room, he left the lights off and the curtains open. He pushed up my T-shirt, pulling it over my head and started kissing me forcefully on the mouth, pressing against my teeth and squashing my lips. He fumbled with the button on my skirt and then I heard a ripping sound and realised the button had popped and the skirt fell to the ground and I tried to think how sexy that was, how masterful, but it was at that point I realised the evening was turning from bright to dark and that I stood at a tipping point and that every moment after this would be altered from what went before, that the mundane would just be a memory of the mundane, that the Lucy I was in this second would never again exist in quite the same way.

He pushed me onto the bed.

'Wait,' I said and when I heard my voice it was weak and quiet and I hated it. 'Wait,' I said, more loudly.

David was pulling at my knickers, sliding his finger and then his thumb deep into me, and simultaneously I was thinking, well this is what you want, isn't it? Isn't it? And if it isn't what you want, doesn't that mean you're frigid? And: just relax, Lucy. This is normal. This is what girls your age should be doing. This is fun.

'Stop,' I whispered, because my throat was constricting and there wasn't enough air to push into my lungs.

I tried again. 'Stop.' But then he was on top of me, his weight pressing down on my ribs, his left hand grabbing my breast and twisting it roughly and he was breathing in heaving gulps of air and his eyes, those green irises I had thought so delicate, were screwed tightly shut as if he didn't want to look at me or himself or any of it.

I clenched my fists and tried to wrestle him off me but he clamped his big hands on my wrists and pressed them down on the pillow.

'Regular little tiger,' he said.

I writhed and twisted beneath him but still he kept pushing against me and my wrists were numb and a white noise started in the back of my skull as he nudged apart my legs with his knee and then letting go of one wrist, reached down and grabbed his dick and jabbed himself into me and I screamed with the pain of it.

'Fucking stay still, will you?'

He slid himself roughly in and out, looking away from me, gaze fixed on a wall hung with a poster of a football team wearing red and white and I was staring at the ceiling willing myself not to cry and trying not to make any more sound than necessary and then, after it was done, I was empty: hollowed out of the last scrap of energy or resistance, as if I didn't exist any more, as if I were just a thing to be used.

David rolled over to one side, turning his back to me. No further words were exchanged. Within minutes, he was snoring. I crept out of the bed, gathered my clothes and walked back to my college room.

The next day, I got a prescription for the morning-after pill.

I avoided the pub and David's halls of residence. For the rest of that term, I saw him only once when we passed in the street. It was December and the air was filled with the jangling chords of festive musak. I was in a parka, my face half shielded by a scarf. He was walking towards me, a bag of shopping in one hand, and I noticed he had a purple bruise high on the edge of one cheek-bone. I started to sweat. I couldn't move. Bustling crowds of Christmas shoppers bumped around me and I just kept staring at him.

He stopped outside a cafe, unaware that I was watching. His face had the same flat, wide quality I remembered. I thought about confronting him, about telling him what he had done to me. But then a pretty girl with long blonde hair and a bobble hat with knitted ear flaps appeared at his side and reached up to kiss him on the cheek and David put his arm around her slender shoulders and they walked across the street and away from me without a backward glance.

I never told anyone this. For a long time, I felt it was my fault I had got myself into that situation. I know now that is common among rape victims. Rape. Important to use the word.

I was weakened by David. The confidence instilled in me by my parents started to dissipate, as if I had been flayed of a layer of skin. I thought I hid it but I realise now that I must have been a shining beacon for men who could use my smallness to make themselves feel bigger.

In my second year, I met one of these. He was a French exchange student, studying abroad for a year. His name was Thibault but everyone called him Lucky because his parents had once thought he looked like a French cartoon character called Lucky Luke and the nickname stuck.

Lucky was charming and clever. He could formulate an opinion on just about anything and deliver it surely, as if it were the only thing anyone could possibly think. We met in a nightclub and snogged on the dance floor and I thought I'd never hear from him again because he was too handsome, too sure of himself, altogether too much in every respect. But he had called the next day. And the one after that. Lucky and Lucy. Lucy and Lucky. Soon, I was his girlfriend, at which point his attentiveness intensified.

He didn't like me wearing dresses.

When I went out with friends, he insisted I call him from a phone box every hour to let him know I was all right. He said it was because he was worried about me. He loved me so much, he wanted to keep me safe, and I didn't question this.

I learned not to interrupt when he spoke.

He didn't like it when I disagreed with him. After a while, I stopped because I genuinely believed he was right and I was wrong, even when it was something I knew more about.

Once, after I went to the hairdresser's and asked them to cut me a fringe, he told me it was ugly and I was stupid to have done it because it would take months to grow out.

'You never think! That is your problem, Lucy! You never think ahead.'

I look back on photos of me with the fringe and I can see he was wrong. It did suit me. It framed my face.

One holiday, we travelled to Nantes and I met his parents. His father was brash and domineering. His mother was sweet and quiet. When his father asked what I wanted to do when I graduated, Lucky intervened and said, 'She doesn't know. She leaves everything too late.' I tried to protest. He took my hand, kissed it and told me, 'You're so funny when you try to speak French,' and then he turned to his father and said something I didn't understand and the two of them laughed and I didn't know why.

We carried on like this for eight months. Lucky issuing demands; me adhering to them in order to keep the peace. By the end, I was doing everything he wanted: not going out; not getting drunk; not wearing the wrong clothes; not seeing the wrong people; not saying the wrong things; not challenging anything.

Of course, he cheated on me. Why wouldn't he when I had earned so little of his respect? So when I walked into his room and found him getting a blow job from a first-year girl with a nose-stud and a heart tattoo on the nape of her neck, I wasn't especially surprised.

But I was devastated. I cried. He tried to win me back, promising it was nothing, telling me she was a slut and nothing in comparison to me. But I must have had some vestige of self-worth left because I told Lucky to fuck off. I Tippexed his number out of my address book. Later, after he'd gone back to France, I found out the girl had been one of many. My friends all knew but hadn't wanted to tell me because they didn't think I would listen. They were probably right. Still, it felt like a betrayal.

After Lucky, I told myself I wanted to be on my own. But I wasn't cut out for it. I needed to be with someone else so I didn't have to examine myself too deeply. I had another boyfriend within a month. I was cautious enough, this time, not to let myself invest too much emotion so that when it ended, it wouldn't undo me. It worked.

And then there was one after that and another one after him. They were only ever six-month affairs that ended when I felt a boy was in danger of encroaching too far, of getting to know me too well.

The irony was that they all seemed intrigued by my aloofness. That's the thing about men: act too needy and they'll withdraw. As soon as you start not caring, they make up the space by caring too much. Stupidly obvious, really.

I felt lonely on my own. But when I was in a couple, I longed for space. I walled myself off, as if my true self were hidden in a secret passageway like a priest's hole a friend had once shown me built into the corridor of their timbered sixteenth-century house. You would knock against the panelling and then – thunk! – your knuckles would sound hollow against the wood. To open the priest's hole, you needed to know how to press on the panel in a certain way: a light nudge with a thumb and then the catch released and the door swung open.

I had my boyfriends. I had the secret space. And that was more or less how I operated until I met Martin.

He was different – safe because, although I knew he needed me, he never expressed it or made me feel obliged to need him back. He was respectful of my mind and my physical space. And if, sometimes, that translated as his own distance and emotional withdrawal, then wouldn't I rather have that than the alternative? Because I could understand it, at least.

V.

I HAVE NEVER BEEN A PROPER SMOKER. At school, obviously, I smoked joints and cadged the occasional Marlboro. But I had never bought myself a packet of cigarettes. I didn't have enough money, at school, and then later in life, when money ceased to be a consideration, I discovered I didn't have the inclination. My proclivities were for the harder kind of drug.

But when Grey Suit offers me a cigarette break, I take it. I want to get out of this room. The plastic of the chair is pressing against the fabric of my trousers and the flesh on the back of my legs is sticky with sweat. There is a dull ache in my right shoulder. I've always been prone to shoulder and neck pain. I went to a chiropractor once who cracked my spine with tiny but powerful hands, before gripping the sides of my face and twisting it violently to the side. When I rose from the massage table, she asked me to swivel my head. I did so, not really understanding the point of it, and I was astonished to find I could move it several more degrees than before. A whole new field of vision opened itself up to me and my first thought was not: how wonderful, now I can see all these things I've never seen before. It was: what have I been missing out on all this time? What have I failed to notice?

'You can take fifteen minutes,' Grey Suit says, almost friendly now that the tape machine has been switched off.

'Thanks.'

Beige Hair gives a tired smile. She pushes her chair back and levers herself upright. Her movements are unnaturally slow and laboured. It is only as she walks to the door that I see the curvature of her belly underneath her baggy blouse.

'You're pregnant,' I say, without thinking.

'Yes.'

'Congratulations.'

'Thank you.'

She walks out of the room and I feel cheated, somehow, that my efforts at warmth, at engaging in a more normal level of social interaction, have been disregarded. And it takes me straight back to school, to that sense of not being part of a larger whole, of not understanding the rules. How difficult it is to be normal.

Grey Suit motions towards the door and follows me out. The corridor is filled with a different sort of air. Lighter, fresher.

'You can go out front,' he says. 'By the car park.'

'Oh, thanks. The only thing is … well, it's silly, I know, but I've left my cigarettes … I don't suppose …?'

'Yeah, sure.'

He takes out a crumpled packet of Camels. I think he is going to offer me one and then disappear into the mysterious back part of the police station, but instead he comes outside with me. We stand to the side of the automatic doors. He proffers his lighter – a silver Zippo with the Harley Davidson insignia engraved on one side. The flame shoots up with a flick of his thumb. I inhale. Smoke sweeps into my throat, clogging the threads of saliva so that my mouth is dry and my eyes prickle.

I can't think of anything to say. Grey Suit doesn't appear to mind. He slouches against the wall, smoking with the cigarette between his thumb and forefinger, like a cowboy. He strikes me as one of those men perfectly at ease with themselves, to the extent that they've never had to question their place in the world. Grey Suit would simply accept a happy existence as his due. He would be easily pleased by physical tasks. A successful rugby tackle would delight him. Putting up shelves would buoy his mood for an entire weekend. He would never think too much or too deeply about the darker side and, in this way, he would navigate his way through life experiencing only half of it and being satisfied. He wouldn't care about not being able to turn his neck all the way round because his gaze would always be forwards.

'Expect you've got better things to do than this,' I say and I try to sound casual, in the manner I think he would appreciate.

He shrugs.

'I mean, an incident at a party,' I persist because all at once, I am overpowered by the need to get him to respond to me, 'it's hardly the case of your career, I'm guessing.'

He drops the butt of the cigarette onto the ground, grinding it into the asphalt with the toe of his boot.

'Oh, I wouldn't say that.'

He doesn't look at me, but instead gazes out at the car park, as if he's spotted something fascinating in between the blue Vauxhall Astra and the Dallas Chicken & Ribs shop on the opposite side of the road.

'Sometimes,' he says, 'the smallest incidents lead to the biggest discoveries.'

It sounds rehearsed, a line he once read in a fortune cookie, but there is a calmness to the way he delivers the words that puts me on edge. A breeze blows an empty crisp packet down a flight of steps. A pigeon waddles and coos. A siren sounds. There's a waft of grease from the chicken shop.

My cigarette has nearly burnt itself out. I take a final drag and cast the butt in the direction of the pigeon. There is a fluttering sensation in my chest as I walk back inside, a discomfiting internal tickle of unknown fingernails. It's excitement, I realise: the first flare of flame as the match is struck. And underneath, there is something else; something I'm less inclined to acknowledge.

Panic at what comes next.

2 May

Drawing room, Tipworth Priory, 9 p.m.

ON THE FIRST FLOOR, the party was even more densely populated than downstairs. A sitting room, decorated in eau de Nil and gilt-framed mirrors, contained a lavish selection of ladies wearing coloured lace. In front of the fireplace, a mustachioed man wearing braces and spats was mixing mojitos to order. Next to him, a girl in a short skirt was shucking oysters, fragments of shell spitting onto the soft carpet like shrapnel.

I slid my way past a novelist whose career had temporarily been ruined by a scandal involving a call girl. He was talking to a singer who had been big in the 80s. The singer was wearing an absurd top hat and had covered his neck and poitrine with black make-up, presumably in the hopes of drawing our attention away from his unfortunate number of chins.

Really, I found myself wondering, where did Ben *get* all these people?

I knew he was an inveterate collector of party guests. Ben's wealth enabled him to move in a certain type of circle. He was always in the newspaper rich lists. He made sizeable donations to the right kind of charities. His cash could be counted on, at silent auctions, to make the loudest noise.

Tatler had run a double-page spread a year ago calling him 'The Most Connected Man in Britain', handily illustrated with a complicated flow chart demonstrating Ben's closeness to various titans of business, media and politics. I had merited a small mention in the bottom right-hand corner, jostling for space amid oligarchs and It girls. It was an old photo, taken when my hair still flopped in front of my face.

'Journalist and author Martin Gilmour' read the caption. 'School-friend and honorary member of the Notting Hill set'.

Ben and I had laughed about it at the time, about the notion that any kind of 'set' existed, as if we were badgers snuffling around in the west London undergrowth for a chi-chi place to live. He pretended not to care about the *Tatler* piece, dismissing it as 'harmless guff' but I could tell he was pleased. He liked to be liked.

I finished the drink in my hand and made my way to the mojito purveyor.

'Mojito sir?'

'Yes,' I said. 'Make it a strong one.'

'They're all strong, sir.'

'Good.'

I felt a pressure at my elbow and then a growly voice saying my name. My heart sank. I knew who it was without having to look. Gilly Rawlings: one of those people one spends a lifetime avoiding only to end up running into with alarming frequency. I shouldn't have been surprised. Gilly described herself as 'a networking queen', which meant she was constitutionally incapable of declining any invitation. I never quite knew what 'networking' involved, other than appearing on various television debates and conference discussion panels to talk about the importance of connectedness in our professional and personal lives. Gilly also hosted a weekly radio programme called *Who Knows Who* and was known for having a large number of followers on Twitter. Two years previously, she had got into some trouble after posting her support for a feminist campaigner who wanted to put the image of a woman on a bank-note (as I pointed out to Lucy at the time, there already was a woman on every bank-note in the form of the Queen. Lucy had greeted the remark with a frosty silence). Anyway, after her show of public support for this preposterously trivial idea, Gilly had received death threats, none of which had come to fruition. Unfortunately.

'Gilly, darling,' I said. 'Mojito?'

'No thanks.' She gestured towards her straining waistline. 'Diet.'

'5:2?' I enquired.

'No, no, no. Fasting? Like an African orphan? Not likely, sweetheart.'

It is at this point that most gallant men would have protested that there was absolutely no need for her to lose weight. But Gilly was short and rotund and all her defining features seemed to melt into each other as though there were no supporting structure underneath, so I stayed silent.

'What a party!' she exclaimed. 'Did you see, just over there ...?' She murmured the name of a celebrity chef who had recently left his wife for another chef a little bit less famous than he was. Personally, I find this modern mania for food incredibly tiresome. Everything is a foam or a root or a smashed avocado or a ragout made from pig's nostrils and offcuts of lamb's testicles. Whatever happened to toast? Just toast. No butter. Maybe a dash of black-berry jam.

'So it is,' I said.

'They tell me – well, I suppose I really shouldn't say, it's only a rumour ...' Her voice dropped and the sentence trailed off.

'Do share.'

Gilly laughed shrilly. She leaned in. Her forehead barely came up to my shoulder. 'A little bird told me the Prime Minister might be coming later. Apparently ...'

I could see her mouth moving but the rest of what she had to say was drowned out by a loud burst of jazz.

'Oh,' Gilly trilled. 'Dancing!' She fell into an expectant silence. It took me a moment to realise she wanted me to escort her down-stairs and shimmy alongside her on the dance floor. I had no intention of doing this and was flicking through my mental Rolodex of available excuses when a bulky male shape appeared in my sightline. I recognised the outline immediately: the set of the shoulders, the stockiness of the legs, the pugnacious silhouette.

The shape approached. I wondered if I could make my escape before it reached me but Gilly was still wittering on and when I looked over my shoulder, I saw the route to the nearest door was blocked by people.

The shape continued its progression towards us. I was surprised to feel my heart pounding, the drum-drum-drum of it pushing blood through my veins with a savage force. How could he have this much impact on me after all these years? A man of such little consequence.

'Oh, Andrew,' Gilly squealed as the shape took form, the blur I'd seen from across the room acquiring focus and sharpness. She stretched up on her tiptoes to kiss him on each cheek, leaving behind a trace of moist lipstick he immediately wiped away. 'Do you know each other?'

'We do,' I said.

'How are you, Martin?'

I looked straight into the meaty face of Andrew Jarvis and wondered how to reply. For a moment, I thought of turning on my heel and leaving. It's what I would have liked to have done in an alternate reality, where I was a different person, a person who existed beyond the shadow cast by his best friend. But it was Ben's party. I should be polite to his guests, however much I loathed them.

'Jarvis,' I said. 'Very well, thank you. And you? I caught up with your latest achievements' – I imbued the word with as much disdain as I could muster – 'in today's *Telegraph*.'

He laughed.

'Oh, you mustn't believe anything you read in the papers.' He wasn't drinking, I noticed. Instead, in one hand, he held a bottle of sparkling Burtonbury water. The seal had not yet been broken on the screw cap. 'Journalists'll write anything they damn well please.'

I let the insult slide. Gilly giggled nervously.

'So, you two, let me see, how would your paths have crossed?' She waved her hands around like a pair of startled birds.

'School,' Jarvis said. 'We were friends at school, weren't we, Martin?'

'Friends is putting it a bit strongly,' I said. He blinked. I laughed to show I mustn't be taken seriously. 'No, I mean, honestly Jarvis, I'm delighted things have turned out so well for you. Couldn't have happened to a more … deserving bloke.'

'Thanks, Martin. Very decent of you. It's an interesting time to be in politics, that's for sure. Lots of big discussions to be had on Europe, welfare, immigration. Did you see that wanker on *Question Time* talking about re-nationalising the railways?'

I nodded. In fact, I never watched *Question Time*, but Jarvis wasn't interested in any kind of response. He just wanted to pontificate, preferably uninterrupted. I have learned, over the years, that it is best to let people like Jarvis bore on until they give themselves enough rope. Sooner or later, they will make a logical error of such appalling proportions that it is easy to step in and take them apart. But one has to wait for the right moment to pounce. That's the secret.

'I said to my wife,' Jarvis was hammering on. 'I said to her: Bitsy, you wouldn't believe what that guy's like in the lobby. I mean—'

He halted abruptly.

'Your wife here, Martin?' he asked, as if the thought had just occurred to him.

'Yes.'

'Really?'

'You seem surprised.'

He narrowed his eyes. His brows were palest ginger, almost transparent. 'Oh no, not at all. Wasn't sure you'd still be together. You just … well, you never struck me as the marrying kind.'

A waitress shoved forward a platter of shot glasses containing a virulent green liquid.

'Thai coconut soup?' she asked.

Jarvis and I took one each. Gilly shook her head regretfully.

'Diet,' she murmured, but no one paid any attention. She raised her voice, determined not to be overlooked. 'So,' she said, directing her gaze at Jarvis. 'Is it true the Prime Minister's coming?'

He shrugged.

'Couldn't possibly say.'

'Oh come on!' Gilly slapped him playfully on the chest. 'You're such a tease!'

He made a show of ruefulness. I remembered, at school, he was always trying to give the impression of being more in the know than he truly was. He should have grown out of it by now.

'Listen, if I could tell you I would, but ...' He tapped the side of his nose with his finger.

Gilly's face went red. Her earrings – large paste emeralds dangling in a chandelier effect from fleshy lobes – started to jiggle, as if responding to some internal pulsation. I thought she might implode with the strain.

'He's coming,' I said.

Jarvis glared at me.

Gilly spun around.

'Really?' she asked.

I nodded. 'Ben told me. They've had to get extra security.'

Gilly was bouncing up and down on the balls of her feet. Her dress had a metallic hem which made a jingling sound as she moved.

'Oh my God,' she said. 'I have to go and tell Marina.'

She gave us both a cursory air kiss and bustled off, abuzz with the glow of gossip to be shared. I watched her go, her wide behind made even wider by the swags of her purple taffeta skirt.

I returned my attention to Jarvis. I could think of precisely nothing to say to him.

'Enjoying yourself?' I ventured.

Jarvis looked at me.

'Extraordinary,' he said.

'Yes, Ben never does things by halves.'

'No, I didn't mean the party. I meant *you*.' Jarvis cracked the seal on his water and took a gulp. 'You've transformed yourself.'

'What do you mean?'

'Just—' He gestured up and down with his free hand. 'This.' He laughed. 'You're not wearing glasses any more, I see.'

'No,' I said, careful to keep the mask of a smile.

'Your hair, it's ...' He leaned in closer. 'It's changed. Darker, maybe?'

I said nothing.

'And your suit,' he smirked. 'Very smart.'

'It's black tie. I fail to see your point.'

'Not just any black tie is it, though, *Martin*?' He gave my name a peculiar emphasis. 'It looks very expensive, very classy.'

I gestured towards the barman to make me another mojito.

'Ben and I share a tailor,' I said.

'But of course you do. Of course!' he exclaimed, amused at some private joke. He sipped his water but his voice, when he spoke again, was even drier than before. 'You've done very well for yourself.'

'Yes. Not all of us can be politicians, of course ...'

'No, that's true.' Another swig of water. 'You always did have this way of looking down your nose at people, didn't you? That time, you know, when you ...' He left the sentence unmade, like a bed he couldn't be bothered to climb back into.

'You were so superior,' Jarvis continued. 'And for whatever reason, Ben was taken in by it. And now ...' He leaned back, sizing me up. 'Here you are. Held close to the ample Fitzmaurice bosom.'

'Yes, well, it's been nice to catch up,' I said, making a move to leave.

He reached out and grabbed my upper arm.

'No, no, listen: I'm happy for you, Martin. Good for you. I don't begrudge you. We've all got to do what we have to, haven't we? It's just ...' He laughed again, that unsettling burble which seemed to emerge directly from his throat. 'From across the room, you looked exactly like Ben. That's why I came over. I thought you were him.'

He let go of my arm and left me standing there. I staggered back and half fell into the fireplace, managing to regain my balance at the final moment.

'You all right, sir?' the barman asked.

'Yes, yes, thank you.'

'Told you they were strong.'

'You did.'

I felt better after finishing my second mojito. I remembered I had left Lucy downstairs. I pushed my way through and found myself in the back corridors of the house. Here, the rooms had been cordoned off from guests by several hand-painted chinoiserie screens.

I breathed in and out, telling myself to calm down. I examined the screens to give myself time to gather my thoughts. From a distance, the silk had looked as though it had been printed with delicate representations of cherry-blossom and single-legged herons in pools of water. It was only as you got closer that you realised the blossom was comprised of a series of naked female breasts and the heron was actually a copulating couple.

I wandered back down the staircase and into the plush, red sitting room, which overlooked the garden. Sofas lined the walls, puffed up with gold-tasselled cushions. A zebra-print rug was flung casually in front of the fireplace. The beat of some tuneless club track was being pumped out of an iPod slotted into a set of silver-plated Bose speakers, which curved into each other like a pair of rhinoceros horns. Why, I found myself thinking, does everything these days need to be made to look like something else? What are we so afraid of?

In the corner, a man in a suit with a pink pocket-square was chatting to a daytime television host who had recently brought out a bestselling fitness DVD. Behind them, I could just make out the hairsprayed bouffant up-do of the wife of a hereditary peer.

Eventually I exchanged my empty glass for a full champagne flute. The waiter had high cheekbones and gelled hair. I caught his eye. He smiled. As he wound his way through the room, I examined the back view – a medium frame with narrow hips. A ballet dancer's poise. Delicate wrists. Probably Eastern European. I watched as he left, the door sliding shut behind him.

When I turned back, Jarvis was staring at me from the other side of the room. He must have followed me, I thought.

Jarvis raised his bottle of water in salute. It might have been the dim lighting or the faint dulling of my senses from alcohol or the fact that I was still recovering from the discomfort I had felt at our earlier conversation. Or maybe it was that he was too far away for me to discern accurately what he was trying to say. Still, I could have sworn that, as he lifted the bottle, he mouthed two soft-edged syllables and when I realised what they were, those two silent words sounded like a cymbal dropped from a great height onto concrete.

I know, he mouthed. *I know.*

There was a rush of cold wind as someone, somewhere, opened a window and let the night flood in.

He couldn't know, I thought to myself. No one knew what had happened that first term at Cambridge apart from me and the Fitzmaurices. None of us had ever breathed a word. Of that I was absolutely sure.

Wasn't I?

Martin

Queens' College, Cambridge, 1993

THE CAR SWUNG INTO THE DRIVEWAY without indicating, the shellacked black of its sides reflecting the blurred orb of a street-lamp. It was already dusk. The evening seemed to fall more quickly here than it had in Burtonbury: the sudden spilling of ink across a blotting-paper sky.

I had been in Cambridge for a few days and was not yet used to the aggressive chill of the wind or the flatness of the surrounding countryside or the constant suggestion of damp in the air. One of my teachers at Burtonbury had warned me about the East Anglian climate before I left.

'The winds come straight from Russia,' the teacher had said. We were all gathered on the lawn in the quad after the prize-giving ceremony and speeches: a melee of mothers in hats and boys in uniform, eating strawberries from plastic punnets and trying to make themselves heard above the syncopated din of the sixth-form jazz band.

'Do they?' I said, bored. I didn't have anyone else to talk to. My mother hadn't come because I hadn't invited her, even though I'd won two school prizes – one for English, one for History. But the Fitzmaurices were there in the audience, smiling as I mounted the stage. Even Fliss, who generally hated this kind of institutionalised rigmarole, was grinning and clapping when my name was announced. Ben, as head boy, was on stage for the presentation of my two silver cups. He winked at me as I passed, but he'd been in an odd mood since the morning and I worried that I'd done something wrong.

173

'Yes,' the teacher was saying. 'No mountain ranges to stop them.'

I stifled a yawn and left the teacher mid-sentence. No need to bother with the social niceties any more, not now that I was leaving.

I returned to Sullies, thinking as I did so that this would be one of the last times I would trace the now-familiar route. As I took the shortcut behind the local church, I heard male voices, sliced through with girlish laughter. There was a hedge between me and the noise. I craned over, and as I did so, I caught sight of Ben on a patch of lawn with his arm around a girl in BGC uniform. Next to him, the bovine form of Jarvis. My hatred snapped into focus.

Jarvis's swollen face was mashed up against another girl's, his lips opening and closing like a fish, his hand underneath her blouse. He looked as if he were eating her mouth rather than kissing it.

I watched for a while. Ben was making his girl laugh, rubbing at her neck with his fingers and thumb. She was tall and skinny and the ends of her hair were dyed red, as if they had been dipped in blood.

My footing slipped. Jarvis, startled, pushed the girl away and turned towards me. His mouth, slack from kissing, tautened into a grin.

'All right there, peeping Tom?'

I flushed.

'I was just …'

'Getting your kicks, were you?'

Ben was staring at me now, his expression unreadable.

'There are easier ways of doing it, you know, Martin,' Jarvis continued. The girl next to him was buttoning up her shirt. 'I can give you a porno mag. Copy of *Readers' Wives*.'

'Leave it,' Ben said, listless.

Jarvis swung round so he was lying on his belly, chin cupped.

'Why're you doing that funny thing with your head?' he asked.

I hadn't realised I was twitching. I made a conscious effort to still myself. The jerky movements lessened.

'Is that what happens when you cum?' he said, grinning nastily. 'Is that your cum face? Twitchy twitchy Martin. Twitchy twitchy twoooo.'

A thrumming began in my chest, faintly at first, then rising to a higher pitch.

'Ben, your parents were looking for us,' I lied.

'Oh shit,' he said, checking his watch. 'I forgot.'

The Fitzmaurices were taking us for tea at the Duke of Clarendon Hotel in town.

Ben stood. The girl with the dipped-blood hair looked disappointed.

'Have fun,' Jarvis said to Ben, his voice hard. 'With your little friend.'

At the Duke of Clarendon, Ben's father George ordered champagne and filled our glasses and we ate crustless cucumber sandwiches. Lady Katherine picked at the food, eating only half of everything. Fliss, who had been so jolly at the prize-giving, seemed now sulky and impenetrable. She stared out of the window, picking at her nails.

'Fliss,' Katherine said, at one point. There was no reaction. 'Fliss, darling, do join in. You're being rude.'

Fliss sighed loudly. There was a difficult silence. Ben reached across the table and poured himself the last of the champagne. His face was tense and I could tell he was chewing the inside of his cheek as he always did when he was troubled or nervous. All day, he had been strangely absent. I felt as if I were looking at him through a screen: that distortion you get when you're finishing a pint and you catch sight of the room, warped and circular when viewed through the bottom of the glass.

His mother started to say something but then George met her eye and gave a tiny shake of the head and she contented herself instead with twisting her napkin with delicate fingers.

'Well, boys,' George said. 'I just wanted to—'

But I never got the chance to hear what it was George wanted to say because at that moment, Ben slapped my shoulder and said, as if we'd already made a plan, that we were going to meet some friends and we'd be back for dinner and see you later and thanks for the tea.

I followed him out of the hotel. Ben was walking at a furious pace, hands in his pockets, shoulders hunched. In the car park, the light was bright. I asked no questions. I had understood, without being told, that this was necessary. That if we had stayed in that airless hotel lounge a moment longer, something would have broken.

'You OK?' I asked.

He nodded.

'Just needed to get out, you know?'

We turned right to take the road down to the Winter Gardens and went to our usual spot by the bandstand. The park was emptying. The daytime visitors had gone, to be replaced by homeless men and drifting teenagers like us.

Ben and I walked to the overgrown rhododendron bush, its flowers dull pink in the evening gloom. We crawled into the branches and settled down on the scrubby dirt. We were only a few metres from the path and could still hear the low chatter of other people's interactions but we were hidden from view.

Ben took out a plastic bag of weed, dry like tea-leaves, then laid out the cigarette paper and the filter and began to roll a joint.

Ben rolled the joint tightly, with deft fingers. He lit it then passed it to me for the first drag. I inhaled, becoming weightless and loose.

'Strong,' I said.

He grinned.

'Only the best for us.'

I reached over and ruffled his hair. I did that sometimes when we were alone. He let my hand rest on his neck.

'You OK?' I asked again.

Ben didn't answer. He took three more long drags before speaking. I counted them. It seemed very important to be measuring everything. Four pebbles by my left foot. One discarded can of Special Brew. Two weeks I'd have to spend without Ben after term ended, before I visited him at home. Five freckles on his bicep in the shape of the Plough constellation.

'It's the anniversary of Magnus's death.'

It took a while to register. The weed was making me higher than I expected.

'Your brother?' I said, the words slow and stupid.

'Yeah.'

I put my arm around him.

'I'm sorry.'

His eyes were filmy. The thought of his crying gave me an ache of longing.

He patted my hand.

'Thanks. Don't wanna talk about it, but needed to say …'

'I'm sure you were such a great older brother,' I said, remembering the lines from that long-ago letter Lady Katherine had written. I wasn't especially interested in what kind of brother he'd been and couldn't summon up any kind of feeling for Magnus, who existed as a flat picture in my mind, devoid of personality or charm, but I knew the right thing to say.

Ben lay back on the ground, eyes closed.

I shuffled next to him, passing him the joint.

A long time passed, or perhaps it wasn't that long at all, and then I turned towards Ben and saw a tear slide from the corner of his closed eye down the side of his face. I watched the tear for a while, mesmerised by the purpose of its movement.

Ben's lips were parted where the joint had been. I imagined I could see the remnants of the smoke slipping from him like a dead person's soul, snaking upwards to the sky. I leaned across his chest and bent my face so close to his I could smell the champagne and the weed and the cucumber on his breath. His lips were dry. I licked them with the tip of my tongue. It was a test, to see what would happen.

Nothing. Ben stayed silent. His eyes were closed, the lids flickering so I could tell he wasn't asleep. I lowered my mouth to his. I kissed him, working my tongue between his teeth so that I could feel the wet warmth of him and at that moment, it felt as if the rightness of what we were doing was self-evident, as if to deny it would be illogical beyond comprehension. I kissed him. There was the lightest twitch of his tongue in response. Then, stillness.

He made no sound. He shifted onto one side, turning his face away. I rolled back, stoned and happy, telling myself this moment would change everything.

But of course, when the weed wore off and we brushed the twigs and leaves from our legs and walked back to the hotel, nothing had changed at all.

Now, three months later, the car came to a halt next to the Queens' College porter's lodge. I already knew, people weren't generally allowed to park there but the Fitzmaurices didn't abide by the same rules as anyone else. The passenger door opened and Ben clambered out with his familiar loping gait. He was wearing a denim shirt, the sleeves rolled up to reveal arms tanned from his three weeks' backpacking through Croatia.

He had gone with James Lewis, who had just finished his first year at Manchester and I had felt a pang of jealousy at my non-invitation. I felt it again now as I noticed the freckles across the bridge of Ben's nose and the deep olive tone of his skin. His hair was lighter too, dirty-blond ends of it catching in the breeze.

But, I reminded myself, we would have a whole three years together at Cambridge. Ben had applied to Queens' because it had a good rugby team and a reputation as a bit of a party college. He'd chosen to read Theology, of all things. I suspected this was a tactical decision – it was easier to get in for the marginal subjects no one else wanted to study. I had applied to read History. There was no question in my mind it would have to be Queens' too. I'd enjoyed the admissions interview and received an ABB offer in the post the following week.

And now here Ben was, back from holiday, on the threshold of his new university life, broad and brown and confident as ever. He had just arrived, I thought, and already he occupied the space as if it had been his to begin with.

I walked out of the half-shadow.

'Ben.'

'Maaaate,' he said and all at once, I was ridiculously happy that he was here, that he had remembered me, that he liked me still. I had spent a weekend on my own in halls, after my inter-railing trip finished earlier than anticipated (some nonsense with a Swedish backpacker who claimed I'd been watching him shower). I didn't want to carry on to the next city after that. Nor did I want to go home – couldn't face it – and although I knew the Fitzmaurices would always welcome me, I had never taken them up on their open-door invitation without Ben being there. They intimidated me, even though I did my best to pretend they didn't.

So Queens' was the only place left.

I had thought I would be one of several students who had done the same thing but when I arrived, it turned out I was the only one. The porter, a bulky bespectacled fellow with a faded anchor tattoo on his inner arm, had been sitting with his feet up on the desk in the lodge, reading a newspaper when I arrived.

'Sorry,' he said. 'Wasn't expecting anyone.'

It had surprised me how alone I felt, sitting in my featureless digs in Cripps Court, the single window overlooking an internal courtyard ringed by vacant rooms, each one with its curtains drawn into a blank gaze which served only to mirror my own emptiness. I didn't have any posters. It had been a matter of some comment at school, where all the other boys had glossy reproductions of a two-dimensional Pamela Anderson and large illustrations of cannabis leaves or Bob Marley or Che Guevara (the irony!) Blu Tacked against the paint. After a while, I enjoyed their mystification at my blank walls but in my posterless room in Cambridge, I had missed Ben with an acuteness that surprised me. It was, I calculated, one of the longest stretches of time we'd ever been apart.

'What's your room like?' he was asking me now, one arm still slung casually around my shoulders. There were other students walking through the car park, carrying cardboard boxes and plastic-lidded crates, and I thought of them looking at us and knowing without doubt that we were two best friends.

'Well, well, well, if it isn't young Master Gilmour.'

The dry, deep tones of Ben's father. He came out of the driver's side, pressing his keyring so that the car locked with a high-pitched beep. It was a black Lexus. 'The run-about', Lady Fitzmaurice called it, as opposed to the more expensive cars – the Bentley, the classic Mercedes and the battered Land Rover used for 'bombing round' the estate.

'Lord Fitzmaurice.' I shook his hand.

'Martin, Martin, Martin,' he said. He had a habit of repeating everything three times. 'I've been telling you to call me George for years.'

I chuckled.

'Sorry. George.'

'Lord Fitzmaurice makes me feel so old,' he said.

'And it should really be Sir George,' Ben chipped in.

'Well, yes, if you're going to get technical about it,' George said. 'But that makes me feel even *older*.'

He slapped me on the back.

'How are you, old chap? Been a while. Are you well? How was the rest of the summer?'

'Dad, seriously, we've only just arrived. Stop with all the questions.'

George held his hands up in a mocking gesture of surrender.

'Sorry I spoke. Listen, chaps, why don't I leave you to it and go and find myself a quiet spot ...' He looked around him. I knew he was scanning the horizon for a pub.

'There's The Anchor, just on the other side of the bridge,' I said, pointing towards Silver Street.

'So there is. *Wunderbar!* I'll be over there and when you've unloaded the car, I'll take you out for a slap-up dinner. Yes?'

I felt a wash of fondness for George, standing there in his baggy corduroy trousers. Whereas Katherine had always been cordial to me, George had from the start treated me with an effusive friendliness.

The first time Ben had invited me to his home had been a couple of weeks after the BGC bop. I had slipped his mother's letter back in his chest of drawers the morning after I read it, playing truant from assembly to do so when no one else was around. Ben had caught up with me at tea, sitting beside me as we ate our toast, and I was astonished that he seemed to want to talk to me. I had thought, after the girl and the music and the kissing, that he would want to be around the other, more popular boys, who knew how to ask about things like fingering and love-bites and hard-ons. But instead he started to ask me about myself, about my family and where I was from.

I gave him a heavily edited version, making sure to emphasise the death of my father and how hard it was to lose a close relative and how grief-stricken I had been and how I didn't feel anyone at school could understand. I left a meaningful pause for Ben to fill with his own admission, but he didn't take the bait. He simply looked at me and nodded and after a while, we moved on to more interesting territory – our favourite subjects, the teachers we hated, the music he thought I liked. He told me in passing the girl he'd kissed had been 'sweet but boring', which gave me a surge of hope. And then I made him laugh. I can't remember what it was exactly, but it could have been an impression of a fellow pupil. I had a good ear and could pick up physical mannerisms and vocal inflections without much bother. It's a skill I still have. In fact, I do a pretty good impression of Ben, although only Lucy has seen it and only once. She found it funny at first and then her laughter stopped because she said it was 'spooky'.

Anyway, the first exeat at Denby Hall was a success. Lady Fitzmaurice forgave me for not possessing any tennis clothes. She wasn't a particularly warm woman, I realised, even to Ben. She would occasionally brush his cheek with the back of her hand, but that was about the extent of her tactility. She told me to call her Katherine, but it took me months to pluck up the courage. The voice in the letter seemed to belong to a different woman and I wondered if she were only able to show herself in writing, when there was a gap between delivery and receipt.

Lord Fitzmaurice, on the other hand, was kind. On the first night, when we were sitting in the drawing room after a dinner of roast lamb (prepared for us by a cook whom no one referred to as a cook, but instead as 'dear old Pam'), Ben's father noticed my interest in the books lining the walls. He took me aside and told me to read Dickens, sending me back to Burtonbury on the Sunday night with a beautiful edition of *Great Expectations*, the flyleaf inscribed with his name. When I turned the pages in bed at night, the paper was soft and thin as moth wings.

I had written a carefully worded thank-you letter, wanting to be neither too effusive nor too curt. I needed to pitch it exactly right. The Fitzmaurices were the kind of people, I imagined, who would set great store by a thank-you note.

I was invited back for the second exeat of term and then it became something of a routine and soon I was spending some of the holidays at Denby too. I remember, during one Easter break, Ben's mother had put on an egg hunt (with the help, as ever, of faithful Pam). Fliss was home too and the three of us were sent off to scour the front lawn and flowerbeds in search of hard-boiled eggs, laid by Katherine's two domesticated hens and stained the yellow of gorse gathered from bushes in the nearby fields.

Fliss and Ben had been winding each other up all morning, making *sotto-voce* comments and mean-spirited jokes. I wondered if their uneasy alliance had something to do with the absence of Magnus, the little brother who was never spoken of. He existed only in photographs and a grand oil painting above the fireplace in the dining room: rotund face, dimpled knees and a smile that revealed tiny, regular teeth. I had asked, once, who he was. I thought it would have seemed odd for me not to notice.

'That's Magnus,' Katherine said. 'He died.'

Her voice didn't change. Ben, sitting on the sofa, rubbed the back of his neck and focused on a point on the carpet just beyond his feet.

'Oh,' I said. 'I'm sorry. What happened ...?'

George went to his wife's side and put an arm around her waist.

'He had meningitis,' George said. 'It was a terrible thing.'

Ben stood.

'I'm going outside,' he said. 'Coming, Mart?'

Magnus was never mentioned in my presence again.

His death had clearly changed the family dynamic in some way I couldn't quite understand. Ben and Fliss's relationship was one of intense affection punctuated by mutual loathing. It all came to a head during that Easter weekend when we were walking round the croquet lawn. The two of them spotted an egg at the same moment, nestling at the bottom of a hoop, and ran towards it, Fliss pushing Ben out of the way to scoop it up, whooping as she did so.

'Oh sod off, Fliss,' Ben said, and he picked up one of the croquet mallets we had left lying on the grass from the night before and threw it with all his strength into the mid-distance. It landed with a splintering crack on the edge of a low wall.

'What on earth was that?' Katherine asked, appearing noise-lessly from the gravel pathway.

'Ben being a dick,' Fliss said mutinously. She was going through a goth phase and had dyed her hair bluish-black and ringed her eyes with kohl. Her T-shirt was ripped at the neck and had 'Black Sabbath' written across the front in faded white.

'Please don't use language like that.'

Fliss rolled her eyes. 'I'm sure you've heard worse, Mum.'

'Stop it, Fliss. I'm not in the mood.' Katherine turned to her son, who was standing with his hands in his pockets. 'I mean, for goodness' sake, you two. It's only an Easter egg hunt. You're acting like babies.'

I could see neither sibling was inclined to make amends. Fliss was scowling and Ben had that faraway expression he sometimes got, which I had come to know was a sign of controlled fury. Heat prickled across my chest. I realised I had to do something to puncture the tension. This was my chance to start making myself indispensable.

'Thank you for organising this, Lady Fitz … Katherine,' I said into the fractious silence. 'I thought it was eggscellent. I would do it all again, but I'm just about fried.'

Katherine looked at me, baffled. I could see Fliss smirking out of the corner of my eye. Ben snorted, but it was a friendly sound. Then Katherine's face changed, the planes of it shifting into a broad smile. She started to laugh, a gentle puttering noise I had never heard before.

'Oh that's very good, Martin,' she said. 'Very good indeed.'

She pressed her fingers to her eyes, which were now moist.

'Mum,' Ben was saying, 'it's not *that* hilarious.'

'No, no, I suppose not, but …' She gathered herself together, wiping away the final tears and then she patted me on the shoulder. 'It is good to have you here, Martin,' she said. 'You've become one of the family.'

As the four of us walked back to the house with our fragile yellow eggs, I was surprised to notice moisture in my own eyes and I blinked, twice, in quick succession, to rid myself of it. It was working, I thought; I really *was* one of the family.

'Earth to Martin, earth to Martin.' Ben's voice brought me shuddering back to the present. Queens'. The porter's lodge. A stack of boxes to be carried up to his room on the first floor of DD staircase.

'DD,' Ben said when he got his room key. 'Just how I like my women.'

'Shame you're not on FF then,' I replied.

'Nah, that's too big. More than a handful and it's a waste. And, you know, they get saggy, the bigger ones.'

He spoke so knowledgeably. Ben had already had sex with four girls that I knew of, whereas I was still a virgin. I didn't care. Most of the girls I knew seemed shrieking and silly. I'd rather read a book. During the last term of school, Ben would ask me about it occasionally, in a circumspect way. I think he was worried about embarrassing me and I knew now I would have to invent a summer romance in order to halt the persistence of the questioning.

After forty-five minutes, we had done most of the heavy lifting. Ben's room came with a kettle, the insides ringed with limescale, but otherwise perfectly serviceable. There was a basin in one corner, obscured by a sliding wardrobe door, and he filled the kettle from the cold tap, put it on to boil, then made the tea. It was only after he handed over a mug patterned with the Liverpool Football Club crest that either of us remembered we had no milk.

'Ah well,' Ben said. 'Put hairs on our chest.'

'Never know what that means,' I replied.

'No. And I probably don't need any more hairs on my chest anyway.' He looked down at the thicket of curls poking out from his shirt. 'You, on the other hand …'

'Fuck off.'

I was sitting on the edge of his bed, blowing on the hot tea, when there was a knock on the door.

'Yeah,' Ben shouted.

A boy wearing an England rugby shirt poked his head into the room.

'Hiya. Just wanted to introduce myself. I'm Jez. I'm your next-door neighbour.'

'Hi Jez, come on in!' said Ben, immediately in his element. He vigorously shook Jez's hand, which was approximately double the size of my face. 'Nice to meet you, mate.'

'You too, mate.'

Over the next few minutes, there was a blizzard of 'mates' flying back and forth between them as they discovered shared interests (sports, mainly), mutual acquaintances (men with single-syllable names from the right kind of families) and a joint love of *Withnail and I*, which they quoted at each other for several more minutes, until Ben remembered my presence.

'Sorry, mate, totally forgot – this is Martin.'

'Hiya, Martin.'

'Hello.' I sipped my tea too quickly and burned the roof of my mouth.

'So how do you two ...' Jez started.

'We're best friends from school,' I said.

I glanced at Ben.

'We should probably go and meet your dad,' I said, putting my mug down on the bedside cabinet with a thud.

'We don't need—'

Jez, affable and stupid as a Labrador, took the hint. 'Sure, sure. I'll catch you later, guys.'

He left the room. Ben began hanging a series of shirts on expensive wooden hangers I assumed his mother had given him. No iron hangers for the Fitzmaurices.

With Jez no longer in the room, the silence between us was crushing.

'Wonder who he supports in the rugby,' I asked. It was a feeble joke, but Ben's reaction took me unawares.

'For fuck's sake, Martin.'

'What?'

'Can't you just, for once, just ...' He hung the last shirt and slid the wardrobe door closed. Ben ran his fingers through his hair – a new gesture, I noted. Probably he'd picked it up from James Lewis over the summer. He looked silly doing it because his hair wasn't long enough.

'What?' I said again, defensiveness creeping in.

He shook his head.

'Never mind.'

I drank my tea. But something had altered, I realised. A stone had been dislodged from the mouth of a cave. When I look back now, knowing all that has gone after, I think I would have to say that this was the start of everything changing. Whether it changed for the worse or the better is a question I have spent the rest of my life trying to answer.

VI.

WE ARE BACK IN OUR FAMILIAR SEATS. Nicky Bridge and Kevin McPherson and me. The dry taste of cigarette smoke still in my mouth. A new cup of tea on the table in front of me. The dull sound of traffic passing by outside where normal people are living in normal worlds thinking normal thoughts.

'Interview resumed at ...' Beige Hair checks her watch. '4.15 p.m.'

She looks at me, not unkindly.

'How're you doing, Mr Gilmour?'

'Fine, thanks.'

'Good. We don't want to tire you out.'

'You're not.'

'Just a few more questions and then you should be good to go.'

I fiddle with the cuffs on my shirt. I am wearing the links Ben gave me for my twenty-first. We were still at Cambridge at the time. By way of celebration, I had invited a handful of friends to formal hall and we wore gowns and downed a bottle of wine each, flinging pennies into each other's glasses in the Cambridge tradition until the final dregs had gone. We ate overcooked beef and a stiff panna cotta and when Ben passed me the small navy box across the long dining table, I was almost too drunk to open it. When I did, there were the cufflinks, studded gold against black velvet. I recognised the engraving immediately. It was the Fitzmaurice family crest.

We had been so close. And now – this.

'For the purposes of the tape, I am now showing Mr Gilmour document 2c from Evidence Folder B.'

Beige Hair slides a sheet of paper towards me. It is in a plastic see-through folder which makes a shushing sound against the laminate as I reach for it.

'Do you recognise this, Mr Gilmour?'

At first, I can't make out what I'm looking at. Lines of figures. Centralised text. A red and white triangular logo in the top right-hand corner. My vision stutters and the typeface wobbles. Gradually, the letters and numbers settle into place and I realise it is an old bank statement. My name at the top: Martin Gilmour. The Queens' College address. I look at the date: January 1994. Three months after we'd unpacked our suitcases into our new student rooms. Back when the years had stretched ahead full of promise and freedom.

'Martin?'

I nod.

'For the tape please.'

'Yes.'

I have twisted one cufflink so roughly it has slipped out of place. I try to manoeuvre it back through the buttonhole. I test myself to see if I can do it without looking but my fingers fumble on the metal.

I know, instinctively, what Beige Hair is going to ask me next and I assess my options for how to answer. I try to calculate what will cause least damage, but it's impossible to know how much they know and so I am lost, momentarily, in a mental hall of mirrors where my previous certainties are distorted, each one a fairground reflection of itself. I have no idea how they got my bank statement. How did they even know where to look?

'OK, Martin, so can you tell us what this payment is here—' Beige Hair taps on the plastic wallet, her nail clacking softly. Clack clack clack.

I lift the bank statement off the table and bring it closer to my face. I want to buy myself some time.

'I'm sorry,' I say. 'Which one exactly?' and I pass the paper back over and Grey Suit groans while Beige Hair smiles pleasantly and

says, 'Of course,' and taps again with her nail. Clack clack clack.
'It's this one, dated 3 January 1994.'

Grey Suit stares at me, one arm slung casually over the back of
his chair.

'Ah,' I say. 'Yes. I mean, it's a long time ago so ...'

She laughs.

'I'm sure you remember a payment that size!' she says, as if we
are good friends having a relaxed conversation. 'Ten grand is a
fortune for a student, isn't it? Especially to an undergrad who's
maxed out his student loan. I mean, no offence, Martin, but you
weren't exactly rolling in it, were you?'

'No.'

'So can you tell us where this money came from?'

I take a sip of tea. It burns the roof of my mouth.

'Well,' I reply. 'It says it right there, doesn't it?'

Beige Hair raises her eyebrows in faux apology.

'Does it? I'm sorry. Stupid of me. What does it say exactly?'

'G. A. C. Fitzmaurice.'

'And who's that?'

I think of George, of his kind face and his bulbous nose and his
leather-bound first editions of Dickens. I think of him sitting in
The Anchor pub on Silver Street, waiting for me and Ben to join
him after we'd settled into our digs. I think of how, when we
walked through the door that evening, he was sitting on his own
with a pint, stroking the head of a stranger's Jack Russell, gazing
into space and the expression on his face was not one of contentment but of loss. Unadulterated loss. And how, when he saw us
coming towards him, his features shifted instantaneously into his
usual pose of get-on-with-it joviality and how that made me sad,
on some level I couldn't immediately access. When he died last
year, I thought of that moment again and again and again. I still
miss him.

I pick up the bank statement. I trace the name with my index
finger. George Alexander Charles.

'George Fitzmaurice,' I tell her. 'Ben's father.'

Notebook of Lucy Gilmour

I SLEPT OK LAST NIGHT, for the first time since I arrived here. It's difficult to get to sleep because of the noises from the other patients. Sorry: residents. That's what we're meant to call ourselves. That's how the staff refer to us, as if this is simply an extended stay in a particularly nice country house hotel.

It's not bad really. The Pines is one of the most exclusive rehab facilities in the country. The central house looks like it could be the backdrop to a well-shot period drama. White brickwork. Georgian windows. Pediments. There is even a gravel driveway and a twee fountain on the front lawn depicting a rotund little boy wrestling with a fish, water pouring from its open mouth.

My room is spartan but functional. Everything is scrubbed clean. I have a single bed pushed against the wall. A basin. A desk. A cupboard with plastic hangers you can't remove. No wire ones, obviously, because they'd be too tempting for the suicide risks. For the same reason, they remove our belts and our shoelaces when we are checked in, as if we are prisoners.

Anyway, no dreams last night. Just empty, blank space, which was a relief after all those panicked subconscious moments when I accidentally stumbled over a cliff edge, only to wake up, moments later, covered in sweat. Yesterday, I asked the doctor to give me a different sleeping pill and he obliged, with the easy accommodation of one who knows he is being paid well over the going rate not to ask too many questions. So perhaps it was the new sleeping pill. Perhaps it was that Sandy, the woman next door, was uncharacteristically quiet – no sobbing or wailing from her side of the partition; no random thumping on the wall.

I try not to engage too much with the other residents. I don't want to make friends. I've had enough of other people for a while.

But I know a bit about Sandy because I overhear the nurses talking about her. She's married to a fading rock star who cheats on her. She's an alcoholic and undergoing some fairly severe withdrawal symptoms. I notice her sometimes in the canteen, sitting at one of the long tables, shaping mashed potato with her plastic fork, adding too much salt, pushing a chicken leg to one side with her knife, slathering it with ketchup and then sliding her plate away, refusing to eat any of it. She has concave cheeks and you can see she was once beautiful but now she is too thin and her skin looks parched and over-stretched and her dyed blonde hair hangs lankly on either side of her face.

This morning I woke up a minute before my alarm clock was due to go off. I felt rested. Outside, it was dark and I could hear the trickle of the little boy and his fish. I stretched, rolling back my shoulders, cricking my neck. I thought, as I always did, of Martin. I wanted to be angry with him, but I never could sustain it. I worried about where he was and what he was doing and whether he was eating properly, whether I'd left enough stuff in the cupboards for him to be able to make do or whether he was eating Indian takeaway every night, dialling the number from the well-worn menu stuck to the front of our fridge. He always had a number 45: prawn jalfrezi. He liked to order a naan, no rice.

We went to a Bollywood party once, a charity shindig organised by one of Serena's friends who was raising money to preserve the Indian tiger from extinction. I wore a sari. Martin, who hated fancy dress, put on a Nehru shirt and was done with it.

I remember Andrew Jarvis was there. I disliked Jarvis because I knew, from what Martin had told me, that he had been a bully at school. In adulthood, I found him mystifyingly pleased with himself: the kind of man who only ever asks a question if it belittles the person who has to answer.

He was wearing a turban and I was appalled to see he had applied brown face-paint from the neck upwards.

'Oh my God, he has literally blacked up,' I whispered to Martin as he came towards us.

'Hello, Jarvis,' Martin said. He didn't extend his hand and Jarvis did not offer his.

'Martin.'

'Didn't expect to see you here,' he continued.

'No? Why not?'

'Didn't realise you knew the Cuthbertsons.'

'Well, there's no reason you should know everything,' Martin replied. I could feel the tension vibrating from him. Not for the first time, I wondered what Jarvis could have done to Martin at school that made my husband bristle with such disdain.

'No, no, of course not,' Jarvis said. 'It's just you're from such different …' He gesticulated with one hand, like a conductor in search of a baton. 'What's the word? Such different … *milieus*. I know Francesca Cuthbertson from way back when. Our families holidayed together in France every year and we all grew up in the same part of Suffolk, you know. Whereas you … I'm sorry,' Jarvis said, making a great show of looking confused, 'I can't remember, off the top of my head, where *you* grew up?'

Martin stood very still.

'Suffolk?' I said. 'How funny. I was reading a newspaper article the other day which said that, statistically, Suffolk is the most inbred county in all of England.'

Jarvis almost choked on his mini-samosa.

'Really?' he said, in between coughs. 'How fascinating.'

'Anyway,' I continued, 'I've just seen Francesca over there and we must go and say hello. Do excuse us … I'm sorry, I can't remember your name …'

'Andrew Jarvis.'

'Of course. Well, see you later, then.'

I walked off with as much confidence as I could muster and Martin followed.

'But we don't know Francesca,' he hissed.

'I know that. You know that. But Andrew Jarvis certainly doesn't have to.'

As for Suffolk being the most inbred county in England? I made it up. But it could be true, that's the point.

I had an unexpected visitor this morning. Visiting hours are meant to be after lunch, from 3 to 5 p.m., but no rule at The Pines is ever strictly adhered to.

No one has come to see me apart from Martin. He has tried on several occasions but I have refused to see him. It isn't just because of what happened. It's everything leading up to that point, all the years I tried, all the times I made excuses and told myself things weren't that bad. All of it came to a head. I looked at my husband on the night of the party and I knew with startling certainty: I do not love you and there is no point in pretending.

It's like tripping over a pebble and breaking a leg. Sometimes the entire course of your life can change because of a single second, because that single second doesn't exist in isolation: it is connected to an infinite chain of minutes, days, weeks, months and years that have gone before. But it's the misshapen second that unravels it. A dropped stitch that ruins a knitted scarf.

Still, I feel bad not seeing Martin. He is trying, after all. I'm not angry with him. I'm just too exhausted to care any more. As for Ben and Serena? If I never see them again it will be too soon.

This morning's visitor took me by surprise and when the nurse announced who it was, I was intrigued in spite of myself. When I walked into the lounge, there was a pot of coffee already laid out and a plate of biscuits on the table by the bay window and there, sitting upright in a chintzy armchair was Lady Katherine, Ben's mother.

I had met her only once before, at Hector's christening. She had been polite but distant, wearing a formal pale grey suit with a pillbox hat and heels with a square toe and a silver buckle. I remember the shoes because they seemed so out of keeping with the rest of her. They were pantomime shoes and she had seemed so buttoned up and elegant.

'Hello, Lucy,' she said, in that low voice. 'How are you?'

I tried to smile. The muscles around my mouth felt tired. I took the armchair opposite her, feeling ungainly in my jeans and striped top from Gap. There was a faded orange stain on the hem. That must have been the spaghetti bolognese from the previous day's dinner, I thought as I sat down.

I saw Sandy across the room, on a sofa with a young man who might have been her son. They were deep in conversation and Sandy had her arm on the sleeve of his leather jacket.

I took a biscuit.

'This is a surprise,' I said.

Lady Katherine gave a tiny nod.

'I imagine it is.'

She lifted her cup and saucer. The cup seemed almost to levitate in her hands. I started to shake and as I poured myself coffee, the milk splashed and spilled over the sides. Fucking Fitzmaurices, I thought, always on their best behaviour even while they were ruining other people's lives. Who did she think she was?

'You seem unsettled,' she said.

'You could say that.'

'I can understand why.'

'I don't think you can.'

Another precise sip of coffee. Pale lipstick mark against the rim.

'Mmm. Well. People we love act in unlikely ways under extreme pressure. People can fall apart.' She looked at me, her grey eyes sharp and steady. 'As I'm sure you know given your … your …' She waved one hand. 'Your current situation.'

I laughed.

'My situation?'

'Yes, Lucy. I'm sure you regret—'

'I don't regret anything,' I said. 'Except possibly marrying Martin in the first place.'

I could hear myself spitting out the words and it felt wrong, somehow. The rage felt misplaced. But it was there, and it seemed I had no control over it.

Lady Katherine turned her head to peer out of the window, generously giving me the opportunity to admire her noble profile. She had a small gold signet ring on her right hand. It was the same one that Ben wore and I knew it was engraved with the family crest. Serena had one too, which Ben had given her to mark the birth of their first child. I always thought there was something curiously medieval about this: as if Serena had only proved herself a true Fitzmaurice by producing an heir.

'I don't expect you to listen to me, Lucy.' She was still staring out the lawn, at the gravel, the grass and the boy with the fish. 'But I wanted you to know that, as Martin's wife, we consider you very much part of the family.'

'You do?'

She ignored me.

'And I hope that you see us in the same way and that you know you can always rely on us for ...' There was a pause. 'Help,' she concluded, turning back to look at me. 'We are more than happy to pay for your stay here, for instance.'

'I thought Martin ...'

She smiled.

'Oh no, dear, no. Martin couldn't afford this.'

She brushed down the stiff fabric of her skirt.

'But, as I said, we're more than happy, given all that Martin has ... well, all that he's done. In return, all we ask for is discretion where it is called for. You understand, I'm sure?'

There was a buzzing in my ears. The sound of a wasp trapped behind a pane of glass. It made sense now. Why she would come. Why she would pretend to care. Why she would deign to visit me in this embarrassing place. She didn't want me to talk. None of the Fitzmaurices did.

Unbelievable, really, how ambitious they were, how unthinkingly they took the world as if it were their due.

'You need to rest,' Lady Katherine continued, 'to get better, and then perhaps you'll be able to see things more clearly ...'

'What gives you the right?' I asked, my voice so low she had to crane forwards to hear me, neck stretched like a long-beaked pelican diving for fish.

'I'm sorry?'

'What gives you the right to play with people's lives like this? To move them around like pawns on a chessboard? Is it because you're rich? Or posh? Or just because you've never had to lift a finger? You've no—'

'I don't think—'

'No conscience. You might've got away with doing it to Martin for all these years but I'm not him. I'm not desperate to be liked. Especially not by people I don't respect. You don't know anything about me. Not one thing. But you have the … the nerve … to turn up here like you own the place, issuing your demands and just expecting me to nod my head and say yes. So tell me, Lady Katherine: where, exactly, do you get off?'

It was the most I had spoken to anyone apart from Keith since arriving at The Pines. The words beaded themselves together in front of me, jewels on a string. There was no hesitation.

'You don't need to worry,' I said. 'I don't want anything more to do with your bloody family.'

I stood to leave and then, without thinking, I turned back and shouted, 'The Fitzmaurices can go fuck themselves.'

Everyone went quiet. Lady Katherine looked appalled. One of the nurses shook her head. But Sandy … Sandy was grinning at me. As I opened the door into the corridor, I could see her pushing up her sleeves and the last thing I saw before leaving was Sandy, limp hair tucked behind her ears, giving me the thumbs-up.

2 May

Marquee, Tipworth Priory, 9.45 p.m.

AT A CERTAIN STAGE DURING THE EVENING, at just the point where the liminal haze of extreme tipsiness slides into the bubbling froth of pure, inescapable drunkenness, the guests began to be ushered outside the house. No one knew why, but we didn't think to question it either. We followed each other like good-humoured sheep, carried along by the drifting current of loud laughter and louder chatter and back-slappings and hand-shakings and huggings and air-kissing: the usual British reserve dissolving like aspirin as the night wore on.

'If you wouldn't mind, sir,' a waiter said. 'The Fitzmaurices are asking everyone to gather in the marquee. It's just this way …' He motioned with the flat of his palm outstretched.

'I know where it is.'

I left the drawing room and joined a crowd of partygoers in the corridor. Jarvis had gone but I couldn't work out where and I didn't want to be surprised by him again.

Lucy reappeared at my elbow carrying two cheeseburgers. She passed one to me, wrapped up tightly in greaseproof paper with 'Ben's 40th' printed on it in red block capitals.

'No gherkins,' she said.

'Thank you.' I took her hand, warm in my cold one, and lifted it to my lips. I was relieved to have her back.

'You OK?'

She looked at me in her direct way, assessing every tiny movement.

'Fine.' I paused. 'I just … ran into Andrew Jarvis.'

Lucy made a face. I laughed.

'Yes. Not my favourite person.'

'And you haven't eaten,' she pointed out. 'Low blood sugar and Andrew Jarvis: a potentially fatal combination. No wonder you look so pale.'

'Do I?'

'Just a bit.' She took a large bite of her burger and a blob of mayonnaise affixed itself to the corner of her mouth. 'Why do you suppose we're being ushered into the marquee?'

'Who knows? Maybe they've got the Pope to do a karaoke number.'

Lucy snorted.

'It'd have to be something by Madonna, wouldn't it?'

'Or the Jesus and Mary Chain.'

'Ha!'

We wandered into the vast white space, lit with garlands of fairy lights emitting a lilac phosphorescence. The marquee smelled of summer weddings and school prize-givings. There was a long stage in the middle of the space and the guests were jostling among themselves to get as close as possible to the front.

Gilly Rawlings jiggled up to us excitedly, an unmanned space-hopper bouncing through the crowds.

'Isn't this *ravishing*?' she said, clearly pleased with herself for picking out such an intelligent word. 'I mean, I can't *believe* the trouble they've gone to. Serena really is a marvel.'

Lucy smiled, then demolished the rest of her cheeseburger, licking the grease off her fingers. Gilly took my arm conspiratorially: she was one of those women who always thought she got on better with men and took pride in the idea.

'What do you think, darling?' she asked me. 'What's going to happen next?'

'Live human sacrifice?' muttered Lucy.

'Not sure, Gilly.' The cheeseburger had gone cold in my hand. I looked around for a bin. Nothing. I wondered whether anyone would notice if I simply dropped it on the floor.

'Oh come now, you must have *some* idea – as Ben's oldest, best-est friend. Who's his favourite band?'

I thought back to those CDs, purchased in Woolworths all those years ago. The effort I'd gone to with money I barely had. For a while the CDs lay around in various dorm rooms, the cases becoming chipped and scratched as they were packed up at the end of each term and then unpacked at the start of every new one, un-listened to but somehow important to keep hold of. Then, when I went to Cambridge, I couldn't find them. They had become part of the ephemeral crap we lose down the back of life's endless sofa.

'He used to like Run DMC,' I said. Gilly looked nonplussed.

'I'd bloody love it if they appeared,' Lucy said. 'Shake things up a bit.'

Gilly, drawing closer to me, dropped her voice: 'I heard a *rumour*,' she started.

'Another one?' I asked mildly.

'… that it might just be …' She turned her back on Lucy and tiptoed up to my ear, cupping her podgy hand as she stage-whispered the name of a rock band beloved of metropolitan thirty-somethings who still wore slogan T-shirts and beanie hats in the hope that they could pass for younger. 'Wouldn't that be *amazing*?'

'Yes,' I said, without enthusiasm. 'Amazing.'

'Are you going to eat that?' Lucy was pointing at my cheeseburger.

'No, go ahead. Might be a bit cold though.'

'I don't mind. Ravenous.'

She chomped her way through her second bap, oblivious to Gilly's disapproving looks. I cast around, searching for another drinks waiter. The buzz of the last mojito was wearing off. I needed another boost to keep the insulating wave rolling over me.

'Well, something's happening,' Lucy said, nodding towards the marquee's entrance where four bald-headed men with earpieces and black shirts were ushering people back so that a narrow pathway was cleared.

'Oooh,' Gilly squealed, dropping my arm as if it were infected and bouncing off towards the action.

'Ugh. She gets worse every time.'

'Lucy …'

'What? I know you can't stand her either.'

'Someone might overhear.'

'Oh bollocks to that,' she said, cheeks pinking. 'Sometimes, Martin, it's good not to care what other people think.'

She was right, of course. She was always right.

Lucy knew me better than anyone but there were many things I never told her. She looked at me sometimes as if trying to make out the shape of a rocky outcrop on a foggy horizon. Sometimes she came very close to seeing me. Almost, but not quite. I think, looking back, it was this that kept her interested in me in a way she hadn't been in anyone else.

The men who had guided us into the marquee were now extending their arms, forming a human fence to hold back the party guests, some of whom had started mumbling about what the fuck was going on and couldn't they just get to the fucking bar and hey, mate, there was no need to push. Someone dropped a plate, the crash of splintering crockery muted by the stretched tarpaulin. There was a hush, and then in walked the Prime Minister and his wife.

There he was: Edward Buller, moving with the attitude of a man who has already assessed the dimensions of the space and found it wanting. His face was eggshell smooth, his hairline receding in the shape of an inverted three, leaving two fleshy petals of skin exposed. His lips were thin, pressed together gravely (he used to smile a lot more, but then the financial crisis had struck and he had assumed a permanently concerned expression: I believe he thought it statesmanlike). His eyes were too small for the rest of him, pressed into the doughy expanse of his features like pebbles in the face of a snowman.

He paused briefly, glancing around the marquee, taking its measure, and then I could see him fix his features accordingly and he unbuttoned his jacket and became jovial, shaking the proffered hands with ease, one palm resting on the other person's upper arm as he did so.

'Good to see you,' I heard him say as he approached. 'Great party. Great to be here.'

Edward Buller got closer and closer to us and I felt a surge of energy, all at once worried that he wouldn't remember me and that I would have to pretend to be a perfect stranger, even though I'd spoken to Gilly plenty of times in the past about how well I knew him. I saw her watching me now with her beady stare as the Prime Minister continued his triumphal procession and I knew that if Edward Buller blanked me, Gilly would note this down and it would become part of her spewing anecdotage at other parties like this one and I would never live it down.

'All he needs now is someone to give him a baby to hold,' Lucy said. 'Wonder if Ben's arranged that.'

I laughed.

'Hi, Eric!' the Prime Minister was saying now, just two feet away from us. 'So glad you could make it.'

He was trailed by his meek wife, Fiona, a slender brunette wearing a mid-calf dress in an ugly geometric print. The *Daily Mail* was forever pillorying Fiona Buller for her lack of style and her habit of recycling old outfits. A few weeks before, she had been pictured at a women's mentoring event wearing a jumper knitted with the design of a poodle across her chest. The *Mail* had run a double-page spread asking fashion experts to give their assessment under the headline 'Paw Show'. One of the stylists had given her 'Canine out of ten for dowdiness'.

'Great to see you,' Buller said to a man with ginger hair. 'You remember my wife, Fiona?' Behind him, Fiona gave a wordless shrug.

The Prime Minister was now close enough for me to smell the metallic edge of his aftershave. I rehearsed what I would say. I thought it best to take the initiative so that, before he had the chance to humiliate me by not remembering who I was, I would say, 'Nice to see you again, Edward,' and then maybe I would follow up with 'Must have been at Ben's' in order to give him the appropriate context. My hand was sweating. I removed it from Lucy's clasp. The Prime Minister had just embraced a woman in a tight brocade dress and was moving towards me, his progress inexorable. He looked up and our eyes met briefly and his gaze was one of complete blankness and I felt my heart rate soar as he came closer and the inevitable moment was upon me and …

'Maaaaate!' Ben had surged out from the crowd and was grappling the Prime Minister into a showy bear hug. All I was left with was a broad sweep of Buller's shoulders and Ben's arms around him. Ben drew back. 'So good of you to come.' His eyes were glistening. Was he – no, he couldn't be – but was he actually on the verge of *tears*?

'Wouldn't have missed it,' Buller was saying.

Then Serena shimmied into the picture, cheekbones pearlescent, and she kissed Fiona lightly on each cheek and said loudly: 'You two never let us down!' so that everyone could see what good friends they were. Fiona took a startled step back.

'I'm going to find a drink,' I told Lucy.

'Good idea. I'll come with you.'

We battled our way back through the hordes of partygoers and into the main hallway where another table had been set up with yet more glasses: long ones, this time, with sugar granules stuck to the rim.

'What are these?' Lucy asked as I handed her one.

'Who cares?'

Lucy sipped hers through a straw. I took a swift gulp from the glass.

'Come on then,' Lucy said, leading the way towards the thumping music that had just started up beyond the dividing wall.

We walked back into the marquee.

Martin

Cambridge, 1993

'MARTIN, ISN'T IT?'

The voice was soft but not hesitant, as if she knew the answer to the question even before she asked it.

I looked up from my textbook. It was on English medieval social history, the pages filled with references to Malthus and patronage and the Black Death and serfdom. Every now and then, I would come across a pencilled note in the margin made by an unknown student who wrote in precise, angular letters. Sometimes there would be a simple underlining and a lone question mark, hanging in the blank space and I would wonder what it was that had attracted his or her attention and whether it had confused them in some way I couldn't yet fathom.

The girl was waiting for an answer and I realised that I had let the silence draw out for a beat too long and I had been staring at her. I blinked, breaking the gaze.

'Yes.'

She was blonde and swishy, one of those women you knew would have been the prettiest girl at school – the ones who arrived at university seemingly fully formed, in roll-necks and tight jeans and high ponytails, at ease with life in a way the rest of us could only admire.

'Hi, I'm Vicky.'

Of course you are, I thought. She would be a Vicky or an Olivia or an Abby or an Alice – any name that suggested horses and dressing-table mirrors and upbringings involving black-tie balls in London where teenagers with recognisable surnames would pretend to be more grown up than they actually were.

I shut the textbook with a thud. The noise of it reverberated across the university library. Groups of students at long wooden desks were bent over foolscap pads like monks from a bygone age, their faces illuminated by the dull greenish tinge of a reading spotlight. Why would Vicky be remotely interested in talking to me, I wondered, putting the cap back on my fountain pen.

'You're friends with Ben, aren't you?'

Ah. That would be it.

'Yes.'

In all honesty, it wasn't the first time something like this had happened. I was used to being the go-between. Usually the girls in question were less blunt. They did, at least, make a stab at pretending to have a conversation with me before bringing up the real purpose of their interest.

'I knew it. He said.'

She was chewing gum. A smell of chemical citrus fruit. She smiled at me, lips and eyes sparkly, ears punctuated by pearl full stops.

'Did he?'

'Yeah, the other night. We were at this sports thing and I said I came to the UL and he said his mate Martin from school was always there and, well, here you are.' Vicky giggled, hoisting up the waistband of her jeans as she did so. 'Sorry. Forgot my belt this morning.'

'But how did you know—'

'That it was you?'

I nodded.

'Ben said you looked like Where's Wally.'

'Oh.'

She laughed. It was a nice laugh. Unforced.

'Don't be offended. It's cute.'

'I suppose.'

She leaned over and squeezed my wrist.

'It is. Promise.'

What struck me most about her pretty face was the arch of her brows. They were so perfectly proportioned, the peak of them situated directly above the last third of her pale blue eyes.

'Fancy a coffee?'

Well, I thought, what harm could it do? I was bored of Malthus. And even if Vicky turned out not to be exceptional company, there were worse ways to spend half an hour. We could talk about Ben. That was never wasted time.

'OK.'

We went to the tea room. She ordered a latte, I opted for a fizzy water; the tea there was foul. We sat at a table by a window. I didn't need to ask her any questions; she simply spoke as if I wanted to know.

She was at Newnham, she told me, studying law. She had a younger sister and brother. She had grown up in the countryside and missed tramping across fields in wellington boots.

'You know, you can do that here,' I interjected. 'The fields around Grantchester ...'

'Yeah, but it's all so flat. I like a good hill. Anyway, sorry. Enough about me. What about you, Martin?'

'What about me?'

'Where are you from?'

'Nowhere you would have heard of.'

She laughed.

'OK, be like that.' She dropped her voice. 'Man of mystery.'

I liked Vicky. I was surprised by that. I had spent so much of my first term at Cambridge avoiding people I couldn't bear. People like Jez, the rugby player, whom Ben had unaccountably taken under his wing. Or Rufus, who had been to Eton and kept talking about the fact he'd been to Eton and whose main affectation was wearing three-piece suits with red waistcoats. Or Jimmy, whose father was the chairman of a gas company and who had long blond hair swept back from his forehead, the ends always on the brink of greasiness, and who spent his holidays at the family villa in Ibiza (the north of the island, away from the tourists and the foam parties). And Jarvis, of course. Jarvis who had followed us to Cambridge like a bad smell.

The four of them appeared to be at the nexus of college social life. As ever with Ben, he gravitated effortlessly towards the centre of any gathering and in doing so, he distanced himself from me without ever making it obvious, without there ever being a point of separation I could put my finger on and say, 'Oh, there. That was it. That was the reason.' And because there was no logic to it that I could see, because he simply seemed to get tired of me in his Ben-ish way, it was all the more painful.

When Ben decided something was cool, it was, and when he changed his mind, it wasn't. That was his gift.

In the tea-room, someone dropped a spoon. A throbbing spot at the corner of my left eye flashed and dimmed.

'Martin?' Vicky was saying. 'Martin? Hello?' She made a knocking gesture. 'Anyone in there?'

I turned to face her. The redness in my head faded.

'Sorry,' I said. 'Miles away.'

'Okaaay. So anyway – are you coming to the Pitt Club party?'

'The what?'

'Wow. Are you, like, stoned or something?'

I shook my head.

'Have you listened to anything I've been saying?'

'Of course I have,' I said, irritable.

'All right, all right. I was just saying, the Pitt Club are having this party tomorrow night and I wondered if you were coming?' There was a pause and I knew what she was about to say. 'And if, you know, Ben was coming?' She tried so hard to be casual about it.

I shrugged.

'He probably is. I mean, he usually does.'

'Great.'

'But I think I'll give it a miss.'

'Why?'

'Not my scene.'

The Pitt was a members' club open only to male undergraduates who had been to Eton or Harrow. In practice, anyone with a posh school, family money or an aristocratic name was let in. They would have drinks parties each term where the men in question would be allowed to ask along a girl (and they would always be referred to as 'girls', never 'women') on the unspoken understanding that she be one of the most attractive members of the university. There was an informal league table of beauty. A handful of girls in our year qualified for inclusion and we all knew who they were. They were talked about in college bars in the hushed, reverent tones usually reserved for film stars or supermodels. Vicky was deemed to be one of them but I had never met the others, who had always seemed to me like mythical beasts: fantastical unicorns who existed only in the collusion of fevered male imaginations.

Although Ben went regularly to these mysterious Pitt Club gatherings, often in black tie for no discernible reason, I had not been invited. He had never suggested taking me, although I would have liked to go. And I, of course, had never asked him because it would have been too humiliating. I wanted him to want me there.

Vicky tapped my hand playfully.

'Don't be silly. Of course it is. Free booze, pretty girls. That's anyone's scene, right?'

I started picking at dirt under my thumbnail with the edge of a packet of sugar. Vicky was still prattling on. 'I mean, I'm going with my friend Louise and she's super-hot so, you know …'

I placed the sugar packet back on the table.

'Oh,' she said. 'Unless … I mean … sorry, that's so presumptuous of me. Maybe you're not …' She pushed the empty coffee cup to one side. '… not into girls?'

She posed it as a question, the words spoken in a rising scale. Too quickly, I rose from my chair and banged my hip against the edge of the table. The china rattled. The sugar packet slid onto the floor.

'Martin!' Vicky reached across and tried to grab hold of my sleeve. I shrank away from her. I walked out of the tea-room as quickly as I could, but my legs seemed sluggish, waterlogged like wool left to soak, and she caught up with me and tried again to put her hand on my arm.

'Don't,' I said, snatching it away from her. 'Please.'

'I'm sorry, Martin.' She was still there, keeping pace with me, and I could still smell her chewing gum now shaded by the scent of canteen coffee, and I wanted to be rid of her and at the same time I wanted her to follow me and I wanted above all not to be alone and simultaneously I desired nothing so much as solitude.

My head began to turn in on itself. I had a clear vision of my mother polishing candlesticks with Brasso and kitchen towel and the way she would examine the left-behind smears of dirt with disgust as if nothing could ever be clean, no matter how hard she tried.

'Martin.'

I kept walking, out towards the open air.

'Martin, stop.'

At the top of the steps outside the entrance to the library, I came to a halt.

'I know you only want to talk to me to get to Ben,' I said. 'You honestly don't need to bother with anything else. I'm fine.'

'That's not true,' Vicky protested. 'Listen, I'm sorry about what I said. It's none of my business and who gives a fuck anyway. I just think you should come to the drinks because it'll be fun and I like you and I'll be there and ...'

Her cheeks were wind-whipped and pink. She did up the zip on her cardigan and pulled the sleeves over her hands.

'You're cold,' I said. 'You should go back inside.'

'I'm fine. Are *you* OK?'

I nodded. She moved towards me and I realised too late what was happening. Before I could step away, she hugged me. The warmth of her. It was the first time I had ever been hugged by a woman other than Fliss. I couldn't move. I allowed her to hold me and then I drew back, embarrassed and inexplicably ashamed.

'Good,' she said briskly. 'I'll see you tomorrow at the Pitt Club then. I'll leave your name on the door.'

'But …'

Already she was moving away from me, turning at the last minute by the UL door to give me a little wave and a smile.

'It'll be fun!' she shouted as she disappeared through the doors. 'Trust me.'

Back at Queens', I went straight to Ben's room and knocked on the door.

'Yeah,' came the languid response. He was spreadeagled on his desk chair, leaning backwards as far as he could risk balancing on two legs. On his bed at the back of the room, set against a long window overlooking the Cam, sat Jarvis.

'Oh. Hello, Jarvis.'

'Hello, Mart,' he drawled. Jarvis called me Mart even though I had never given him permission to do so. He simply shortened my name as if it were his own possession. He was studying one of those fake degrees invented for the purposes of dense individuals with a facility for sport. Land management or something. Jarvis had sailed through the interview process because the university wanted him on their rugby team and he was at Robinson, a horribly modern college on the edge of town with nothing, as far as I could see, to recommend it.

Behind him, punters pushed their way through the waters, disappearing and reappearing behind a forest of slim-trunked trees. Autumn leaves lay golden brown on the ground.

'All right, mate,' Ben said, not getting up. The two of them exchanged a quick glance and I had the uneasy sense that they had been discussing me.

'I won't stay—'

'Shame,' Jarvis said, smiling.

'—but I just ran into Vicky and she wanted to check you were going to the Pitt Club drinks tomorrow.'

Jarvis sat forward on the bed. He was wearing chinos and a pale blue shirt and a pair of Vans trainers he thought were cool.

'Is she now?' he asked.

Ben let the chair fall back to the floor.

'Vicky …' he mused. 'Remind me …'

'She's blonde,' I said. 'Newnham. Law. Said you told her I looked like Where's Wally.'

Jarvis guffawed.

'Oh that's very good, Ben. You know, Mart, there is a distinct resemblance …'

The back of my neck felt hot. I wanted to tell him to fuck off. I wanted to stride over to the other side of the room and slap his smug face with such force that his spittle would stain the walls. But I didn't. I forced myself to meet his smile with my own. The key to defeating an enemy like Jarvis was to remain calm at all times (Sun Tzu: 'It is the unemotional, reserved, calm, detached warrior who wins, not the hothead seeking vengeance.')

'Yeah, yeah, I remember. Fit Vicky.'

There was a deliberateness to Ben whenever he was in Jarvis's company. He assumed Jarvis's speech patterns and his fashionable faux cynicism and he was always careful never to seem too close to me, as if our friendship would undermine him. I found it all extremely trying. It made him look so desperate.

'Cool,' Ben said now. 'Thanks, mate.'

He stared at me and I realised I was expected to leave the room.

'I'm going, too,' I blurted. 'Vicky's put my name down.'

Jarvis sniggered. Ben looked surprised.

'Cool, cool. The more the merrier.'

'So I thought we could meet somewhere before, maybe. And go together?'

Jarvis, *sotto voce* from the bed: 'I bet you did.'

'Um. I think it might be easier to meet there. A bunch of us are going to Grantchester and I don't know when we'll be back, so …'

'How are you getting there?' I asked. Like me, Ben was one of the few students who did not have a bicycle. He laughed.

Jarvis interjected: 'Why, Mart? Are you worried about sweet little Ben being all on his lonesome without his big, brave Martin?'

'No,' I snapped.

'Rufus has a car,' Ben said. 'We're driving.'

'Fine,' I said and I felt myself spin as if dropping from a very great height. 'See you there then.'

The door closed behind me to the sound of suppressed laughter.

The Pitt Club was situated, somewhat incongruously, above Pizza Express on Jesus Lane. You had to buzz to be let in. I walked up the staircase in a suit Katherine had given to me – an old one of George's. It was too big for me across the shoulders. I had hemmed the legs in a rudimentary fashion with a needle and thread from an old sewing-kit my mother had given me to take to Burtonbury. In Epsom, my mother had always done the darning and stitching – those tiny necessities one never pays much attention to until one is faced with a hole in a sock and no one around to fix it. At school, there was always a matron on hand to help.

But Cambridge was a baffling place of new experiences. It was harder to know what to do.

Lager, for instance. I had never liked it but I knew, as a man, I was expected to drink it. At the college bar, I started ordering Stella because everyone else did. But then everyone switched to Kronenbourg halfway through term and somehow the right people just knew without having to ask why. I was constantly trying to keep up and failing to do so. It was that first term at Burtonbury, all over again.

'Name?' A man in white tie was standing by the door at the top of the stairs with a clipboard.

'Martin Gilmour,' I said.

'Gilmour,' the man echoed, drawing out all the vowels. 'Yes, here you are. Go on in. Cloakrooms to the right as you enter.'

The room was packed with men, jostling for space in black jackets, laughing and shouting and raising their glasses to be filled. The light was muted. There was a fire surrounded by a brass grate with an upholstered seat on which three girls in dresses of blue, green and red were sitting. I stood in the threshold for a second, taking it all in. I unwound my scarf. The cloakroom turned out to be an unattended space with coats strewn across sofas. One amorous couple was locked in a clinch, rolling around on a pile of abandoned clothes.

'Excuse me,' I said as I left my coat on the sofa furthest away from them. They did not respond. I stared at them, pretending to check the buttons on my shirt. The boy had his hand rammed up the girl's velvet skirt. Her tights were halfway down her thigh, the elastic digging into her dimpled flesh. His mouth was on hers, her lips wet and red and too big for her face. Her hands were in his hair, her back arched so that her breasts pressed into his chest. A ladder in the 10-denier nylon ran up from her ankle to her knee, the trail of it lengthening with each push and shudder.

'Do you mind?' A voice from behind me. 'We're trying to leave our coats.'

I left hastily.

'Fucking weirdo,' I heard as I walked into the crowd.

I took a glass of champagne from a waiter, scanning the room for Vicky's blonde head. I couldn't see her anywhere. There was music playing: a jazz track with syncopated beats and the background strumming of a double bass.

'Can I help you, sir?'

A man with bent-forward shoulders and an oily smile had appeared at my elbow.

'Looking for anyone in particular?'

'Ben. Ben Fitzmaurice.'

'Of course, sir. He's just over here.'

He led me through the braying male conversation. I recognised Ben's back before he turned.

'Mr Fitzmaurice, your friend …' The man hovered his palm towards me. 'I'm sorry, sir, I didn't catch your name.'

'Gilmour,' I said for the second time that evening. 'Martin Gilmour.'

'Maaaaarrrrttt!' Ben said, slapping my back with such force that champagne from his glass splashed against my chest. 'So great to see you, buddy! Why don't I top up your drink? Have this—' He passed me an open bottle of Veuve Clicquot. 'Here, let me introduce you. You know Jarvis, obviously …' Jarvis slyly arched an eyebrow. 'And this is Rufus and Jordan and Tom, and this right here, this vision of wonder …' He was slurring his words. I had never seen him this drunk. His eyes were unfocused, the pupils greatly dilated. 'This is Vicky.'

'We already know each other, silly,' Vicky was saying, playfully batting away Ben's hand. 'Yay, Martin, you came!' She reached across and kissed my cheek, her mouth cool as paper. Her long blonde hair was wound up in a complicated arrangement on the top of her head. It made her look older and yet extremely young at the same time, like a little girl playing dress-up in her mother's clothes.

She took my hand. 'I'm going to introduce you to Louise,' she said, manoeuvring me away from the group. She leaned towards me. 'God, that guy Jarvis is such a fucking letch. Thanks for saving me. Are you having an awful time?'

I shook my head.

'Good! Does that bottle have anything in it?'

I realised I was still holding the Veuve. Vicky proffered her glass and I filled it, taking care not to let the bubbles slip over the side.

'So where's your friend Louise?'

'Oh, she's not here. I just said that to get away from them.'

We took a seat perched on the edge of the fire grate. At our lowered sightline, all we could see were torsos and cummerbunds and manicured hands with bright red fingernails.

'Thanks for inviting me,' I said.

'Don't be silly. It's lovely to have someone normal here.'

What a strange thing to say to me, I thought. I'm the least normal person I know.

The evening wore on and the noise in the room grew louder and the champagne kept being poured but I had stopped drinking after that first glass, aware of my own sense of unease in this place of supreme assurance. At some point, Vicky left my side to go for a cigarette and never returned. I didn't mind. Being sober in a roomful of drunks allayed some of my disquiet. I could resume my usual role of observer without interruption.

The man with the sloping shoulders came and sat where Vicky had been. He moved too close to me, so that his leg pressed against mine.

'You all right, sir?'

I didn't respond.

'We can find a quiet spot if you'd rather. Just the two of us.'

He grazed the back of his hand lightly up my trouser seam. In spite of myself, I felt a twitch of response. I stood, quickly.

'Some other time then, sir.'

I went in search of Ben. Eventually, I found him in the cloak-room, hands on Vicky's buttocks, drawing her to him and kissing her neck while Jarvis looked for their jackets.

'Are you leaving?' I asked.

'Mate! Martin! There you are.' Ben pulled away from Vicky and strode over. He seemed so unaffectedly happy to see me that I felt a surge of the old fondness. 'Where have you been all night? This guy,' he announced to no one in particular, 'this guy right here,' he poked me in the chest, 'is my oldest, dearest friend. Aren't you, Mart? Aren't you?'

'I suppose I am.' I was delighted to see Jarvis bristling. 'For my sins.'

'You're always there,' Ben continued. 'Always fucking there. Every time I turn around' – he made a show of swivelling his head, his eyes wide with surprise – 'there you fucking are. My old mate Mart. You really, really, really, really love me, don't you?'

There was an edge to his voice.

'You can say that again,' Jarvis said.

'Can we all just go now?' Vicky pleaded. There was a black hyphen on her face. I squinted to make it out and saw it was an eyelash.

Ben, glazed, responded after a short time delay.

'Yes, my sweet, yes we shall. Now, where are the keys?'

'What keys?' I asked.

'The car keys.'

'A car? Since when have you had a car?'

'Since none of your fucking business,' Jarvis said.

'Jarvie, Jarvie, Jarvie, leave him alone. It's not my car, Mart; it's Rufus's. I'm driving it back for him.'

Ben staggered slightly.

'That's not a good idea,' I said. 'You're drunk.'

'Am not.'

'He's fine,' Jarvis said.

'Clearly, he's not fine.'

Suddenly Jarvis was in front of me, his face an inch away from mine, his nose so close I could see the shivering tendril of a single nasal hair.

'Why don't you fuck off out of here,' he said, his voice low. 'And leave the grown-ups to it?'

'Leave him alone.' Ben grabbed Jarvis by the shoulder and pulled him back. Jarvis swung round, fist already formed. Ben flinched, a second too late.

'Jarvis!' Vicky shrieked. 'Don't.'

He dropped his fist and stalked out of the room.

'Fuck off, the lot of you,' he said. 'Fucking pricks.'

The three of us looked at each other. The balloon of nervous tension in my chest began to deflate and we started to laugh.

'What a dick,' Vicky said.

'Agreed.'

'Oh, he's not that bad,' Ben said, picking up his coat. 'Nothing like a fight to sober you up.'

And when I peered into his face, searching it for clues, wondering once again where I lay in the spectrum of his love, back in the grip of the usual insecurity, I saw the drunkenness had gone, dissipated like mist. So when he jangled the car keys and led us outside, I refused to question it. I wanted to be his best friend again. I would have done anything for him at that moment.

Which is why, when we got to the silver Audi parked around the corner, and when he opened the passenger door for Vicky and when he asked if I wanted a lift, I got into the back seat without allowing myself the luxury of a second thought.

He turned the key. The engine started. Click of an indicator. Beam of headlight. Ben gripped the steering wheel and slid the car into the night.

VII.

'GO ON.' Beige Hair sits absolutely still across the table. Grey Suit blinks at me slowly.

Beyond, the dim sound of a faraway argument, the rattle of the breeze across the window. My leg is jittering up and down, a frantic metronome beat. The sole of my shoe sticks and rises with each motion.

I wonder how much to tell them and what it will mean if I do. If I let it all out, it will certainly be the end of my friendship with Ben, although perhaps that is already over. It will result in the destruction of my public reputation, or at least what little there is of it. As for my marriage? There is no going back. I think Lucy realises she can't keep butting her head against the wall. I will never change. I will never be able to love her the way she deserves. And even if, deep down, she always knew that, I still feel responsible. She is the one person in my life, other than Ben, I have come closest to loving.

Perhaps it is because I am thinking of Lucy and perhaps because, in my mind's eye, I can see her face with its kind eyes and worried expression and I can imagine pinching the lobes of her ears, each one soft with the lightest spray of down, and perhaps because I can hear her saying to me from across the void that the Fitzmaurices never really cared, not really, and that I should stop protecting my best friend who turned out not to be my best friend after all … perhaps it is because of all this that I almost decide to be honest for the first time in twenty years about what happened that night.

Besides, they already know about the money, don't they? I'll have to explain that.

'Go on,' Beige Hair says again.

Just enough to get them digging, I think. Just enough to turn their attention away from me and Lucy, and set them off on another scent. Towards Ben. Two for the price of one.

'All right. I will.'

Martin

Cambridge, 1993

BEN SAID HE WAS GOING TO DROP Vicky off at Newnham, but why didn't we take a spin around town first and let the car run for a bit? Vicky giggled and placed her hand on Ben's leg, massaging his muscles, taut from rugby and early-morning rowing. I watched mutely as she moved it further inwards so that I knew the tip of her little finger would be approaching his groin. On cue, Ben moaned.

'Stop it,' he said in a way that meant exactly the opposite. 'I need to concentrate.'

He glanced in the rear-view mirror and caught my eye and smiled. I looked out of the window, a patina of drizzle now speckling the glass. I should be in the front with him, I thought; I should be the one with the hand on his thigh.

Vicky turned on the radio. A beating bassline filled the car. My head hurt with the weight of it. Ben kept driving, up Jesus Lane and then onto Newmarket Road where the tarmac widened and he pressed down on the accelerator and we sped smoothly along, overtaking a coach that had drawn into the kerb. I opened the window and the night air rushed in, blowing back my hair and numbing my face. I tried to lose myself. I tried to remind myself that this was what being young was about but I kept being pulled back into the moment, the curious tension of it. Vicky removed her hand from Ben's leg and drew her sparkly jacket closer to her. She took a cigarette out of a sequinned bag.

'Can I?' she asked.

'You can do anything you want, beautiful,' Ben said.

Onwards the car went, slicing across the roundabout, motor purring as we turned right, then down to Parker's Piece where the moon cast its spectral light across the grass. The space between us and it seemed infinite.

Music blared out from the radio. The windscreen wipers swished and squeaked. Swish. Squeak.

Red traffic light. Amber. Growl of acceleration as Ben pushed on the pedal before the green had fully flicked into play. A pedestrian about to cross the road stepped back, alarmed. I pressed my forehead against the window as we passed, trying to block everything out.

We turned right instead of left. Away from Newnham and Queens' and before I could ask where we were going, Ben hit the accelerator and we were rushing into a road with cars parked on either side and a pub sign clattering in the wind and then he turned abruptly left, wheels screeching, and I saw a sign for Orchard Street and the image of an apple tree lodged itself in my head along with the thump and thud of the music and Vicky's sharp giggle and the acrid smell of tar and Ben's laugh and the sight of him inclining his head towards her so that he was no longer looking through the windscreen and now we were in a narrow, narrow street with hardly enough room to squeeze through and still he was speeding, pushing down on the accelerator, and the car engine revved and whirred and screamed with the force of the movement and the houses blurred into one long line of paint and I could just make out a swipe of blue shutters before the memory of them kaleidoscoped inwards and there was nothing but bright, white light as the car careened out into the main road and smashed violently into a fence.

Suspension.

We turned over, the roof of the car slamming onto the pavement. The seatbelt cut into my windpipe and I gasped for air. Vicky cried out but the sound was more gurgle than shout. Glass shattered, silver spores of it falling across my face. The car juddered and spun back onto its wheels with whiplash force. The seatbelt released its grip. Air pushed back into my lungs. Vicky's head snapped and lolled, hair falling. Ben in shadow. Wetness on my chin. I reached up, removed my hand, saw it was blood.

Silence.

In front of me, Vicky sat motionless. Ben was slumped over the steering wheel. The windscreen had split in two. Jagged pieces of glass yawned open like a mouth. I tried to say his name but could make no sound. I jabbed at the seatbelt clip to release it. It was stuck firm. I kept slamming my hand down until finally it snapped back.

'Ben, Ben! For fuck's sake, Ben!' I was shaking him, my hands grabbing hold of anything – his hair, his neck, his chest. 'Wake up. For fuck's sake. Don't ... don't fucking do this ... don't.'

His eyes opened. He looked at me for a moment with complete incomprehension. I could tell his nose was broken, purplish bruises spreading across his face, blood across his teeth.

'What ...?' he started.

'Get out!' I shouted. 'Get the fuck out of the car.'

'But, Vi—'

'Forget her. We'll deal with it. Get the fuck out of the fucking car.'

I pushed my weight against the buckled metal of the door and fell out onto the pavement. I attempted to stand and found my leg was unable to take my weight. My right foot was twisted, the ankle swelling beneath my sock.

No time to worry about it. No time.

I dragged myself round to the driver's side, grabbed the door handle and pulled with all my strength until it gave. Ben sat there, dazed, a grey tinge to his face.

'Ben,' I said, more softly this time. 'Ben. You need to come with me.'

He looked at me blankly.

'Trust me.'

He took my hand and I levered him out onto the pavement.

I looked back at the car. Vicky stared at me through bloodshot eyes. A whimper. It was a noise so faint it erased itself and I told myself it had never happened. She was dead. She was already dead.

'Listen to me,' I said to Ben. 'I only had one glass of champagne. If anyone asks, I was driving.'

He was shivering.

'Do you understand?'

He said nothing.

'Do you understand?' I asked, this time louder.

He nodded and then crumpled to the pavement, knees hitting the stone with a crack. He started to crawl back to the car and I realised he was trying to get to Vicky. Her dress was spotted with blood. One hand lay unnaturally upwards on her lap, the palm glinting like a pallid pool of water in the moonlight.

I don't remember much of what happened after that. There were lights and sirens and a gathering crowd. I was told later that a taxi driver had been the first on the scene. According to his witness statement, the cabbie thought there had been two fatalities because he could just about make out the girl in the car and Ben was lying prone on the pavement in a spreading puddle of his own blood. I was the only one standing. Apparently I kept saying: 'It was my fault. It was my fault,' and when the taxi driver tried to reach out, I stepped back and told him not to touch me. He was the one who called the emergency services. When they arrived, he told the police he had never seen anyone in a state of such profound shock.

I'm not sure I agree with his analysis. I recall being calm but not shocked, exactly. I was completely certain of what I was about to do and what would happen because of it. Part of me had known the outcome as soon as the three of us got in the car outside the Pitt Club and perhaps, even before that, if one were to go back through the years and attribute some degree of fatefulness to the human condition, perhaps then a case could also be made for the idea that I was always intended to take the fall for Ben at the moment he most needed it. That was my purpose.

It was destined this way. It was why I had been sent to Burtonbury, why I had found that letter, why I had become his friend and met his family and why, now, he would forever be indebted to me. It was why I was different from everyone else in his life: Jarvis, Rufus, Jez, Vicky, even Fliss. The gratitude would bind us together. I would save him from himself. It would be our secret and he would spend the rest of his life paying for it.

Paramedics arrived and put blankets around our shoulders. We were taken to Addenbrooke's Hospital and given cups of sweet tea while the police questioned us. We stuck to our story. I said Ben had had too much to drink and had passed me the car keys outside the Pitt and asked me to drive. I had got lost, I said, being unfamiliar with the one-way system in Cambridge, and I had been trying to get back to the centre of town when I ended up on Orchard Street. It was dark, I said, and rainy, and visibility was poor and I hadn't realised how fast I was going but I wanted to get Vicky back to college as soon as I could since she was tired and wanted to go to bed. So maybe I accelerated more than I should have done but I hadn't meant to, not really, and just as Orchard Street gave into the main road, a fox had sprinted out into the middle of the greasy tarmac and without thinking I had swerved to avoid it and then, I said, and then … I lapsed into silence. I willed myself to cry but no tears came. I tried to think of something to say about Vicky, some admission of sadness, but I came up with nothing.

I think, looking back, this might have worked in my favour. It was taken as further evidence of my severe state of shock.

At some point, Ben's parents arrived, white-faced, slack-mouthed, rushing into the hospital ward in a flurry of raincoats and anxious protestation. They wanted to know everything all at once and something about their manner, about their sheer, imperious confidence seeped into the atmosphere. Everyone they met was in their thrall. They were glorious in their self-assertion. They took control without imagining it could be any other way. Ben was moved to a private room. George insisted the police stop questioning me as I was quite obviously in no fit state to be interrogated.

From then on, everything became much easier to navigate. The Fitzmaurices dealt with the police. They got their family lawyer involved. They spoke to Vicky's parents on my behalf. A financial settlement was swiftly agreed. Vicky's family, whom I never met, treated the whole episode as a tragic accident. I was formally arrested by the police on a careless driving charge but, in the end, the Crown Prosecution Service deemed it wasn't in the public interest to pursue it any further. Not enough evidence. And the family's wishes to let it be must have counted for something. I was given a one-year driving ban and a fine, paid for by Ben's family. Otherwise, I emerged unsullied and received a letter informing me no further action would be taken.

I don't quite know how they managed it, but I suppose money and power and a hint of aristocratic presence will go a long way. They could be very impressive, that family. The rest of that term passed in a haze. And when, at Christmas, I had nowhere to go, the Fitzmaurices invited me to spend it with them at Denby.

On Christmas morning, I woke in a four-poster bed in one of the prettiest guest bedrooms. I had never been put up there before. Usually, Katherine led me to a small room on the top floor with a brown carpet and shelves filled with old children's books and threadbare teddy bears. I never minded. It made me feel as though I were properly part of the family: not someone the Fitzmaurices had to stand on ceremony for. And there was comfort, too, in the modest size of my quarters. I didn't feel lost when I could reach out and touch the walls at night. I was cocooned by the vast sweep of the tiled roof.

This time, I had been taken to my new room without explanation. When I mentioned it to Ben he grinned but his eyes were dim. His face still bore the strain of what had happened several weeks previously. He was out of his neck-brace now but there remained a shadow of a bruise on his neck where the seatbelt had caught. The back of his hand was criss-crossed with steri-strips. We were intimate again, the closeness of our friendship now re-established by what we had been through, but he seemed caught behind a sheet of ice that would not melt, no matter how hard I tried to get through it. I put it down to trauma. He was always rather fragile, I told myself, whereas I was made of stronger stuff. I was more used to life's dark corners.

My new room at Denby had windows overlooking the lake. In the morning, I drew the curtains and saw each pane of glass lightly dusted with December frost. The radiator clanked into life and I could hear the ancient tapping as the pipes started to work. I grabbed a towel from the stack left by the housekeeper on the chest of drawers (two bath towels, one hand towel and a flannel I never used) and walked into the en-suite. I splashed my face with cold water, then turned on the bath taps, selecting a sample-sized bottle of bubble bath from the basket on the side.

'Lily and geranium,' I read out loud. 'Hotel Belfort, St Tropez.'

I slipped out of my pyjamas, leaving them on the floor for someone else to pick up and fold (this was one of the joys of staying here, I had discovered. It had taken me years to get used to it but then Ben had explained that the cleaners got embarrassed if you didn't leave them enough to do. 'It's a kindness, really,' he had said).

Just as I was about to dip my toe into the warm, frothy water, there was a knock at the door from outside.

I wrapped the towel around my waist and padded back out into the bedroom.

'Come in,' I said, my voice still gravelly from sleep. I thought it would be Ben, but when the door opened, it was George who revealed himself standing in the corridor. He was wearing dark blue slippers and a striped dressing gown with a cord belt. I felt suddenly underdressed, aware of the draught.

'Happy Christmas, old chap.'

His face was weary, thick grooves on each side of his mouth. His hair was whiter and thinner than I remembered it. The puddle of a yellow-brown liver spot on his temple.

'Happy Christmas, George.'

'Mind if I come in?'

'Please …' I hastily removed some clothes from the little wooden-framed sofa at the end of the bed.

'Oh don't worry about that,' George said. He came and sat in the place I had just cleared, his bones cracking as he lowered himself down. 'Just wanted to have a chat before …'

He waved his hand vaguely. I didn't know whether to sit or stand and in the end went over to the window and tried to lean against the ledge in as relaxed a fashion as possible. But there was a strangeness between us. We were both trying to ignore it and yet it kept coming back.

I thought over the previous evening. Ben and I had arrived by train from Cambridge. Katherine had picked us up in the car, the back seat covered in dog hair. We had eaten fish pie for dinner in the kitchen. Fliss was there, cracking jokes in her dry, laconic way. George had asked how the term at Cambridge had gone and I was able to tell him that my Director of Studies had already predicted a first in my Part I and Ben had chipped in saying that his parents shouldn't expect to hear the same from him because he'd been too busy partying and he said 'party' as if the 't' were a 'd', an affectation he had picked up from Jarvis.

After dinner, Katherine had suggested we 'sit soft' and we had gone to the red sitting room and the fire had been lit and the conversation had continued. In one corner, a tall twinkling Christmas tree. There was no tinsel, I noticed. Just white fairy lights and uniformly sized baubles in ivory and gold.

Ben had gone to bed earlier than the rest of us. He said he was tired and I said it wasn't surprising, really, after everything he'd been through.

'What do you mean?' he asked. 'Everything I've been through?'

'I just meant, you know, the car crash. You're recovering.'

'So are you.'

My ankle was still badly sprained and wrapped in a swathe of bandage that smelled of hospital chemicals.

'It's been bloody tough for both of you,' George said. 'Bloody tough.'

'It's nothing,' I replied.

Ben smiled. The smile didn't reach his eyes.

'You're so resilient, Mart.'

'Someone has to be.'

I meant it as a joke, a small note of levity to lift the atmosphere, but it didn't work. Ben stretched his arms up and out, leaning backwards and groaning as he did so. The groan turned into a yawn.

'Darling, go to bed,' Katherine said from her spot next to Fliss on the window seat. 'Martin's right. You're shattered.'

'I'm only looking after you,' I blurted.

There was a fractional pause. Kindling crackled on the fire. George sneezed. Fliss examined her fingernails. And then Ben laughed: a brittle, social laugh, deployed to defuse tension. He slapped me on the shoulder. I winced.

'As ever, Mart, as ever. What would I do without you?'

He walked out of the room. Shortly afterwards, Katherine followed. George, Fliss and I stayed chatting for a bit, soaking up the warmth. Then George announced he was 'off to Bedfordshire' and put on the fireguard before shaking me by the hand and kissing the top of his daughter's head. Fliss and I didn't say much. At one point, she rolled herself a cigarette and started to smoke it out of the window and some of the ash was blown back by the night breeze and scattered like snow across the carpet.

'You shouldn't do that in here,' I whispered, trying to keep my voice light.

She laughed.

'What are you going to do, Martin – spank me?'

I looked away.

'You're so easy to embarrass,' she said. She flicked the cigarette out of the window, pulled it to and came and sat next to me, her leg against mine. Fliss laid her head on my shoulder. Her hair smelled of wet leaves. My neck became stiff and heavy. I slipped to the edge of sleep, drawing back with a start as my head fell forwards. I noticed Fliss's hand on my chest. She was breathing deeply, a trail of air catching in her throat like a growl every time she exhaled. I said her name. She woke shaking her head.

'Shit. What was I saying?' She thumbed the corner of her mouth, checking it for saliva. Her face had a blurry quality, jumbled and out of focus.

'Nothing.'

Fliss grinned.

'Well that's lucky. Because I was having the filthiest dream.'

She tilted her face up towards mine questioningly.

'No?'

I moved her hand gently back to her lap.

'No, Fliss.' I stood. 'Nothing personal.'

'Yeah, yeah, that's what they all say.'

'I don't—'

'I'm fine,' she snapped. 'You go. I'm going to stay here for a bit.'

She swung her legs up onto the sofa and curled in on herself. She was wearing denim shorts and opaque tights and a lumberjack shirt over a T-shirt printed with the image of a screaming skull. She looked so young lying there, so defenceless.

'Night, Fliss.'

She didn't hear me. I think she was already asleep.

And now here George was, acting oddly, saying he wanted to speak to me. For a moment I wondered if Fliss had said anything. Ben's sister had her charms, but she was nothing if not unpredictable. A fragment of a Burtonbury chemistry lesson came back to me unbidden. Francium: the most unstable of all the naturally occurring elements. No more than a single ounce of it present in the earth's crust at any one time. Boiling point unknown. Fliss wouldn't have accused me of ... of ... no, she wouldn't. Would she?

'You've been a great friend to Ben,' George said abruptly. 'We – Katherine and I – are more grateful than we can say.'

'It's only—'

'Please.' He raised his hand. 'Let me finish, Martin.'

The window ledge was pressing into my naked back. I pushed harder against it until it began to be a dull pain.

'In many ways, you are part of the family,' George continued. 'And we would like to – to—' He pulled at the lobe of his ear and I realised he was nervous and that I had never seen him in a state of anxiety before. 'To formalise the arrangement, as it were. Katherine and I are aware that you are in a financially precarious situation. Your mother ...' He paused, ever tactful. 'I understand she is not in a position to help you and we would like to do so. I don't know if you have plans after university' – I shook my head – 'but I'm sure, from the sounds of things, you will take a very good degree and it seems only fair that we, as a family, support you in your future endeavours. Katherine and I would like to make a contribution towards that.' He shuffled his feet. 'As I say, you've been an incredibly *loyal* friend to Ben.' He left a tiny space around the edges of that word, emphasising it most particularly. Then he turned and looked directly at me. 'This would be a way of ensuring that might continue.' We met each other's gaze.

'Of course,' I said.

George's face softened. He clapped his hands together.

'Splendid,' he said and the torpid air between us became suddenly lively with promise. 'I'm glad we understand each other.'

'We do,' I said quietly. I walked over to him and although I had never done anything like it before, I put my arms around George and hugged him. My bare chest itched with the scratchiness of his dressing gown. He smelled of sweat and ginger Roger & Gallet soap. He was bulkier than Ben and, at the same time, his flesh was more flaccid and hung loosely from his bones. George patted me awkwardly on the back.

'Ah, ah, there. Really. There's, uh, no need, Martin. Really,' he said again, trying to withdraw and subtly push me away. But each time he shifted back, I moved forwards to fill the gap. The towel between him and my nakedness seemed suddenly thin and flimsy. I had tucked the hem of it into itself like a knot. It could quite easily slip and fall to the ground.

231

I knew I was making George uncomfortable and I delighted in it. After years of painstaking effort, the power balance between us had shifted perceptibly in my favour. He knew what I knew about his son. He knew the damage I could cause. Naturally, I'd never do anything – wouldn't dream of it because Ben was after all my best friend – but I'd have been lying if I said I hadn't hoped for some kind of acknowledgement from the Fitzmaurices of what I had done. It was a noble act. It deserved gratitude. And while I hadn't expected to make any monetary gain from this sorry situation, now that George outlined it so logically, it seemed at once to make perfect sense. I was like a son to them. It was only right they should treat me as such.

'Right,' George said. 'That's quite enough of that.' He pushed me away, more forcefully this time, and, amused, I allowed him to disengage. The colour in his cheeks was heightened, each one mottled by a tracery of burst capillaries.

'Thank you, George.'

'Let's say no more about it.' He patted me on the shoulder. At the door, with one foot already in the corridor, he turned. 'I'll need your bank details in due course,' he said, as casually as someone asking where the dishcloth was.

'Yes,' I said. 'Oh, and George …'

'Mmm?'

'Happy Christmas.'

'You too, old chap. You too.'

Three weeks later, my bank account received the first quarterly payment of £10,000.

Notebook of Lucy Gilmour

HE THOUGHT I DIDN'T KNOW ABOUT THE MONEY. Poor old Martin. Half the time, he's just a naive person pretending to be suave. He believes I don't notice. But I notice everything. When you're married to someone you don't trust, you have to do a lot of noticing. When you wake up to the fact that, despite your attempts to see the best in everything your husband does, he is not a particularly nice person, you need to be on your guard. You need to store up the scraps, to gain power in increments. And you need not to let on you know.

You need to keep acting sweetly and stupidly and looking sad at the appropriate moments, as if life has defeated you, as if the stuffing has been knocked out. I was good at that. If you make yourself small and unobtrusive, it's amazing what you can get away with. Martin left me pretty much to my own devices. We were, thanks to the Fitzmaurices, comfortably well off, so I didn't need to worry about work: the odd bit of freelancing here and there; some proof-reading; a bit of web design.

'Were you happy?' Keith asked me this morning, his tone scrupulously calm.

Was I? Not exactly. But I wasn't unhappy either and it's possible the entire notion of happiness is overrated anyway. Contentment with flashes of happiness is the most we can hope for. I knew why I had married Martin and I knew he would never be emotionally available and there we had it. I didn't expect it to turn out the way it has, but I suppose all it proved was that I am deeply fond of him. A rooted affection that comes from understanding someone so well. I knew his flaws. The biggest one of them all was his blind devotion to the Fitzmaurice family.

It would have surprised Martin to know how clearly I saw him. He thought he was so good at keeping secrets – especially when it came to the money. But it's not as if you can ignore big lump sums of cash regularly appearing in your spouse's bank account, at least not when you know he's written the access code down in his Moleskine diary and all you have to do to log on is copy out the numbers faithfully, type in the name of his school and then make an educated guess at his password, which wasn't difficult at all. Do you want to know his password? Do you really? It's pathetic. It's 'Fitzmaurice' followed by the day and month of his birthday.

Like I said, pathetic. He was so desperate to be one of them. So madly, fatally desperate.

'Did you ever tell him how you felt?' Keith asked. He had heard about the fracas with Lady Fitzmaurice in the visiting room and wanted to delve deeper into my relationship with them. I looked at the framed print above the fireplace. It was one of those 1950s tourism advertisements: a painted scene of a yellow motor car driving through Alpine countryside with 'Switzerland' printed in bold red letters across the bottom.

'Did you deliberately choose that for its neutrality?' I asked.

'I'm sorry – what was that, Lucy?'

'The poster. Switzerland. Famously neutral. As all the best therapists must be.'

I caught a twitch of a smile on his face. He removed his round-rimmed spectacles and cleaned them on the edge of his shirt. Without them his face looked exposed and vulnerable.

'I hadn't thought of it like that,' he said, finally sliding the glasses back up the bridge of his nose. 'But now that you've pointed it out, I rather like the idea.' He uncrossed and recrossed his legs. 'So. Did you ever tell Martin how you felt about the Fitzmaurices?'

I sighed. He was impossible to divert. The truth was I hadn't ever raised it with Martin because I hadn't wanted to embarrass him. His sense of self was so intricately bound up in the idea of being part of the Fitzmaurice family that confronting him about being little more than their paid chattel would have been his undoing. He wouldn't have accepted it and I might have said something unkind. Of course they don't love you, Martin. They're using you! They're exploiting *your* love for *them*! You know what these payments are, Martin? Hush money, pure and simple.

That's how it would have gone. And then the whole fragile edifice would have crumbled. Besides, it was nice not having to worry about money. There. I said it. And if the price for that was the occasional stilted and awful dinner party at Ben and Serena's, then I just had to suck it up. Didn't mean I liked it though. Not. One. Bit.

Naturally I thought about the girl. Victoria Dillane, killed in a car accident at the age of eighteen. Life tragically cut short. No promising career as a lawyer. No marriage or children. Just a funeral in a rural church in Somerset. No flowers, please. Donations to the Red Cross.

It was covered in all the local papers. It didn't take a genius to work it out. I could see from Martin's bank statements that the first instalment of cash came in 1994. I had a hunch something had gone on between the two of them before I came on the scene. Otherwise, why the money? Why the constant oscillating vibrations of their love–hate tension?

So I sought out a connection. I typed Martin and Ben's names into Google and searched backwards. There were plenty of distractions to sift through at first – social diaries detailing dreary parties they had both attended in their twenties; a photograph of them in *Tatler* magazine at a polo match; some archived rugby match reports from their schooldays and one small item in the *Burtonbury Gazette* with the headline 'Scion's Son Off To Cambridge' with a snapshot of a grinning, teenage Ben.

It took a while to find the relevant newspaper article but then there she was: Victoria Dillane.

The incident had been major news in Cambridge for weeks. It helped that she was so photogenic. There seemed to be a ready supply of photographs: smiling, young face looming out brightly from above her black matriculation gown; standing by a pony, hair netted neatly underneath a riding hat; looking away from the camera at a sunset on a family holiday to the south of France; laughing and wearing a clingy pink dress on the occasion of her school leavers' ball. I looked them all up online. There was plenty of stuff about Victoria but only one cached entry made reference to the passenger in the car: 'Ben Fitzmaurice, the eldest son of Lord and Lady Fitzmaurice, and an undergraduate at Queens' College Cambridge was travelling in the back seat at the time. He escaped serious injury.' A couple of short items mentioned 'an eighteen-year-old male driver' who had been arrested on a charge of careless driving. The driver, it was reported, had passed a breathalyser test and blamed the sudden appearance of a fox in the road for losing control of the wheel. There was a news-in-brief some months later saying that the case had been dropped by the CPS.

That was it. It was hard not to think that someone, somewhere, had done a very effective clean-up operation. And that an integral part of that clean-up involved keeping Martin Gilmour quiet.

Which raised all sorts of questions, didn't it?

VIII.

I GIVE THEM JUST ENOUGH TO PIQUE their curiosity – the car, the Pitt Club, Vicky, the slipperiness of an unfamiliar road – and when Grey Suit asks me who was driving, I look him in the eye and say: 'No comment.'

That should do it, I think. It's up to them to fill in the blanks. I don't see why I should make it too easy for them.

But this should set them along the right course. After all, even two police officers as dense as this pair can't fail to be a little bit excited by the careful trail of breadcrumbs I've left leading them into the heart of the labyrinth. Ben Fitzmaurice. Aristocratic scion. Wealthy socialite. Future MP. I can see the cogs whirring in their over-exerted little minds: there'd be a lot of media coverage, wouldn't there? And surely they'd be commended for doing their jobs so thoroughly. An award, perhaps: the professional equivalent of a feather in the cap.

'Yes, sir,' I can imagine Grey Suit saying as a florid-faced superior pins some ridiculous medal to his lapel. 'At first, we thought it was just a domestic incident but then we ascertained the facts and saw it was a much larger crime.'

I have no loyalty left to Ben. For years, he traded off an arrogant certainty that I wouldn't say anything. That is now over. It has to be. After what happened that night at the Fitzmaurice party, I don't feel I owe the ungrateful little shit anything. And when he falls from his great, self-appointed height, I will be there to see it.

I think of the *tricoteuses*, those women who sat next to the guillotine during the French Revolution and knitted during the intervals between public executions. Knit one. Purl one. Knit one. Purl one and soon I'd have my own Phrygian cap to wear while he bled.

'It must have been a very traumatic episode for you, Martin,' Beige Hair says.

We have just returned to the interview room after a short break and she smells of tuna mayonnaise and something else, some background note of manufactured saltiness – smoky bacon crisps, perhaps. You'd think she could have popped a mint in her mouth.

'It was very upsetting,' I say. But I hadn't been especially upset at the time. I was sad about Vicky, I suppose, but I had barely known her and afterwards, in the confusion that followed, I was so worried about Ben's well-being that I didn't have much time to wallow in my own feelings.

After the accident, we waited by the car's crumpled carcass until the paramedics came.

Ben didn't say much in the back of the ambulance on the way to the hospital. His shoulders were wrapped in a metallic blanket, the sort marathon runners wear after they cross the finish line. His face was pale apart from a scratch running from the outer edge of his eyebrow to the centre of his forehead. At one point, I remember, I reached out and touched the side of his face. He let my hand rest there and then shifted to one side, the blanket rustling. I had wanted to reassure him, but we both knew it was overlain with so much else. I was aware that we had reached some pivotal point in our friendship: that from now on, no gesture would be taken at face value. It would always represent something else.

'At the same time, Martin, I'm guessing it was a bonding experience,' Beige Hair says. 'I mean, as tragic as it was, when you go through something like that, it brings you closer?'

Again, the unnecessary sound of a question mark at the end of a statement.

There is a pause. Beige Hair glances at me expectantly.

'Wouldn't you say?'

'We were already close.'

Grey Suit, who has been staring at me throughout this exchange, now makes a point of turning to look at the wall.

'So,' he says, still looking at the wall. 'Why were the Fitzmaurices paying you all this money, then?'

'Like I said, I was a son to them—'

Grey Suit gives a forced laugh; a showy guffaw intended to demonstrate how ludicrous he finds me.

'I've got a son, Martin, and I don't pay him £40,000 a year.'

'Possibly because you don't have that kind of money at your disposal,' I say coolly.

Grey Suit's eyes harden.

'Even if I did,' he says slowly, 'I wouldn't give anyone that kind of money without a very good reason.'

I sigh.

'How much longer is this going to take? I already—'

'Shall I tell you what I think, Martin?'

'I'm sure you're going to whether I like it or not.'

'I think Ben was driving the car that night. I think he'd been drinking. I think he took the wheel and drove the car off the road because he was so hammered he couldn't even see straight. And you—' He jabs his finger at me. 'You decided to take the blame for him. And you know what that is? That's wasting police time. That's obstructing the course of justice. That's helping someone get away with murder—'

'Hardly murder,' I mutter under my breath.

'I'm sorry – what was that?'

'Nothing.'

'Serious charges, Martin. Serious charges that you don't seem to be taking that seriously. So I want you to think very, very carefully before you say anything else.'

Grey Suit sits back. I imagine his heart beating with such force beneath his chest that it sucks the skin out of shape.

Beige Hair interjects, her voice soft.

'You were acting from the best of motives, Martin,' she says.

'You wanted to save your friend. But now? Now, it's time to tell the truth, yeah?'

My face is blank but underneath, I feel adrenalised: a surge of cortisol roaring through my bloodstream. I'm glad they're taking the bait. And when Ben Fitzmaurice is hauled up on murder charges, I suspect he and Serena will be very sorry they underestimated me.

'Why does he deserve your loyalty?' Beige Hair asks. 'Help us to understand, Martin. We need to know what happened.'

'I can't see what any of this has to do with it. It's ancient history.'

'But it's all connected, isn't it?' she says.

Yes, yes it is. I'm aware, even as I'm doing this, that I will go down too. But I'm ready. It's inescapable. If I thought DC Nicky Bridge were clever enough to understand, I would tell her the problem is that everything is now so deeply intermeshed I no longer know where I finish and where Ben starts. We are, in the end, just two chambers of the same poisoned heart.

2 May

Marquee, Tipworth Priory, midnight

WE HAVE BEEN DANCING FOR TOO LONG. My feet are tired, the hard leather of new shoes pinching my toes and rubbing against the tender part of my ankle where the nub of a blister is starting. Lucy is whirling her arms above her head, spinning around so that the hem of her dress flares out. She is holding a glass of champagne aloft and as she moves, drops of it spill out onto strangers' shoulders and I spot one balding gentleman looking startled, then baffled before taking out his pocket handkerchief and using it to mop his shiny pate. He leans in to an elderly lady with grey-blonde hair set like concrete around her face, and he says something in her ear and points up to the marquee roof and she follows his gaze and cranes her scraggy neck and then they huddle more closely to each other and leave the dance floor, transmitting wordless disapproval as they go. Lucy, oblivious, whirls on.

There have been several speeches, each one delivered from the central stage by Ben's friends and family. I wasn't asked to say anything. I pretended not to mind and told myself it was because Ben knew I had a horror of public speaking but I was hurt. Especially when Andrew Jarvis took the microphone and delivered some boorish nonsense about what a 'legend' Ben had been at school. Nauseating.

Serena stood in her shimmering dress and dabbed at her eyes and apologised for being emotional and then told us what a great dad Ben was and how lucky she was to have him and then, horrifyingly, she said, 'This one's for you' and a small jazz band appeared from nowhere and Serena, who had never as far as I knew sung anything in her life other than in the shower, launched into a patchy rendition of 'My Funny Valentine'. Everyone cheered and applauded but, really, she was barely in tune the whole way through.

Ben bounded onto the stage and kissed her, placing his hand on the arch of her naked back. The buttons on his shirt were coming apart and his eyes were simultaneously floating and focused and I could tell that he'd taken some coke and that he was surfing the crest of a wave of his own manic confidence.

He gave a brilliant speech. Of course he did. At one point, he invited his mother on stage. I hadn't known Lady Katherine was at the party but there she was, walking up the stairs in her recognisably upright way: a posture that was half-diffidence, half-elegance and entirely untouchable. Her hair was white and looked as if it would crinkle to the touch. She was wearing a belted jacket and skirt in raw silk. Her face was powdered and her neck was weighted down by an enormous emerald and diamond necklace.

I hadn't been in touch with her since George's funeral. His death had made her even more unapproachable. At the door to the church, she had taken my hand as if it were something rotten. I had kissed her lightly on the cheek and said how sorry I was and she had nodded and said, 'I know, Martin. Thank you.' But there had been no warmth and over the months that followed, I realised I didn't want to see her again. Perhaps it was grief. Whatever it was, I had the uncomfortable sense that when Katherine looked at me, she saw something I was trying to hide.

I stared at Ben on stage, bathed in a halo of light, grinning and boyish and charming. I thought, briefly, of Magnus: the dead little brother, that small boy with the pudding-bowl hair I had only ever seen in pictures, whose existence was never mentioned by the family. The Fitzmaurices grew their silence like scar tissue.

After the speeches, a purple curtain suspended across the back of the stage was cut loose. As it dropped, we heard the strains of a popular song currently dominating the charts and then, emerging from the shadows, we saw the silhouetted shapes of the world's biggest boy band taking formation. All five of them were dressed in matching floral-printed suits. I guessed Gilly had been wrong about the middle-of-the-road rock band.

'We gotta get through what we gotta get through,' they sang, wholly committed to the nonsense of the lyrics. 'You gotta help me and you know it too-oo-oo.'

Lucy threw herself into it straight away. It had always surprised me how much she loved to dance. You wouldn't expect it of her, but there she was, mouthing all the words, stamping her feet in time to the beat. Before long, a crowd had gathered around her and I could only just make out the back of her neck and the glinting clasp of her necklace.

I wasn't going to join in but then I saw the Prime Minister and his wife on the outer edges of the circle. Edward Buller was doing his best to shimmy his hips but was too stiff to make it seem natural. His wife clicked her fingers and shrugged her narrow shoulders, pecking at the music like a bird. I slid towards them. The song ended and everyone stopped, embarrassed they'd been caught out by the silence, and then a new guitar chord struck up and we resumed our positions, becoming once again a heaving mass of movement.

I moved closer. I could see him out of the corner of my eye. The music swooped and swerved and bounced. I reached out and placed my hand on the sleeve of Edward Buller's jacket. He didn't notice. I tugged at the sleeve.

'Edward,' I said, raising my voice so it could be heard. 'Ed.'

He turned, his face lightly coated with sweat.

'Yes?'

'It's Martin. Martin Gilmour.'

Behind him, his wife had stopped dancing.

'Of course,' he said. 'Of course, Martin. How are you?'

I knew he didn't remember me but I was so relieved not to have made a fool of myself that I played along.

'Good, thank you. I think the last time we met was at Ben's summer party a few years ago.'

'Ha! Must have been, yes. Must have been.'

I realised I was still holding on to his jacket sleeve and he was trying to pull away. I let it go.

'Well, very nice to—'

'I'm Ben's best friend,' I blurted out. 'From Burtonbury.'

The smile on Buller's face froze and then dropped.

'Darling,' his wife was saying, 'we really should go and get some food.'

'Yes. We should. Enjoy the party – ahh …'

'Martin,' I said. 'Martin Gilmour.'

'Great meeting you.'

He pumped my fist up and down. As he left, I noticed his social smile stuck back in place like a nicotine patch.

I stood there for a moment surrounded by people but circled by that familiar loneliness. Drink, I thought. I must get more drink.

'Sweetie!' I heard Fliss's voice and then felt her wrap her arms around me from behind. I was awash with gratitude.

'Fliss, darling.' Too late, I realised she had her face pressed as closely as possible to mine and then her lips were on my mouth and she was trying to kiss me.

'Fliss,' I said, extricating myself. 'No.'

She threw her head back, roaring with laughter.

'Oh Mart, I keep forgetting. You're not into me like that. I know, babe, I know. But you can't blame a girl for trying.'

Her hair was glittering, full of tiny shiny scraps of silver that she had threaded into plaits. She hugged me and I could smell her body odour. She was one of those women who didn't believe in anti-perspirant. Her mustiness was part of her attraction. It was unregulated, like the rest of her.

'Gorgeous Mart,' she drawled and then, suddenly serious, she added: 'You know, whatever happens, you have to believe I …'

She stopped and put the tips of her fingers to her mouth and then Serena, silently, was at her side, a toned, tanned arm around her sister-in-law's shoulders.

'Felicity,' she said. 'There you are. I have to kidnap you, I'm afraid. Family photograph.' She looked at me. 'You don't mind, do you, Martin?'

'No, no, of course.'

They disappeared back into the tidal pull of the party. I left Lucy on the dance floor and walked back into the main house.

'Gimlet, sir?'

A waiter passed me a glass. It was the one from earlier, who looked like a ballet dancer. He smiled at me, accentuating the groove underneath each cheekbone.

'You looked like you needed that, sir.'

'Mmm. I did.'

I let my eyes trail over his chest, down towards the trousers, the buckle on his belt, the shoes scuffed with mud from the garden. And when he moved away from me, I followed him through the doors and the long warren of corridors until we got to the temporary kitchen that had been set up by the caterers and I could feel my heart thumping with expectation and I wanted to reach out and touch him because I was worried, then, that this was not happening and he was not real and then he turned and smiled at me again and so I kept following.

He put down his tray on a steel table and carried on through the kitchen, moving with that same fluid grace, and beyond the tent was the grassy lawn and the maze in the distance where the ghost of the monk was said to walk and then there was a low wall and he sat down and lit a cigarette and offered me a drag. I took it, sharing the space where his mouth had just been and then we were kissing and his tongue was in my mouth and I could taste his smoke and my smoke and the sharp, cool juniper of the gimlet and his hands were in my shirt, tracing the concavities between my ribs, and I let him do everything and I tried not to think too much about what it meant and I tried to let my mind unfurl and expand and be consumed by this moment and I felt all the strange conflicting thoughts that had jangled in my cerebral cortex since the beginning of time, I felt them start to evaporate and blow away in the night's blackness.

Behind us, the sound of whooping and the thud of a low, persistent bass note.

He knelt on the grass in front of me, unzipped my trousers, pushed them down to my ankles and then, as if he owned me, as if he knew exactly what I needed, he pulled me towards him roughly and took my cock in his mouth. I groaned. He slid his mouth up and down, stroking the tip with his tongue. I pushed my dick back into his mouth, holding his head in my hands so that I could push further into him. I wanted to fuck every part of him, to ram my dick against the back of his throat until he couldn't contain the size of me. He sucked and licked and cupped my balls and I moved my hands from his head to his shoulders, wanting simultaneously to push him away and pull him into me, wanting to say yes and no and yes and no and then, with his mouth wet and smooth, I came and there was nothing but the bright, white bliss of release.

A second of silence. Another.

I disentangled myself.

The waiter, still on his knees, looked up at me.

I couldn't bear it.

'I'm sorry,' I said, 'I don't know what happened. Too much to drink. You see, I'm not … I'm not … like you.'

He wiped his mouth with the back of his hand.

'You are wrong,' he said, his voice accented and precise. He shrugged his shirt back into place. 'You are exactly like me.'

He left me sitting on the wall. For a long time, I didn't go back into the party.

Notebook of Lucy Gilmour

AT FIRST, I DIDN'T EVEN NOTICE HE'D GONE. I was so used to Martin disappearing as and when he felt like it that it took a while to register his absence from the marquee. Besides, I was having fun. The music was great.

I was dancing with a man I'd met once before at one of Ben and Serena's awful soirees and although I couldn't for the life of me remember his name, he turned out to be a pretty good mover. When the boy band left the stage and the DJ started, things heated up. The man drew me closer to him and somehow managed to manoeuvre himself so that my legs were straddling his left thigh. He started nibbling at my neck.

'What are you doing?' I said.

'What does it look like?'

'I'm married.'

'So am I.'

'OK, but ...' I disentangled myself. 'No offence,' I said.

'None taken.'

And we carried on dancing as if nothing had happened. It's not that I wasn't tempted – I was – but I'm constitutionally monogamous. The idea of cheating brings me out in a rash. I'm pretty sure Martin's never cheated on me.

Anyway, the music was pumping and there I was having fun for the first time that evening. For the first time in months, actually. Then Ben came up behind me and put his hands proprietorially on my shoulders.

'Hi, babe. Know where LS has got to?'

And that's when I saw he wasn't there. He wasn't anywhere in the marquee either. Or in the main house. Wherever I looked, I couldn't find him. Arguably it didn't help that I couldn't exactly walk in a straight line. I kept going up to people I thought I knew and asking them if they'd seen him and it was only afterwards I realised I didn't know them at all, it was simply that they were famous and that's why I recognised them. I was drunk. Drunker than I'd been in a long, long while. But the only way to withstand it was to drink more, I told myself, and I swiped a bottle of champagne from one of the tables and started sipping it straight from the neck.

I wandered through the main hall, past the enormous fireplace, and then outside onto the front lawn where the cloakroom girls were slouching and giggling and the purple and white lights were still beaming across the front of the house. In the trees, the gasping sound of a couple; a tangle of legs and arms. I stood for a moment on the gravel feeling the prick and crunch of it through the thin soles of my party shoes. I looked up at a full moon. I lifted the bottle of champagne to my lips and took a sip. It had been an all right night after all, I thought to myself. Much better than expected. In the tipsy headiness of that moment, I caught myself thinking that life wasn't all that bad, when you thought about it.

A bird made a noise. An owl, maybe. I was useless with birds and had always found the flap of their wings and the sharpness of their beaks disturbing: alien beings with their feathers and tiny, darting black eyes. I turned in the direction of the sound and saw the outline of the chapel and beyond it a dark mass of space where Ben had said the maze was. The darkness shifted and a human shape became visible, walking rapidly across the grass until it was swallowed up by the shadow of the house.

'There you are.'

Serena.

'What are you doing out here all on your own?'

She appeared beside me, the skirt of her silver gown bunched up in one hand. Hair was falling loosely from her chignon in a way that made the disarray seem intended. Her eyelashes were dense and spidery. When she blinked, she did so slowly, as if they were too heavy for her face.

'Taking a breather,' I said, refusing to be embarrassed by the bottle of champagne I was holding.

'Mmm.'

She summoned over a man in a black suit brandishing a walkie-talkie.

'Carlos, darling, do you have a cigarette I can cadge?'

'Of course, madam.'

He took out a packet of Marlboro Golds from his inside jacket pocket and offered her one, stooping to light it for her. Serena took a long drag. When she removed the cigarette from her mouth, it was sticky with lip gloss. She shivered and closed her eyes in rapture.

'God that's goooood.' She offered it to me. 'Want some?'

I shook my head.

'That's right. I always forget you don't smoke.'

(I don't think Serena ever actually forgets but she pretends to do so in order to demonstrate that I'm not important enough for her to think about.)

'Looks like you're pretty well covered in the drinks department anyway,' she continued, craning her neck to see the bottle.

'It was going spare,' I said.

Serena didn't reply. She was a woman unafraid of silence. She took her time finishing her cigarette and then stubbed out the butt with the toe of her silver stiletto.

'Cleaners'll pick it up. That's what we pay them for, right?' She stared at me. 'We need to talk to you.'

She took my wrist, holding it tightly and started leading me back into the house.

'What the ...' I tried to shake her off but her grip was strong. 'Where ...'

'Shhh,' she said. 'This way.'

She pushed through a door I hadn't noticed before and we found ourselves in a narrow corridor, away from the rest of the party. The hallway was dimly lit. At the far end, a bulb flickered arrhythmically. Clearly the interior decorator hadn't got to this bit yet.

'I don't know where Martin is,' I said. 'He'll wonder where I've gone.'

'Oh he's here already,' Serena replied, pulling me along. 'Ben found him.'

She guided me into a room about half the size of the kitchen with a desk along one wall and floor-to-ceiling shelves which were empty of books. A large scene of Venice hung to my left, the oils dulled by cracking varnish. There was a bulky shape in one corner covered by a dust-sheet and an unlit fireplace in front of which were four leather armchairs. Ben and Martin sat in two of them, facing us as we approached.

'Found her,' Serena said. Ben grinned but the grin made no difference to the rest of his face. Martin angled his head towards me but didn't turn. He seemed to be focusing on some unfixed point in the mid-distance. The atmosphere was skewed. Something was wrong.

I clutched the champagne bottle closer to me and walked over to sit in one of the armchairs.

'What's going on?' I said, and that was when Ben started to speak.

3 May

Study, Tipworth Priory, 1 a.m.

BEFORE A THUNDERSTORM HITS. Electric current in the air. A certain heaviness in the sky, squeezing your head like a tightening clamp. The water waiting to fall. A mass of it accumulating in the belly of a cloud, droplet upon droplet until the skin breaks. A storm 'gathers' like a crowd or the bunched-together pleating of a skirt, each stitch adding volume, each person adding density, until it reaches the point of being too big to contain. And then? Explosion.

'Come and sit down, darling,' Ben said to Lucy. I heard her walk into the room, my wife's familiar footstep, and part of me wanted to get up and push her back outside, to warn her not to venture one inch closer. I couldn't look at her. Every time I tried to meet Lucy's eye, I thought of the waiter outside, kneeling in front of me on the night-damp grass.

I was angry at her, still, for believing I was good enough. That I had it in me to try.

She sat on the armchair next to me. She had a bottle of champagne in one hand and for a brief moment this afforded me the flicker of a smile. Lucy crossed her feet. I focused on the straps of her new shoes. I knew that, as soon as we got back to the hotel room, she would take these shoes off with a sigh of relief. She would have a bath, no matter how late it was, and she would wash her face with a scrap of white muslin and brush her teeth before going to bed. In all the years I had known her, Lucy had always done this. A creature of routine.

I thought of the Tipworth Premier Inn with longing. How I wished we were back there right now, lying on the cheap foam mattress, with nothing to do except fall asleep. Instead, we were here, in this room, listening to the dying sounds of the party outside, waiting for someone to say something.

Serena perched on the edge of Ben's armchair, draping an arm around his shoulders. Her dress fell to the floor like a mermaid's tail. Her earrings glinted in the low lamplight. Outside, there was the sound of dismantling. I wondered where it was coming from. Too early for the marquee to be taken apart by the Fitzmaurice minions.

The guests had started to trickle out into the night, back to their normal lives. The beneficence of Fitzmaurice hospitality would soon be just a glittering memory to be held up occasionally to the light and the events of the last five hours would collapse into vague reminiscence. The party would dissolve from solidity into a series of dissolving half-questions: 'Do you remember …?' 'Wasn't it fun when …?' 'Didn't we meet at …?'

They were dazzling, these Fitzmaurice parties, and then they were nothing. The fizz of a sparkler burnt to its end and then discarded, a bent piece of metal suddenly revealed for its disappointing self.

Next to me, Lucy took a sip of champagne straight from the bottle. I circled her wrist with my hand. I felt safer with her here.

'Sorry to drag you guys away from all the fun,' Ben said. He leaned forward in his chair, elbows on his knees, hands steepled together. The shoulders of his jacket bunched up. He looked like he was about to explain something in the manner of a trendy lecturer, one of the popular ones the girls have crushes on and the male students want to go for drinks with.

Serena was stroking the back of his neck as he talked. I found the soft movement of her hand intensely distracting. Stroke. Stroke. Stroke. Up. Down. Up. Down. It was a gesture of intimate possession. With every trace of her fingers she seemed to be staring more directly at me.

See what I have, Martin? See? He's mine.

Ben coughed.

'There's something I—'

'We,' murmured Serena, her hand still moving.

Ben corrected himself: '… *we* want to talk to you about.'

And because I was trying to pretend that this was normal, because I still wanted it to be so, because I so desperately wanted our friendship to go back to how it had been when we were boys and nothing had yet complicated it, I said 'Montenegro?' as calmly as I could, even though I knew it wasn't to do with that, and that the prospect of investing in one of his schemes had been used like a bribe to get me into this room.

Serena was still stroking his neck.

'Darling, would you get me a whisky?' Ben asked, and Serena unfolded herself from the chair and went to a drinks cabinet in the corner. I heard the ice clink against the glass. The sibilant hiss of the soda syphon.

'You know, LS, how much we value your friendship,' Ben started again. His pupils were dilated. A tiny pulse at the corner of his mouth was twitching. 'That goes without saying.'

Next to me, I felt Lucy bristle.

'But friendships evolve, don't they?' he said as Serena handed him the drink and resumed her perch, one arm outstretched across the top of the chair. 'And I – we – wanted to talk to you about …' He lifted the glass to his lips but didn't drink. 'About going forwards. There are various …' He made a show of searching for the right word but I sensed this was a well-rehearsed speech and the hand movements were part of the masquerade. Too studied to be real. 'Various complications we need to discuss with you.'

He shifted in his seat, pulling up each trouser leg with a pinch at the knee. Serena twiddled the hanging globe of one earring with her fingers, swinging it lightly to and fro.

'I've been asked by Ed Buller to stand for parliament,' he said.

Lucy made a sound that was somewhere in between a gurgle and a snort.

'Ben,' I said, 'that's wonderful news. You'll be fantastic.'

I meant it, too. I forgot to calculate what this news might mean for me. Because of course Ben wanted to stage this announcement with the appropriate build-up and gravitas. He was a Fitzmaurice, after all. They pretended they never courted attention but they always did. Why else would they have wanted me around so much growing up? It was because they had this innate desire for an outside observer, for a misfit who could double-source their smugness. I was their mirror, placed at just the right angle to provide them with their most flattering reflection.

And now, Ben needed my help. That was why we had been asked here.

I felt lighter. Stupid of me to question our friendship after all this time. I thought back over the party and realised how tense I had been, how everything around me had seemed to shake and vibrate with unease, how I had latched on to Lucy as ballast. I should have had more trust in Ben. My Ben. He was still *my* Ben.

'It's a great move,' I carried on blindly. 'I can't think why you haven't done it before. You're so electable. You've got the ideas, the mind and—' I laughed. 'The charm.'

'But Ben,' Lucy said, 'don't you need to have opinions to be a politician? What do you actually believe in?'

His face hardened. He tried to smile but couldn't.

'Lots of things.'

'It's just I've never really heard you outline a political philosophy,' Lucy continued, the 's' in philosophy sliding around like a marble on glass. 'I'd love to hear it.'

'He doesn't have to justify himself to you of all people,' Serena said quietly.

'What does that mean, Serena? "Me of all people"? Am I not worthy of his ... his ...' Spittle was gathering at the corners of her mouth. Lucy wiped the flecks away with the back of her hand. 'Is my vote somehow less valuable, is that what you're saying? I'm sorry if I'm not up to the Fitzmaurice standards. I realise I don't have a title or a TV career or millions of pounds' worth of cash, but—'

'Lucy,' I said. 'That's enough.'

She glowered at me. The skin around her clavicle was stretched and pink.

'You're drunk. Please. You're embarrassing yourself.'

She shook her head.

'You've no idea, Martin. You've no fucking idea what's coming.'

She sat back.

'I don't know what you—'

I was interrupted by the sound of Ben standing and walking to the fireplace. He leaned against it, clasping his hands easily in front of him. Where did he learn all this stuff? Or was he somehow born with it?

'The reason Serena and I asked you here tonight was to say that we're incredibly grateful for all your many years of loyalty and friendship,' he said, not catching my eye. 'But we're entering a new chapter of our life, one which requires a degree of ...' He cleared his throat. 'Discretion.'

'You know you can always trust me, Ben,' I said. 'You don't even have to—'

'Please.' Pause. 'Let me finish.' The tumbler of whisky was on the mantelpiece, the ice slowly melting in the heat. 'A career in politics is something I've worked towards all my life, but as I'm sure you can appreciate, it doesn't come without its associated risks. One of those risks is that my past life will be raked over by unscrupulous members of the tabloid press and I need to be sure, Ed needs to be sure, that nothing embarrassing will ever come out.'

And then I thought of her. A glimpse of a half-remembered moment. Blonde hair swept up. Head snapped forward. Blood on the windscreen. Legs twisted. A semi-colon of broken glass on the hem of her blue, blue dress. A crumpled, lifeless thing where once there had been the full, vibrant youth of Vicky Dillane.

'Vicky,' I said, and it all made sense.

'Please don't mention that name,' Serena said. Her voice trickled down my neck. I glanced at Lucy. So Serena knew, even though I had thought Ben and I had an unspoken pact that no one else would ever be told. He had betrayed me. And I, stupidly, had never thought to do the same.

Ben, pale in the lamplight, turned towards the wall.

'I know you have been very loyal, Martin, and I trust you feel the Fitzmaurice family have rewarded you handsomely for your efforts.'

'For Christ's sake, Ben, it wasn't an effort—'

'But the time has come for us to part ways.'

Somewhere in the back of my head, a string was stretched taut. It pinged with a single high note and then it snapped.

'What?' I was bleating, pathetic. 'What are you saying? What the fuck are you saying?'

My brain folded in on itself. The few things I had once held certain started to collapse. I was swimming in darkness. Above me, the rain had started to fall and I didn't know where the wetness began or ended or where to find the straight line of the horizon and I was disappearing, as if my skin were becoming the liquid that surrounded it and Ben was on the shoreline: unreachable and watching.

'You will, of course, be suitably compensated,' he was saying. 'It's unfortunate, but there we have it. It would be better, for all of us, if this evening marked the end of our public friendship. You know, of course, that you will always have our deeply held affection, but—'

'But you want him to fuck off out of your life and never breathe a word about the fact you killed someone,' Lucy said, her voice rising. 'Where the fuck do you people get off?'

I stared at her. So she knew as well.

Ben recoiled. Serena rose so quickly she seemed almost to be levitating.

'You really are a foul-mouthed bitch,' she spat, launching into Lucy with venom. 'I don't know how Ben's put up with you all this time. You've always been so superior, always acting so meek, like butter wouldn't melt. Do you think I didn't notice? Think I was too stupid, did you?'

'Darling—'

She brushed Ben aside.

'I'm done,' Serena said. 'They're not worth our time.'

Lucy took a swig from the champagne bottle.

'You're a joke,' she said.

'Well you're a fat, ugly nobody,' Serena shrieked. Her face, usually so composed, was twisted and shrunken. The veins on her neck throbbed.

'Sweetheart.' Ben came to his wife's side and put his arms around her. 'Please. Let's try and keep this civilised, shall we?'

A high-pitched buzzing sound started up in my right ear. I shook my head, trying to silence it.

'Are you saying …' I started and then I had to stop. I gasped for air. My throat was constricted and the next words came out as a whisper, 'You don't want us to be friends any more?'

Ben made no move to come towards me. Was I imagining it or was there a ghost of a smile on his face?

'Well, look, Martin. You have to admit we haven't exactly been close for quite a while now. I know we got on when we were boys but, if we're honest, we don't have a lot in common, do we? I mean, I have the utmost respect for you but I think it's time to go forwards and follow our own paths and—'

Going forwards. That phrase again. That meaningless phrase.

'He's been trying to get rid of you for years,' Serena hissed. 'How do you think it will look if he's publicly associated with a … with a … well, with someone who killed an innocent young girl?'

I couldn't tell if she really believed what she was saying or whether it was the narrative that most suited her purpose.

'You're a leech, Martin,' she continued. 'A leech. And I'm not just talking about the money – although, God knows, that's been a small fortune. You exploited us all! George, Katherine, Fliss …'

At the mention of Fliss's name, I felt tears start to form.

'Does Fliss …' I ventured. 'And Katherine. I mean, is everyone else in agreement?'

Ben nodded.

'George … George never would have allowed this. Ben, you know I didn't …' I couldn't bring myself to say it, to say Vicky's name. 'You know I took the fall for what you—'

He spoke over me, unmoved: 'I'm sorry you're taking it so badly but, really, there'll be a healthy sum in it for you. I'm not going to leave you in the lurch, financially speaking.'

'But Ben,' I pleaded. 'Mate. It's never been about that. Never.'

He was impassive. I pushed myself off the chair and knelt on the floor in front of him.

'You must know that, you must. You're my best friend. I … I … I'm nothing without you.'

'For Christ's sake,' Serena muttered. She turned to Ben. 'Didn't I tell you? Tragic.'

I wanted to reach out, to touch him, to grab the edge of his jacket. I needed to feel the physicality of him, to pull him down so that he could look me in the eye. I was sure that if only I could touch him he would understand, he would become my Ben again, rather than this stilted facsimile of himself.

'Ben. Ben.' I kept saying his name. 'Ben. Please. Please don't do this.'

'Get up, Martin.'

'I'm nothing without you.' The words kept coming without my being able to stop them. But it was true. I existed only in relation to Ben. I had constructed myself around his edges, brick upon brick, assessing each concrete millimetre for what it might mean to him and what it might bring me back. I had wanted so desperately for him to need me that I had forgotten to defend myself from loving him.

I looked up at him. On his face, something like pity.

This was it then. He didn't love me. He never had. I felt very tired. I closed my eyes, sat back on my haunches and waited for the pain to pass. In a moment, I told myself, I would get up. In a moment, I would stand and push back my shoulders and breathe in and out and pretend it didn't matter. I would erect the necessary facade and no one would be able to get close to me. I knew how to do it. I had done it before.

I stood. I was crying. The final humiliation. I covered my face with my hands, not wanting Ben to see.

'We'll arrange for a substantial sum to be transferred to your account,' he was saying. 'In return for which you'll agree to sign a confidentiality agreement drawn up by my lawyers ...'

'So,' I asked stupidly, 'the Montenegro deal ...?'

He looked at me as though he had only just become aware of my presence.

'Martin,' he said, almost kindly. 'There was no deal. It was a way of getting you to stay. But of course, I'm sure I can see a way of letting you in,' he said. 'If that would ... help.'

He went on speaking. On and on and on in the same dry, toneless way. He was so far away from me, so alien. I wondered if I had ever truly known him or had I been deluded all these years, a pawn in a game that was being meticulously played out around me, of which I had no knowledge.

'... will be enough ... financially secure ... appreciation ... great sadness ... realistic ... hope for the future ... elections ... have to think of the party ... sad state of affairs ...'

Disconnected phrases and words seeped into the room. I could make out only half of them. The walls shrivelled and squeezed inwards. The floor spun. I stumbled back to my chair and sat heavily on the leather, waiting for the movement to subside.

'It was never about that,' I said, more to myself than anyone else. 'It was never about the money.'

I could hear Serena's intake of breath and I could imagine, from the backlit cocoon of my hands, the set of her features. She had never liked me. I had never been able to win her round. I hadn't thought it mattered. I hadn't thought she mattered. Wrong again. I had been so focused on fighting the battle, I had forgotten to identify the enemy.

Eventually, the words stopped and there was silence.

Outside, the unnatural sound of a woman giggling.

Then Serena spoke.

'Right. I think you two should be getting back. We'll have our lawyers contact you next week. Where was it you were staying?' She dripped contempt from every pore. 'The Premier Inn, wasn't it?'

'You know,' Lucy said. 'You can't treat people like this.'

'I'm sorry?'

'You should be.'

'No, I meant—'

'You think you're so bloody special. The Fitzmaurices. Like you were born to rule over the rest of us. You think you can chew Martin up and spit him out when you get bored? You can't. You fucking can't. You'll destroy him. Ben,' she said, appealing directly to him, 'he's done nothing but love you all his life, you know that.'

Serena laughed sharply.

'Oh we've all known that for a very long time. It's embarrassing.'

'You've got no heart.'

Serena smiled. She moved with deliberate slowness to the window, the sequins on her dress shifting shape like the sea.

'You know what you need, Lucy?' She picked a stray thread from the curtain and held it between her thumb and forefinger, examining it carefully. 'You need a child. It would make you less … less …' She pretended to search for the right word. 'Bitter.' There was an icy pause. 'Shame you can't find a real man.' Her voice was rising. 'Shame we all know Martin would rather fuck my husband than his own wife.'

The words hit me with full force. I stood. My body felt leaden. Serena came towards me.

'Did you think we didn't notice?' she said, face twisted. 'Wake up, Martin.'

Without warning, she brought the flat of her hand across my cheek and slapped me.

The sound of it radiated outwards like a tuning-fork note.

I didn't see Lucy get out of her chair. By the time I noticed she was standing with the champagne bottle in her hand, it was already too late. A beat passed. Another. Something popped like a bubble and I realised my wife was screaming – a sound I had never heard before. I blinked, then looked at her. Her teeth were bared and the muscles in her arm were gleaming. I was fixated by those muscles. Where had they come from?

She was shouting. The words slipped into each other until they became white noise. She was pointing the finger of one hand towards Serena, moving closer with every jab. Jab. Jab. Jab.

Serena took one step back, then another, then her ankle twisted and her high heel slipped from under her and as she was falling, Lucy launched herself across the room.

'You bitch,' Lucy was shouting. 'You fucking, fucking bitch!'

Serena was flailing. She gripped hold of Lucy's wrists and tried to wrestle her off but Lucy kept pushing her until Serena's back was shoved against the wall.

I couldn't move. Out of the corner of my eye, I saw Ben sprint across the room but Lucy was already raising the champagne bottle, holding it high with one arm stretched upwards, every tendon strained and flexed. I had a moment of pure admiration for the beauty of that arm, for the strength I had never known was there, and I felt pride. Sheer, generous, loving pride. Ben tried to reach out and grab Lucy's wrist but it was too late. Because then Lucy smashed the bottle against Serena's beautiful head.

A gasp. A whimper.

An earring skittered across the parquet floor.

Serena sagged forwards and slumped to the ground.

Lucy dropped the bottle. It didn't break. Rivulets of red trailed across the yellow label.

There was silence.

I moved towards the window and took Lucy's arms, pinning them behind her. I could feel her shaking, the delicate shivering of her flesh. She looked at me wildly. A bruise was forming on her lower lip.

'Shhh,' I said. 'Shhhh now. It's all right. It's all right.'

Ben was on the floor, his ear pressed to Serena's chest shouting at me that we needed an ambulance and would I fucking call a fucking ambulance Martin and there was the rush of footsteps and a sudden crowd of people around us and in the midst of the confusion, I pushed Lucy towards the door and slipped out of the room. In my hand, I had the champagne bottle.

Outside, I flung it hard and long into the lake. The bottle landed with a faraway splash. I held Lucy more tightly to me.

In the darkness, we walked the length of the gravel driveway and out of the gates. I felt detached, as though removed from my own skin, watching these two solitary figures at a distance. What struck me most as we walked was my absence of guilt. For the first time in my life, I had not seen it as my obligation to shield Ben from the worst of what was to come. I was no longer his 'Little Shadow'. Beneath my ribcage, my heart seemed to expand. And behind us, the outline of Tipworth Priory receded against the early-morning sky.

IX.

Tipworth Police Station, 6 p.m.

GREY SUIT IS LOOKING AT ME SCEPTICALLY.

'So let me just check I've got this right.'

There is a scrap of something green stuck in his teeth, which becomes visible when he talks. I wonder how long it will be lodged there before he notices or before someone tells him. I wonder if I should be the one to do it and then I decide not to. It is enjoyable, this feeling of knowing something he doesn't. It gives me the edge.

He glances at me across the table and waits.

'Please,' I say, gesturing for him to carry on.

'You and Mrs Gilmour were summoned to the study after the party at around 1 a.m., is that right?'

'I wouldn't say "summoned" exactly.'

'Right, right, but that's where you went to meet with Lord and Lady Fitzmaurice? To discuss the Montenegro deal?'

I nod.

'So, you have the discussion, all very amicable and business-like, Lord Fitzmaurice outlines the project, you say you need to go away and discuss it with Mrs Gilmour?'

'Yes. I've just told you all of this, why—?'

'We just want to be clear,' Grey Suit says. 'Get the chronology straight. You understand.'

'It's for your own good, Martin,' Beige Hair pipes up, drawing her jacket closer and crossing her arms. She has a silver bracelet on her left wrist, one of those chunky things weighed down by ugly charms one sees advertised every Christmas and Mother's Day.

I point at it.

'That's pretty.'

'Thank you,' she says and immediately pulls down her sleeve to cover the bracelet so that it no longer affronts my line of vision.

'You leave the study at about 1.20, 1.30 a.m.,' Grey Suit says.

'Around then, I think. I can't be completely sure.'

'You close the door behind you and walk down the corridor and it's as you're walking away that you hear a scream and a thud.'

'Yes.'

'So you turn back to check on what's happened and upon re-entering the study you see …' He stops. 'Remind us what you saw.'

Upon re-entering. I shudder. Pointless officialese.

'Serena was on the floor, her back against the wall and Ben was sort of half crouching over her. He was shouting for an ambulance. He clearly knew something was seriously wrong.'

Grey Suit leans back. He hooks his index fingers into the belt loops of his trousers. A stale smell of instant coffee pervades the room. I can't wait to get out of this stuffy little box of implication and incrimination.

'Tell you what I'm struggling with, Martin.' He assumes a storybook expression of confusion: creased forehead, knitted-together brows, uncertainty as drawn by a children's illustrator. 'The four of you had a perfectly reasonable discussion, and then you and Lucy leave, and within a matter of seconds – not even minutes, but *seconds* – something so terrible happens between Lord and Lady Fitzmaurice that he knocks her out with such force she ends up in a coma, even though—'

I try to speak. He waves me quiet.

'Even though not one of the hundreds of guests at the party that night we've questioned saw anything amiss between them. There was no sign whatsoever of marital tension.'

'Well. Ben's anger is a fickle beast.'

'What does that mean?' Beige Hair asks.

'It means he doesn't often show what he's actually feeling,' I say, cautiously dropping the breadcrumbs that will take them further and further into the labyrinth. 'I've seen it happen before.'

'You have? When exactly?'

I shift in my seat. I want to appear uncomfortable, as if it pains me to drop my best friend in it and yet I know that it must be done.

'I can't go into it,' I say.

Beige Hair and Grey Suit exchange a knowing look. Good. They have their suspicions. They have all the pieces, and they know about the bank payments – the Fitzmaurice hush money – so now they just need to slot it all together. Shouldn't be too hard.

What was it they said about the best way to complete a jigsaw puzzle? Go for the corners first. Well, I've given them the corners. And if they want to send me down too, then so be it. But I suspect they're not all that interested in me. It's Ben's scalp they want.

'Are you suggesting something happened at university, Martin? Something between you and Ben? Something to do with the car crash? Something that might, you know, explain these generous payments into your bank account?' Grey Suit asks and I notice that there is an undertone of agitation to his voice, as if he is trying not to show how excited he is. 'Because if something did happen – if, for instance, you took the blame for something that wasn't your fault and if, hypothetically speaking, you're scared of dropping someone in it – then this really is the time to tell us the truth. You have to tell us, Martin.'

I place my hands flat on the table. I drum the passing seconds with my fingers. One. Two. Three.

'I don't think I do,' I say, enjoying their mounting anticipation and meeting it with deliberate calm. 'I don't think I have to tell you anything at all. The last time I checked, I wasn't under arrest.'

Beige Hair stares at the floor, a light flush on her cheeks.

'Speaking of which,' I continue, 'are you planning on charging me with anything? Because my patience really is wearing a little thin.'

Grey Suit coughs.

'We appreciate your co-operation,' he says. 'We won't keep you much longer.'

'Thank you.' I smile. 'By the way, you've got something in your teeth. Just—' I part my lips and mark out the relevant spot in my own mouth with the tip of a precisely placed fingernail, 'there.'

Lucy

IT'S SAD, IN THE END, saying goodbye to Keith. When I first came here, I was so resentful of our sessions. I hated having to explain myself, having my every response probed and prodded as if it were an interesting piece of scientific tissue. But now I've grown used to him. I've found it helpful, I suppose, unpacking some of what went on.

Unpacking. That's one of his words.

'Can we just unpack that a little, Lucy?'

This afternoon, he said: 'I've been impressed by your progress, by your willingness to do the work.'

It was the most forthcoming he'd ever been with me. There was a pressure behind my eyes and I realised I was on the verge of tears and that I hadn't cried (not properly, at least) for what felt like a long time.

'So you don't think I'm a danger to society, then?'

He smiled. The corners of his eyes crinkled behind his spectacles.

'No, I don't. And I've said so to the powers that be.'

'Hope they believe you.'

I haven't told him everything. I haven't lied, exactly. I'm a bad liar. My father once said I had honesty writ large across my forehead. But I am capable of making deliberate omissions, of leaving gaps and silences unfilled by explanation. Besides, it doesn't just concern me, what happened that night in the Tipworth Priory study with Serena. There's what it would mean for Martin, too. If I said anything it would lead to the unravelling of a lie he told to save his best friend; a lie which dropped like a stone through water and sent out ever-widening circles of cause and effect.

I have never spoken to Martin about the girl, Vicky Dillane.

I wonder if anyone other than her parents still thinks of her. Probably not. Maybe a handful of friends who recall her smile on anniversaries and birthdays, whose stomachs lurch when her name comes up. But other than that, she is a forgotten casualty, a chipped-away memory flattened by the Fitzmaurice might. She deserves to be more than a footnote to someone else's history.

You know, it wasn't just for Martin's sake or my own that I did what I did that night. It was for her too. For every woman whose voice has been silenced.

And I'm not meant to admit this, I realise, but hitting Serena with that champagne bottle felt good. It felt like one of the most empowering things I'd ever done. I regret it, of course I do. I don't want to be the kind of person who willingly causes harm to others, especially not to another woman, but in that moment, it seemed the only way to make myself heard. It seemed the only thing the Fitzmaurices would understand. Aggression met with aggression. Something they couldn't buy their way out of.

Martin and I walked back from the party along dark country roads. I took off my shoes. The cool roughness of tarmac under my feet felt solid while the rest of the world was still shimmering. We didn't speak but Martin took my hand in his. It was unlike him, this gesture of intimacy, and I knew that by offering it he was telling me that he understood. He didn't blame me.

Back at the hotel, we lay on our twin beds fully clothed and facing each other, our cheeks pressing down on buoyant synthetic pillows. We agreed to our version of events. We didn't know then how serious the injury to Serena was but we thought there would probably be some sort of investigation. The papers would have a field day.

He said I should go away for a bit, let him handle the fallout and then he suggested coming to The Pines. Martin had been here for a stint in his twenties. Rehab. Paid for by the Fitzmaurices, obviously. He said, apart from anything else, it would do me good. He said he was worried about me and that perhaps I needed some time and space 'to come to terms with things'.

'What things?' I asked.

The light behind the nylon curtain had tilted from bruised black to the greying white of dirty laundry.

'I know ...' Martin hesitated. 'I know how much you wanted children.' He couldn't look at me. 'I'm sorry. About what happened.'

The miscarriage.

'I think ... I mean, I thought ... It was a mistake I didn't want to make.'

I closed my eyes. Pinpricks of light played across the lids.

'You can't control everything, Martin.'

I realised my marriage was over. I think I'd already known for weeks, months leading up to that point. For so long, I hadn't wanted to be alone. Especially not after the miscarriage, when I doubted my own worth, when I needed someone – anyone – to attach myself to.

I had underestimated the power of the Fitzmaurice allure. Being around people like that – wealthy, privileged, beautiful, selfish people – is not good for the soul. They look inwards while giving the pretence of generosity. They are careless with the rest of us. It is not consciously malicious, it is simply a lack of imagination for other people's lives. But the impressionable among us – the misfits, the insecure, the bitter and the vulnerable – we are swept into their golden currents, as weak swimmers overcome by a shining tide. We want to be them while hating them for being it.

But after that night, I didn't want anything more to do with them. I wanted to be out of it. I wanted to wash myself of their lies.

That conversation in the hotel room was the closest I'd ever felt to Martin. Funny, really, that for so long the idea of Ben had been a wedge between us and then, in the course of a single evening, we were bonded by our mutual fury. It was the arrogance of it that enraged me. Chewing up a person and spitting him out when he was no longer useful.

It doesn't justify what I did, but I write this to state the reason for it, to remind myself I am not mad.

Serena had got to me the most. She was so unfeeling. For years I had put up with her undermining smugness and her litany of casual put-downs. She hated Martin without his even noticing. I could never figure out why Ben had married her but now I think that it was to mask his own weakness. Serena was strong and Ben … well, Ben never really knew his own mind. He needed others to make it up for him: his father, his mother, his wife, even the bloody Prime Minister.

Still, I wonder why he didn't just drop us both in it: tell the police it was me and Martin and leave us to rot. It would have been the Fitzmaurice word against ours and it doesn't take much of a leap of logic to know who the police would choose to believe. Perhaps some residual loyalty to Martin prevented Ben from dealing the final blow. Or perhaps he has a longer game plan. Perhaps he wants Martin to owe him a favour for some, as yet, unrevealed reason. I don't know. But I do know that, whatever happens, Ben Fitzmaurice will carry on being as beloved as ever.

That's the problem with charm. It means you get away with stuff. It means you never have to develop a real character because no one remembers to look for one. They're too busy basking in the glow of your attention. They're too busy being impressed.

At the end of our session, Keith stood up and gave me a hug. The neck of his jumper smelled of Persil washing powder. He patted me lightly on the back.

'Good luck, Lucy,' he said.

I tried to say something in response, but the words lodged in my throat. I walked out into the corridor with the scratch of them still there and then I found my way back to my room and closed the door behind me and lay down on my bed and stared at the ceiling.

I knew I wouldn't stay married to Martin. I couldn't. It had gone beyond a point of return. I was a different person from the woman who had married him: the wife who had for so long played the game. When I thought of that long-ago Lucy, it was as if I were imagining a character in a book.

She had changed, over the years. She had been stuck behind a pane of glass and then, without warning, she had punched her way out.

Here she was – here *I* was – and Martin was no longer part of my story. It's not that I had any sort of resentment towards him. I just didn't love him any more.

I started to pack my case: shoes first, then the few T-shirts and jeans I had brought with me, each item rolled up so that it didn't crease. Books. This diary. I put my sponge bag in last, bulky with pill bottles and hairbrush. I shut the top and pressed down hard so that the zip slipped smoothly around the edges.

I took one last look at the room, then rolled the case into the corridor. The carpet was thin and fuzzy. It reminded me of teenage stubble: the wispy facial hair of a boy trying too hard.

There was the sound of a door closing. I turned just as Sandy tapped me on the back.

'Lucy,' she said in her rasping voice. 'Are you going?'

I nodded. 'Last session with Keith this morning. Honourable discharge, I guess.'

She grinned. She was wearing lipstick in an unflattering coral shade. It was too young for her face and bits of it were leaking into the puckered skin around her mouth. Her leather jacket had tassels hanging from the arms. It smelled of having been worn in too many smoke-filled bars. Her hands were jittery.

'Will you—' I paused. 'Will you be OK?'

'Oh yeah, don't worry about me. I'll be fine.' Sandy smiled sadly. 'I always am.'

'If you ever need anything …' I started, but then I didn't know how to finish the sentence. It was just one of those things you said, as a matter of politeness, and it felt fraudulent in this setting.

She took my hand in hers. She shrugged, her bony shoulders coming up around her ears like eagle wings, and without saying anything more, she disappeared back into her room.

When she had gone, I opened my hand. There was a tiny folded scrap of lined paper lying there. Written inside, in shaky black pen, was: *Don't let the bastards get you down* followed by two exclamation marks.

I smiled, then re-folded the paper carefully and put it in my shirt pocket. I thought of Martin. I couldn't stand there with him while the world collapsed.

Don't let the bastards get you down.

I wheeled my suitcase down the corridor and out into the open air.

X.

JUST IN TIME, SERENA WAKES UP.

Most generous of her, I must say.

In fact, it is the first time I can recall that Serena has ever done anything that might be remotely advantageous to my prospects.

Beige Hair and Grey Suit are summoned out of the interview room by a superior. For a while, I am sitting there on my own, listening to the sound of raised voices in the corridor. When they come back, they seem annoyed.

'We've been informed that Lady Fitzmaurice has regained consciousness,' Beige Hair says as she presses the stop button on the unwieldy tape recorder. 'She's told us she slipped.'

I smile. Good.

'As I said: it was an unfortunate accident.'

Beige Hair purses her lips. Grey Suit gives a snort of laughter.

'Yes,' he says, 'well …'

So the police let me go. They have to. I don't admit anything and without any detail, they can't possibly know what happened behind those closed doors in the study that night. Ben and Serena are never going to say anything. Of course they're not. They don't want the attention or the scandal. They don't want tabloid journalists sniffing around, making phone calls, asking awkward questions. They're still hoping I'll agree to their absurd arrangement and keep my mouth shut. I've taken to ignoring Ben's increasingly urgent phone calls. In his desperation, he's even cut me into the Montenegro deal. *It makes no difference*, I want to scream, *you're wasting your time – I've seen how little I mean to you and I cannot un-remember it. I refuse.*

I glance down at my feet. One of my shoelaces is loose. I will have to re-tie it before leaving, I think. Across the floor, Beige Hair is wearing flat ballet pumps in ersatz leather, the flesh of her plump feet spilling out over the edges.

'Must be a relief,' Grey Suit says.

'Naturally.'

'Them being such good friends and all.'

He glares at me, the dislike barely concealed. I meet his stare coldly. His collar is too tight for his neck. I wonder how easy it would be to reach across and push the knot of his tie up until it squeezes all the breath out of his oesophagus and how long it would take for his face to turn red, then purple, then lose colour and I imagine how, at first, he would flail and try to get me off him but I wouldn't relent and then his limbs would get slower and heavier until his only choice was to fall still. How long would all that take? Couple of minutes, probably. The line between life and death is so very faintly drawn.

Not that I'd ever do it.

But I like to picture it. I like to remind myself that I have the capacity to react.

When the interview is over, Beige Hair thanks me for my help. She tells me I'm not to leave the country and she has no doubt they'll be speaking to me again soon. At this, her nostrils flare. She's thinking of Ben, I can tell, of arresting him for that tragic yet indubitably glamorous long-ago crime. It's bound to make the papers. Beautiful young girl. Drunken university poshos. An important family who tried to hush it up.

She shakes my hand briskly. She is like an understudy desperate to get on stage now that the leading lady has been taken ill.

Her fingers are surprisingly small and delicate. I will rather miss her stolid, reliable presence. Grey Suit grunts something unintelligible before leaving the room. Beige Hair is left to gather up the remaining papers from the table, some of the sheets dense with Lucy's neat handwriting. I'm glad she stuck to our story. My loyal wife.

It's nearly 7 p.m. by the time I get out of the police station and the sky is streaked silver with cloud. As I walk into the car park, I can hear excitable whoops from schoolchildren who have presumably been hanging around since school ended. A gaggle of them in navy blue uniforms are huddled in the doorway of the fried chicken shop across the road, counting out pound coins in cupped hands. Where are the parents, I wonder?

A car draws up. In the back, a familiar shape. The driver's door opens and a plain-clothes detective goes round to the passenger side. I see someone shift from the seat and the policeman places a protective hand over the doorframe so that whoever it is doesn't hit his head on the metal.

The person emerges in gradations: a thatch of curled brown hair; loafers; checked shirt that I know has a small hole in the elbow. Ben.

I step behind a wall. The detective is saying something in a friendly manner. Ben grins and nods and twinkles in his ever-charming way. What self-possession, I think; what casual arrogance. And I can't help but admire it still even though I know that his confidence will be short-lived, that everything he once thought certain is about to crumble around him once he steps over that threshold and into the police station.

My heart beats out a quickening rhythm and I imagine walking up to Ben and jabbing him in the chest. I know something you don't know, I want to say. You're losing. You don't even realise what's coming. I will grind your self-satisfaction into dust. You will fall and you will know I have betrayed you and that will be my triumph.

I walk out of the gloom. I take the steps slowly so that he has time to lift his head and register my presence. The smile slips from his mouth.

I stop. I stare. I meet his gaze and hold it. I think of all the times he has made me feel less than him. All those unkindnesses I had

275

tried to convince myself were imagined. All those looks exchanged with Serena, the meaningful suppression of half-conceived sighs. All those offhand jokes made at my expense, until the caricature of me became more believable than the reality, until I became Little Shadow – a person without his own persona, simply a darkening of the imprint left by another, bigger man. I thought of the anxiety it had caused me, the tension I had to pretend didn't exist, of the effort I had made.

I think of a teddy bear, arcing across a room, and a door opening and the first time I heard his voice. I remember a tiny black spot on the cuff of his shirt where a pen had leaked its ink.

I had loved him.

I force myself to breathe.

Inhale. Exhale.

Across the car park, Ben's expression shifts from raw anger to a more muted discomfort. He doesn't even care enough to stay furious with me, I think. As if I am nothing. As if I never meant anything to him.

The detective is talking now and Ben is leaning in closer to hear him and I can hear the murmur of their chatter and it all sounds so easy, so fluid and I realise that Ben is yet again familiar with the unspoken codes of conduct, the unexplained hierarchies of the police station. He'll be telling them he's sorry for the inconvenience and he's sure they can get it all cleared up and yes, thank you, he'd love a cup of tea, white no sugar, and yes, that's kind, his wife is much, much improved although we had a scare there, I'm sure you understand, and yes, the whole thing was an unfortunate accident and they're terribly sorry for wasting your time but Serena had been drinking – they all had! It was a party! – and she'd slipped and hit her head against the fireplace and knocked herself out and there we have it, these things happen don't they and they're just very lucky it wasn't more serious and thank you, *thank you* for taking such trouble to investigate and he was sure they had far better things to do and he was sorry, *so sorry*, and if there was anything he could do by way of recompense and would they accept a few bottles of wine, maybe, from his cellar at Tipworth, just as a token of his gratitude? No? Well then, another time. They'll be up here again soon, now that the renovations have been done and Tipworth is such a lovely quiet town, isn't it? The perfect place for Serena's recuperation. The kids love it. They can run around in a way they never can in London. Do you have kids? Oh well then you know what we're talking about don't you …

The usual patter. Ben does it so well. But he doesn't know what awaits him on the other side of the police station door. Because no amount of charming chit-chat will save him then.

The pair of them walk past me. I am just fifteen metres away from them, maybe twenty. Ben doesn't flinch. There is a sharp red shaving nick on his chin. He takes the steps up to the station entrance two at a time. The automated glass doors swish open and they walk inside.

Wordlessly, I follow. Grey Suit is standing in the lobby. He raises an eyebrow.

'Can I help you, Mr Gilmour?'

'Uh, yes, yes,' I say. 'Would you mind terribly if I used the gents before I head off?'

I can see him dislike me just that little bit more.

'Right. I'll take you through.'

His plodding footsteps lead me back down the corridor, past the interview room and the coffee machine. When we get to the lavatories, Grey Suit gestures towards them with a flourish.

'Here you are, sir.'

'Martin, please.'

'Martin,' he says, flat with disdain.

'Thank you. I know my own way out.'

He nods, then turns back down the corridor.

I am alone at the urinal. I don't need a piss but I wash my hands to make it sound convincing, should anyone be listening. The dryer is one of those eco affairs that pushes out powerful jets of air without ever actually drying anything. I wipe my damp palms on my trousers.

I leave the gents and continue further along the corridor. I have a powerful inclination to go upstairs. It's probably some hangover from my schooldays: the inbuilt knowledge that all the important stuff happens on the higher floors. That's where the senior staff will have their offices. And if I know Ben Fitzmaurice at all, that's exactly where he'll be heading.

I run up the stairs, trying to keep my footfall as light as possible. My mind is filled with a single urge: find Ben, watch him squirm, witness his takedown. I want to see the smugness leak from him as realisation dawns.

The layout upstairs is a carbon copy of the ground floor: a long corridor lined with thin carpet, doors leading off on either side. But these doors have nameplates on the front, each one prefaced by letters intended to denote rank.

I stand, back pressed against the wall, and I see Ben being ushered into one of the rooms by the detective. He is holding a cup of tea. China mug. No polystyrene for him.

'This way please, Mr Fitzmaurice,' the detective is saying. 'We won't keep you long.'

'Thank you,' Ben says and his voice is the special one he uses when talking to traffic wardens or nannies.

I can just about make out another voice from inside the room: low and rumbling, like a wheeled suitcase on tarmac. The door begins to close. I walk rapidly, trying not to break into a run. I catch a glimpse through the narrow opening of the door: a uniformed officer with silver on his epaulettes. He is shaking hands with Ben.

'Detective Chief Superintendent,' Ben is saying. 'Good to see you again.'

Good to see you again?

The words land like a grenade.

Sweat on my back. Dryness in my throat.

Of course, I think.

Of course they know each other. What was it that had first brought them together? Doubles at the tennis club? A shared box at the opera? A cosy seating arrangement at a black-tie charity function?

I start to panic.

I note the smoothness of Ben's voice, the relaxed bearing of his shoulders, the way the policeman stands to greet him, as if Ben were doing them a favour. And because of all this, I know within the space of a single second that nothing will change.

Not one thing.

And then it strikes me with shattering force what a bloody fool I have been.

All this time, I've been playing the cards without remembering the deck was stacked against me. Stupid, stupid Martin, I hear my mother saying. Always forgetting who's really in charge. Always believing he's better than he is.

My chest prickles with heat. I allow myself a small, pointless sob.

The door slams shut.

I know, in this instant, that the careful trail I have laid in my police interview will come to an abrupt halt in that room. Dullards like Beige Hair and Grey Suit won't stand a chance. I was stupid to think they would. You can't take on a man with such powerful friends. You can't possibly pit yourself against the power of the status quo. Reputation. Charm. Wealth. The knowledge of how things work.

You're born into it, if you're one of the lucky ones.

And if you're not? You can waste all your life trying.

Or you can end up like Vicky Dillane: cast aside like a piece of junk.

Or you can end up like me.

I turn and retrace my steps. Grey Suit nods as I leave. The doors open into a rush of evening air. A siren blares.

The schoolchildren have all gone now. The lights are on inside Dallas Chicken & Ribs where I can make out a man in a green tabard lifting a basket out of the deep-fat fryer.

I cross over the road to a minicab office. The woman inside

is wearing a headset. She asks where I'm going and calls me 'love'.

I just want to go home.

'The railway station, please.'

'That'll be five, ten minutes. Take a seat.'

I sit on a hard bench and pick up a dog-eared gossip magazine, the pages slightly damp to the touch. It is as I turn the page that I notice my hands are shaking.

It was all for nothing. The whole fucking lot of it.

XI.

Two Years Later

I AM WARMING THE TEAPOT WHEN THE PHONE RINGS. I have poured two inches of boiling water into the green enamel pot and am swirling it around, taking care not to lose any from the spout, just as my mother taught me, and when the call comes through, I'm half minded not to take it. I have my morning routine carefully planned. Make the tea. Feed the cat. Open the back door with a jolt because it always sticks a bit and then water the garden.

I have a damson tree that is about to flower. It has been a mild winter and the plants are in a state of indecision. There were crocuses in February. Everyone talks about global warming. I'm disinclined to believe it. Climate just happens, doesn't it? No one thought the ice age was anything to do with aerosol cans and exhaust fumes.

I find the garden peaceful. I like pottering around, doing all those little things one must to keep it going. Pruning. Tending. Watering. Watching. I used to think, looking at Lady Katherine taking nail scissors to the ornamental window boxes, that it was a waste of time. But now I see it has its merits. The quietness of it. The patience that is required.

Sometimes, as I'm bending to water the pots, I will see a tame fox standing on the roof of the neighbour's shed. The fox looks tense and wary and ready to run should I have the temerity to move any closer. I even have a bird table. I leave nuts and toast crusts out for the sparrows. This late-flowering liking for wildlife has surprised me too. I could never see the point of creatures before. Humans seemed to me to be the only things worth spend-

281

ing time on. I suppose it's because I was trying to be a successful one. Looking back, I think I'd have to say that I failed in that. I failed quite conspicuously.

The phone rings again and I put the teapot down on the side of the sink and I tighten the knot on my dressing-gown belt and I walk into the corridor in my slippers, deliberately taking my time in the hope that whoever it is will lose patience and hang up. But they don't. The ringing sounds persistently through the cottage. I reach the dining table and pick up the receiver.

'Hello.'

My voice is croaky and I realise with the absent-minded shock of the solitary that I haven't spoken to anyone for several days.

There is a moment of static and then a faint clicking sound, as if someone's bones are cracking. Then: 'Hello, Martin.'

I recognise her voice immediately.

'It's Lucy,' she says.

I let the weight of the silence sag between us. There is so much to say and, at the same time, there is nothing at all.

'Oh,' I reply. 'Lucy. How …' I look around the room, casting about for clues as to what to say next. My eyes alight on a post-card, propped against the mantelpiece. It is a Giorgione portrait of a young man. His brows are heavy, his mouth slightly agape. He looks at me, challenge expressed in the jut of his jaw. 'What a surprise.'

From the other end of the line, a low chuckle. She always had a dry, gentle laugh. It is nice to hear it again.

'It's been a while, Martin. How are you?'

'Oh, fine,' I say, feeling suddenly self-conscious. I've been wearing the same pyjamas for over two weeks now. I haven't yet got around to doing the laundry. There is a faint brown-red stain on the dressing-gown lapel. Baked beans, I think. Or maybe tomato pesto. I don't know. I don't really care. I'm rather enjoying my slink into slovenliness. There is no one to impress any more, no need to put on a front.

'Good! That's good. Are you writing?'

'No. Haven't found the inspiration.'

I can hear her muttering to someone else, talking about closing the fridge door and no, she didn't know where the car keys had got to and why didn't he look over there – no, not there, over there. Then: a man's voice. I hadn't known she was living with someone else. But then, why shouldn't she be? She didn't owe me anything. And I had never sought to find out. It's just that I thought she was mine.

'Sorry,' she says. 'Domestic issues.'

'Ha.'

'So, no writing …?'

'No. I mean, not books. The odd bit of journalism here and there. I've started doing book reviews for the *FT*.'

'That's great.'

'Well, it's not exactly going to change the world but it keeps me occupied.'

I don't tell her about the writing that takes up most of my time. I don't tell her I wake up every morning and sit at my laptop and write this. I fail to mention that I'm writing down everything I can remember about Ben. I don't tell her I've been tap-tapping away at my own curious obsession. I don't know what it is, exactly. Not a book. Not a memoir. A reckoning, maybe. A purge. The satisfying of a need I have to get it all down.

The cat winds itself in and out of my legs, pushing against my calves with sinuous intent. I sit on the sofa and it leaps up onto my lap. I automatically start to stroke its striped back, feeling the arch of its spine. I should really give it a name. It has been two months now since it appeared in my garden and refused to leave. I tried to ignore the cat at first, shutting it out of the kitchen, refusing to leave food for it. But it stayed there, obstinately, and every morning I would wake and come downstairs and look out of the kitchen window and see the cat shivering heroically on the lawn. After three days, I relented and let it inside. No name though. By not giving it a name, I continue to refuse the cat permanent status. It is, I told myself, just a temporary visitor. It doesn't mean anything. It doesn't mean I am going *soft*.

'I wanted to call you, Martin, because, I've … well, I've got something to tell you. I wanted you to know.'

She sounds anxious. I picture her looking up at me with that wrinkle across the bridge of her nose I know so well, eyes weathered by worry, lips pressed in a tight, imploring line. I had once found her willingness to please so annoying. Now I wonder why I was so cruel to her. She had only ever tried to love me. It wasn't her fault I was unlovable. That I chose not to receive it.

'I'm pregnant, Martin.'

'Oh.'

I push the cat onto the floor and kick it away with the tip of my foot. It squeals and slips underneath the sofa. There is a beat of static.

'Are congratulations in order?'

She laughs.

'Yes! I'm very happy about it. We actually had a few cycles of IVF, so …'

'In that case … congratulations.'

Outside, a delivery van draws up. It is driven by a shaven-haired individual who parks on the pavement. I hate the way they do that: mounting the kerb as if the rules don't apply to them. He slams the driver's door shut but the window is still open and I can hear the thudding bass and electric whir of an irritating pop tune disturbing the quietness of the street.

Everyone is so self-involved these days. No care ever given to how other people might like to exist. No boundaries. All the noise bleeding into leftover silences; all that ceaseless, frenetic activity filling every available space with teeming nonsense. Status. Favourite. Tweet. Filter. Scroll. Like. Update. Feed. Feed. Feed. The world reduced to the bite-sized attention spans of the lowest common denominator.

I wait for Lucy to say something else. I find the phone so difficult because there are no visual clues as to how the other person is reacting. I'm not sure why she's called to tell me. What she does with her life now is her own business. The divorce was quick and mutually agreed. We didn't even need to get lawyers involved. Nothing more needed to be said. I could see it in Lucy's eyes: some internal switch had been flicked. She saw me for what I was and I understood. I don't blame Lucy for attacking Serena. Lord knows, I'd often thought of doing the same thing myself. I can understand only too well what it is to reach a boiling point and then move beyond it, to the place where heat is so intense it feels cold, like the froth of liquid nitrogen pressed to a wart.

'Thank you, Martin.' Lucy's voice brings me back. 'I wanted to tell you. I thought you should know. I mean, I realise you were always ambiguous about children ...'

She expects me to deny this or offer reassurance but I can't. She's right: I didn't ever want children of my own. When Lucy was pregnant, I had vivid dreams about the baby being handed to me and the ghost of Sylvia staring up at me from the infant's mewling face. The miscarriage, when it came, was a relief and I couldn't hide it. I would have been a terrible father. The idea of in-vitro fertilisation, of wanting a child so much you are willing to fuse it in a petri dish, is anathema to me. I never would have done that for her. Never. And I realise she knows this, without it ever having been said.

'So,' I start, racking my brains for an appropriate thing to say. 'When are you ... due?'

'August,' she says. 'We're past the three-month stage, so that's a relief.'

'We?'

'My partner. Will. He's a carpenter.'

I let out a bark of laughter.

'How useful.'

I can sense Lucy stiffen.

'Actually, he's incredibly artistic. He makes bespoke pieces for clients. That kind of thing.'

'Oh. Well. I'm pleased for you.'

'Are you?'

'Of course.'

'That's kind, thank you. And thank you for everything else. I never really did say how much I appreciated, you know, what you did.'

She means the police. The fact I didn't tell them what really happened. Because, in the end, it turned out I wanted to protect her and this had surprised me as much as it did Lucy.

'It was nothing.'

'It wasn't.'

We stop. I hear the letterbox clatter and a thud on the doormat. The only post I get nowadays is junk mail and canvassing leaflets from the local politician who is a woman called Chloe with short, spiky hair. Chloe looks young enough to be my daughter. She's standing for the Lib Dems and although she won't win, I think I will vote for her. Anything has to be better than Edward Buller's Tory party.

'It's nice to hear you, Lucy, but I should really get on. I've got a deadline.'

'Of course, of course. Sorry to disturb you. I just …'

'I know,' I say. 'I know.' I wonder what to add, then settle on 'thank you', which sounds wrong but is all I can manage. The cat jumps back onto the sofa and starts kneading its paws aggressively on the fabric of my dressing gown. I glance at it and the cat stops and stares back at me in perfect stillness. I clear my throat. 'You are a very kind person,' I add, heat rising up my gullet. My head twitches involuntarily, once, twice. I wait for it to pass.

'Goodbye, Martin,' she says and there is a catch in her throat.

I hang up. I listen to the dialling tone, then replace the phone.

I go back into the kitchen and flick the button on the kettle to reboil the water. The cat follows, indignant at my lack of attention. I tip out some Whiskas into its bowl. Jellied brown chunks of indeterminate gunk. The label on the pouch claims it is chicken and beef. I raise a spoonful to my nose and sniff it. I wonder sometimes if I could make a stew out of Whiskas. It smells pretty good. Too good for stray cats at any rate. Actually, what I'd really like to do is make dinner out of cat food and invite someone round to eat it, only telling them after the final morsel has been consumed what it consisted of. The flaw in this plan being that I don't have anyone to invite.

The person I'd most like to play the prank on is Ben, of course, but we don't talk any more.

I haven't seen him since that day at the police station, the day when I realised Beige Hair and Grey Suit were never going to be up to the job of proving a case against him. But I have charted his progress at a distance. I have kept tabs on what he's up to. I was wrong to leave it in the hands of incompetent middle-men. And so I have been deliberately biding my time. When it comes to it, I will be prepared. Sun Tzu: 'To know your enemy, you must become your enemy.'

He stood for parliament. Ed Buller parachuted him into a safe seat as a preferred candidate after the death of an aged politician who left a sizeable portion of his money to the local church. Ben sailed through with a nice majority. His maiden speech in the House of Commons a few months ago was on penal reform, arguing against a mooted proposal to give prisoners the vote.

I watched him on BBC Parliament. He was wearing his hair a new way, the front of it swept back with too much gel and it made him look older and less trustworthy. The camera light glinted distractingly on his hair as he spoke.

He had already mastered the emphatic hand gesture – those earnest, open-palmed punctuations so beloved of telegenic politicians schooled in the art of public relations and media-friendly headlines. He smiled in the right places and nodded his head when a sentence required it. There was something mesmerising about him. There always had been, even at school. His teeth were very white. I wondered if he'd had them done.

Since then he's been appointed junior minister. He's said to have the ear of the PM. A recent opinion piece in the *Telegraph* tipped him as one of ten possible future leaders, alongside that meaty oaf Andrew Jarvis who somehow seems to have clung on in there despite my regular anonymous calls to various tabloid news desks tipping them off about his mistress in London. So far, no one has taken the bait.

The tea is brewed. I pour myself a cup and add a dash of semi-skimmed from the fridge. The cat, masticating noisily, is fully occupied. I walk upstairs, the floorboards creaking gently as I go. The cottage I find myself in seems perpetually on the brink of collapse. The walls bulge in unlikely spots and no surface is entirely straight. When I leave my phone to charge on the bedroom floor at night, I will wake the next morning to find it has slid several inches to the right. Sometimes I feel I'm subsiding too: a ship listing before it sinks.

On the first floor, there is a small landing with three doors leading off it: bathroom, bedroom and my study. Holding my mug of tea in one hand, I push open the door to the study and take a seat at my desk. My computer is positioned so that I can see beyond it into the garden when my attention wanders. There is a soft chirruping of birds from the other side of the window. A spider's web hangs in one corner, fragments of silk glistening in the morning light.

I think briefly of Lucy, of the probable swell of her tummy, the stretch of her pale skin over the expanding thing underneath. I have always found pregnancy a strange notion: the idea that a woman could grow a whole new being in her belly and that this alien collection of cells, this embryonic person no one yet knew, would be ballooning into her most intimate parts, unfurling and filling, greedily swallowing fluids until it got too big to contain, like a tick, gorging itself on blood. In any other context, it would be thought of as a tumour. Yet instead of being terrified, we are expected to embrace it. Bearing children is treated as some sort of sacred rite of passage. But I see it as an impossible gamble. Because who knows what one might produce?

I spin my chair and look at the wall behind me. I have covered it in long rectangles of brown packing paper, purchased from

Ryman and unrolled and Blu Tacked onto the paintwork. I'm working on a timeline. I've plotted every important juncture of Ben's life along a horizontal axis, accompanied by the relevant date written out in black Sharpie and any press cuttings or further details I have found online. There's nothing much from his school-days, other than the odd report I stole from his trunk of possessions at Denby Hall and the copy I made, all those years ago, of Katherine's letter ('*All best love, Mummy*').

But things start to get interesting at around the time Vicky Dillane was killed. There were quite a few newspaper articles written back then which I'd had no idea about. I had been so insulated from the aftermath by the Fitzmaurice family. I had thought it was a kindness on their part but, of course, it was pure self-interest. By cocooning me, they protected themselves. The less I knew about what had really gone on, the better. The fewer questions I asked, the easier it would be to smooth over the inconsistencies. Because it seems astonishing to me now that the police never investigated further. I knew the Dillane family had been bought off to not pursue the case. I know that wealth and class can manipulate but I had never fully grasped the extent of it. The power it gives you is immense. Nothing is immune, not even the truth. Especially not the truth. But what will they think when I reveal what happened; when they find out their daughter was killed by the callousness of a drunken young man who is now an elected politician? What will they *do*?

In recent months, there have been so many articles and interviews to rip out of the papers and stick onto the wall that I've had to open another roll of brown paper just to accommodate them all. Ben's face now stares out at me from smudges of newsprint wherever I look. Here he is appearing before a select committee, looking tired and harassed and hunching over a file of papers. There he is judging a charity dog show, holding a West Highland terrier called Monty who is trying to lick his face. Here he is accompanied by his beautiful wife Serena, resplendent in grey silk, to the opening night of a Prince's Trust gala. Serena made a good recovery from her accident. If you look closely enough at photos of her face, you can see she has a thin white scar that runs from her hairline to the outer edge of her right eye. Otherwise she appears to be back to her glossy, glassy, untouchable self. There he is posing with his four children in the kitchen of his constituency home, wearing an apron (an apron of all things! I had never once, in all the time I knew him, seen Ben cook) embroidered brightly with 'Keep Calm and Carry On Baking'.

And then – my favourite one – a much-reproduced school photo from our final year at Burtonbury. Ben was head boy by then and Jarvis was his deputy. They are sitting side by side on the front lawn at Sullies. Ben has his legs open, hands placed solidly on each knee. Jarvis is shiftier-looking: his tie askew, his gingery hair matted at the temples. They are grinning.

I remember them snorting with unexplained laughter just before the shot was taken. Jarvis had leaned across and murmured something in Ben's ear and I, standing directly behind them, had craned to make out what was said but hadn't been able to hear. I'd been jealous, and I had reached out and grazed the tips of my fingers across the shoulder of Ben's blazer, just to feel it was there, just to remind myself of what it was to touch him. Ben's head snapped round.

'Mate, what are you doing?'

'Sorry. There was a bit of fluff on your blazer.'

Jarvis glared at me.

'Thanks, Mum,' Ben said, and Jarvis laughed and then they both turned back at the same time to face the photographer who took the photo moments later.

It's a picture that has been used again and again in various newspapers to illustrate the cronyism at the heart of Edward Buller's government. Every time it is printed, the frame is cropped close so that you can only see the arms and torsos of the other boys. But I know I'm there, standing to the left of Ben's head. There is an ink spot just above the top button of my blazer. If you squint, you can almost see it. What you can't see is the thump of my heart or the tremble of my hands. What you can't see is the ferocity of my love or the path that's about to open out in front of us. You can't see the course our lives are about to take. You can't see where it ends, in a grubby little police station with a polystyrene cup of tea and a woman with beige hair and a man in a grey suit.

At least, that's where Ben thinks it ends. It doesn't, not really. He and I aren't over. We have not had our final reckoning. I will not let him get away with it even if he's charmed every police officer in the country. He believes I still orbit around his dazzling sun.

I do not.

You wouldn't think it to look at me, but I am angry. I am quietly, lethally furious. And I am ready. I can feel the thrum and vibration of atoms splicing together. The reckoning will come soon.

As for me, I think I'll cope rather well in prison. I will write. I will think. Besides, I've spent a lifetime learning how to survive in institutions. I'll be able to assimilate in a way Ben will never manage, a thought that brings me immense satisfaction. For once, he will not know the rules. It's curious but I realise that, in my anger, I am also content.

The cat, sated by breakfast, pads into the study. It springs onto the top of the filing cabinet where I keep a stack of old newspapers and back copies of the Cambridge alumni magazine. The cat curls in on itself, sweeping its tail in front of its paws like a shield. It closes its eyes. A tiny triangle of pink tongue is just visible. It begins to purr, a low reassuring rumble.

What will I do with the cat?

I turn to my desk and fire up the computer. I click on the document icon on the desktop screen. I look at the bottom left-hand corner of the page: 53,823 words. I like to monitor this figure. It gives my thoughts solidity and heft. It reminds me that all of it happened, that it cannot be denied if it exists in black 11-point Arial.

I try not to think of the cat.

I settle down to type. I need to edit my notes on the police interview. I want to ensure I have all the details correct, that the chronology is accurate. I take a sip of tea.

I try not to think of the cat.

Who will feed it when I'm gone?

I stand. My head twitches. Once, twice. I brace myself for a third but it never comes. I go to the filing cabinet and place my hand over the cat's warm, sleeping head. I feel the fragile bones of its skull under my palm, the gentle rise and judder of its breathing and I think of that bird, that long-ago bird in the playground at my primary school.

I let my hand rest on the cat's head for a second longer. Then I stroke its back and tickle its chin. The purrs get louder, then stop altogether.

I tighten the belt of my dressing gown.

I sit back down at the desk.

I continue to write.

Outside, a world awaits.

Acknowledgements

Thank you to my agent, Nelle Andrew, for her strength, spirit and indefatigable refusal to accept second best, whether it be restaurant tables or plot structure. Also for teaching me that mayonnaise really does go with everything.

Thank you to my incredible editor, Helen Garnons-Williams at 4th Estate, for believing in me from the very first sentence I wrote and for having the most brilliant insights into both work and life.

Thank you to the whole team at 4th Estate, including Alice Herbert, Tara Al Azzawi, Michelle Kane and everyone who worked so hard on my behalf. Thank you also to my dear friend, Cormac Kinsella.

Thank you to the brilliant Carina Guiterman at Little, Brown for reading my manuscript when she should have been preparing for her sister's wedding – and apologies to Carina's sister for distracting the bridesmaid.

Thank you to the Beauman family – my darling Francesca, and her parents, Nicola and Chris, for their astonishing generosity and friendship over the last two years. I wrote a large portion of *The Party* in Nicola and Chris's beautiful Cambridge house and I finished the last chapter at Fran's home in Los Angeles (with minor interruptions when I was being tied up by children). I can never repay that debt in full and I appreciate it more than I can say.

Thank you to Sarah Langford and Detective Sue Hill for explaining the ins and outs of police interviews and the Crown Prosecution Service. Any mistakes are, naturally, my own.

Thank you to my earliest, most trusted readers and writerly support team, all of whom combine serious literary talent with extraordinary kindness: Olivia Laing, Francesca Segal, Viv

Groskop and Sebastian Faulks, whose many wise and pithy insights I would like to claim as my own.

Thank you to my parents, Christine and Tom Day, for too many things to list. Your support means the world to me.

Thank you to Emma Reed Turrell, for everything.

Thank you to my friends: I couldn't be me without you.

And thank you to Jasper Waller-Bridge, for running into the street and for being in my corner every day since then. This one's for you, with all my love.

London, February 2017